M. C. Rudasill

Age of Decision

Our choices echo through the ages.

Literary Lights Publishing
TALLAHASSEE

© Copyright 2009 Michael C. Rudasill
All rights reserved.

No part of this book may be reproduced, stored in a retrieval system, or transmitted in any form or by any means - electronic, mechanical, photocopying, recording, or any other - except for brief quotations in printed reviews, without the prior permission of the author.

This is a work of fiction. With the exception of obvious historical references to public figures, locations, and events, all characters and incidents in this novel are the products of the author's hyperactive imagination. Any similarities to actual people – boring or convivial, living, dead, or searching for a brain among the legions of the undead – should be considered coincidental.

ISBN: 978-0-9727127-6-7

Library of Congress Control Number: 2009906554

Book One: The Ultimate Paradigm
Book Two: Age of Decision

I dedicate this book to my wife Susann and to our Creator, the cardinal One, through whom all good things will abide forever, untouched by any shadow of calamity. Without Him, this passing universe – with its tales of honor and infamy – would never have been imagined... or so artfully engineered.

Cold Summer Rain

The cold summer rain did not fall lightly. It dripped dismally to earth, as if it oozed from a wound in the face of the heavens.

Ignoring the rain, the officer stared intently through the windshield and wiped away the fog, squinting at the object of her displeasure. Raked by the blue-disco swirl of her bubble lights, a battered pickup truck idled unevenly in the roadway, its flickering left taillight revealing the reason for the traffic stop. Pelted by water, it leaked erosive rivulets of rust onto the glossy pavement: fenders hunched against the gathering dusk.

She stepped out of her car and cautiously approached the truck with one hand resting lightly on the gun at her hip. Pausing at the corner of the tailgate, she carefully studied the two men in the cab. The driver faced forward; the passenger gazed pensively at the officer's reflection in the large, rain-streaked mirror on his door.

She detected no signs of danger. To all appearances, the men did not pose any threat. But appearances could mislead, and they did not reassure her.

Something feels wrong, she informed herself cautiously. A faint buzz of electricity tingled her scalp. Her skin crawled with anticipation. *What's wrong with this picture?*

In the distance, the thunder rumbled uneasily. *Is this how it feels before lightning strikes?* She smelled a strong, musty odor: a distinctive bitter tang. *What is that scent?* In a flash, her mind connected the dots.

Cocaine!

Before she could duck, the rear window exploded outward. She glimpsed a fountain of spraying glass as a freight train smacked into her neck, stunning her soul and knocking her world out of kilter.

The officer flipped backwards as if cracked in the face by a well-aimed baseball bat.

SHE DID NOT NOTICE THE SECONDARY SHOCK as her body hit the pavement. She felt no pain as her head bounced heavily against the asphalt.

Softly, hypnotically, her consciousness began to fade. A call should have gone out, but her radio remained silent.

Officer down.

The rainfall segued from drizzle to downpour. The officer's eyes clouded over, wandering aimlessly behind fluttering eyelids.

Something had gone wrong, but she could not imagine what. Something had happened... something bad... something evil. She could not make sense of it.

A clamor of distant shouting – a tumult of angry voices – drifted past her face like a wayward cloud trailing just beyond her reach. Muffled apparitions slipped through the grasp of her mind, sliding like smoke though her fingers. Wayward wisps of fear haunted the fringes of her awareness as she teetered at the edge of a deep, delicious sleep. And yet, for all that, she did not yield.

A trickle of consciousness began to seep back into her being. *God help me; it hurts... what's happening to me?*

On the rain-slicked street, the view had turned grim. The fallen officer lay flat on her back with her head turned 45 degrees to the right, the bend in her neck partially compressing a gash that leaked warm blood onto the roadway. An unseemly crimson puddle pooled beneath her head as her blood mingled promiscuously with the pelting rain. The downpour increased, assaulting the earth in deadly earnest as the rain pulsed relentlessly from the swollen sky.

The officer's right eye stared dully at a huge drop of rain about to hit the pavement. For some reason, she perceived it with uncommon clarity. Encapsulated in its core, she saw a glassy piece of hail as smooth and misshapen as the clouds above her.

The solitary drop, magnified and captured in the light of her flickering awareness, struck the asphalt full force and exploded upwards. The sight seemed hypnotically intense: exotic and strangely beautiful. Like a passage from a cinematic poem, the raindrop rebounded from the blacktop in sinuous slow motion, shattering into splinters of light that unfurled delicate tendrils, like the petals of a flower. Softly, slowly, the petals lazily wilted back down to the surface of the glistening road.

Her vision faded. She could not awaken, and could not turn her head. But somehow, in spite of her wounds, the officer sensed that the worst was yet to come.

She moved her lips, but failed to utter a sound. A large red bubble emerged from her mouth and popped silently, punctured by the rainfall.

As the dark mist closed in, she struggled helplessly, her instincts warning of a greater danger. At the edge of her thoughts, a predator waited. Her mind tried to gather its strength as her consciousness drifted away.

With the delicate footfall of a hungry wolf, the killer began his careful approach.

Dawn of Awareness

Jamie awoke with a start and gasped, reaching for her neck. She struggled to her feet and groped for the gash where the bullet had torn tender flesh. She found no wound, no scar: just smooth flesh in the prime of youthful good health.

Looking in the mirror above her bureau, she confirmed that her neck was undamaged. From the looking glass, an unblemished countenance returned her gaze – unkempt, but gracefully poised: perfect oval face, creamy skin, cascading burgundy hair, and a startled natural beauty with blue eyes opened wide in dismay.

To all appearances, the face in the mirror reflected privilege and power. To those accepting such stereotypes at face value, Jamie offered the lily-white picture of a sheltered soul enjoying the life of a princess. Her remarkable beauty impacted those she encountered with startling intensity. After meeting Jamie for the first time, some could recall little but the effect of her loveliness.

Appearances deceived in Jamie's case, and the facade in the mirror belied a bitter reality. Long ago, before she could walk, evil had drilled a bloody nest deep into her infant soul. Nightly rapes and vicious beatings had been simple facts of life from the crib until her escape from home at the ripe old age of 16.

Age and empowerment had delivered Janelle "Jamie" James from the terrors of youth, but the price of survival had been high. Each night as she slept, cruel memories swarmed from the abyss of her haunted past. They arose like ghouls, anxious to afflict her soul, as if enraged by the fact that she had escaped their grip during her carefree waking hours.

Jamie had long downplayed the abuse she had suffered during her fractured, wasted childhood. Forgetfulness had protected her from the type of pain that could drive a soul to madness. To this day, to look at her, one would scarcely guess the truth.

It was only a dream, she told herself, staring at her neck, so clean and unblemished. *But it was so real!*

She shuddered in revulsion, wet with morning sweat that crawled slowly down her neck. Her heart pounded in the aftermath of the nightmare. *Only a dream.*

The sunlight battered her eyes, bullying its way into her universe: intense and aggressive. Against her wishes, Jamie's husband had left the blinds open in their spotlessly clean bedroom.

Remembering her dream, she felt a moment of fear. *Was it a warning about Donny?* She reached for her telephone and punched in her husband's number. He picked up at the first ring.

"Hey babe, what's up?" Hearing Donny's voice, she felt reassured.

Her husband Donny – a tall, blond Florida cowboy – possessed the practical virtues of patience and persistence. During the past five years, she had found him to be an interesting study in contradictions: dependable but never boring, as faithful as the sun and occasionally as brazen.

"I just called to say hi," she told Donny. Not wanting to burden him with unneeded drama, she paused. "You left the blinds open," she added. *Keep 'em on their toes.*

"Jamie, are you awake? Before noon?"

"Ha ha. Funny."

"Uh, listen, can I call you later? I've gotta go into the courtroom."

"Sure."

"Are you okay?"

"Sure. Why wouldn't I be?" She bluffed.

"No reason. Just asking."

"I'm okay, okay?"

"Listen, Jamie, if it's important, we can talk now."

"It's not that important. Don't drive me crazy, Donny. Just take care of yourself, okay?"

"Okay, babe. I'll be in court all day. I'll call you later. I love you."

"Back at ya, pal." She slowly hung up the phone.

Nightmares had plagued her for years, but the intensity of this dream had exceeded them all. It felt like a premonition. She remembered it and shuddered, cold in spite of the morning warmth. *Officer down.* She would tell Donny later, when he got home.

Jamie's husband – a sheriff's deputy – served on the road patrol. She hated his job with a passion… but he loved it, so what could she do? She refused to ask him to quit a job that he loved.

She arose and pulled on her robe, walking to an old oak desk in the corner of the room. Reaching beneath a drawer, she found a small, worn business card and gently detached it from the tape that secured it safely out of sight.

She read the card and smiled wryly. *Ira Freeman, Martial Arts and Crafts.* Years ago, someone had written a telephone number on the back. She turned the card over and mulled the message scrawled below the number. "Need help? Call me. Nightmares cured, or your money back." She smiled and shook her head. *Nightmares cured? I could use that right now.*

She should have told Donny about the card when she received it in the mail, but she had held her peace. Donny might lose his career if the authorities believed that he knew the sender's identity without reporting it. Jamie had decided to live with that risk, but did not expect Donny to do the same.

Jamie felt certain that 'Ira Freeman' was an alias for a notorious outsider who had saved her life once, years ago. Since that time she had married, earned a bachelor's degree, and started coursework for a doctorate in Forensic Psychology. She had recently begun an apprenticeship in the Florida Department of Law Enforcement's witness protection program… the same FDLE program that had once hidden her away in the wilderness, safe from certain death.

As the years passed, Jamie had not forgotten those who helped in her time of need. She would not betray their trust.

As Jamie suspected, Salvatore Benuto – a person of interest in a notorious Tampa arson murder – had mailed the business card to her. A decorated veteran and a former cop, he did not have the typical resume of a person of interest in an unsolved federal terrorism case; but he remained one, nonetheless.

A few years ago, Sal Benuto had hit a patch of black ice on the highway of life. When a Mob assassin had killed his only friend, he had gone mad, destroying the underground headquarters of Tampa's most powerful Mafia family. In the wee hours of a nondescript winter morning, he had used high explosives to detonate a deserted city block in the hardened cobblestone heart of Ybor City, Florida.

Sal had taken fiery revenge on Tampa's premier Mafia family, the Provencentis… smoking a select array of Cigar City hoods like burning stogies stubbed into the Mob's evil eye. He had excised part of the Mafia malignancy – Ybor's Strangler Fig – like an inflamed carcinoma torn unceremoniously from the body politic.

After he punished the Mob, on the run from Tampa authorities, he had not sought his own personal safety. Instead, he had traveled south to Oree County to guard Jamie's safe house as she waited to testify against Joe Boy Provencenti. Before the trial ended, Sal Benuto had saved her life.

The Italian gangs of Ybor City still ruled organized crime in the Sunshine State. A new don had taken the reins of the Provencenti family. Having turned the page, the wise guys no longer mentioned Sal Benuto's name. Federal agents suspected that he was a terrorist, and by the letter of the law, they were correct.

The feds knew him as a person of interest. His friends knew him as Streetcar.

Jamie was his friend. And on this beautiful summer morning, when all seemed well in her brave new world, she did not trust appearances. Her instincts had sounded an alarm, and she believed with uncanny certainty that her vivid dream held a portent of trouble to come. Somehow she knew that beneath the shallow surface, evil had turned in her direction.

She felt the threat in her marrow. Evil depraved had turned her way: denuded of decency, unimaginable and unavoidable, inexcusable, relentless, unmentionably obscene.

She sensed it down deep in her soul.

Soon – very soon – she would call upon Streetcar for help.

A Fish in Hand

"The red worm ain't catchin' zip, Big Daddy." The boy held the offending invertebrate at arm's length, his tender face wrinkled in profound disgust. The slender youngster's dark red hair matched the color of the translucent lure on the end of his hook. He had the look of a true child of nature: tousled, unkempt and ungainly, with faded freckles barely visible beneath his tan.

"Zip ain't on the menu, kid," the burly old timer replied gruffly. "I'm glad the worm ain't catchin' it." The big man smiled crookedly and scratched his chin with an oversized, sun-spotted hand that bore the imprint of a faded Harley Davidson tattoo. He was a big man with a wide face framed by an impressively long, wispy white ponytail. Bear-like but gentle in demeanor, he hunched over his spinning rod like a giant clutching a twig.

"This fakey ol' worm stinks, big-time," the boy added.

In response, the old man sniffed officiously. "That's a good lure, Junior. I caught a big bass with it last week."

"It's the fish, then. They're a bunch'a idjits."

"Fish don't bunch, they school. And you mean idiots, not idjits."

"Well, they're a school full'a idjits."

"Not the first, and not the last."

"Idjits," Danny reiterated playfully, tweaking his grandfather.

"Idiots? The way they've avoided your worm argues against that claim. And don't ever use that word to describe human beans, Danny. Okay?" They observed a moment of silence as the child considered his grandfather's request.

"You mean human beings, not beans… right, Big Daddy?"

"What?"

"You said beans. It's human beings, not human beans."

"I said beans, and I meant beans. Like pintos, only human."

They grinned at each other. The old man mussed his grandson's

hair, and the child carefully slicked it back into place.
 "Grandpa... about tonight..."
 "Yeah?"
 "What time is Daddy gettin' home from prison?"

Window of Importunity

No one would have believed it, but it had happened anyway. After a hard-fought campaign, Delia Rawlings had snatched victory from the jaws of denial, triumphing in the evil stepmother of elections to take her oath as Florida's first black, female sheriff.

Delia had tried to avoid issues of race and gender during the long campaign, but they had been unavoidable. Like dyspeptic bulldogs, the reporters had locked down upon the color of her complexion and refused to let it go. A sour boilermaker from America's past – the mixed legacy of liberty polluted by the bitter dregs of race-based slavery – had plagued her morning after.

A handsome woman, Delia did not blend easily with the crowd. She stood tall and straight: square of face and strong-featured, with a hawk-like nose, generous lips, and a remarkably clear complexion. Her skin glinted in the summer sunlight like polished ebony: blacker than black, lustrous and smooth.

For more than a week after officials counted the final ballot, swarms of foraging reporters remorselessly sniffed through town like armadillos rooting for one last, tasty morsel. Delia had avoided them in full knowledge that their hardened shells and comical meanderings could lull observers into forgetting that they possessed powerful claws adept at tearing their prey.

The fanfare over race and gender had eventually faded like the wake from a manatee-slicing powerboat, fouling the air as it chugged off into the sunset. Oree County had quieted down, and the sheriff had gratefully slipped into a dull routine of too much work and not enough play. Delia loved her job, reveling in the mundane details of police work. But she also loved to have fun.

On this particular evening, she planned to relax. She would leave work early to visit her brother at his new house on the Alafi River, adjacent to Cutler County. She looked forward to breathing the clean country air during the long drive through the South Central Florida countryside.

She did not know that during her drive, she would encounter an unpleasant surprise. On a remote rural highway, evil would seize her by the throat. Attempting to enforce the peace, she would confront the outer limits of human depravity.

Before the evening was over, as hail pelted painfully from the sky, Delia Rawlings would face disaster.

The Facts of the Case

The old man soberly considered his grandson's inquiry. *What time is Daddy gettin' home from prison?* The boy had asked the same question at least five times today, but he patiently answered one more time.

"Your daddy should be home by ten tonight." The boy mulled over the information as if it were fresh news.

"Why didn't you or Mama go to pick him up?" he inquired. He knew the answer, but the act of asking somehow reassured him.

"He didn't want us to pick him up at that nasty old prison. He never wanted us to go anywhere near it."

"But you visited him there. So did Mama." The boy stated his case with the confidence of a prosecuting child who has found a flaw in the argument of an elder.

The old man expertly cast a lure across the small lake, landing it delicately at the edge of a dense cluster of waterweeds. High above the shimmering surface of the water, the sun emerged from behind a fat white cloud. The sticky warmth pressed sleepily upon their shoulders, lulling and relaxing.

"Yeah, I visited him all right, and so did your mama. But he didn't like it one bit. Your daddy can be as stubborn as me, and that's saying something." As he listened to his grandfather, the boy threaded and tied a new lure with enviable dexterity. He bit off the extra length with gusto and spat it out before speaking again.

"You're stubborn too. Right, Big Daddy?"

"I'm afraid so."

"That's why you were a beatnik, right?" Casting his line away from his grandfather's, he watched as it fell beside a royally gnarled cypress log.

"Yep," Big Daddy replied. "I'm as stubborn as a mule. That's why I was a beatnik, and that's why I raced hot rods when I should have been helpin' my daddy."

"Like I help you. Right, Big Daddy?"

"Sure, Junior. Like you help me."

As the child reflected on his extended family, he remembered his uncle Pete. The very thought annoyed him.

"Uncle Pete ought t'have gone to prison instead of Daddy. Those drugs was Uncle Pete's. I saw him put the suitcase in Daddy's car. I was little, but I remember."

"I know."

"Me and Daddy was waitin' for Uncle Pete in the diner. Daddy didn't know that Uncle Pete put them drugs in his car."

"I know."

"Uncle Pete slipped out the back exit when the cops showed up."

"I know, Danny, I know. It was wrong, and it cost your daddy five years of his life."

"It stank." The precocious child used bad grammar deliberately. If his mother had caught him mangling English in this manner, he would have been in big trouble. But his mother had driven to town, and Danny was 11 years old, fishing with his grandfather on a wonderfully hot summer day.

"You told the judge, but he didn't believe you," Big Daddy continued. "The prosecution had a theory, and your story didn't fit, so your daddy went to prison instead of your uncle Pete. It weren't your fault. It just happened."

"Uncle Pete could've told the truth and gotten Daddy off the hook."

"I know."

"Why do I have to call him Uncle, anyway?" He grimaced. "Kenny Brantley said he's Daddy's cousin, so he ain't really my uncle. He's my second cousin."

"When you was born, Pete asked if he could be your uncle. He didn't have brothers or sisters… no wife, no kids. You're his favorite."

"Next to Aunt Marcy."

"Yeah, next to her," Big Daddy said, sighing deeply. "She may be the only person on earth he really loves. When she was little, Pete was her hero." *Before she grew up.*

"I like Aunt Marcy."

"We all do."

"When's she gonna visit?"

"I don't know." The old man sighed deeply. "It's complicated."

"Everything's complicated around here."

"She's made a new life. I don't think she wants to be anywhere near your uncle Pete, to tell you the truth. He creeps her out."

"He creeps me out, too. He creeps everybody out."

"I know. But he lives right down the road and he's family, so we're sorta stuck with him."

"I reckon Uncle Pete's been good to me since daddy's been in prison. Even if he did cause the whole dang mess."

"True."

"He takes me to target practice all the time. I like shootin' things. Mama lets me go 'cause he's family and all."

"I know."

"Uncle Pete don't like Mama. I hate that. I told him, too."

"Do you know why he acts that way?"

"Cause he's sick up here." Danny tapped his head knowingly.

"He's sick in the soul."

"He don't like Mama 'cause she's Jewish. He told me, and I yelled at him. He just laughed."

"It's rotten."

"It's stupid."

"It's just plain wrong."

"Why is Uncle Pete like that?" In response, his grandfather sighed and squinted at the horizon, scowling sourly.

"It all goes back to Pete's daddy, my older brother, Dean Ray Johnston. Dean Ray wasn't like Mama or Daddy. He was a nasty little boy who grew up into a big, nasty man, and he raised your uncle Pete to be mean just like him. He tormented little Petey until he became mad… like a pit bull that's been poked with a stick. I tried to stop it, but I couldn't. You see this?" He pulled up the strand of thick white hair that hung over his right temple.

"Wow! What's that from?" The boy marveled at a deep, poorly healed gouge in his grandfather's scalp.

"That's where Dean Ray like to have brained me with a steel tie-rod. It happened back when little Petey was four years old. Dean Ray almost killed me that time."

"That's crazy!"

"You're tellin' me? I lived it."

"Why'd he do such a crazy rotten thing?"

"He said I was interferin' with the way he was raisin' Petey."

"How's that?"

"I told Dean Ray that he should give the little guy a break. He rode Petey night and day, cussin' him like a dog."

"That's nasty."

"Yep. I should'a gone to the law, Danny, but I didn't do it 'cause my mama asked me not to do it. I should'a done it anyway. Not that they'd'a done anything about it. I never saw anything physical from Dean Ray, just a bunch of yellin' and cussin' and name-callin'. That was bad, but they wouldn't have done nothing."

"Wow."

"I failed your uncle Pete."

"Do you think you're the reason that Uncle Pete's an idiot?" Surprised by Danny's question, Big Daddy laughed spontaneously.

"I'm afraid I can't claim the credit. He's all growed up now. It's his choice, and he's a still a racist, through and through."

"I hate all that racial stuff."

"Me too. But we can hate that stuff without hatin' your uncle."

"It's hard."

"I know." They stared into the lake as a fish swirled the water.

"Why can't we just make him change?"

"He's a grown man. If he was hurtin' anybody, I'd turn him in to the law, but he's not doin' that as far as I can tell. He swore he ain't messin' with dope anymore."

"I hope it's true."

"A racist hurts himself more than anyone else. He's like a man drinkin' poison to spite his neighbor."

"Uncle Pete seems healthy as sin to me." Hearing this, Big Daddy shook his head.

"He's poisonin' his soul."

"Well, I don't like him 'cause he don't like my mama."

"Your mother said it best. She said we're not required to like our enemies... just to love 'em."

"Mama's too nice for her own good."

"She's a wise woman."

"I know."

"It takes a lot of forgiveness to hold a family together, Danny."

"I'm half Jewish."

"Yep."

"Why don't Uncle Pete hate me?"

"I don't know. He's given you a pass for now, maybe because of what he did to your daddy. But listen up, Danny." The old man grasped the boy's shoulder and looked into his eyes. "His hate runs deep. Some day, he might turn mean."

"Maybe I should turn mean first. He's been rude to my mama!" Hearing Danny's words, the old man smiled.

"What would your mama want you to do?" The boy hung his head, disappointed with the question. Danny's mother believed in turning the other cheek. She loved her enemies and prayed daily for their souls. *Mama's too good for her own good,* Danny reminded himself. He looked up at his grandfather.

"If Uncle Pete had told the truth, Daddy never would have gone to prison."

"I know."

"He's an idjit."

"Danny, please don't call people idiots... even Uncle Pete."

"Yes, sir."

"How many times has he taken you shootin' in the past five years?"

"About a billion."

When it came to shooting, Danny had not needed much

coaching. He was a natural. After years of rigorous practice, he could respond expertly to any combat scenario his uncle could dream up.

"Maybe Pete's reformed," the old man suggested

"You're too hopeful," Danny replied.

"He's been stayin' out of trouble, and he volunteered to pick up your daddy today. Maybe there's hope."

"Huh," the boy grunted skeptically. "I'll bet there's somethin' in it for him." Danny's grandfather, a genial giant who assumed the best about people, gazed soberly at his grandson.

"I'd hate to think you're right."

"Right as rain, Big Daddy."

"Hey Squirt, what's that fish doin' with your bait?" He pointed to the middle of the pond, where the boy's line bobbed in the water.

"Oh, no," the child cried, jerking the rod too rapidly and snatching the bait from the fish's mouth. Deeply grieved, he stared up expectantly at his grandfather. He looked as if he believed that with a word, the former Bohemian hot rod mechanic could alter the course of history and give him another chance to set the hook.

"Well, *that* one weren't no idjit," Big Daddy observed dryly. In spite of his stubborn good humor, a dull ache welled up within him. *What time is it?* He looked at his watch. *4:00 PM*

Pete would pick up Dan at the prison in South Florida soon. *In six hours, they'll be home.* A nagging sense of foreboding grew as he considered these things. Winston "Big Daddy" Johnston looked out across the pond, past the dense brush at the water's edge and the low ridge beyond. *It took nerve for us to plant citrus on that ridge. If we get another hard freeze, it'll kill those trees right down to the root.* He lifted his gaze and stared at the distant horizon, trying to distract himself but failing in the effort. *Pete's picking up Dan at the prison,* he reflected ruefully. *The man who should'a been in prison is picking up the man who served time in his place.* He shrugged his shoulders abruptly, as if to dislodge his doubts.

Feeling a breeze on his cheek, he looked up toward the eastern horizon. There, above the edge of the earth, he saw a small, dark cloud.

One Pickup, Fully Loaded

By four o'clock, the public bus had left the parking lot of the Micco Bay Correctional Institution. Dan Johnston, free man, sat in a small patch of grass at the edge of the parking area, leaning back against the trunk of a large live oak tree. He stared upwards, trying to glimpse a cardinal that cheeped softly as it flitted from branch to branch, hidden behind a veil of glossy leaves. Dan smiled ruefully and flipped a twig into the air, closing his eyes with a sigh. *For five years I've been stuck behind four walls. Now that I'm free, I'm stuck without a ride.* From his small patch of shade, he patiently monitored the entrance of the parking lot.

A few minutes after the bus left, he stood and stretched. On his feet he resembled one of the Great Blue Herons in the lake that sprawled to the north of the prison. Dan Johnston did not merely stand, as other men might stand, rising to their feet in blessed anonymity. He loomed large: as tall and thin as an upright rail that had been curiously sculpted to resemble an attentive crane with its head on a swivel, looking around to avoid trouble. He slouched so badly that his neck appeared to curve backwards, an illusion accentuated by a prominent Adam's apple. He had a long, thin face crowned by a full head of fine brown hair, a dark tan, neat brown moustache, and thin but prominent nose.

Staring away from the parking lot and out across the lake, he heard the truck before he saw it. He looked away from the lake as his cousin, Pete Johnston, wheeled into the parking lot in a cloud of dust, at the wheel of a battered, beige Chevy pickup with oversized wheels and a small rebel battle flag in the middle of the rear window. *There's old Pete. Still a bonehead after all these years,* Dan reflected grimly. *Why didn't I let Big Daddy and Sarah pick me up?* He knew the answer before he asked the question.

The shame of jail had almost crushed him. Only his immediate family had kept the faith, and he did not wish to burden them with another visit to this pestilential hellhole.

Recently, when Pete had visited Dan in prison, he had apologized for letting him take the rap. "No one would've believed me," he offered weakly. "But I should've tried." The apology had seemed bizarrely out of character, but Dan had forgiven him immediately.

Dan trusted people. He resembled his father in that regard.

Dan's cousin Pete, on the other hand, trusted no one. Since early childhood, Dean Ray Johnston had shaped little Pete into the image of hard-nosed, racist cruelty. Dean Ray, now deceased, had earned notoriety as the Great Grand Dragon of the Armed Faction of the Ku Klux Klan, a remorselessly radicalized, neo-racist offshoot of the original Klan. Young Pete had been Dean Ray's ablest protégé.

As he thought of these things, Dan gathered his meager possessions and waved at the truck that rolled in his direction. In spite of his thinness, he had powerful, sinewy arms, and if you ignored his pallor, prison had left little mark on him. His smile remained quick, his teeth crooked but healthy, hands delicate but powerful: the calloused tools of a skilled sculptor who had spent five years perfecting his art in a sweltering prison workshop.

The rusty pickup rolled up and stopped with a squeal of brakes. Pete emerged from the driver's side as tall and tan as ever, with tight yellow curls bouncing around his smiling face like freeform coronas orbiting an unkempt sun.

Pete Johnston resembled a Neanderthal trying to pass as a respectable Southerner – a genetic legacy from the prehistoric mists. His brow jutted over his eyes like a porch roof built to shed rain. Oversized biceps carelessly bulged from his sleeveless T-shirt, eager to flaunt their thick mat of pale brown fur. Racist tattoos peeked through the hairy foliage like vermin beneath a hedge.

Like Dan, Pete Johnston possessed his own peculiar genius. Unlike Dan, however – and without the knowledge of his family – Pete had invested his talents in a succession of extremely successful criminal enterprises. On this particular trip, he was combining illicit business with family duty.

"Danny, you look terrific," Pete cried exuberantly. He clapped his cousin on the shoulder, and they hugged. Pete opened the dented passenger door. "Let's hit the road. This place gives me the creeps." Tossing his bag on the floorboard and climbing inside, Dan glanced over his shoulder at the neatly stacked boxes in the truck bed.

"Are those cucumbers?"

"Yep. Jimmy Wilmington has a new produce business, and he asked if I'd pick up a load."

"Jimmy Wilmington?"

"Go figure. He's got a little stand on Highway 52 across from Pig City Barbeque. He asked me, and I figured, why not?"

Pete lied easily and well. His own cousin could not detect the fabrication. As far as Dan knew, Pete remained a ne'er-do-well, happy-go-lucky shade tree mechanic who enjoyed a carefree life unencumbered by responsibility. Pete played the role like a professional actor, a redneck savant performing Shakespeare in the Swamp.

In the bed of the pickup truck, he had stacked tall wax boxes of aromatic cucumbers, two high and four abreast, tying them down tightly with nylon ropes. No one would have guessed that in the bottom row he had packed more than 80 pounds of high-grade Colombian cocaine… the first delivery of the summer from his criminal cohorts in northern Colombia.

Whenever the first coke of the season arrived, Pete liked to pick up a sample. His reasons went beyond an interest in quality. He used the opportunity to spend face time with his leadership team. His personal presence, backed by his terrifying reputation among the criminal cognoscenti, inspired the kind of respect that kept employees from skimming profits and turning informant.

To Pete, 80 pounds of cocaine amounted to chump change. He would drive to Orlando tomorrow to drop off the drugs with a distributor he had known since high school, leaving the truck at a scrap metal business in Longwood.

As a sober drug dealer, Pete transcended the stereotype. He possessed a phenomenal IQ that had failed to cure his racism. He hated to get stoned, but he loved the money down deep in his soul.

Over the years, a bloody fountain of drug money had yielded a secret fortune in cash that had led to untraceable international influence. Drug money had paid for the armory Pete had stockpiled to supply the Great White Nation during the race war that filled his warped dreams. A crude gusher of drug money had lubricated the wheels of his multi-national organization, strengthening his control over a few, well-paid political contacts.

Pete popped the clutch and the old truck burned rubber, rocking out of the parking lot and onto the two-lane country highway. Remembering Dan's plight – five years of incarceration for a crime that he himself had committed – Pete just had to smile.

He usually minded his manners when carrying dope, but lately success had bred pride, and he had become careless. Today, he felt like a million… a number that happened to match his bi-weekly income.

Pete had no way of knowing that on this day, within a few hours, his dreams would careen to an end. And when the sky began to fall, he would have no one to blame but his own inveterate, vain and profane, flamboyant and cold-blooded self.

Rendezvous with Infamy

A powerful storm front moved into Oree County just before dark. In the cab of their antique pickup, the air had actually turned cool... unheard of for August in this part of Florida.

"Feels like a big storm's comin'," Pete drawled unconcernedly. He appreciated a break from the heat. "A real whopper."

"Maybe a tornado will take us to Oz."

"Ya think?" They grinned, temporarily forgetting the history of betrayal that tainted the air between them.

Pete blinked and adjusted his rearview mirror.

"Ssssst," he hissed angrily. "Who's back there?" Dan turned to face his cousin and cast a careful eye to his left, scanning the highway behind the truck.

"It's a cop car."

"Great!"

"No big deal. Mind your manners, and you won't get a ticket."

"Right," he replied skeptically. "This is Oree County, Danny. Do you know what that means?"

"We're almost home. That's what it means to me."

"To you, maybe," Pete said, licking his lips and nervously glancing in the rearview mirror. The squad car was right on their tail. "To me, it means we're in the stompin' grounds of a certain black African lady sheriff who happens to hate my guts." When he pronounced the word African, he mangled the pronunciation in profound disdain – 'A-free-can' – as if he spoke the ultimate insult.

"I wish you wouldn't use that tone."

"Tone?"

"Yeah, tone."

"Shut up!"

"It makes you sound like an ignorant racist."

"Shut up, Danny! Who are you, Oprah?"

"Sure. Call me O."

"Well, O, I guess my tone is rotten. But it ain't my fault. It's society's fault. I have low self-esteem."

"And Pete, about the N word." *I know it's comin', so I'd better nip it in the bud.*

"What?"

"Nobody says that anymore. Nobody but hip hop artists and members of the Aryan Nation." *As far as I know, you might be a charter member,* Dan did not add. "And you don't know anything about the Sheriff of Oree County. Maybe she's a good cop."

"Don't be a fool. Do you remember that phony preacher who used to be sheriff here?"

"The one who was murdered by the Mob?"

"Yeah, him. He had it in for me. He chased me for years, but he couldn't touch me because I avoided Oree County like the plague. Now his black African girlfriend is the sheriff."

"I read about her in the Palm Beach Post. She's Florida's first black female sheriff. She got elected fair and square."

"It was rigged."

"That's progress, Petey."

"Shut up!" He slammed his hand on the steering wheel. "Don't even go there." Pete squinted in the mirror, blinking against the glare. "There's no way the cops would know this truck. I just bought it yesterday."

"It's no big deal. What're they gonna do, arrest you for driving on a public road?"

"You don't get it," Pete murmured, grimacing tensely.

"What are the odds that the sheriff's in that car?"

"Stranger things have happened. There ain't that many cops in Oree County."

"Who cares? You can't do anything about it, so why worry?"

The wind picked up. Random bursts of rain began to slash across their windshield. Pete chewed his gum furiously, his eyes flashing periodically to the rearview mirror.

Dan waited for a reply, but his cousin did not utter a word.

Trafficking Stop

In the pall of the gathering storm, the darkness had intruded ahead of schedule. As a result, Delia Rawlings found herself speeding as she drove toward her brother's house. *Tornado warning with possible hail, and I'm running late... why didn't I just cancel dinner?* Even as she considered these things, she knew the answer. Lately, she had sorely missed the comforting presence of her former friend and mentor, Sheriff Tommy Durrance. He had died violently, and she still felt the loss, but she did not want to wallow in it. Ready to forget her woes, she looked forward to an entertaining evening with her brother and his happy little family.

Slowing down behind an old pickup truck with a single working taillight, Delia heaved a monumental sigh. *I never get a night off.* She could have passed the rattletrap without a second glance, but that would not have fit the code of ethics that had put her into this uniform, in this county, in this squad car, at this particular moment. *I'd better write him a warning.*

As she turned on her car's flashing blue lights, gusts of wind tossed the tops of trees near the road. Her nostrils flared at the scent of water, and the cold summer rain began to fall.

"Great!" Pete cried, slamming his fist against the dashboard. "She's lightin' me up!"

As Dan glanced to his right and studied the cop car in the oversized side-view mirror, he did not sense trouble. He failed to notice when his cousin reached surreptitiously below the front seat, quietly pulled out a long-barreled revolver, and laid it across his lap.

Pete slowed the truck and pulled over, guiding it into the entrance of a wide, rock-strewn road. Dan's eyes wandered toward the brightly lit agri-business construction site in an empty field at the end of the rocky road. Two storage silos towered in the distance, illuminated by streetlights. *I wonder who built those silos? A lot of things have changed in the past five years.* He glanced in the side mirror again and watched the officer as she approached the truck, apparently oblivious to the gusting wind and rain.

The officer, a tall, dark woman in her mid-40s, approached the truck cautiously. With her right hand resting lightly on the gun at her hip, she glanced at Dan Johnston's reflection in the mirror. For a moment, their eyes met.

Dan studied her face from an artist's perspective, admiring the way her dark green uniform contrasted with her severe, swept-back hair and her clean black skin. He smiled at her, relaxed and happy.

This officer held no ordinary position. This was the Sheriff of Oree County.

PETE JOHNSTON COULD SHOOT like an evil Annie Oakley. Practicing regularly on his private range, he had perfected a number of extraordinary shots. He referred to one of his most impressive tricks as the "mirror shot."

He regularly practiced the mirror shot in a variety of positions, using a rogue's gallery of reflective devices: mirrors large and small, reflective surfaces in a variety of shapes: convex, concave, or otherwise contorted. Once, he had placed five bullets inside a bullseye at 20 yards while gazing at the reflection in a stainless steel coffeepot.

In the passenger-side mirror, Dan gazed without suspicion or concern as the sheriff paused at the rear of the truck, checking them out. He turned to his cousin and smiled.

"I'll bet this bomb has a bad tail light." His smile disappeared instantly, replaced by a look of sheer horror.

Petey had a gun.

Pete Johnston held a long-barreled, stainless steel revolver of a type he preferred when shooting targets. He squinted carefully, focusing on the officer's reflection in a handheld mirror as he sighted down the barrel, concentrating intently. The pistol pointed through the window behind them, with the barrel resting at the junction of his neck and shoulder. Pete's tongue protruded slightly as his thumb slowly tightened on the trigger.

Dan's jaw dropped open. With wretched clarity, he saw what would happen next. His heart sank like a stone in a drowning pool: below the seat, through the rusted floor, down through the asphalt and beyond, as if it melted down into the molten magma in the core of the earth. His head swirled, sickly and faint.

"No!" he screamed at the top of his lungs. His hand flashed out to knock the weapon away, but before he could touch the gun it fired loudly, blowing through the rear window in a plume of splintered glass mixed with bitterly cold rain.

With a single, well-aimed shot, Pete Johnston ended Dan's dream of a quiet and peaceful life.

The bullet hit home.

The sheriff flipped backwards, as if cracked in the face by a well-aimed baseball bat.

"No!" Dan screamed reflexively, opening his door and jumping out of the cab. "You idiot! You bloody, stinkin' idiot!"

The rain began to fall in earnest. Hail began to strike the vehicles with loud clacks, rebounding against the asphalt.

"Shut up, Danny!" Pete jumped out of the cab and walked to the back of his truck. Ignoring the painful pellets of ice, he daintily donned a pair of cotton work gloves, humming tunelessly as his lanky cousin began to run in circles on the rocky roadbed. Dan looked like Ichabod Crane after a glimpse of the horseman: beside himself with shock and terror.

"He shot her!" Dan shouted toward the sky. "My God, he shot her! Help! Help!" In response, a frighteningly loud thunderclap shook the earth, and the downpour increased in intensity.

Pete opened the door of the squad car and rummaged inside as hail rattled off its metal skin. He emerged in a minute with a grin, holding aloft a videocassette and a loaded shotgun.

"Why, looky here little Danny. We're in the movies!" He felt careless and exultant. "That black African ain't dissin' *me*!" He laughed harshly at the thought. "Just one more thing."

Glancing at Dan, Pete smiled at his panicked expression. When he had pulled the trigger, he had defied all that his cousin stood for. In spite of that fact, he savored the certainty – born of experience – that Dan would muster neither the courage nor the skill required to stop his rampage. Pete despised Dan as a hapless wimp. But this time, he had it wrong.

Something had happened to his mild-mannered cousin.

Something nasty – something unspeakable – had happened to Dan Johnston in the joint. When an inmate had attacked, Dan had found the will to survive. He had fought like a tiger, neutralizing his adversary in seconds. Now, with his back to the wall, he felt the hot power rising from deep within. *No way, Pete! Not this time!* With his mind racing to find a solution, he noticed a pile of lime rocks at his feet. Bending down, he scooped up a jagged chunk of rock the size of a baseball.

Pete Johnston slowly approached the fallen officer, footsteps crunching on the hail. His bullet had struck a passing blow, slashing a crimson crease across the right side of her neck. She had suffered a concussion when she fell, and her consciousness flickered like a failing candle. Blood oozed slowly from the side of her neck, feeding a glistening maroon puddle beneath her head.

The downpour increased. Beams from the squad car's headlights fluttered like startled butterflies beneath the full weight of the storm. Wisps of steam curled upwards from the warm asphalt like spirits freed from the earth: grasping tendrils that added a haunting touch to the storm-bowed beams of light.

Pete Johnston bent over the officer and assessed the wound like a professional. *I must have nicked a vein. One more shot ought'a finish it.*

Pete's assault had been a pragmatic action as well as a crime of passion. He felt certain that he would escape, free and clear.

Pete had always escaped. For almost 15 years, he had dealt drugs with élan, savaging whomever he wished whenever he wanted, while playing the role of an incompetent shade tree mechanic.

Pete had purchased the truck under a fictitious name from a

senile old codger who could scarcely sign the title. The authorities could not trace the paperwork to him. He had no criminal record, and felt certain that he could not be linked to this shooting.

He tucked the pistol into his belt and slipped the crime scene videotape into a spacious pocket in his baggy camouflage pants. Stepping in front of the fallen officer, Pete expertly jacked a round into the chamber of the shotgun and raised it to his shoulder. Pausing briefly, he smiled. "Hasta la vista, tar baby!" he said as he began to squeeze the trigger.

LAUNCHED IN ANGER, hurled swiftly through the air, the projectile stuck the skull squarely. The brute impact bludgeoned the bone, split the scalp, and knocked Pete Johnston off of his feet. The gun swung up, blasting harmlessly in the face of the falling rain.

Even a man in Pete's superb physical condition could not immediately shake off the effects of such a blow. The blunt force of the heavy rock simply knocked him silly. His world spun as he lay on his back in the middle of the road, moaning ever so softly. He struggled in vain to remember his identity, his location, and the mission at hand.

If someone had told Pete Johnston the truth, he would not have believed a word. In his wildest dreams, he could not have concocted a more unlikely story.

Little Danny Johnston had finally stood up to his older cousin Pete. Using the power and skill perfected as the best pitcher in the history of the Micco Bay Correctional Institution, Dan Johnston had slammed Pete in the temple with a 98 mile-per-hour stone projectile, generously greased with fear.

The blow had stunned Dan almost as badly as his cousin Pete. Now, as Dan watched, adrenalin gave way to dread as Pete staggered to his feet, struggling to come to his senses.

Like a scrawny outcast challenging a dominant bull, Dan charged into the roadway and tackled Pete, lifting him high onto his shoulder before slamming him to the asphalt with all of his might, head first. Struggling for his life, he wrenched Pete's revolver out of his belt and tossed it away. The gun skidded into the glare of the squad car's lights, spinning slowly to a stop.

As Dan grabbed the barrel of the shotgun, Pete's hand clamped down tightly on the stock.

Wake-Up Call

"Who's there?" Pete shouted blearily as Dan tried to pull the gun from his grasp. Dan kicked Pete in the head: once, twice, as hard as he could, forcefully attempting to wrench the weapon from Pete's convulsive grasp. After an eternity, the gun popped free, and Dan backed away, aiming it at his cousin. He panted heavily, the long barrel swaying as he shivered in fear.

Within the blink of an eye, Pete Johnston awoke.

He did not rouse slowly. He did not blink groggily and wonder where he was. Instead, like a mechanical soldier, he blasted into consciousness: fully awake and ready for battle. He stood upright in a motion so swift that Dan could barely follow it. On his feet, he squared his shoulders with uncanny self-control, like a video-arcade villain preparing to battle an inexperienced child.

"You stinking, sorry, no good piece of dirt," Pete began to hiss methodically. He uttered the words as if they were a magical, murderous chant: an evil incantation that Dan had never before witnessed.

Pete's vision sharpened, focusing on his target. *My own cousin. I've got to kill my own, stinkin' cousin.*

The sound of Dan racking a shell into the shotgun's chamber stopped him for a moment. Dan backed away, ready for his move.

"Give me the gun, Danny boy," Pete murmured softly. He stepped toward Dan, hoping to close the distance between them.

The mouth of the barrel erupted, blowing a hole in the pavement at Pete's feet and spraying him with stinging particles of dirt. He stared at Dan, beginning to realize that he had underestimated him.

"You've grown some grit, cousin."

"Get into the truck, Pete! Get out of here!" Dan shouted, jacking another round into the chamber. "Go on! Git!"

"My pistol," Pete hissed. "I'm not leavin' without my pistol." *It's the only piece of evidence,* he did not add.

Dan looked at the pistol, swung the shotgun towards it and blasted away with another round. As the revolver spun from the impact, he pumped another shell into the chamber. When it stopped spinning, Dan could see that the blast had blown off the trigger.

"Okay," he said, backing up several additional steps, "get your pistol and get out of here. If you don't get out of here, the next load will be in the middle of your big, ugly gut."

Pete flinched with ill-contained anger and slowly approached his cousin. Squatting carefully, he gingerly reached for his gun.

"Pick it up by the barrel and throw it into the truck bed," Dan instructed, gesturing with the barrel. Peter tossed the pistol contemptuously between two boxes of cucumbers.

"What do you have in those boxes?" Dan asked angrily. "What's in there?"

Pete sneered at Dan, filled with contempt. "What do you think?"

"Doesn't anything matter to you? I just wasted five years of my life in prison! What about this officer's life? What about her family? What kind of monster are you?"

"See ya later, Bozo," Pete rasped. He had paled with anger, and he looked as quick and dangerous as a rattlesnake trapped in a corner.

"This is the end, cuz," Dan added. "There ain't no later."

"Whatever. But listen up," he hissed, speaking slowly and deliberately. "If you ever, and I mean ever, tell anybody what I just did, I won't just kill you." He spoke flatly, with the volume of his speech increasing gradually. "I'll kill your whole stinkin' family." Dan raised the gun to his shoulder and aimed carefully at the middle of Pete's torso.

"Go, or I'll kill you myself, right now."

"I'll go. But if you talk, I'll kill your whole family! Do you hear me?" By now, he was shouting. "I'll kill your weepy little brat and your pretty little Jew-girl wife. I might even throw in good ol' Uncle Beatnik for free." Pete shuddered with anger.

"Go." Dan took the slack out of the trigger.

Pete spit fiercely at his cousin and stalked away. Opening the driver's door, he jumped behind the wheel.

Dan stepped backwards a safe distance from the truck. With the shotgun raised, he drew a bead on the back of his cousin's head. *I could kill him now, and my family would be safe.* He did not pull the trigger, for he lacked the will to kill his cousin in cold blood.

Pete gunned the truck, leaned out of the window, and turned back to Dan. "Keep your mouth shut!" he shouted as he popped the clutch. The truck careened away, spraying gravel across the crime scene with profligate disdain.

Hearing a moan, Dan looked down at the Sheriff of Oree County. She tried to raise her head: a bad idea if ever there were one. The flow of blood turned into a torrent as her damaged flesh finally split wide open. Crimson fluid burst from the officer's neck like a bloody wildcat gusher that crudely pulsed toward the sky before collapsing into the dark puddle beneath her head.

Dan dropped to his knees beside her. He dropped the gun and pressed the palm of his hand against her neck, desperately trying to save her precious life.

It took both of his hands to stop the flow. After the blood staunched, he bent over and groped with his teeth until he managed to compress the button on her shoulder radio.

"Sheriff, is that you?" A tinny voice asked from the other end of the radio signal.

"Officer down!" Dan moaned. "Officer down!" In response, a voice crackled in the tinny speakers.

"Where are you?"

"On Highway 93 near the Cutler County line," Dan shouted, "an officer's been shot. Send an ambulance. Hurry! She's dying!"

"This is a police frequency, sir."

"I know that!" he barked. "I'm using her radio, you moron! She can't talk; she's been shot!" Another, more mature voice interrupted from the other end of the line.

"Who's the officer?" the voice asked.

"I don't know her name," Dan shouted hoarsely.

"She's the Sheriff of Oree County!" He wearily closed his eyes, numbed by the tumultuous tide of events.

The intensity of the downpour increased. The rain fell recklessly, remorselessly pelting the earth. As the traumatic shock from the attack began to ebb, Dan's senses returned with full force.

The hardened hail smote his head and arms, making him wince as the ice chilled his soul. The sheriff tried to move, and Dan pressed his elbow gently against her, leaning over to shelter her face from the force of the blast.

"Don't move," he cried urgently. "Please, sheriff, please; don't move!" He continued to press both hands against her neck. Having finally stopped the gusher through the application of pressure, he feared that further movement might widen the fragile wound. "Can you hear me? Blink twice if you can hear me."

The Sheriff's eyes, wandering and unfocused, regained their clarity as she heard his voice. She looked at him with sudden understanding, beginning to realize what had happened. She blinked slowly: once, then twice, and closed her eyes. *Someone shot me. I remember now… the shooter was closing in for the kill. Who is this guy?* She tried to speak, moving her lips weakly.

"Please, don't move," he shouted above the metallic clatter of hail rattling against her squad car. The hail rained down with persistent, percussive force as the wind increased in intensity. The water began to whip sideways, smacking painfully into their faces. They squeezed their eyes shut against the blast.

Officer down.

The hard truth seemed unavoidable. Dan felt it deep in his bones. He and the fallen sheriff were bound together at the neck. If she died, he might as well volunteer for the electric chair, for he would lose the only witness to his innocence. *Old Sparky, here I come,* he reflected bitterly.

"Don't die," he said aloud to the officer. He cradled her head in his lap. His hand throbbed, but he dared not move it. He could feel her every pulse, every beat of her heart. The palm of his hand had become a wall for her shredded vein, effectively holding the sheriff's life inside her body.

"Please don't die." *Does she have a family?* he wondered. *She didn't deserve this.* A wave of pity washed over him. Her lips moved slightly. Her eyes rolled upwards, and she softly fell asleep.

Dan did not hear the approaching siren. He did not see the lights as Deputy James Cumberland's squad car slid to a stop. But he heard the percussive clatter as the car door slammed open and the deputy leaped out, crouching low and ready to shoot.

A Crime Scene to Die For

"Step away from the Sheriff, or I'll shoot!" the deputy shouted at the top of his lungs, scanning the empty roadway for accomplices as he crouched behind the door of his car. His vehicle had slid to a stop in the oncoming lane, providing an excellent view of an exceptionally nasty crime scene.

Squinting through the veil of rain, the officer scanned the dark, deserted country road. Sheriff Rawlings' car idled beside him, its front door open and bubble lights flashing. In front of the empty car, in a beleaguered oasis of artificial light, a strange man cowered on the pavement. The sheriff's head was in the man's lap, and his hands appeared to be wrapped around her neck.

"Back off or I'll shoot!" the officer cried.

"I can't let go!" Dan shouted. "She'll die!"

"Let her go and step back!" the officer cried, risking all to save the life of his sheriff. He scuttled toward Dan Johnston with a curious sideways motion, stopping a few feet away. He moved like an angry crab: primed and prepared to attack.

"Let her go!"

"I can't! She'll die!" Dan screamed, frightened out his wits, but unwilling to doom the fallen sheriff. "She's lost too much blood!"

The officer scuttled the last few steps and pressed the gun against Dan's temple. He punched the safety off and mashed the end of the barrel viciously into his soft flesh. Pain shot like lightning in a visible flash that arced across Dan's field of vision.

"Let go, or I'll shoot!" the officer screamed at the top of his lungs.

"I can't! Look at my hands! Look at my hands!"

The officer glanced at Dan Johnston's hands and began to realize the extent of the problem. Dan had applied compression to the side of the sheriff's neck to stop the flow of blood. If he removed his hands, a deadly fountain would add to the crimson puddle beneath her head. The unpleasant truth could not be avoided.

If Dan had obeyed the officer's orders, he would have signed Delia Rawling's death warrant.

FIVE MINUTES LATER, the approaching ambulance turned off its siren and silently navigated a flickering barrier of squad cars. The ambulance pulled up to the sheriff's car and stopped.

Lit by multiple headlights, three Oree County sheriff's deputies surrounded the fallen sheriff with their weapons drawn, aiming at the head of a man who sat on the ground with Sheriff Rawlings' head in his lap. Jumping out of the ambulance, the first paramedic to reach the scene – a slight woman carrying a large medical case – ignored the drama and pushed past the deputies to kneel beside the fallen officer.

"How long ago did this happen?" she asked Dan Johnston.

"I don't know," Dan answered dully. "Twenty minutes? A half hour?" For Dan as well as Delia, the shock had begun to set in. His arm ached dully. His hand felt numb, and his back was killing him.

"We got the call ten minutes ago," a deputy growled, edgy and confused.

On her knees, the paramedic carefully looked at Delia's neck without asking Dan to remove his hands. She saw the puddle of blood and shook her head, glancing up at him soberly.

"You've stopped the blood." It was an observation, not a question.

"Yes, ma'am."

"My partner will be here in a second. We'll take over, okay?"

"Sure."

"Don't let go of her neck until we tell you. Do you understand?"

"Got it. Don't let go until you tell me."

"All right," she said with a sigh as she prepared the I.V. "How did this happen?"

Joint Action

"Open up," a voice shouted to the jailer. "It's Major Albritton." The steel door slid open with a clang, and Major Robert 'Alibi' Albritton walked slowly into the hard tile hallway. He stalked heavily down the hall, glowering and intense, the clack of his boot heels echoing ominously against the bare concrete walls. He reached the control room and paused, his hand pressing against the glass on the heavy steel door as he looked at the clock. *It's 6:00 AM, and all is definitely not well.*

"Open up," he barked impatiently, and the door slowly slid open. He walked into the room and stopped, looking the occupants up and down. The men, sworn deputies all, feared to meet his gaze. They stood at attention and glanced at the major obliquely out of the corners of their eyes, furtive and guilty like hounds that had sucked the yolk of a forbidden egg.

"What're all of y'all doin' here at this ungodly hour?" he enquired bluntly, without the usual handshake and smile. The men looked nervously at one another, unsure of how to respond. Normally, two men would work the graveyard shift, but four men stood in the guard station shifting nervously from foot to foot. The senior guard on shift, Sergeant Bill Chandler, cleared his throat uneasily.

"Ah… you know, it's a big deal, what's happened, Major Albritton. The slime bag who shot the sheriff is here. We didn't want him to escape during the night shift, so the boys came in early… just to help out."

"The slime bag who shot the sheriff?"

"Yes, sir."

"He's here? Right now? In custody?"

"Uh… yes, sir."

"You're sure?"

"Yes sir."

Alibi paused and pulled out his handkerchief. He wiped the perspiration from his face methodically, struggling to keep his composure. Carefully folding it, he returned it to his pocket and looked up, riveting all three men, one at a time, with his angry stare. *It's hot in here,* he reflected. He did not speak the words aloud. Small talk suited neither his mood nor his mission.

"Have any of you boys touched the prisoner?" They looked away and did not answer immediately.

"Which prisoner?" Bill Chandler asked with a weak grin.

"Don't you play with me!" Alibi blurted angrily. "You know who I mean."

"Sorry, sir."

"The janitor just came over to my office. He said he heard somebody screaming bloody murder down here." Blinking nervously, the guards did not respond.

"Did you boys mess around with the prisoner?" They looked at one another fearfully, filled with trepidation. "Tell me now," he added, speaking with a tone that made their skin crawl. "Don't make me wait, or it'll be worse."

"He got a little noisy," Bill replied. "We had to shut him up so the other inmates could sleep." His voice trembled. "That's all we did."

"You shut him up? Well, let's hope you did it by the book, boys. 'Cause if you roughed him up, I won't wait for the Oree County Dispatch to get hold of it. I'll press charges myself, up close and personal. Do you understand?" He was shouting by the time he finished.

"Yes, sir."

"Good."

"But the sheriff was shot. She might die," Bill bleated defensively, "and he's the one who did it."

"How do you know that? Are you the judge and jury?"

"No sir, but . . ."

"Did you know that her car has a new surveillance system?"

"Uh... we heard the shooter got rid of the video tape."

"The tape was part of the old system. We left it in her car for backup while she was testing the new system. And guess what? The new system worked like a charm."

"Like a charm?"

"You bet. The entire crime was captured on a hard drive in the trunk of her car.

"That's great."

"The hard drive was damaged when lightning struck her car during the storm, but Kenny just finished restoring it. And would you boys mind guessin' what we saw, recorded on that computer?" Bill gulped audibly, afraid to hear the answer.

"What?"

"Your prisoner didn't hurt Sheriff Rawlings. That boy laid everything on the line to save her life." The jailers glanced at one another in obvious dismay. "He's not a criminal. He's a hero."

"They told us that he shot her," the sergeant wheezed weakly.

"Take me to his cell."

When the door to Dan's cell swung open, even the jailers gasped.

They had played his face like a piñata.

His eyes, swollen tightly shut, bulged like rotten, blue-black grapefruit. His lips had swelled until their prominence – splayed wide and impossibly meaty – prevented him from speaking clearly. His neck showed dark bruises, and although they did not know it, he had suffered a hairline fracture of his right elbow. He could barely lift his swollen arm, and it throbbed like a rotten tooth.

Dan stood when the deputies entered. Swaying erratically, he flinched in fear. He would have raised his hands to defend himself, but he thought they might mistake it for a threatening gesture.

Dan had served time in the joint long enough to understand that frightened cops are the deadliest kind. Although this was a county jail... not a state prison... the same principles applied. Some guards were professionals, and others were merciless hacks. At this miserable lockup, he had learned the hard way that these guards were hacks who demanded respect and the fear bred by violence.

"Dan Johnston?" Alibi asked.

"Yes, sir," Dan drawled tenuously through his swollen lips, unsure of what was about to happen.

"I'd like to thank you for saving our sheriff's life."

"What?" he mumbled hopefully, scarcely able to believe what he heard.

"I'd like to thank you for saving Sheriff Rawlings' life."

"She's alive?" he slurred as blood began to ooze from the corner of his mouth. He wiped it away impatiently, frustrated with his impeded speech. *Ouch!* His skin burned to his touch.

"Yes, sir, she's alive. And you're a hero, son." Hearing his words, Dan nodded blissfully. *Oh, yeah.*

"We have a video that shows the whole thing. You risked your life to save the sheriff. I want to thank you personally."

"Jus' glad she's alive," Dan mumbled.

"I'd like to apologize for the unprofessional behavior of these men." He glared at the officers.

"O-gay," Dan slurred, nodding happily. *Man, that hurts.*

"Mr. Johnston, we're real sorry," the sergeant began to mutter. Too hard-hearted to muster a sincere apology, he attempted to bail himself out with a show of feigned remorse. Dan ignored his half-hearted attempt to minimize liability.

"Ride-o," he slurred through the pain. "You're afraid of a lawzoot." In spite of it all, he started to laugh. *Ow!* The agony hammered his nervous grid, gouging his ribs like hot iron.

Dan turned his wounded face to Major Albritton and attempted unsuccessfully to open his right eyelid. "Could y'all spare a Motrin?" he asked. The major answered immediately.

"I've got some in my desk, Mr. Johnston. Why don't you come with me? I'll drive you to the hospital myself, if you'd like." He bitterly eyed the jailers. "If not, we can call an ambulance."

"Le'me think."

"We'll call your family right away."

"Ogay. Can we leave now?"

"Yes, sir."

Taking his elbow, he led Dan Johnston carefully out of the cell. "By the way, Mr. Johnston, you may want to consider the FDLE's witness protection program. We know that your life was threatened at the scene of the crime."

"You heard that?"

"It's all on the video."

"Good." They walked down the hall side by side, their footsteps ringing off the concrete walls.

"We've contacted the FDLE and they're sending an officer. They've got a file on your cousin, but they could never get enough proof to charge him with anything. Until tonight."

"He fooled me. He fooled m'family. I feel like'n idjit."

"It's not your fault."

"I know."

"We'll get him."

"Good." They arrived at the end of the hall. A buzzer sounded and the door opened. Alibi Waldron gestured toward the open doorway.

"Just let us know what you want us to do for you. You're a free man, Mr. Johnston."

"What did you say?"

"You're a free man, Mr. Johnston."

Major Albritton turned one last time and gazed back down the hallway, where the four jailers stood, shocked into silence. "Let's get out of here before I show those boys how to use a nightstick properly," he growled.

When Dan Johnston smiled, the pain felt terrific.

Two Years Later

Witness Predilection

"So tell me, are you coming to my party?" Jamie leaned back into the cushions of the couch as she kicked off her shoes. *That sure feels good.* She stared toward the roof as she tried to imagine the expression on her friend's face. "Well, are you coming or not?" she asked testily.

"Don't you have to study nowadays?" Delia Rawlings enquired hopefully. "Do you really have time to throw a party?"

"I've finished all of my coursework. I've taken a hiatus to work with the FDLE's witness protection program. Didn't I tell you?"

"You don't tell me anything anymore. Since you married that cowboy, I'm out in the cold."

"What cowboy?"

"You know… the cute one who works for me. What's his name?"

"Very funny."

"You aren't laughing."

"Okay, you're avoiding my question. Are you coming to my party, or not?"

"How could I not come to your party, Jamie?" Delia asked with a smile. "Aren't you my BFF?" *That girl is relentless.*

"I suppose," Jamie sniffed haughtily. "So, what are you doing tonight?"

"You are one nosy girl."

"Granted. So? What are you doing? Would you like to come out to the ranch? I'm cooking a roast."

"Sorry, honey, I can't come tonight. I'm going out."

"Going out? Who's the guy?"

"Don't ask, 'cause I sure ain't gonna tell." Delia smiled secretively, enjoying her friend's unrelenting curiosity.

"Then don't tantalize me with a little bit of information, okay?

You're giving me just enough to make me curious."

"You're always curious, like the curiously dead cat."

"Dead cat? That's nice."

"Curiosity got your tongue?"

"Clever. So, who's taking you out?"

"Let's make a deal. If you don't ask anymore about my big evening out, I won't ask whether you've been assigned to my case."

"Delia, I'm an intern, for goodness sake! Your case is a really big deal."

"You're a doctoral candidate, little girl. They didn't hire you to write parking tickets."

"A doctorate doesn't impress 'em down at the cop shop."

"Then let's put it this way. Are you assigned to my case?"

"If I were, I wouldn't tell you. The less said the better. You're the victim, and Dan Johnston's family is under witness protection. That's all you need to know."

"The last I heard, I was still the Sheriff of Oree County."

"Oh, excuse me. I forgot to salute."

"I give up."

"Thank you!" Jamie replied emphatically. Glad that the topic had turned away from her biggest case, she gazed at her nails distractedly. *I need a manicure.*

"I'm 22 years older than you," Delia continued. "Who made you the responsible one?"

"You know the answer. I was 50 by the time I was 20. That makes me older than you."

"Okay, let's get back to your party. What should I bring?"

"Just bring yourself, officer. And just in case you don't know, I've got a surprise guest comin' in from out of town."

"Who?"

"It's a surprise! You're pushing it!"

"Maybe I am." Delia Rawlings said softly, distracted by her reflection in the bathroom mirror. *Should I put more makeup on my neck?* The thick purple scar from the gunshot wound stood out vividly. As happened sometimes, the impressive nature of her reflection mildly surprised her. She remained attractive in her middle years: a handsome, dark-skinned woman pushing 50, tall and athletic. Against her neck, the scar from the healed gunshot wound spread an angry, purple tendril... a faded fingerprint from the frustrated hand of death.

"Did you hear the news?" Jamie inquired. "They've delayed Peter Johnston's trial again." *If we're going to talk about the trial, let's stick to the public record,* she reasoned.

"Yeah, I heard."

"It's strange, don't you think?" Jamie continued. "First, he fired his defense team. Then his new lead counsel died in that accident."

"Very strange."

"Is he trying to delay the trial? The coincidences keep piling up. It looks mighty fishy to folks like us."

"We're not the trusting kind."

"Not by a long shot. It sets off my alarms."

"Yes," the Sheriff replied. "It's sad any way you look at it. Win Johnston's family will never be the same."

"They've been through hell, or the next worst thing," Jamie clarified. "Did you hear about Win's heart attack?"

"Heart attack? Win?" The news shocked Delia.

"I'm afraid so."

"Oh, no. He's such a great old guy. Is he okay?"

"They're keeping him in the hospital. It's pretty serious."

"Win was always so good to me. Remember that terrific letter to the editor he wrote during my campaign? Seth published it in the Oree County Dispatch. That letter may have won me the election."

"I don't know how much more Win can take," Jamie added. "First Dan went to prison, and then his nephew Pete tried to kill you. After that, Dan's family went into hiding. Then, Martha died."

"That is one sad family."

"You know the saying. One bad apple plagues the whole barrel with its rot."

"That's not how I heard it."

"You heard the sanitized version."

"Cute. Do you think Win will recover?"

"I hope so. But enough of this sadness! Let's talk about happier things."

"Let's."

"You won't forget about my party, right?"

"Party? What party?"

"My party, two weeks from now, on Friday the 4th of July. Write it on your calendar, okay?"

"No illegal fireworks?"

"Donny's getting a permit. I made him."

"You made him? Why am I not surprised?"

"Hey, I'm a law enforcement professional now, Delia. Just like you."

"I know, honey. That's the part that scares me."

Graveyard Shift

On the evening of July 4th, in a county almost 100 miles away, a towering sheriff's deputy strode down a hallway inside a modern county jail. The big man moved with impressive solidity, dominating the sterile public area.

When they built the jail, the taxpayers had sought security, but had created sterility: shiny white tile floors bordered by flat ivory walls glaring beneath the harsh glow of cheap fluorescence. The hallway seemed to drift uneasily beneath the pulsating lights as though possessed by a troubled spirit, like a ghostly scene from *One Flew Over the Cuckoo's Nest*.

The big deputy swaggered as he walked, dominating the hallway: a looming, beefy slab of a man as thick in the shoulders as a prime cut swinging from a hook. He swayed like a palm tree in the air-conditioned breeze wafting through the Broward County Jail in downtown Fort Lauderdale, Florida.

Down the hall, just around the corner, a guard on duty in the lockdown pod glanced briefly at his watch and frowned. *11:58 PM. Where are those jerks?* The next shift started at midnight, and the jail did not tolerate tardiness. The guard did not know that at this very moment, relief lumbered in his direction.

Behind the pale, super-sized deputy strolled Paul Larson, a recent hire who had acquired his job the old fashioned way: through questionable political connections. Paul contrasted sharply with his companion. Thin, tanned, and of medium height, he wore a thick crown of curly brown hair and a quick, cunning smile.

"Happy Independence Day, Larson," the big man grunted over his shoulder.

"Unhappy, you mean. We have to work Friday night, the 4th of July, when we should be watchin' fireworks and knockin' back a few cold ones. We're chumps, Mack. Chumps."

"I don't mind. Me and Emma'll be chillin' in the Keys next week."

"You lucky dog."

"Tell me about it."

"Hey, I want to clean the windows in the control room. Can you help me get some cleaning supplies?"

"Sure." The tall guard paused and fished through his pocket, searching for the key that would unlock the janitorial closet.

"Thanks, Mack."

The big man inserted the key and swung the door open. The smaller man pointed into the closet and flipped on the light. "The Windex is on the top shelf in the back. Could you get it? I can't reach."

Big Mack entered the closet. Moving the buckets aside, he worked his way to the rear wall as his partner glanced up and down the hallway.

"Perfect," he whispered.

"Here you go," the big man said with a smile, holding out two bottles. He squinted toward his companion, who stood silhouetted against the brightly lit doorway. To his surprise, he noticed that Larson held a pistol in his hand.

"How'd you get a gun in here?" he asked, perplexed. "That's totally against the rules."

"The guys at the front door are as stupid as you, that's how," Larson leered. As the gentle giant stared at him with a look of perplexity, Deputy Larson slowly squeezed the trigger.

The well-silenced gun coughed delicately as it launched a heavy bullet from the barrel's mouth. Mack had no time to duck.

The bullet entered his nasal cavity and split the back of his head open like an overripe melon, exploding outward with a ropy spray of brain and bone and gristle. Big Mack collapsed, instantly and completely. Against the wall where he had stood only moments before, a gruesome bas-relief of shattered humanity oozed slowly toward the earth's gravitational core, crawling down to join the victim on the hard tile floor.

Paul Larson grinned and tucked the smoking gun behind his back, hiding it in his loose-fitting pants before he stepped backward and carefully locked the door. *These porcelain handguns are just too good,* he reflected.

Shutting the closet door, Larson strolled around the next bend in the hallway and waved at the two guards in the control room. They pressed a button and let him into the pod, surprised to see Larson without his reliable partner.

"Where's Mack?" the lead deputy asked nervously, licking his lips. The other deputy in the control room remained silent, taking his cues from his more experienced partner.

"He had a fender bender comin' to work. The lieutenant will be sending someone up to take his place in a couple of minutes."

"I'd better stay 'till he gets here," the senior guard offered half-heartedly.

"Nah, go on home. We've only got one prisoner."

"He's a nasty one."

"He can't be too nasty, eh? They took him alive." They laughed.

"You're crazy, Larson."

"Like a fox guarding the henhouse." He winked. "The chickens don't have a chance."

"This guy's up for murder one now. They made a DNA match with a cold case in Cutler County."

"That's old news. I can handle this knucklehead."

"Okay, you've got it. Just be sure to stay in the control room until your backup arrives."

"Sure."

The two deputies left the pod, glad to turn their backs on the depressing lockdown unit. Guard duty in a lockdown unit could drive a man crazy: long days filled with screaming inmates and the heavy atmospheric threat of untold bodily harm.

"Witless chickens," Larson whispered as the door shut behind them. As soon as they were out of sight, he reached down, unlocked a drawer, and grabbed a set of handcuffs and leg irons. Placing his key into a slot in the console, he turned it, flipped two switches, and pressed a button to open the only occupied pod.

Out of the cell stepped Pete Johnston, as tall and cool and hairy as ever. *He's as hairy as an ape,* Larson mused, smiling crookedly. *It's downright obscene.*

"What took you so long?" Pete Johnston asked blithely.

"Step lively, Pete; we've gotta move fast." Larson opened the door to the control room, and Pete Johnston stepped inside, standing silently as Larson affixed iron shackles to his legs with well-concealed transparent packing tape.

"Watch it, Pete," Paul Larson instructed tensely. "If those shackles fall off in front of anyone, we're dead."

"Who are you… my daddy?"

"Just pretend I'm the boss for a few minutes, okay? Pretend that I'm a bull with attitude."

"If you were that, I'd have to kill you."

"Never mind." Larson grinned wickedly. *Fat chance, big guy.*

"I'll pretend that you're the lead goat."

"Good enough. We'll be swimmin' in goat's head soup if we don't make it out of here."

"Lead the way, goat boy!"

"Right." Larson hurried Pete through the control room door. "Open the main door when you hear the buzzer, okay?"

"Yo." Larson pressed the buzzer, and Pete swung the door open. Larson hurried out of the control room and stepped past Pete. "Let's get out of here," he said tensely as they walked down the hall toward the elevator.

When the elevator doors opened, they saw an overweight guard with his hands folded on his belly. Larson recognized him as Abe Stoller, the recreation officer on the night shift. Abe stared in surprise as they stepped into the elevator.

"You're exercisin' an inmate this late… by yourself?"

"Not by myself, Abe. You'll be there. Not to mention the fact that we've got a thundering herd of Broward's finest downstairs."

Pete Johnston, looking down from his hirsute height, ogled the perspiring, overweight guard like a cruel child inspecting an insect.

He smiled and winked, licking his lips.

"They've changed his exercise protocol," Larson stated officiously. "They want to be sure he's in the yard alone 'cause of all the threats. You heard about what happened last month, right?"

"The fight over the television? We all heard. This Neanderthal almost caused a riot." There had been a fight over a Jerry Springer show in the high security unit, and race had been the primary factor. As a result of that riot, and due to several tips regarding smuggled weapons, the authorities had moved Pete Johnston into his own, private lockdown pod.

"You shouldn't call me a Neanderthal," Pete whispered to Stoller. "That hurts my feelings, bad." He paused for a moment. "Real bad."

"Shut up," Larson interjected sociably as the elevator stopped at the top floor and they stepped into the hallway.

"I feel like an organ grinder chained to a monkey," Pete sneered, winking at Abe Stoller.

"Shut up, Johnston!" Larson barked the words loudly, barely able to suppress a chuckle. *I'll make you pay for that one.*

Paul Larson and Pete Johnston had been friends since their first year at the University of Miami, before Pete had dropped off the grid to pursue extra-legal entrepreneurial development in the field of illicit narcotics. The two longtime associates, after years of lethal partnership, shared the intuitive understanding of hunting wolves: lifelong members of the same bloody pack.

He'll make me pay for that wisecrack if he gets a chance, Pete thought with a grin as they stepped up to the door that led to the concrete exercise yard. Signaling to the guard in the control room, Stoller pressed a buzzer and opened the door to the workout area. Paul Larson and Pete Johnston entered the state-of-the-art exercise yard for high security inmates, surrounded by a tall fence topped with rolls of razor wire. Perched atop the building, the exercise yard was further secured by a 15-story drop to the streets below.

"Looks like you've got the yard to yourself," Abe said to Pete Johnston without enthusiasm as he walked down the steps and strolled out onto the open concrete. Paul Larson paused in the gate, turning to address the overweight guard.

"I'm going to get some air out here with the prisoner."

"Suit yourself." Stoller replied, picking up a magazine and leaning back in his chair, almost hidden behind the bulletproof glass. Half-blinded by the flashing lights of the security console, Stoller read in peace for several minutes, glancing at the concrete recreation area from time to time.

Abe did not hear the helicopter until it had poised directly above the exercise pen. At first, the thumping seemed dim and distant, but the sound swiftly grew in strength. He put down his magazine and looked up as the spotlight turned on and a beam of light raked across the basketball court. To his astonishment, a small black helicopter hovered above the razor wire. As he watched, unable to comprehend the unfolding tableau, the chopper dropped a cable with two harnesses attached. The cable fell neatly into the middle of the yard.

"No!" Abe cried as the tumblers in his mind clicked into place. At that moment, his telephone rang.

Paul Larson and Pete Johnston caught the rope and swiftly climbed into the heavy harnesses. Snapping their hooks securely, they waved with both hands at the helicopter.

Abe punched the emergency alarm and frantically picked up the telephone. "They're getting away!" he shouted.

"Who? What's happening up there?"

"The prisoner's getting away! The cop-shooter! Peter Johnston!" Abe's blood pressure surged, placing him at the cusp of a coronary. "There's a chopper up here!" He threw the phone down and fumbled with his keys, desperate to unlock the riot gun beneath the counter.

As he jacked a round into the chamber of the shotgun and ran out of the guard station, the two men rose into the air, swinging from the end of the cable. They gazed down at Abe Stoller and laughed dismissively as he dashed into the exercise yard and drew a bead on them. They had already risen beyond the effective range of the scattergun, but he planned to pepper them with painful shot, nonetheless.

As Abe sited down the barrel, he realized that Pete Johnston pointed in his direction. In Pete's hand, he saw a pistol.

A light flashed from the end of the barrel, and the overweight guard gasped as a ton of bricks plowed into his chest. He dropped the shotgun and tumbled down the steps, crashing onto unforgiving concrete as the thump of the departing helicopter drummed delicately – like a gypsy moth – against the failing gates of his awareness.

Independence Day

At 11:45 PM, 14-year-old Danny Johnston abandoned all efforts to sleep and decided to sneak a smoke. As he had on many sleepless nights, he entered his bedroom closet and stealthily used the strong wooden shelves as steps to climb upwards. Carefully sliding aside a small attic door, he boosted himself into the heart of his own, secret haven.

During his years in the state prison system, Danny's father had come to despise air conditioning, considering it one more layer of security between his incarcerated body and the fresh air of liberty.

In a way, Dan remained in prison. He and Sarah and Danny had received new names and a new life, but they lived alone in a remote area, far from family and friends. In spite of this, they had struggled to build a life worth living. Their family remained intact, clinging together like an island economy in an ocean of strangers.

When the Johnston family had entered the witness protection program, Big Dan had insisted that they live in an old fashioned Florida house with a large attic to dissipate the summer heat. He had also requested a roomy barn where he could continue his life's work: creating metal sculptures great and small, drawing inspiration from whatever school of art captured his fancy at the moment.

During the past few years, Dan Johnston – a brilliant sculptor – had matured from artistic copycat to aesthetic rebel. He had welded, ground, and polished his way through a veritable smelting pot of styles: realism, impressionism, surrealism, and an evolving style of his own that he called "heavy metal fusion."

The large attic fan that cooled the venerable Florida home on hot summer nights provided noisy cover for Danny whenever he wanted to sneak a cigarette. For good measure, the airflow vented the smoke outside.

Danny loved the old attic with its huge, rattling fan. As his eyes adjusted to the darkness, he could see the shimmering beams of moonlight slicing though the slow-moving blades. Groping until he found a string, he turned on a bare 60-watt bulb. Blinking in the glare, he knew that he was home free.

One could see in the unfiltered light that Danny had grown like a weed during the past two years. He looked tall and lanky, with a fuzzy shadow on his face that required a bi-weekly shave. His fire-engine-red hair had segued to a darker shade, and his freckles blended into the tanned complexion of a typical teenager in the sun-blasted clime of South Central Florida.

He quietly slid the attic crawlway door back into place and sat down in a worn vinyl lounge chair, reveling in the moment. This, indeed, felt like his personal throne room.

Taking his time, he thoughtfully lit a Marlboro with an old-fashioned kitchen match. He began to puff languorously, filling the dusty air with rich curls of forbidden tobacco smoke. *If Mom knew I was doing this, she'd kill me,* he reflected with a furtive smile, *and Daddy'd finish off what's left.* He leaned back and exhaled, watching the smoke swirl luxuriously around the dusty bulb.

A loud bump in the house below startled him, and he almost dropped his cigarette. Sitting up, he carefully brushed hot sparks from his lap. *What was that?* His parents slept soundly, and when awake they moved gracefully. They never so much as stubbed a toe, and they certainly never went bump in the night.

Dousing the light, he buried the smoldering butt in a coffee can filled with sand and carefully crawled across the attic floor. Pausing, he slid aside a piece of cardboard covering a crack where the wall met the ceiling in a corner of his parents' bedroom. He could not see, so he held his breath, listening carefully.

At first, he heard nothing. But then, at a volume so low that he wondered if he imagined it, a man's voice spoke softly in the darkness. He could not make out the words. *That must be Dad,* he reassured himself, crawling back toward the trap door that led to his bedroom. *I'd better get back in bed.*

As he prepared to slide the trap door aside, another male voice answered the first. The new voice came from his bedroom, only a few feet below his perch. Hearing the low-pitched, unfamiliar voice, Danny Johnston froze in terror. An unfamiliar rush of sheer horror seemed to roll down his body from head to toe: hypnotically evil, paralytic in effect.

"He's not in the closet," the raspy male voice stated emphatically. "Let's check the attic."

Dodging the Needle

For his escape from the Broward County Jail, Pete Johnston had chosen a Dauphin of recent French manufacture: a reliable, turbine-powered aircraft owned by one of his proxy corporations. His men had retrofitted the chopper with Czech military hardware, and had stored it for the past several weeks in a secure hanger in Davie, Florida. The helicopter was sophisticated and deadly, much like the sociopath it now bore through the sky, cradled in its aluminum womb.

Within four minutes after the Dauphin snagged its cargo atop the jail, the Broward Sheriff's Department had rerouted an airborne helicopter from the site of a Miramar robbery. The law enforcement chopper had a chance to gain a good angle on the westbound flight path of the retreating Dauphin, but they did not have sight contact, and the French bird had speed to burn: far too much for the sheriff's creaky aviation relic. If it had not been for a high-flying eye-in-the-sky reporter, their pursuit would have failed. The airborne reporter responded instinctively, tracking the Dauphin from high altitude on a reporter's hunch as the bird of prey streaked away from the shimmering downtown area, flying due west toward the darkened, distant Everglades.

The sheriff's helicopter, flying at full speed, pursued using an interception vector conveniently provided by the thrilled eye-in-the-sky reporter. As an experienced aviator, the reporter had provided expert information.

Alarms sounded inside the jail. Quickly realizing the extent of the threat, the Broward Central Dispatch team called the local Homeland Security hotline. Within five minutes, Homestead Air Force Base had scrambled an F-15 interceptor from the Florida Air National Guard's 125th Fighter Wing.

The Broward Sheriff's Department helicopter intercepted the

Dauphin at Cooper City, less than five minutes from the Everglades. Flying directly into its path, the chunky old chopper almost struck its sleek target. Enraged, the pilot of the Dauphin spun the craft around to face his awkward, outdated adversary. For a moment, the French helicopter paused in a steady hover.

As the reporter's video would later show a shocked nation and a smug, self-righteous world, what happened next would be vile, astonishing, and unhealthily entertaining. The law enforcement chopper wheeled sluggishly toward the French helicopter as a missile scorched from the Dauphin's left launch tube. The missile streaked rapidly toward its target and delivered a fiery body blow.

At the moment of impact, the law enforcement helicopter seemed to hesitate, as if pondering the plunge into disaster. And then, without further fanfare, it exploded with a blinding blast of light, accompanied by a terrific boom and a strangled gasp from the dumfounded eyewitness in the sky.

Ignoring the aftermath, the Dauphin turned west and accelerated toward the heart of the Everglades. The terrified reporter fled east toward his home airport. He had filmed enough footage. The story would go national, and he would reap a rich reward.

The pilot switched the Dauphin's engines to silent mode as he approached the Sawgrass Expressway, scanning the terrain below for the three small landing lights that would mark their destination. Within seconds, he saw the lights that marked a long lake bordering the Expressway. He pulled back on the throttle, slowing down to a relative crawl. They had to move quickly.

"Get ready to jump!" he shouted, turning on the autopilot and climbing into the back. "We have to jump at the same time, okay?" *I'll bring the chopper down after we jump,* he did not bother to add.

"Okay." Pete shouted.

"Ready!" He pointed to the lake below the open door. "Jump!"

As the three men jumped out of the open door, the pilot pressed a button on the cell phone in his hand. A techie in his employ had rigged a diversionary device, and the signal from his phone triggered a time release that would disengage the autopilot in three seconds.

They plummeted into a warm South Florida lake, skipping hard across the surface and swimming to the weed-strewn shore as the helicopter began to wobble like a drunken pilot staggering from an airport lounge. Soaking wet, they ran toward the Sawgrass Expressway. A tractor-trailer idled beneath an overpass, its driver checking the tires as he waited to receive his illicit human cargo.

The helicopter struggled through the sky above the Expressway. The sudden exit of all on board, followed by the disengagement of the autopilot, had mortally destabilized its flight. Barely clearing the west traffic lanes, it crashed into an open field on the far side of the multi-lane highway.

As they climbed into the cab of the big rig, they felt a satisfying jolt as the chopper exploded. The blast shook the earth. The flames lit up the inside of the cab. They could feel the heat against their faces.

"Good timing," shouted Pete from his perch in the sleeper compartment. The big diesel thundered, and the driver slipped the clutch and smiled smugly. "Our next stop is an airstrip near Kissimmee," he stated laconically.

"Caiman Islands, here I come," Pete whispered silently.

"Ooh la la," crowed Larson.

"Home free," Pete boasted, smiling brightly.

Or maybe not, big boy, thought the slippery Paul Larson. He flashed an infectious smile and uttered a devilish chuckle.

"You'd better shut the curtain," the driver warned. "The cops will be thick around here within a few minutes."

"Just give it the juice, pal," Pete sneered. "We'll be off the Sawgrass Expressway before they know what hit 'em."

It had been a bad day for cops in Broward County… especially for their families. Two fathers, one mother, and an unmarried jail guard with a co-dependant bulldog would not come home tonight. Pete's minions had executed his plan to perfection. He had pulled off the most brazen crime in the history of the Sunshine State. If you happened to be a sociopath, the future looked bright.

Pete Johnston, disciple of death, had successfully dodged the needle.

Terror Mismanagement

Who are those men? Danny wondered, frozen in terror. *They're coming up here!* The quiet tread of careful footsteps could be heard in the house below as the men searched for the steps to the attic.

Weak with fear, shaking so badly that he could scarcely crawl, Danny slid aside the small door and climbed down into his bedroom closet. He moved slowly, filled with dread. He felt as if he were swimming through the deep end of a drowning pool, struggling against a calamitous current of fear.

Danny had wondered lately if God existed. Now, his terror removed all doubt. He began to pray fervently. *Please, God; please Jesus, help me!* He prayed fervently, returning instantly to the faith of his mother. *I don't want to die.*

As he heard the doorknob jostle at the foot of the attic steps, Danny slid the door shut above him. Shivering involuntarily, he climbed down the shelves and dropped to the floor. For the moment, the moon had passed behind fast-moving clouds. In the oppressive silence, his bedroom felt dark as a tomb. *Mom! Dad!* he thought in panic. He felt pressure building in his chest, and his throat tightened in fear.

Danny ran quietly down the hallway toward his parents' bedroom. At any moment, he expected a dark form to pop out from a doorway and grab him, but he forced himself to move. At the door of their bedroom, he paused.

"Mommy?" he whispered softly, stepping into the room. "Daddy?" He heard no answer.

Something was wrong.

The room seemed uncannily dark and silent. Feeling his way through the darkness, he circled the edge of the room, moving toward the window. As he moved, he stared: transfixed by the sight of two large, shadowy lumps sprawled ominously across the king-sized bed.

Just as he reached the window, the full moon emerged from behind the clouds.

In Danny's world, time stopped still… dead still.

He saw his parents clearly.

His mother lay on her back as if she slept: eyes closed, unmoving. Her face reflected a profound peace, as if she had gently slept through the shock of her own death. The killer's well-aimed bullet had punched a clean, precise hole in the middle of her forehead. Her brunette locks swam in a shallow sea of blood, an obscene crimson halo that slowly increased in size. The bloody puddle spread outward relentlessly, polluting the clean white sheets.

Danny's father lay on his stomach, sprawled sideways across the bed. His head and arm dangled below the open nightstand drawer where he had reluctantly stored a handgun against the risk of such a night. Three neat holes had been drilled in Dan Johnston's back. His fine-featured face bore a fixed expression of shock mingled with pained disbelief.

Danny heard a piercing scream that seemed to emerge from somewhere in the distance. He wondered about the origin of the desperate outcry, for the voice seemed vaguely familiar.

As if awakening from a nightmare, he recognized the sound of his own, horrified shrieks. Attempting to get away from the sight, he stumbled backwards toward the open window. He tripped and fell against the aluminum screen, knocking it through the opening. Instinctively, he caught the window frame and avoided a nasty fall onto the steeply pitched roof.

He turned to the bed and stared again, scarcely believing his eyes. *Dead. Both of them… dead.*

He knew the killers would be coming, but for a moment he did not care. His eyes wandered to the floor, where his father's pistol lay unused beside his open hand. *He almost got 'em,* Danny thought idly, and his anger began to build. Having lived under the threat of sudden death for two years, his emotions now rapidly transitioned from disbelief into rage.

The anger demolished his fear. *I'll kill them!*

He heard a faint sound. *They're coming!*

As a surge of dread triggered a sickening flood of adrenaline, Danny dropped to the ground and scooted nimbly beneath the huge, low-slung bed.

The Turn of the Worm

The killers in the attic almost dropped their guns in glee when they heard the little boy scream. This was what they lived for!

"Let's complete the trifecta," the larger man whispered. "The payoff will be outstanding."

"After you," his younger colleague offered graciously, sneaking down the attic stairs behind his mentor.

In the hallway below, the big man signaled his companion to check the child's room as he approached the master suite. *The kid should be easier than the father.* It had taken three well-placed rounds to stop Dan Johnston, who had managed to dig a pistol out of his nightstand before expiring.

The killer stepped into the master bedroom. At first glance, in the pale moonlight, everything appeared as he had left it. Dim, ethereal light poured in through the open window at the right side of the bed.

Reaching into the room, the lacy curtains waved imploringly in the thin rays of moonlight. They resembled weakly petitioning arms: a ghostly plea that fluttered limply in the warm summer breeze, begging him to end the slaughter.

That window had a screen, the killer recalled. *Now it's gone.* He looked out the window and shook his head. *The kid got out the window. Pretty smart.* He deeply regretted this development.

Tonight's job had been a package deal for both parents. The Chicago Capo had tossed in the boy at the last minute. His death, while not part of the original deal, would bring a generous bonus. *We've got to catch that kid if we can.* The shorter killer appeared in the doorway, interrupting his reverie.

"What happened to the boy?"

"It looks like he got out through the window. Let's make sure he ain't in the house before we start tracking him." They paused and smiled at one another. *This is as good as it gets,* they reflected, contentedly guessing one another's thoughts. *This kid is ours.*

WHEN DANNY SLID BENEATH THE BED, he stirred up dust inside the narrow space. On his stomach, with the bed pressing firmly against his back, he had little room to breathe. His allergies began to flare up, tickling his nose without mercy.

As the killer came into the room, his scraping footsteps assaulted Danny's nerves like kisses from an open grave. The boy's fear grew exponentially as the seconds ticked by. Waves of terror rolled over him from head to foot. The shockwaves of fear seemed rhythmic, beyond his control, like the tides: drumbeats of adrenalin that ebbed and surged like the sea, compressing his chest and rendering each breath more difficult than the last.

As Danny struggled to regain his self-control, he heard the rich resonance of a single drop of blood hitting the bedroom carpet. Turning his head toward the sound, he saw an automatic pistol lying on the carpet beside his father's open hand. The black pistol contrasted sharply with the pale, lifeless fingers dangling loosely beside it.

A low voice whispered from the doorway.

"I'll check downstairs. Let's be quick."

"Okay. I'll be down in a minute."

The big man began to search the master bedroom. He opened the closet door, shoving aside clothing to grope the back wall. Danny used this noise for cover. Weeping softly, shaking convulsively, he slowly reached for his father's gun.

"MY BONNIE LIES OVER THE OCEAN," the killer began to sing with a coarse, rumbling baritone voice, almost purring the words down deep in his chest. "My bonnie lies over the sea." He paused, staring at the bed. Then, he shook his head, holstered his gun, and turned toward the door.

Beneath the bed, Danny could no longer suppress his allergies. The persistent tickle inside his nose had become unbearable. *I can't,* he thought urgently, but to no avail.

Danny sneezed just before the man stepped out of the bedroom.

"Whoa!" the killer cried enthusiastically, "Gentlemen, start your weapons." Walking to the dark side of the bed opposite the open, moonlit window, he meticulously pulled up his trousers and knelt on the floor. *I should be prayin' for mercy instead of killin' for money,* he thought as he knelt down.

Immediately he paused, questioning his sanity. *Where the hell did that come from?* But the idea had not come from hell.

"Sayonara, you sneaky little worm." He lowered his forehead to the carpet, flicked on his flashlight, and looked underneath the bed.

The killer had hit the jackpot. He saw the kid, as pale as a ghost. At the sight, he smiled beneficently. *Here's our bonus money.*

He could almost taste the money as the scrawny child blinked in the glare of his bright flashlight. But as he raised his gun to administer the coup de grace, he noticed something peculiar about the boy's expression. *He ain't afraid. He's concentrating.* He squinted curiously at the child. *What's in his hand?*

In a flash, he recognized the object in the boy's hand.

Too little, too late.

Danny's handgun exploded in the killer's face, punching a heavy bullet through his open right eye. The bullet plowed through his brain and exited messily through the back of his skull, spraying the carpet with gore before it lumbered to a stop in a beam inside the bedroom wall.

"Uhhh . . ." he exhaled as he began a disastrous plunge into the abyss. He fell helter-skelter into an open pit that swallowed everything, even the echoes of his own, terrified wail. The pit surrounded him with palpable darkness... with hopeless loneliness and a smothering stench that was – indeed – as hot as hell.

The killer had medical insurance. He had a dental plan. He even had an IRA. But he had not planned on this.

The arms of hell embraced him as he shrieked in soundless horror. The fiery man had become, to his own astonishment, quite literally a man on fire.

"Joey!" his companion called in vain. When he heard no reply, he raced up the steps and burst into the master bedroom.

He gasped at the scene, stunned and dismayed. Big Joe, his longtime partner in mayhem, lay crumpled on the floor: face down, as lifeless as a discarded crash test dummy. With the last bloody pump of Joe's failing heart, his shattered skull spewed a final, ponderous gush onto the pale beige carpet.

The cause of death looked obvious, with no formal inquiry needed. Someone under the bed had shot Joey's lights out.

The hit man jumped atop the bed, lowered his gun to the carpet and fired swiftly, rotating his wrist to cover the entire area beneath the bed. He emptied a full clip before slamming in another and emptying that one, too: 22 shots in all.

"Thanks a million, Joey!" he shouted bitterly to his dead companion. "Now I have to lug your beefy carcass outta this place." He well remembered their instructions: 'no witnesses, no evidence, or no final payment.' Not that they needed instructions.

"Confirm the kills," he said aloud, beginning to run through the checklist. He suddenly felt exhausted.

What a drag, he reflected. *Joey finally got whacked. We had a lot of laughs. We made a ton of money, too.*

The killer knelt quickly on the carpet, ignoring the beautiful moonlight in the clear summer sky as he shined his flashlight beneath the bed to confirm the boys' death. To his surprise, he saw nothing but dust: filthy clumps competing with ponderous motes that circled listlessly in the air, trapped by his probing beam.

The space beneath the bed was empty.

The killer heard a quiet click behind him. *The closet!* With a sudden burst of awareness, he tried to roll away from the bed.

Right here, right now, inside of this humble house in a quiet rural area, the killer's years of experience failed him. Against an opponent with superior skills, he flunked his final exam.

Danny knew exactly what to do. His demanding Uncle Pete had drilled him relentlessly, training him to shoot accurately under extreme duress. Now, the practice paid off. His first shot hit the killer in the side as he tried to roll away from the bed. He squeezed off the next shots automatically.

Danny emptied the clip into the killer's thrashing body, drilling him in the head more than once for good measure. It all seemed surreal to him, as if he were playing a video game. He felt no emotion: neither anger nor fear, dread nor regret... absolutely nothing as the shots rang loudly in the high-ceilinged room and the scent of burning gunpowder flared hot in his nostrils, familiar and bittersweet. When he ran out of bullets, he continued to squeeze the trigger, clicking the pin against the empty cylinder. After a few hollow clicks, he threw the pistol down and sat on the floor at the foot of the bed.

Danny began to shake, sick with anger and disgust. He ached, raw and torn with unimaginable grief. He could not process what had happened, could not bear to think about his parents. He started to cry. He had reached the end of his life... or of life, as he knew it.

In the past, evil had damaged his family, but it had always survived. Tonight, at long last, evil had destroyed his parents' wartorn lives. *I have to live,* he told himself. He wanted to run into his mother's arms, but they were quietly cooling on the bed, locked in the grip of death. *Mom and Dad would want me to live.* He remembered his uncle, and the anger welled up, hot and bitter. *Uncle Pete did this. He's gonna pay!*

Danny fought to regain his self-control, choking back sobs and turning his mind away from the carnage. He felt numb from head to toe. For the moment, no adult could advise him to avoid bitter thoughts of revenge. No one could tell him to lay aside his wrath. His senior advisors had left the building.

"You stayed with Daddy to the end," he whispered to his mother. "Just like you promised." Abruptly, the tears stopped. Standing on shaky legs, he staggered to the nightstand, shielding his eyes from the carnage on the bed as he groped for the ammunition in the drawer. He found two heavy boxes of cartridges and squeezed them tightly in his left hand. As he turned to leave the room, he almost tripped over the twisted body of a fallen killer.

Stooping to pick up his father's gun, Danny ran as if his life depended on it.

The Death of the Party

At 12:40 AM, Sheriff Rawlings sat on the back porch at Jamie's remote farmhouse, enjoying the sounds of the warm Florida night as they discussed their plans for the rest of the summer. The fireworks had ended, but Delia remained as the last diehard reveler in attendance at Jamie's much ballyhooed 4th of July party.

To the sheriff's surprise, her cellular phone rang. *Nobody calls me this late.* She flipped it open.

"Whoever you are, this had better be good," she drawled, smiling and winking at Jamie. As Jamie watched, the sheriff's face paled and her mouth fell open. "Are you sure?" She shut her mouth and looked at Jamie, pursing her lips. "I'll be right there." At that, she stood abruptly and snapped the phone shut.

"I have to go, Jamie. There's been some trouble in Broward County."

"What happened?"

"Peter Johnston has escaped."

THE LONG HIGHWAY TO HEADQUARTERS in Pezner ran in a direct line from Jamie's ranch into town – as straight as a rifle shot. The sheriff's car barreled down the narrow country highway through dark swamps, overgrown hammocks, and moonlit, wide-open cattle plains. The road had no lights, and the wilderness seemed stripped of inhabitants. As she drove, the darkness pressed heavily against her car, launching shadowy butterflies in the pit of her stomach.

This is creepin' me out, she reflected miserably. *Why did that man have to escape?* She could not imagine what she might do about it, but she would return to her headquarters. She had to act decisively... even if she could not see, touch, or find any adversary around her.

Delia's fellow officers, friends, and family would share her burden. Fulfilling her chosen role, she would stand beside them as a comforting presence. She would project stability and calm as they heard the news and telephoned the station, asking what they could do to help. Like her predecessor and mentor, Sheriff Tommy Durrance, she would faithfully stand her post – even when she had absolutely no idea of what to do next.

Jesus, show me what to do. Help me handle this wisely, she prayed. That much, at least, she had learned over the years. Pray for help. You'll need it.

When her cell phone rang, she flipped it open immediately. "Rawlings."

"Sheriff, where are you?" The voice of Major Robert 'Alibi' Albritton revealed his concern.

"I'm heading north on 319, about 20 miles south of town," the sheriff replied.

"We're sending a car to meet you."

"Pete Johnston doesn't scare me. He won't catch me by surprise again." Alibi spoke to someone in the room before he answered.

"We just received some more bad news from the FDLE."

"What?" Delia asked, unconsciously raising the pitch of her voice.

"Someone reported a shooting at the Johnston's safe house. We're waiting for more information." The sheriff almost swerved off the road. *I can't believe it!*

"How's that possible? They were hidden by the best! Nobody knew where they lived. *I* didn't even know."

"I know."

"Are Dan and Sarah okay?"

"We don't know yet."

"What about the boy?"

"We don't know, Sheriff. The FDLE said that somebody called 911 and reported four deaths. They think the caller might have been the boy."

"Four deaths?"

"That's what the caller said. Nothing's been confirmed."

"How did it happen?"

"I'm sorry, Sheriff; we just don't know. The FDLE told me they had no agents near the house. It was deep cover, and they were thought to be safe."

She remembered what she had learned about Dan Johnston's family in the past two years. The family had suffered for five long years while Dan served time as an innocent man, unjustly convicted. And yet, in spite of that, he had risked his life to save hers.

"John Engle is driving out to meet you," Alibi added. "He's gonna follow you here. Just to be safe."

"Okay, Alibi. Just to be safe." *Just to be safe? Where have I heard that before? I remember... Tommy Durrance said those words on the night that he died.* She punched the accelerator and turned on her lights.

Delia did not wish to admit it, but she felt glad that her deputies were driving out to meet her. Dreadful events had occurred tonight, and the evil genius of Pete Johnston seemed to lurk behind every dark tree.

She felt fear, but she would not be cowed. The sheriff stood ready to fight.

Sheriff Delia Rawlings, armed and dangerous, had a score to settle with the outlaw, Pete Johnston. The wheels of justice might turn slowly, but they would turn irrevocably: gears gnashing silently, night upon day upon night, as death drew near and the jaws of hell opened wide to receive its grim delivery.

Delia Rawlings knew that some day soon, the wheels of justice would grind Pete Johnston beneath them. Heaven would repay his venom with the punishing pulse of judgment. And when judgment arrived for Pete Johnston, she planned to help out in any way she could.

Runaway

To put it mildly, Danny had left in a hurry. In spite of his rush, however, he had managed to extract the cash from his father's safe. He quickly crammed it into his backpack, along with his mother's cell phone, some clothing, his wallet, his father's semi-automatic handgun, two boxes of hollow-point 9 mm cartridges, and his favorite stuffed bear. In the kitchen, he dialed 911 and shouted into the receiver.

"This is Danny Johnston. My parents have been murdered. We were in witness protection, but it didn't work. I just killed both of the hit men. Rural Route 2, Box 28." Leaving the phone off the hook, he ran out the back door.

The full moon emerged from the clouds as he slipped into the orange grove behind the house. The tall orange trees, casting dense black shadows in the moonlight, lined the broad rows of white sand far into the distance. Aside from an occasional slithering snake or browsing bunny, the entire tableau lay still beneath the pale moon.

Turning away from his grief, Danny paused to consider his path. He sensed his newfound independence with an unexpected sense of elation that startled him, quickly followed by a surge of guilt. On his own, he would have to find his way.

He ran through the orange grove, high-stepping through the silky piles of sugary sand. The sensation felt familiar from his many hunting trips in these groves. It comforted him somehow: the loose, peculiar pull of finely ground silica beneath his feet. After a long run, he reached the Alcon Citrus Processing Plant.

For a moment he stopped, hidden among the trees as he watched the road and the large plant. Beyond a tall chain-link fence, steam rose wispily beneath the streetlights in the deserted truck yard. The stainless steel tubes of the cold-pack evaporators towered over the surrounding terrain of rolling hills and orange groves. They stood more than 100 feet in height, commanding the horizon as far as the eye could see. To Danny, the inanimate towers seemed to stand watch over the darkened land: silent sentinels that impassively ignored the lonely child.

Past the towering evaporators, he could see a halo of light on the horizon. The light emanated from the Eastside Gas and Go, a massive truck stop of local fame. He began to run, impatient to leave the area that he had come to call home.

Danny arrived at the truck stop 40 minutes after the murder of his parents. He did not know that the Davis County Sheriff's Office had broadcast an alert with his description. If he had known, he could not have cared less.

For reasons that might be forgiven him, Danny Johnston had lost faith in the criminal justice system. He no longer trusted the FDLE witness protection program, the local sheriff, the police, the highway patrol, or any other official in green, tan, gray, or blue.

Arriving hot and winded, he paused across the highway from the truck stop. He stared at the huge parking lot, marveling at the sheer size of the largest truck stop in Florida. Craving anonymity, he felt reassured by its vastness.

Ducking the low branches, he entered the shadows beneath an orange tree, dropped his backpack, and pulled out his mother's cell phone. Turning it on and paging through the phone book, he found the name he sought: *Jamie*.

JAMIE KNEW NOTHING ABOUT THE ATTACK on Dan Johnston's family. After Delia left, Jamie cleaned her kitchen in serene ignorance, pausing only when her cell phone rang on the coffee table. She picked it up, tossing her hair out of her eyes with her left hand. *Who's calling this late?*

"Delia?"

"Hi, Jamie. This is Danny Johnston… the son, not the father."

"Danny?" She felt temporarily disoriented. "Why are you calling this late?" She looked at the clock. "Is everything okay?"

Jamie liked and respected the entire Johnston family, but she had come to love Danny and Sarah. A kind, gracious beauty from an old Southern family of Jewish descent, Sarah Johnston had become a dear friend. Her father and mother had disowned her for marrying Dan, the nephew of the notorious racist Dean Ray Johnston. Dan had shared nothing in common with Dean Ray, but they had not been willing to listen.

"I've got some bad news," Danny said to Jamie. To his surprise, his throat tightened up, and tears tried to well in his eyes. *I can't afford to cry,* he thought fiercely. *I can't cry!* He successfully resisted, clamping a lid on his agony.

"What is it?" Jamie asked, instantly alert.

"My..." he fought, but could not say the words. *God, help me!* he prayed. He had never been very religious, but he was becoming more so by the hour.

"What is it, Danny?"

"Okay," he said, regaining control. "Okay, this is the thing. My dad and mom have been murdered."

"Murdered?" She shouted the words, completely taken by surprise.

"Yeah. Murdered. But I just killed the guys who did it."

"Danny... are you playing some kind of game?" *Has he gone crazy? Would he joke about something like this?*

"No. Sorry, Jamie, I'm not playing. It really happened, and now I'm gettin' the heck out'a Dodge."

"Where are you, Danny? Please tell me! I'll come and pick you up." Jamie felt frantic. She loved the Johnston family, and had invested dearly in their survival.

"You're a nice lady, Jamie. You were a good friend to my mama. That's why I called you. But you can't help me now. If the government couldn't keep us safe, what can you do?"

"Where are you, Danny?"

"I don't want to say."

"Okay then; where are you going?"

"I'm going to visit Aunt Marcy in Tallahassee. Big Daddy's in the hospital with a heart attack. Grandma's gone, so Aunt Marcy's the only kin I've got left." He paused and looked around warily, peering through the dark leaves of the orange tree. "Don't tell anybody where I'm going. Okay?"

"I have to tell them, Danny. We need to protect your aunt."

"Like you protected us?" He paused, ashamed of his words. "I'm sorry, Miss Jamie. It wasn't your fault."

"Okay, listen," she rubbed her forehead, buying time. In the entrance to her kitchen, her husband Donny watched her patiently. He could see that something had shaken Jamie badly, and he would soon enough learn the extent of it. "I'll tell the authorities that you called me, but not where you're going, okay? At least, not right away." *Even if I lose my career for it,* she reflected bitterly. She had to admit the truth to herself. *Danny's right. We failed him.* "I'd like to call your aunt and tell her that you're coming. Is that okay?"

"Okay, thanks. I gotta go now. I'll call you from Aunt Marcy's."

"Okay."

"Thanks for caring whether we lived or died."

DANNY TURNED OFF THE PHONE and shouldered his backpack. Trudging out of the orange grove, he crossed the highway and walked into the garishly lit parking lot of the truck stop.

As he approached the restaurant, a two-toned, blue and silver PT Cruiser caught his eye. The driver had parked in front of the truck stop's restaurant, engine idling.

In the driver's seat sat a healthy, smooth-shaven man in his late 20s or early 30s. To Danny he looked vaguely familiar. He was tall, with a five-o'clock shadow, clear eyes, and a head full of thick hair: stylishly long and unusually black and glossy, as if dyed by professionals for a television commercial. He tapped the steering wheel rhythmically, humming under his breath, seemingly immersed in the music inside his car.

Outside the car, a booming bass line could be heard above the backdrop of idling trucks and slamming doors. The driver smiled at no one in particular, nodding blissfully to the beat as he glanced around the parking lot.

Meeting the boy's eyes, he nodded before returning to the open map on his dashboard. He appeared to be alone. Acting on instinct, Danny decided to take a chance.

The Ride

"Excuse me," Danny said, tapping on the windshield. The young man behind the wheel looked up from his map and rolled down the window.

"Can I help you?" he asked skeptically. In spite of his youth and his dark good looks, the man's violet eyes revealed a jaded world-weariness beyond his years. His ebony hair, hanging straight to his shoulders, glistened in the dim light as if posing for a camera. The hair seemed too perfect, like a glossy Goth toupee.

"Are you going north?" Danny asked hopefully.

"Do you recognize me?" the man replied.

"No. Should I?"

"I guess not." The driver sighed heavily, obviously relieved. "You're mighty young to be hitchhiking after midnight." He noticed how the boy glanced around nervously. *What's his story?* the man wondered. No stranger to trouble, he recognized the signs of recent trauma behind the boy's innocent expression. "Where are you going?"

"To my aunt's house in Tallahassee," Danny replied uncertainly. *This guy seems okay. But what if he won't give me a ride? What if another killer is out there, following me?* Danny had excellent instincts, and he applied them astutely. He decided to tell the truth: or rather, to tell part of it.

"I'm running away from a violent situation," he said, knowing that the words would provoke the right action from any decent soul. "I need to go to a safe place." *Don't we all,* the man reflected. He half-heartedly tried to stare at his map, but could not ignore the boy's words. Danny spoke again.

"If you're going north on I-75, you can drop me off at I-10," he added hopefully. "I can hitchhike from there."

"Get in, kid," the man said, unlocking the doors as he folded the map and stuffed it into the center console. "I've got nothing but time on my hands. Did you say that your aunt lives in Tallahassee?"

"Yeah."

"No problem. I'll drop you off at Aunt Bee's door."

Danny climbed into the passenger's seat and leaned back into a blast of air conditioning. *Cold air and leather seats... thank you, God.*

"Buckle up. We're gonna make up for lost time."

The car jolted backwards, stopped abruptly, and rocketed out of the parking lot, whipping swiftly onto the ramp that led to I-75 north. Judging from the comfort of the ride, they did not seem to be speeding, but soon Danny glanced at the speedometer and noticed that it read 100 miles per hour.

"Is this some kind of special PT Cruiser?" Danny asked, attempting to turn from the agonizing memories of less than an hour ago.

"Yeah. It's a DreamCruiser Series 3. It'll be a classic someday."

"It's a pretty cool ride. Did you trick it out?"

"Nope. It came like this from the factory. It's one of my favorite rides. Dirt cheap, nice little turbo: the works."

"Sweet." Danny murmured. As they crested a hill, the boy looked to his right. He pondered the beauty of the darkened countryside: orange groves, woods, and watery marshes lit by scattered streetlights and the nebulous auras of distant homes.

"So, tell me, kid. What are you runnin' from?" As the driver asked the question, he rummaged in the driver-side door and retrieved a pack of cigarettes, shaking one out. He clamped it between his lips and pushed in the lighter before catching himself.

"Aw, shoot." He looked at the boy and bit his lower lip. "I almost forgot. I quit smokin' five hours ago." He said the words regretfully, wistfully gazing at the pack in his hand. He hit the button to roll down the window and quickly threw out the rumpled pack, along with the unlit cigarette. "Oh, man! I just littered. That's a big fine."

"You could've given me that smoke. I could use one right now."

"You're too young for such a nasty addiction. I'm trying to quit, and it's one of the hardest things I've ever done."

"You don't strike me as a quitter."

"Ha, ha. Very funny, kid."

"Why are you quitting? Do you believe all of those stupid statistics?"

"You're a real wise guy, aren't you?"

"Yeah. So why are you quitting?"

"I've been tryin' to quit all of my bad habits. It ain't so easy for a guy like me, kid."

"Why do you call me 'kid'?" Danny asked, curious. He had grown like a weed in the past two years. He was large for his age, with a wispy beard beginning to haunt his chin. People usually mistook him for an older teen. "Do I look like a kid to you?"

"My grandmother's best friend used to call me 'kid'. I'm just passin' it along." He paused, reflecting on times past. "I ran away from home when I was about your age. What are you, 13?"

"Good guess." Showing the remarkable resiliency that some children possess, Danny had compartmentalized the bloody murders of his parents for the time being, and had moved on. "How old are you?"

"29."

"My name's Jimmy Preston. No, I lied. It's really Danny Johnston," he offered, putting his fears aside.

"Preston, but really Johnson?"

"Not Johnson, Johnston. Danny Johnston."

"What's with the different names?"

"I've been in witness protection lately. It didn't work out, so I'm going back to my real name."

"Ha! That's a good one."

"What's your name?"

"Drew."

"Drew what?"

"Marks. Drew Marks."

"That sounds familiar. Haven't I heard it before?"

"Maybe," Drew replied. *Please, don't be a fan.*

"Oh, I remember. That's the name of that stupid rock star who got busted in Spain for heroin: the lead singer in Blunt Trauma. The case was thrown out on a technicality... probably a technical bribe."

"Are you a fan?" Drew asked hopefully.

"Are you kidding? No way! Blunt Trauma's for stoners and head-bangers," Danny continued. "Not that there's anything wrong with that. Ha!"

"Funny."

"Have you ever seen Blunt Trauma live?"

"Uh... a few times."

"They're like, the grossest, grodiest head-banger band ever. Their lead singer once stapled his eyelids shut. He just stretched them out and stapled them to his cheek with a staple gun during a live performance. I saw it on video. Gross!"

"I'll bet that hurt," mused Drew, rubbing the scars on his cheeks.

"They're a bunch of old guys your age, but they're still, like, crazy popular with the metal-heads at school. They have this musically deprived Grateful Dead-type cult following. My daddy calls them a 'legion of blown minds'."

"Yeah?"

"Yeah. I was watching them on 'One Hit Wonders' the other night, but Daddy made me turn it off. He doesn't want me to hang out with druggies, even on TV."

"Your father sounds like a very wise man."

"He got himself killed." Danny stated bluntly. Stunned by the thought, he stared out the window, looking lost. "He couldn't save us."

"I'm sorry to hear that." Drew knew better than to ask questions about such a tender subject. His own father had died when he was ten, and the memory still lingered like a dull ache in his bones that stirred when bad weather rolled in.

"Daddy didn't want me hangin' out with druggies," Danny repeated softly, his eyes glazing over.

"He was right. It's not smart to hang out with druggies." *Ask me for proof, and I'll show you the scars.*

"You know, you look exactly like the lead singer in Blunt Trauma. And you have the same name. Are you related?"

"What do you think? How many Drew Marks can there be?"

"Really? You're related to him? You're his spittin' image."

This guy just won't quit, Drew thought. He reluctantly realized that the boy had cornered him.

"I'm the man," he sighed, coming clean. "I admit it. I'm the famous Drew Marks, recently of the amazing one-hit wonders known to our socially impaired cult following as Blunt Trauma."

"No kiddin'?"

"No kiddin'."

"Daddy says that you guys are the dumbest hop-heads to ever smudge a TV screen."

"Hey, watch it!" It annoyed Drew to be mocked by a child he was transporting out of the kindness of his heart. "Don't insult the help."

"You should talk. You're a big old, foul-mouthed dope fiend!" Danny guffawed disrespectfully. "I've heard your records."

"You don't know what you're talking about."

"I know your lyrics," Danny cried gleefully. He loved to tease adults, and did it whenever he could get away with it.

"My girlfriend back in sixth grade was a big fan of yours. She played your CD, "Shock Therapy," until I was sick of it. Some of those songs are still stuck in my brain. I know the first verse of "Love Zombies" by heart:

> Pull the plug, the party's drained
> Down the sewer of my brain.
> Rattle loud the ball and chain
> And shriek of dreams come true:
> Putrescent dreams of you.

"PU!" Danny cried, laughing so hard his sides hurt. "Something stinks! Who could ever believe that was a hit?"

"Cork it, kid!" Drew interjected. "Love Zombies was a monster hit. It was the biggest hit ever by a Metal band... in the entire history of rock."

"Oh, wow, like, you mean, the biggest Metal hit since the dawn of time?" Danny sneered sarcastically. "They didn't even invent Heavy Metal until the '70s. I saw it on VH-1."

"You're an impertinent little wretch." Drew feigned indignation, but his heart was not in it. Deep inside, he knew that the kid was right. Who would have believed that such a song could be a hit? The lyrics expressed a manically depressive theme as putrid as the poetry was puerile. *But at least,* Drew reassured himself, *we kept the music real. We played straight-ahead, Ska-influenced Retro Metal. That's worth remembering.*

"You've got nerve, kid," he admitted grudgingly. *I like this squirt.* "So, you said you're going to Tallahassee?"

"Yeah. I'm gonna visit my aunt."

"Aunt Bee? Eighty years old, with her hair in a bun?"

"Ha!"

"Not Aunt Bee? Auntie Em, then?"

"Obviously, you've never met my aunt."

"That's right. I don't really know you. And you don't know me either, though you seem to think you're an expert based on VH-1."

Danny looked at him thoughtfully. The man had a point.

"You're right. I don't know you. So fill me in. Tell me your story, and I'll tell you mine. Tallahassee is more than 200 miles away. That means we've got almost two hours before we get there." Hearing this, Drew laughed under his breath.

"You don't miss a trick." Drew adjusted the mirror and eased up on the cruise control, coasting to a more defensible 80 miles per hour. "Okay. I'll tell you my story; but first, I want to clear up a misconception."

"Fire away."

"First of all, I'm not a druggie anymore. I've been clean for 104 days. I've been walkin' the line since rehab, just like a regular boy scout."

"Congratulations."

"Thanks." He glanced at Danny with a rueful smirk. "Do yourself a favor, kid. Don't mess up your life like I messed up mine."

"So, what's the famous Drew Marks doing out here in the middle of nowhere? Shouldn't you be touring Europe or something?"

"It's a long story."

"We've got time."

"Okay," he exhaled, wondering where to begin. "Well, I guess I was naive. After rehab, I thought I'd hook back up with my band. I thought we'd pick up where we left off."

"And?"

"I got a lesson in the flip side of loyalty."

"What happened?"

"When I tried to call them after I got out of rehab, I couldn't reach 'em. They weren't taking my calls. I finally reached our road manager, and that's when I learned the truth." He stopped, drumming his fingers on the steering wheel. *I wish I had a smoke.*

"What?" Danny asked impatiently.

"I learned that the band – the band I helped found – had dropped me like a hot potato."

"No!"

"Oh, yeah. They kept the name I invented. They kept the logo I designed. They've got a new lead singer, and they've started a new project in the recording studio that I helped build."

"Really?"

"Unfortunately, yes. I drove down to our studio in Miami to talk last week, but they barely gave me the time of day. If I hadn't owned a piece of the building and the equipment, they would've called the cops."

"What's their excuse?"

"What do you mean?"

"Daddy says that every idiot has an excuse."

"I guess *I'm* their excuse. Due to my erratic behavior before rehab, they've officially pulled the plug on our relationship. They've dumped me. They've moved on."

"What did you do before rehab?"

"I was out of control."

"Details! Give me details."

"I got sloppy drunk at the Grammies last year. I made fun of them in front of Usher."

"That's juicy. Is that all?"

"Well… I insulted their girlfriends in public a couple of times. Just kidding, you know, but they weren't laughing. Last summer I passed out in the punch bowl at our drummer's wedding. After that, I wrecked our bass player's car. The usual stuff."

"Stupid human tricks."

"Yeah, but it's not like they're innocent lambs. They're still doin' the same drugs I was doin' before rehab."

"They'll hit bottom, one way or the other," Danny observed. "Daddy says the bad stuff always catches up with you." He referred to his father in the present tense, his heart ignoring the bitter facts.

"True. What goes around comes around." He nodded. "I thought they'd give me another chance, but no such luck."

"Bummer."

"I guess I'm better off without 'em, but it still hurts. The ironic thing is that they're still gettin' high. I couldn't hang out with them, even if they wanted me back in the band, so why should I care if they've dumped me?"

"Sometimes it's best to move on."

"Our whole band should've gone into rehab. They're burying themselves under a mountain of dope."

"Like you did."

"Yep. It's pitiful."

"Curiously pathetic."

"But my sympathy is tempered by the fact that it's their choice."

"My Uncle Pete was a drug dealer. He made some real bad choices." *He made the wrong choice tonight,* Danny reflected.

"Well, I'm clean now. I'm as clean as a mountain stream, and it feels great. Let that be a lesson from an old man of 29, kid. Don't waste your time gettin' wasted." Danny grew thoughtful.

"Big Daddy – he's my granddaddy – he used to be a big drunk.

But he quit, too. Just like you." The boy shifted uncomfortably in his seat. "He hasn't been drunk in more than 20 years." He hesitated remorsefully. "I shouldn't have called you a drug-head, since you ain't one anymore. Sorry about that."

"No problem."

"Thanks"

"All right, kid. I told you my pathetic tale. Tell me yours. What's put you on the highway after midnight, running away from home?"

Aunt Marcy

Sometime after midnight, Marcy awoke from a deep sleep, startled to consciousness by the sound of her telephone ringing off the hook. Rolling over in bed, she turned on the light and reached for the receiver.

The light revealed a lovely young woman: blond and slender, with tousled hair, perfect oval face, and sleepy green eyes. Dressed in an oversized Tweety Bird slumber shirt, she did not look like a sophisticated and successful attorney who served as an advocate for the poor. She looked like a refugee from a college slumber party.

"Hello?" Given the hour, she asked the question as politely as she could manage.

"Is this Marcy Johnston?" The voice was that of a young woman, like herself.

"Yes. To whom am I speaking?" She began to gather her wits. *What time is it?*

"This is Jamie Hawkins. We've never met, but I'm your brother's caseworker."

"Dan's caseworker? Why are you calling me?" In her heart, she knew the answer.

Marcy's stomach seemed to leave her body and sink through the mattress. Her head began to pulse, spinning out of control, dizzy and faint.

"Why are you calling me?" she repeated, unintentionally raising her voice.

"I just spoke to your nephew, Danny. He told me that he's hitchhiking to Tallahassee. He wants to stay with you, and I told him I would call you."

"Danny? Hitchhiking? At this time of night?"

"Yes."

"That's crazy!"

"I know, but he refused to let me pick him up. He said he's lost faith in the system." Jamie paused. "We're looking for him."

"What's happened?"

"Are you sitting down?"

"Of course. I'm in bed, for goodness sake!" Marcy almost screamed the words. "What's happened?"

"I'm so sorry, Marcy. We haven't confirmed it yet, but Danny just told me that both of his parents have been killed."

"MARCY, CAN YOU HEAR ME? MARCY?" She turned her face toward the voice and blinked.

She realized that she was sitting on the brown leather chair in her living room. Her friend Chesterfield sat in the love seat, leaning forward with his chin in his hand and his elbow on his knee, looking like a better-dressed version of Rodin's famous Thinker. A handsome man in his 50s, Ches wore a nondescript gray polo shirt, gray slacks, and glossy black shoes: neat and natty, even at this hour.

"Marcy?" he repeated. "Are you okay?"

"Ches?"

"Yes, Marcy?"

"How did you get here?" She looked down and saw that she was wearing her jeans and a blue tee shirt. *How did I get dressed? I was talking on the phone.*

"You called me and asked me to come over," Ches replied. "Every light in the apartment was on when I got here, and you were sitting there, staring into space. I've been trying to get your attention for the past 20 minutes."

"What do you mean?" She could scarcely process his words.

"You've been sitting right there for the past 20 minutes, staring at the wall without responding, and I've been freaking out the whole time." He took her hand. "Marcy, what on earth is wrong?"

"Oh, Ches," she said as her memory returned. "Dan and Sarah have been murdered."

"What?"

"And Danny's out there on the road somewhere. He's coming here, Ches. They've been killed, and I don't know what to do."

A Desire Named Streetcar

He sat upright in his chair, almost asleep. When the telephone rang, the sound startled him. He had not expected this type of interruption, for his telephone had not rung in years.

He had purchased the cellular phone several years ago. It was old and awkwardly oversized, but it possessed one particularly useful trait: due to its age, the phone did not include a GPS locator. If anyone tried to trace a call, they would not be able to zero in closer than the nearest tower.

Age had rendered its battery anemic. If he had not decided to spend the night in the only shepherds' hut with electricity on the ranch, the message might have languished in his voice mail for weeks.

For the past few years, Salvatore "Streetcar" Benuto had lived a simple life. Following the seasons, he had crossed the farthest reaches of a vast Montana ranch, leading sheep from pasture to pasture. Tonight's shelter, high in the mountains, was located less than five miles from the main house where his friend, Wally Hamilton, lived alone.

Streetcar had acquired enough of the Basque language to converse with his fellow shepherds, but he sometimes went for days without speaking. When not working, he preferred to spend time with his elderly Maine Coon cat. Every night, he would rub the cat's fur as he read in the harsh lantern light beside a hot fire. Some nights, instead of reading, he would lay on his back for hours, gazing at majestic swarms of vivid stars scattered in clouds across the clear Montana sky.

"Hello," he said into the phone, his voice cracking from disuse.

"This is Jamie," a woman's voice announced. She sounded strained, as if she had been crying.

Streetcar abruptly stood up, turning to face the door. He

balanced on the balls of his feet, on full alert as if a bear were about to break into the hut. To those who did not know his history, the reaction might have seemed comical.

"Jamie?" For a moment, he felt disoriented, taken back into his dark and compromised past. Years before, his life had entered a troubled phase marked by a disjointed mix of violence and retribution, selfish vengeance and noble self-sacrifice. At the sound of Jamie's voice, the memories returned helter-skelter, like an involuntary video montage. "What's wrong?"

"I need your help," she said. She stopped, unable to continue.

All was not well in the Sunshine State. Huddling in a shadowy nook between the newest shops in the county – a drug store and a spotlessly clean Dollar Mart – Jamie nervously glanced around the deserted parking lot. Skittish and uncertain, she jumped at the sound of a gum wrapper rattling ominously across the sidewalk, driven by an errant breeze. In spite of the warmth, she pulled her collar close. She looked as if she stood in a freezing winter wind, not a summer breeze swirling past a sheltered nook.

On her way to the Oree County Sheriff's Department, in the dark hours after midnight, Jamie had pulled over to use this pay phone, driven by desperation. Since the day when Sal Benuto had dropped off the grid to avoid awkward questions from the federal authorities, she had never attempted to contact him. But now, she had crossed the Rubicon.

She knew that her call could lead to trouble. Some might accuse her of aiding and abetting a terrorist: groundless claims, but career ending, nonetheless. She had placed her call from a pay phone using coins, preferring to play it safe.

"What's wrong?" he repeated softly. He imagined Jamie as he had first seen her on a tumultuous day long ago in the heart of Ybor City: pure and innocent, scarred by evil, but untainted by its power. In Jamie, he had found an unconquered spirit plagued by predators, but unwilling to yield to their madness. From that first meeting, he had loved her as one might love a beleaguered little sister. She looked up to him, also... to him... to a former street person despised by strangers. She trusted him, and he would not abuse that trust.

At the sound of Streetcar's voice, Jamie began to cry. She wept silently, the tears sliding down her face and wetting her collar. She could scarcely utter a sound. Her throat tightened. Her breath felt short, compressed: squeezed by the pressure of the moment.

"I need..." she started to say. She paused again.

"Just a minute," Streetcar said. To give her time, he walked to the window, looking out at the Basque shepherds who sat beside the fire under the open sky. *I've been protecting these sheep for years... keeping in practice, I guess.* Smiling at the irony he shook his head.

"Okay, shoot."

SOMETIME AFTER 3:00 AM, a call from an old friend awakened Richard J. Collins, the recently retired former Deputy Director of the CIA. He could not have imagined that the call came from an old buddy... a comrade-in-arms from his days in Vietnam.

Sal had called Rich from his second cell phone. Years ago, during a fit of prescient paranoia, he had purchased both phones using different aliases. He had maintained their accounts ever since, and now he put them to good use.

"Rich, this is Sally." Richard Collins sat up in bed. Gently, to avoid awakening his wife, he climbed out of bed and wended his way from the bedroom to his study, navigating by the shaky rays of a nightlight. In the study, he shut the door securely.

"Who is this?" he asked skeptically.

"It's Sally. It's really me, Rich."

"Sally? Are you crazy?" he whispered fiercely. "Why are you calling me? You're wanted for questioning by the federal government... the same government I've served my entire life!"

"Yeah," Sal answered. "It's a real mind-blower, ain't it?" Rich almost hung up, but at the last moment he paused and returned the receiver to his ear. The voice on the other end, an unwanted blast from his Vietnamese past, remained intimately familiar in spite of the years that had passed between them. Inexorably, the husky voice continued to speak.

"You've come a long way from the streets of Philly, Rich. I've followed your career like a proud big brother."

"Sal, come on. You're killin' me here! I can't believe you're calling me. On my home phone, no less!"

"I wouldn't bother you if it wasn't important, Rich. Besides, this is the kind of thing you'd want me to call about."

I doubt that, Richard Collins thought bitterly.

"I have to tell the authorities about this call, Sal," he said brusquely, biting off the words. "First thing in the morning."

"Yeah, sure. Do whatever you gotta do, Rich."

"They'll find you, Sally. They'll find you, and they'll hurt you."

"Some day, maybe. But I'm gonna turn myself in eventually, so it don't matter anyway. My life's over, Rich." He paused and stroked the cat in his lap. "I'm just waitin' 'til the cat dies."

"Until what?" he replied incredulously. *Until the cat dies? He sounds crazier than he did back in 'Nam.*

"I've got a cat, and he depends on me. That's all I mean."

"Oh... okay. I get it."

"I made a vow. After he dies, I'm gonna turn myself in."

"A vow? To who?"

"To God, Rich. Who else is there?" He smiled grimly. "That don't sound like me, huh?"

"We've all changed."

"We sure have. You're a big shot now, but I guess I'm a shot that backfired. Through the breech, right in the face."

"Where are you, Sal?" *This guy needs help.*

"You'll find out soon enough. But whatever happens, I want you to know somethin', right up front. The guy I've been stayin' with, for the past few years... he's a mutual friend, Rich. He don't know nothin' about my past. Nothin'. He don't even own a TV. He's not a big fan of the papers, either."

"So what do you want from me, Sal?" Rich had wandered into the kitchen. He opened the refrigerator and blinked as he stared into it's bright interior, searching for Maalox. *Why me?*

"Have you ever heard of a guy named Peter Wayne Johnston?"

Richard Collins' antennae went up immediately.

"Of course I have. He's the redneck who assaulted that sheriff in Florida a couple of years ago. They say he might be behind a string of unsolved murders down there."

"That's the guy."

"He's even more of an outlaw than you are."

"And that's sayin' somethin', ain't it? Anyway, this Peter Wayne Johnston escaped from jail a few hours ago. His cousin was hiding in a witness protection program, scheduled to testify against him. And guess what? At about the same time the goon escaped, his cousin and his wife were murdered. Shot down like dogs."

"No!"

"That's what I heard."

"That's terrible."

"Yep. They had a kid, too. But the good news is, the kid got away. He's on the run now. So anyway, I'm thinkin' that maybe the kid has lost confidence in the system. He probably won't be too anxious to go back into the witness protection program."

"How does this come back around to me?" Rich rubbed his brow worriedly, beginning to see the writing on the wall.

"I need you to send a specialist to Florida."

"What? Are you crazy?"

"We need somebody to protect that kid, Rich. We need the best guy you've got. Maybe there's somebody you worked with who owes you a personal favor. Maybe he can do it for free, huh? I don't want the government mixed up in this."

"Who's this *we*, Sally?"

Streetcar did not answer his question.

"How did you learn about this stuff?"

"This is like the U. S. Army, Rich. Don't ask, and I won't tell."

"Okay, okay… then I'll ask you something else. Why me, and why now? I'm retired!"

"I need your help, Rich. I've lost a few steps. I'm pushin' 60, and I don't think I'm good enough to protect the kid."

"That makes sense." Rich sighed heavily, rubbing his eyes.

"Besides, he's in Florida. I made a promise not to go there."
"A promise?"
"Yep."
"This is crazy, Sal," Rich replied weakly.
"Do it for old time's sake, Rich. Please." *For old times sake... like when I saved your life,* he did not bother to add. Rich's sigh of resignation could be felt from Philadelphia to Montana.
"If a child is in danger," Rich stated by rote, "it isn't a mission for a private citizen. It's a mission for the government."
"We don't need an army, Rich. We need one good man. The government tried and failed. The government needs back up, and so does the kid."
"I hear you," he sighed, passing his hand over his eyes. *I think I'm getting a headache.*
"It's Florida, Rich. Every citizen in Florida has the right to protect human life with deadly force if necessary. It'll all be street legal."
"I know the law in Florida. But I don't know about this."
"Whatever you decide, keep it on the Q.T., okay? You know, the part I told you about the kid, and me askin' you to help protect him... okay? Don't tell nobody nothin'. I'm countin' on you."
"What *should* I tell the agency, Sal? I've worked with some of those guys for years. They'll know in a heartbeat if I'm holding back."
"Tell 'em the truth, just don't tell 'em everything. Tell 'em I called. Tell 'em I said I'm lonely and I'm gettin' ready to go on the move. That's all true. Tell 'em I've been workin' with foreigners and I'm dyin' to speak English for a change. That's true, too. After they figure out what I've been doin' for the past few years, your story will match what they learn."
"I hope you're right, Sal." *I'm risking my retirement... but you saved my life.*
"I know I'm askin' you to bite the bullet here. But if you're smart, the bullet won't go off."
"Great analogy."

"You'll be helping a crime victim in need. There's nothin' in it for you or me... nothin' except doin' the right thing. And if you pick the right guy to protect the kid – if he's good enough – he doesn't even have to break the law. It'll all be on the up-and-up."

"Okay, Sally." *This is unbelievable.* "Is there anything else?"

"The kid's name is Danny Johnston. His story will make the national news. He said he's going to visit his aunt in Tallahassee. Her name is Marcy Johnston. They'll probably be goin' to his parent's funeral some day next week. Beyond that, I don't know."

"Any other requests?" *I can't believe I'm going along with this.*

"Please, get lawyered up before you report that I called. I don't want to get you in trouble. We haven't talked since 'Nam."

"I know that and you know that, but who'd believe it now?"

"I'm sorry I dragged you into this, Rich." On the other end of the telephone, Rich heard his friend sigh.

"Okay, I'll help you protect this kid, Sally. But you're askin' a lot from a retired guy."

"I know. By the way, uh... buddy..."

"Yeah?"

"Thanks."

Salvatore Benuto turned off his phone and paused briefly. *Rich to the rescue.* Abruptly, he swung into motion: tying his boots, throwing on his jacket, and taking a backpack from the wall. Pulling a drawer from a rugged chest at the foot of the narrow bed, he dumped its entire contents into his backpack.

He knelt and pried a board from the floor in the corner of the room. From the hole, he fished out a .45 automatic, several boxes of ammunition, and four large silencers. Placing them in the backpack, he stood and wearily eyed the big cat that slept soundly on the bedspread.

"Bad news, Cat. We've gotta go." The cat did not respond. He continued to sleep, eyes and paws twitching. He had slept a lot lately, and Streetcar worried about that. Bending over, he gently picked him up. Curling him inside of his aluminum-framed backpack, he zipped it partially shut so the cat's head poked out the top. Bending over, he shouldered the heavy load.

Streetcar opened the door. The shepherds looked up, surprised to see him emerge fully dressed and wearing a backpack at this late hour. The Maine Coon cat peeked at them from his perch in the backpack, mildly curious but half asleep. Streetcar reached back and stroked the big cat reflexively with his fingers as he began to speak to his companions.

"I have to leave." He spoke haltingly in their native Basque tongue. "It's an emergency. I won't be coming back." The leader, a tough man in his mid-60s, stood.

"Right now?"

"Yes."

"Can we help?"

"Yes. The police will visit after I'm gone. They'll want to know about me. Tell what you know. The less said, the better. Please, don't lie for me. They will punish you if you lie."

"We have no fear of men. We will not lie to them," he added with a smile. "We speak Basque. That should slow them down." He winked and gestured toward his companions. "For years, we knew you were hiding here, living among us in the high plains. We have our families and friends, but you have no one. You seldom leave the high country."

"I didn't know you'd figured it out," Streetcar replied, marveling at the man's words. "You guys sure know how to keep your mouths shut."

"Like you." They nodded at one another, smiling wryly.

"Thanks for not asking questions."

"It is not good for a man to hide. Hiding takes a toll on a man."

"You're right," Streetcar replied. *I'm only waiting 'til the cat dies. I can't just abandon him.* As if he knew his owner's thoughts, the ragged old cat began to purr in his ear.

"I have to get moving," he said reluctantly. The big Maine Coon began to twist playfully inside the pack, clawing at his best friend's silver necklace.

The Basque elder stepped away from the fire, reaching out to shake his hand. "Why don't you take the mustang? He can see in the dark like a cat. The moon is bright, and the trails are familiar."

"Thank you, Domingo."

"Go with God, Salvatore."

The Matter at Hand

"Okay," Danny replied to Drew Marks. "I'll tell you my story, but you've got to promise that you won't dump me after you hear it."

"What makes you say that?"

"Do you promise you'll give me a ride, no matter what?"

"Well... sure, I guess. Why not?" *What's this kid up to?*

Danny sighed and looked out the window. He had begun to remember, to feel the pain. He needed a distraction, even if it involved telling this stranger his story.

"Okay, then. This is what happened."

THE CLEANER HAD ACTED SWIFTLY. Tonight's job had turned ugly, but he had straightened it up like the pro he was.

A born killer, he had worked for years as a top mechanic for one of the biggest outfits in the country. He was the real deal, a specialist brought in for high-profile jobs. Whenever a job went bad, he fixed it. If the primary contractors dropped the ball, he would execute in their place. As a bonus, his bosses occasionally asked him to kill the primary contractors after they finished their dirty work.

The cleaner received most of his jobs through an old-school capo in Chicago who lived by Omerta, the ancient Sicilian code of silence. Only their boss, one the most powerful Mafia dons in the country, had knowledge of his jobs.

For years, he had served Chicago's Brucci crime family as their most elite killer, earning an astronomical rate. He had already earned a bundle on this job by ensuring the execution of the independent contractors. To his surprise, however, a mere boy had killed his intended victims. To earn his fat paycheck, he had merely burned a little midnight oil to light up the Johnston's rustic Cracker tinderbox. For sport, he had followed the boy's footprints through the orange grove, emerging in time to watch from a distance as Danny climbed into a distinctive two-toned car that took the northbound ramp onto I-75. After the PT Cruiser sped away from the truck stop, the cleaner slogged toward his car. He had hidden it less than a mile away: a convenient coincidence.

As he moved, he gazed down the gap between straight rows of orange trees to view his fiery handiwork. Almost two miles away, flickering above the horizon, a false sunrise revealed the location of the fast-burning wooden house. He smiled to hear the sirens of distant fire trucks. *What a mess.*

He had planned to kill the hired guns on the following day, but his instincts had warned him not to wait. He had entered the house warily, scarcely believing what he found. From the position of the bodies, it appeared evident that the boy – a mere child – had done the job, polishing off two Mob mechanics like a pro. *He must have killed 'em with his father's gun. Tell that one to Dr. Freud.*

Realizing that the crime scene contained too many loose ends, he had verified the identities of the deceased, scrounged up some fuel oil, and kindled a fire to hinder the investigation. The old house, built of cypress and pine, had gone up like a torch.

The cleaner toiled slowly through the sand until he reached his car. On the surface, it looked like a nondescript Chevrolet Monte Carlo. But the car possessed speed to spare, and he was prepared to use it. He fired it up and fastened his seatbelt, easing onto the highway, turning north toward the truck stop and the interstate beyond.

I hope they come through with another contract, he reflected, punching a number into his cell phone as he turned onto the ramp, heading north on I-75. The phone automatically encrypted the transmission.

"Pick it up," he whispered impatiently. After four rings, a voice answered.

"Hello." He knew the voice. He had reached his Chicago capo.

"The job went south, but they took care of the main assignment," the cleaner stated flatly. "I cleaned up the job site."

"You cleaned it up?"

"Affirmative." The killer punched the gas.

"What went wrong?"

"They didn't earn their bonus."

"Do you think that you can take care of it?"

"I'm already on it. But this is an extra. I'll need a triple commission." *Wired to my Swiss account, as you know. The feds'll be on this like maggots on a corpse, so you'd better move fast.*

The situation would become too hot to handle if the feds began to protect the boy. *If the Capo wants it done, now's the time.* The professional allowed himself a wicked smile. The price of this job had just blown up like a prized pig at a state fair.

"Stay on it," the Capo rasped. "I'll call you right back."

"Right-o," the killer replied glibly, looking at the speedometer. It read 140 miles per hour and climbing, but one could scarcely tell from the smoothness of the ride.

At 3:00 AM, all of the Independence Day fireworks had sizzled out. The holiday traffic seemed to have abandoned this rural stretch of I-75. He gazed ahead intently, whipping past the occasional tractor-trailer, pickup, and SUV. *Where is that two-toned PT Cruiser?* He itched for adventure, excited by the prospect of easy money and a quick, clean kill. *This is sweet,* he mused, glancing down as the needle edged past 150 mph. The tachometer showed that he was well below the red line. He still had more power under the hood.

"God bless Detroit," he said aloud, sarcastically biting off the words. *As if there is a God. Hah! I might as well invoke the blessings of Baal or the lightning of Thor.* "Thor bless us, everyone," he added in a high, piping voice, twisting the words of Tiny Tim from Dickens' Christmas Carol. Unlike Tiny Tim, however, he did not dream of plum pudding. He dreamed of a bloody jackpot at the end of a gilded rainbow.

The cleaner's attention did not stray far from his work. He scanned the road ahead, diligently seeking the distinctive taillights of a late-model PT Cruiser. He had earned his bones long ago. He knew that this was just a job… but it was a job that he would execute with professional precision and élan.

"I'm getting filthy rich in this business," he said aloud. "Maybe I'll give the proceeds to charity." He grinned at the idea. "Or not!"

Charity had nothing to do with the matter at hand.

Top Wolf

"Okay; just finish it. No loose ends." The politician blurted the words brusquely and slammed down the telephone. He stepped away from his desk and hastily stuffed a stack of papers into his briefcase, vexed beyond measure.

"What happened?" a soft voice asked. The owner of the voice lay sprawled across a leather couch, untroubled by the late hour or the grim nature of their business. A wiry, nondescript man with soft brown hair, he had innocent looks that belied a Machiavellian mind. With the obligatory double chin and retreating hairline of a middle-aged bureaucrat, the savvy political operator cultivated a bland appearance that effectively cloaked the corruption of his soul.

Over the years, Timothy 'Timbo' Holder had grown into much more than a skilled attorney and lobbyist. He had become an urbane legend. The highly paid confidant of presidents and kings lived life on the edge as a political action figure, par excellence. In his time, Timbo Holder had unearthed and spread tons of political dirt on both sides of the aisle. As a prominent D. C. player, he knew where the bodies were buried at home and abroad. He had ruined the reputations of more than a few members of the body politic, and the steps of his past could be traced by following the trail of predictably shallow, unmarked political graves.

Hearing Timbo's question, the handsome politician looked up from his papers. In the Washington dog pile, Senator Howard Bedford stood head and shoulders above the pack: a tall, slim, American Standard breed: finely coiffed and manicured, yet somehow homespun and down-to-earth. His subtle blend of sophistication, authority, veiled temper, and lap-poodle friendliness cried 'politician' to the observant and 'moral chameleon' to the wise.

"We have trouble in paradise," the Senator said to Timbo, his face contorting into an Andy-of-Mayberry approximation of an arch expression. "They bagged the big fish, but the little fish got away."

He loves this cloak and dagger stuff. Timbo sneered inwardly, hiding his thoughts with a politically acceptable frown. *Why doesn't he just say it out loud? If anybody's listening, they've got the goods on us anyway, so why the secrecy?*

"Good enough," Timbo replied, playing along. "Let the little fish swim. Who cares?"

The politician paused and stared at his desk for a moment, then looked up at his advisor. "I told my contact to finish the job. That is one little fish we can't afford to throw back."

"You said 'finish him off?' just like that?"

"Yeah, just like that. Why not? It's a freebie." *Not that I won't have to pay later.*

"There aren't any freebies, especially with our friends in Chicago."

"Well, this one's free… for now, at least."

"They shouldn't be contacting you directly, Howard." Annoyed by his comment, the Senator cut him off with a wave of his hand.

"We've been through this. My phone line is protected, and no Chicago judge in his right mind would order a tap on the other end. You remember who I am, right?"

"You? Right. You're Mr. Clean."

"That's right. I am Mr. Clean."

"That's what this mess is all about. You have to keep your image clean at any cost."

"Yes. It's a two-edged sword."

"That's one way to put it."

"What's your problem? Are you developing a conscience at this late date?"

"Maybe. I agreed that we should eliminate that drug-dealing white supremacist from your past. I just wish we'd left the innocent bystanders out of it."

"Give me a break! I told you the story. Pete's cousin Dan was trying to blackmail me! He would have bled me dry. If the press had caught a whiff of my childhood association with Peter Johnston, they'd swarm like jackals on a wounded boar. Nobody would care about the truth." *And you swallowed my story whole.*

"I sympathize, Howie. I just wish we could have handled it some other way."

"Did *you* come up with another way to handle it? Did *you* cook up a solution in your two-thousand-dollar-per-hour head?"

"No," he admitted.

"Well, there you have it. I was blackmailed. You offered no solution, so I came up with one. As a result, we're in this together."

"I know. But I still wonder if we did the right thing."

"The right thing? You must be kidding!"

"I wish I were."

"Okay, let's review the facts. Pete Johnston and I haven't seen each other since my junior year in high school." *And you bought that whopper.* "He was a white supremacist who became a big-time drug dealer. Any hint of my high-school friendship with that man would have ruined my career. And his cousin, Dan Johnston, was blackmailing me!" The senator lied well, with an innocent expression that could not be read, even by Timbo.

"It would have killed your career," Timbo sympathized.

"If that happened, what good could I accomplish?"

"None," Timbo sighed. *As if it matters anymore.*

"We had to get rid of Dan Johnston, and we had to make it look like Peter Johnston did it. Unfortunately, that meant that we had to involve his family. Was it a bad thing? Of course. But it was necessary for the greater good. Thanks to our friend in Chicago – a connection that you provided, as I recall – we were able to time the killings to coincide with Peter Johnston's escape."

"This is the nastiest thing I've ever been associated with," Timbo stated dispiritedly. "You're right, of course. He blackmailed you, and you had to save your reputation. But, for the life of me, I can't imagine how you ever got mixed up with Peter Johnston."

"We grew up down the road from each other. We were kids, and you know how kids are. Kids can be friends with anyone – even if they disagree with everything their friend stands for." *Not that I disagreed. We swore a blood oath to defend the master race, and we shanghaied Dan to witness our vows. That's why Dan had to die.* "The Johnston family was rotten to the core," the senator added innocuously, "but how could I know? I was just a kid."

"That racist creep deserved to die," Timbo replied. He looked closely at his associate, sniffing him out like a beta wolf eyeing an untrustworthy alpha. *What are you hiding?*

"Without a doubt, Peter is an evil man," Howard responded. "It's a tragedy that he wasted his talents. He was a genius in his way, but he chose the wrong fork in the road. He never evolved, and the world left him behind." *And you don't know the entire story. I had good reason to be mixed up with Pete when I was a poor boy trying to climb the political ladder. He had tons of money, and he funded my first three campaigns.*

"Well, the threat is now dead," Timbo said. "Thank God."

"God had nothing to do with it," Howard hissed. He looked out the window and fought to regain his composure. *Peter, my Aryan brother! If you knew what I know, you would forgive me. The Jewish conspiracy is strong. They heavily oppress the Middle East. Soon, if I play my cards right, I'll have my hands on levers of power that can unseat the Jews forever.*

Howard Greenlee Bedford possessed the instincts of a true politician. When the notoriety of Pete Johnston – his best friend forever – had threatened his goals, Howard had destroyed the living evidence with impressive finality.

Pete Johnston had supported the Senator since the beginning. The drug dealer had remained anonymous, keeping his distance as Howard's red-hot political career ascended like an Apollo moon shot. Pete had supported him discreetly, seldom asking for favors. But now, the risk of their association had become too great.

Howard Bedford would have murdered a battalion of friends to protect his own, squeaky-clean image. If necessary, he would leave a trail of bodies from Key West to the steps of The Hague.

From his youth until today, Howard had risen through the ranks by dint of relentless ambition, deceitful word-craft, and carefully cloaked greed. Recently, international politicians had placed him in the running for the appointment of a lifetime: a seat in the newly formed International Parliament at The Hague, Netherlands. There, as the appointed representative for the United States, Howard Bedford would wield unprecedented influence over such institutions as the War Crimes Tribunal and the International Criminal Court.

The international political community had offered him the chance of a lifetime. And so, to protect his spotless reputation, he had seized upon a rare opportunity to eliminate his biggest threat.

Timbo Holder knew a powerful Chicago don, and Howard Bedford had turned to him for help. Except for one loose end, they had executed their plan flawlessly.

Less than an hour ago, Mafia assassins had murdered Pete's cousin Dan and his wife, Sarah. Howard had always hated Dan, and he had not flinched at the decision to kill him. Pete Johnston would soon be history also, compliments of a discount package deal from Chicago.

No trail would lead to Howard Bedford. Law enforcement officials would assume that Pete had escaped cleanly after ordering the murder of Dan's family. They would hunt for the dead among the living. In the end, only three men would know of his part in this blood-drenched affair: the Senator, Timbo Holder, and one discreet Chicago don.

Howard Bedford's image would remain pristine. His racist past would stay buried. Only one small blemish, one little child, remained as the last piece of the puzzle. *And soon, he'll be gone like the rest.*

To ensure finality, Howard had made another bloody decision: he had decided to kill the child. His reasoning was sound, if evil. From the beginning, although he had pretended otherwise, the Senator had intended to kill them all: Dan, Sarah, and the boy.

Three years ago, during a final visit to Cutler County, Howard had dropped by Pete Johnston's house after dark to shore up funding for his first national campaign. Pete had promised him that they would be alone, but upon entering Pete's home, Howard had been surprised to see Pete's nephew, Danny Johnston, sitting at the kitchen table. Danny had ignored the adults as he busily loaded shells for target practice. But the boy had taken one good look at Howard Bedford, and that amounted to one look too many. If the truth got out, the boy could ruin Howard's political career.

The Senator hated loose ends. *I've got to play it safe. If that boy ever talks about seeing me with Pete, my career will be dead.*

Howard smiled and looked at his watch. Soon, the living evidence would be destroyed. The great Senator Howard Bedford would remain unstained in the eyes of the public. The people of America, that ignitable human fodder that fueled his ambitions, would continue to view him as the ultimate rarity: an honest politician... as wise as a fox, but as pure as the driven snow.

Road Kill

"So, that's what happened. It was all over by midnight, I guess," Danny summarized. "After I killed those men, I ran through the orange grove. I saw you at the truck stop, and now we're halfway to Tallahassee."

The car hurtled swiftly through the countryside on a relatively empty stretch of I-75. Although the clock read 3:22 AM, neither of them felt sleepy. Drew blinked and scratched his head, considering the boy's story. *Could he be telling the truth? No way!*

"That's an amazing story," he said.

"You don't believe me, do you?"

"I didn't say that."

"It's okay. I don't blame you. I wouldn't believe it, either. But it happened to me, so I don't have any choice." Anxious to change the subject, Drew focused on another issue. He adjusted the rearview mirror and jerked his thumb over his shoulder, pointing at the highway behind them.

"Can you believe that guy back there? He must be going 150 miles per hour. Two minutes ago, he was a speck in the distance. Now, he's ready to pass us."

Danny turned around and gazed directly at the approaching lights. *Could it be?*

The car whipped past them, then pulled in front and slowed until the PT almost kissed its bumper. Danny grew tense.

"Don't pass. Slow down, and see what he does."

"Sure, why not?" *I'll humor the kid.* He slowed down, dropping back. To Drew's surprise, the dark Monte Carlo also slowed. Once again, their bumpers almost kissed.

"Slow down again," Danny suggested.

"Okay." He eased up on the gas, glancing at the speedometer as it dropped from 50 to 45. The other car followed suit.

"Great," Drew hissed. "He's a road rage freak." He looked at Danny, recalling the boy's wild tale of mayhem and murder. "This is a random kook, kid. Don't worry about it."

"He's after me," Danny stated without emotion. Drew looked at the boy in obvious disbelief. "It's obvious, isn't it?" the boy added dryly.

"Look, kid. I don't quite believe your story, okay?"

"That's okay. But you'd better be ready now, whether you believe me or not. This guy is going to try to kill us. And I mean, like, right now, okay? Right now."

"Forget about it," Drew blurted, irritated beyond measure. He hit the gas and the turbo spooled out smoothly as they whipped past the Monte Carlo and sped down the interstate. He glanced down at the speedometer. *110... 120... 130...140.*

"He's coming!" Danny shouted, reaching into his backpack as he rolled down the passenger window. In the rearview mirror, the headlights rapidly approached.

"That's crazy. He must be going 200 miles per hour!" Drew kept the PT in the right lane, pedal to the floor.

As the car pulled up beside them, Drew glanced at the driver. Shocked and dismayed, he noticed that the man's right hand held a sawed-off shotgun. He did not realize that Danny had rolled down the passenger-side window, or that Danny had a gun in his hand.

"Look out!" Drew shouted at the top of his lungs, stomping on the brakes. The PT jerked as if it had struck a wall as a magnum load of Number One buckshot blew past the front of their windshield, barely missing them.

As the brakes slammed him forward against the window frame, Danny held on for dear life. Rebounding from the blunt force, he managed to pop his head out of the window and squeeze off a quick shot that blew a hole through the rear windshield of the other car. Brake lights came on, and the Monte Carlo began to screech to a halt.

Drew hit the gas as soon as the Monte Carlo's brakes took hold, and they rocketed past the larger car. But a sinking feeling in their stomachs informed them that the trick would not work again. Momentarily, Danny slipped back into the passenger's seat.

"What are you gonna do?" the boy shouted anxiously, staring through the rear windshield at the approaching headlights.

"Get ready to follow my lead," Drew said. He felt angry, but unafraid. A sign on the next hill read, 'Exit 41.' Drew knew this exit well, for it led to the Highway 54 shortcut to Tallahassee. Because Highway 54 skirted the north side of the Miccosuki River, the entrance to the exit ramp began just past the river's bridge and circled steeply back toward Highway 54. The circular ramp to the two-lane highway could be treacherous, especially at night.

The exit ramp presented drivers with several warning signs, followed by a 360-degree curve. Years ago, when Drew had first taken the turn, he had almost lost control.

They approached the exit rapidly, ripping along at almost 150 miles per hour in the left lane of I-75. Behind them, in the right lane, the Monte Carlo quickly gained ground.

"When I hit the brakes, fire at will," Drew growled, disgusted at the thought of a complete stranger trying to kill them. *We were minding our own business!*

At the last possible moment before they passed Exit 41, Drew Marks stood on the brakes. His timing was flawless. The Monte Carlo whipped past, and Danny fired four quick shots at the driver, who ducked just in time.

Drew released the brakes and hit the top of the ramp at 40 miles per hour, accelerating sharply. They had survived the interstate, but an unlit country highway lay ahead.

The killer braked, cursing at the top of his lungs. Angry enough to bite the head off a rattlesnake, he almost wept with frustration.

Things had not gone well.

Squealing to a halt, he slammed the car into reverse and sped backwards, skidding to a stop just past the entrance to the ramp. Heedless and angry he hit the gas, burning thunderous clouds of hot rubber.

He hit the top of the ramp at 45 miles per hour and continued to accelerate around the tight curve with torrid abandon: first 65, then 85 miles per hour.

As he whipped around the last part of the steeply banked turn, concentrating intently to stay on the road, the killer noticed something ahead. He could scarcely believe it.

In the middle of the road, the car that he had been chasing shined its bright lights directly into his eyes. The car completely blocked the one-lane exit ramp.

Brilliant! his mind perversely shouted, admiring the elegance of his adversary's solution. He could not brake, but if he hit the car at this speed he would be a dead man. To the left of the PT Cruiser he saw the guardrail: to the right, a steep drop-off. He could not pass to the left; that would be suicidal.

"No!" he screamed, swerving right. As the Monte Carlo rocketed past the parked car at the cusp of the steep inner bank, it seemed to magically balance for an instant, deftly clinging to the gravel shoulder. His right wheels almost fell over the edge, but somehow held fast. He cut the steering wheel back to his left and regained the ramp, but at that point, the car began to fishtail.

The rear bumper kissed the rail as the car prepared for lift off.

The Monte Carlo lost its stability completely, spinning in a circle, as its back wheels broke loose from the road. The front end struck the barrier one last, terrifying time.

The car went airborne.

It flipped majestically, cart-wheeling violently over the top of the steel guardrail. The airborne car landed hard, bouncing heavily down the steep embankment: crashing and crunching through the tall grass before tumbling to a sudden, sodden stop.

At first, the car began to burn slowly.

A small fire started in the engine compartment, visible beneath the crushed hood. Then, gradually, the flames began to spread.

Leaving his hiding place, Drew clambered back up the slope and hopped behind the wheel of his car.

"Danny!" he shouted wildly. Ignoring his cry, the boy stepped past the PT, climbed over the guardrail, and hopped down the steep bank, hypnotically approaching the burning car. He held his father's automatic handgun loosely in his right hand, ready to finish the job. *What has happened to me?* he wondered dully. He watched the scene from a distance. He saw himself carrying the gun, silhouetted against the flames. He felt no pain, no fear, no doubt: only a dead certainty that he wanted to finish this job.

Danny knew that his lack of emotion showed proof of an abnormal state of mind, but he did not care one whit. He had suffered enough pain for one night. He longed to dish it out.

As the boy approached the car, Drew watched the twisted drama in a state of suspended disbelief. He noticed the gun in the boy's hand, the barrel pointing toward the ground. The outline of the child's form seemed surreal: as black as pitch against the glow of the burning car: the very image of unhealthy, unholy obsession.

The flames began to spread.

Danny felt the hot hand of the fire pressing against his cheek, applying pressure against his fevered mind: pushing him, holding him back from his goal. He reached the driver's side of the car and saw that the roof had been crushed down to the steering wheel. He could not catch a glimpse of the killer inside. *I need to finish him off,* he remembered. He felt no anger now. He felt inestimably practical. *My gun still has two in the clip and one in the pipe*, the boy remembered, thinking like a true professional.

Drew flashed his lights and honked the horn, trying to catch Danny's attention. When that failed, he backed the car to the foot of the ramp and doubled back to pick him up, pulling off the road and laying on the horn. The PT's pitiful horn beeped in limp futility, comically underpowered, but unwilling to give up the fight. Drew Marks, on the other hand, felt suddenly empowered by a belated dose of terror.

"Kid," Drew shouted with remarkable volume and piercing power. "Let's go!" At that moment, the wrecked Monte Carlo burst into flames, knocking Danny back like a punch in the gut. The bright flare of light raked firebrands across his field of vision, searing his eyes with a vivid, orange aura. A surreal shriek, haunting enough to chill even Danny's icy blood, arose from within the car as the killer began to burn to death. Coming to himself, Danny turned and ran toward Drew's PT Cruiser. He climbed in and slammed the door, finally beginning to tremble.

"What are you waiting for? Let's get out of here!"

Market Flux in the Skin Trade

When his phone rang, Sonny DiAngelo answered quickly. He expected to hear confirmation of the boy's death, but what he heard startled and shook him.

"Help!" a voice shouted maniacally. In the background, a crackling sound could be heard. "I'm burning!" the voice shrieked, quavering with abject horror.

"Who is this?" Sonny asked stupidly. He was a pale, heavy-set, thick-browed man with a shiny, bald, radically sloping forehead and hairy forearms sized to match a massive belly. A clever, creative, and insightful man occasionally prone to bouts of uncharacteristic stupidity, Sonny served as the Capo Bastone – a.k.a. under boss – for Chicago's preeminent Mafia family. Tonight, as usual, he lounged in a white knit shirt and dark grey Dockers as he waited to receive news of a job well done. In lieu of words of success, however, his telephone brought troubling news. The Capo gazed at Don Brucci quizzically, then glanced furtively in the direction of their elegantly dressed companion.

"You have to hear this," Sonny stated after listening for a few more seconds.

"Put him on speaker," the Don suggested. "James is aware of our situation." Don Antonio Brucci spoke with a deep, gravelly voice that did not match the dapper splendor of his appearance, thin and regal and characteristically natty. He nodded at the other man, a short, dark Sicilian-American of medium height. The visitor had a wide face and mouth with dark-red, generous lips that bulged like well-fed leeches grazing on the verge of his mouth.

This visitor possessed big league credentials. James Biggliatello, a.k.a. Jimmy Biggs, had long served as a caporegime in the most powerful family in New York City, closely allied with the Chicago family run by Don Brucci. Jimmy Biggs, a made man, could be trusted to take family secrets to the grave... and to hell beyond.

In sharp contrast with the dark-skinned captain from New York City, Capo Crimini Antonio Brucci, the top Don in Chicago, made little impression upon first appearance. A small, slim, eminently well-dressed and thoroughly world-weary man with rimless glasses and a puffy crown of pure white hair, the Don looked like a retired scholar or a former captain of industry. The delicate hair frosted his pate like vanilla icing spread over tanned skin the color of overcooked bread crust. The Don's face, thin and expressive, featured long folds down each cheek and deep crows-feet at the corner of each eye. Although their meeting had lasted past midnight, he had neither loosened his tie nor removed the jacket of his natty navy suit.

He must sleep in that suit, Sonny reflected as he punched the hands-free button before placing the telephone in its cradle.

"Help me, please, I'm dying!" a voice shrieked through the tinny speaker, competing against a loud, crackling background noise. Sonny leaned forward nervously, deeply concerned.

"That guy's in trouble," the Don suggested with a slight smile, glancing at Jimmy Biggs. "What's that sound in the background? It sounds like fire."

"Sonny, can you turn it up?" Jimmy asked, leaning forward. For Jimmy Biggs, this amounted to interesting entertainment.

"Don Brucci," Sonny DiAngelo blurted spontaneously, staring at the numbers on the telephone display. "It's the cleaner. It's Paulo."

"Hmm," the Don responded sagely, bemused but not greatly surprised. *These things happen.* "Take it off mute," he ordered. As Sonny released the mute button, the Don spoke loudly.

"Paulo, this is Don Brucci. I'm with Sonny and a friend of ours from out of town. Did you finish the job?"

"Help me!" the caller screamed, his voice becoming more shrill and hopeless. "I'm burning!"

"I think you're right, Don Brucci," Jimmy Biggs observed. "That sounds like fire."

"Maybe the fire cat's got his tongue," the Don suggested with a wry smile. Jimmy Biggs guffawed. Sonny DiAngelo stared at them in disbelief. *How is this funny?*

"Help," the voice moaned pathetically.

"I think he's dying," the Don added happily.

"Ask him if he can see the devil," Jimmy Biggs suggested, provoking a guffaw from the normally self-possessed Don. They smiled at each other, enjoying the moment. Experiences like this did not happen every day.

The tinny voice in the speaker unleashed a stream of obscenities as the background roar increased in pitch. The voice shrieked one last time, oozing a sizzling gusher of tortured agony followed by a delicate tremolo that increased before ending with a haunting, high-pitched squeal, punctuated by a grotesque burble.

At this point, quite mercifully, the call ended. For several seconds the men sat in silence, reflecting on the strange and unsettling experience.

"Wouldn't you know it?" the Don finally asked, raising an eyebrow. "They dropped the call."

"He can't get a refund, either… not where he's going." Jimmy mocked, shaking his head. "That's one hell of a rip-off."

"Don Brucci," Sonny stammered, stunned and dismayed. He attempted to say more, but failed. His mouth opened and shut haplessly, issuing a sound like moist potatoes mashed with a fork. The Don took the lead and addressed his companions jovially.

"That phone call was… well, let's just say that it was rather unusual," he opined. "I'm guessing that Paulo wrecked his car. Perhaps the crash triggered his cell phone, and it called our number. Who can figure out these fancy phones?"

Sonny stared at the Don with his mouth open. Slowly, his brain found traction and his mouth wheezed into motion.

"He was one of the best mechanics in the country," he stammered. "If somebody killed him, I'd like to know who did it."

"No one is impervious to death. These things simply occur. My consigliere is on his deathbed, and Pavarotti has lost his high note.

Perhaps it was just his time."

"He was one of the best," Sonny repeated dully.

"Yes, he was one of the best. But accidents happen. They happen to the best and the worst of us. There are better men than Paulo in the world. For instance, this man sitting with us is better than Paulo." The Don nodded at Jimmy Biggs, who smiled and nodded back. "But I would not impose upon his hospitality by asking him to help us with our business. He has important work to do for our friends on the East Coast.

"There is another man in Canada," the Don continued, "a most magnificent killer. You know of whom I speak." The Don's suggestion frightened Sonny. He cleared his voice.

"I've heard about him, Don Brucci," he wheezed fearfully. "Should I contact our friends in Canada?" *Please say no.* Sonny DiAngelo knew his limitations. The Don referred to a killer unlike any other, a sociopath who combined remorseful effectiveness with a choirboy's face in a package so dreadfully sadistic, so twisted and cruel, that those who knew of him were reluctant to mention his name. Wise guys in the know used an oblique – if comical – nickname for this particular Canadian killer: 'Chucky,' the killer doll.

"Let us think this through," Don Brucci suggested, looking upwards as he touched his fingertips together. "Paulo is dead. He was sent to clean up the crime scene if needed, and to minimize our exposure by eliminating the schlubs who did the job.

"Our primary targets have been eliminated, in spite of witness protection. We did all of this with a little help from our friends, the Domellas," he said, nodding at Jimmy Biggs. "We worked under color of permission from the Provencentis, so we would not appear to violate their territorial rights. We knew that Don Provencenti disapproved of Peter Johnston, so we persuaded the Provencentis to allow us to do the job on him."

"How'd you pull that off?" asked Jimmy.

"Remember Billy Bones?"

Years ago, someone in Florida had killed Billy Bones, a small-time Brucci operator. Authorities had never found the killer.

"Sure. Billy was shot in the head sitting in a car in a parking lot. It was in Orlando, right?"

"Correct. We told Don Provencenti that we had proof that the redneck, Pete Johnston, whacked Billy Bones over a good drug deal gone bad. That's how we received permission to bring our boys into Provencenti territory to do the job on Pete."

"How'd you know that the Provencentis didn't do Billy Bones themselves? He was whacked in Provencenti territory. Everybody knows he hated their consigliere, John Dicella."

"Just between us," Don Brucci replied with a wink, "we whacked Billy. That's how I knew the Provencentis didn't do it."

"Sweet. But how'd you get Provencenti buy-in?"

"I told Don Provencenti that the vendetta was personal. After all, Billy Bones was my brother-in-law."

"Nice."

"The Provencentis didn't have a clue of what we were up to. They agreed to let us take care of the redneck drug dealer only. They never imagined that we'd whack government witnesses."

"I guess that's just tough on them."

"Yes, it is. But to get back to my story, we now plan to wrap up the loose ends. Interestingly enough, I've learned something useful as this process unfolded: my powerful friend, who asked that we execute these jobs, is an obsessive perfectionist.

"About an hour ago, Paolo volunteered to take out an additional target – a teenaged boy – for an additional fee. My powerful friend agreed immediately, and I agreed to foot the bill. I can wet my beak in his purse later. Because Paulo's contract represented an extension of our original deal, I offered no guarantees. I downplayed our chances of success. After all, the job was an add-on… not properly planned.

"Now it appears that Paulo has failed to finish the job. But he may have done us a favor. The price to kill the remaining target has now gone up.

"This is a great opportunity. If we can execute this last little target, a very powerful man will be greatly in our debt. Best of all, the Provencentis will take the heat."

"What should we do, Don Brucci?" Sonny asked.

"Call Don Ardianella in Toronto," the Don ordered, shooting a sidelong glance at Jimmy Biggs. "Ask for the man we spoke of."

"Anything else?"

"Tell them that we will confirm as soon as possible. Tell them the job will be very high profile, but extremely lucrative. Don Ardianella loves money. He'll do what you ask."

Jimmy Biggs had leaned forward anxiously during the last part of their conversation. Unable to bear it any longer, he spoke up.

"Don Brucci, may I speak freely regarding this matter?"

"Of course."

"I have listened with great interest. As you know, our families have been faithful allies for many years. If the man who asked for this favor is so powerful – strong enough for even you to speak of him with respect – we would like to assist you. I would like to personally volunteer my services on behalf of our family."

The Don eyed Jimmy cannily. *I had hoped you'd say that.*

"I must warn you, James. This target might not be found in an open city like Miami. He may hide out in the heart of Provencenti territory."

"Can you arrange the consent of the Provencentis?"

"I don't think so. Don Provencenti called me a few minutes ago, and he made it quite clear that he feels betrayed. The Provencentis will not tolerate another major contract within their territory. They gave us an inch, and we took a mile by murdering government witnesses. They will give us no more inches."

"Some say the Provencentis have gone soft," Jimmy suggested. The Don laughed quietly.

"Don't underestimate them. Don Provencenti is young, but he is a clever man. They say that he combines the strategic gifts of his father, the charm of his mother, and the financial talents of a young Meyer Lansky."

"They say a lot of things. I say different. He's not one of us. He's a half-breed, not a true Sicilian."

"Perhaps, but his father was a true Sicilian, so we must consider him as one of us. It cannot be denied that he's a brave man: a man of respect. In tonight's matter, however, he has behaved unwisely. I'm afraid that he does not trust my judgment. If he did, he would recognize a great opportunity."

Biggs turned red in the face as he heard Don Brucci praising Don Provencenti. He reacted angrily, the words exploding from his mouth.

"With respect, Don Brucci, I think that Don Provencenti is overestimated. Yes, he can be brave when cornered, but even a jackass can be brave when a lion attacks.

"I knew him when he was a hippy musician... Ace Feldmann: a longhaired freak, a stoner and a clown. He's run the Provencentis into the ground. He's not a gangster; he's a punk."

Hearing this, Don Brucci leaned toward Jimmy Biggs, his face full of fatherly concern. "You think so? Really?" he asked innocently. *Good, very good. If New York approves this hit, ignoring Provencenti disapproval, it will strengthen my hand and weaken their dominion in Florida.*

"Please, let me do the job, Don Brucci."

"Do you think Don Domella will approve your involvement?" Don Brucci referred to Don Luigi Domella, the Capo di tutti capi of New York City's most powerful crime family.

"I'll ask him right away. I can't speak for him, but I think he will approve." Jimmy's smile revealed crooked, egg-brown teeth that peeked from behind his blood-red lips like shy snails hiding behind twin leeches. "If the Provencentis will not assist, they can hardly fault us for proceeding without their help."

"Very well. I'll contact my friend to see if he wants us to add a contract on the boy. If so, I'll arrange a deal benefiting both of our families." As the Don finished speaking, a clever idea occurred to Jimmy Biggs.

"Don Brucci, I've got an idea," he exclaimed excitedly. "It is dangerous, but it could be very helpful."

"What?"

"If we execute another contract in Provencenti territory after tonight, it will provoke a response. The jackass will fight."

"Go on."

"We must weaken Don Provencenti's hands."

"What do you suggest?"

"Let's throw a wrench in the Provencenti's friendly relations with Florida law enforcement."

"Go on."

"The Provencentis operate discreetly. They have a few key contacts in crucial positions. They stay off the radar."

"Yes."

"Let's put them back on the radar," Jimmy said excitedly, leaning forward in his chair. "Of course, we could never rat them out. That would be unmanly."

"Of course. What do you suggest?"

"The Provencentis were once involved in an ugly public trial."

"Yes."

"Let's use our connections with the press. Let's bring that trial back into the public mind. The redneck drug kingpin came from the same part of Florida. Let's imply the events were linked. Let's stir the pot and make them look bad. If they're distracted by the spotlight, it's more likely that the Provencentis ignore our intrusion." In response, Don Brucci's eyes widened.

"Eureka!" he cried, jumping from his chair

"Eureka?" Sonny asked.

"I know how to distract them!" the Don almost shouted, filled with glee. "Why didn't I think of it before?" Such excitement from the reserved Don Brucci astonished Sonny, who stared in disbelief.

"What do you mean?" Sonny asked, glancing suspiciously from Don Brucci to Jimmy Biggs and back again. Biggs and Brucci thought too quickly. He could scarcely keep up with them.

"This is too perfect," the Don gloated. "If I didn't know any better, I'd say it was Providential!"

"Providential?"

"Sonny, you lox. Don't you read the executive briefs?" the Don scoffed at his Capo and lifted an executive summary from his desk. "You gave me this brief earlier today. Take a look! Put two and two together. How can we make the Provencentis look bad?"

"Of course," Sonny said as he remembered the brief. "That's a fantastic idea!" The Don nodded at his Capo and turned to Jimmy Biggs, eager to explain.

"Do you recall the name of the key witness years ago at the trial of Joseph Provencenti? She was a young woman in the Florida Department of Law Enforcement's witness protection program."

"Her protection wasn't so great, was it?" Sonny suggested. "She almost got whacked by Joe Boy Provencenti."

"I knew Joe Boy," Jimmy replied with a smile. "He was a real gangster. Not a loser like Ace."

"Yes, he was," the Don agreed. "But do you remember the name of the government's key witness against Joey Pro?"

"That was years ago," Jimmy recalled. "What was her name? Joanie? Janie Jones?"

"You have a very good memory. Her name was Janelle James, but they called her Jamie. Jamie James."

"Right."

"Well, guess what? Since that trial, Janelle James has married and started a career in law enforcement." He threw the executive report on the desk in front of Jimmy Biggs.

"It's right there on the first page of our report. Our contact in the Florida Department of Law Enforcement is very thorough." Jimmy picked up the report and began to read. The smile emerged suddenly, illuminating his swarthy face. "I see what you mean."

Sonny picked up the report and read from the cover page. "Witness protection subjects: Daniel and Sarah Johnston. Florida Department of Law Enforcement Case Number 13784, managed by FDLE Special Agent Janelle James Hawkins."

"Janelle James Hawkins," repeated the Don smugly.

"Too good to be true," Biggs breathed.

"But true nonetheless. A few years ago, Janelle James testified against Joseph Provencenti, Jr. It's all in the public record. Do you see where this is heading?" In response, Biggs clapped his hands.

"Brilliant! If we kill her, the cops will think the Provencentis were behind the whole deal." He practically salivated at the prospect.

"Precisely."

"Perfection!" breathed Capo DiAngelo, awed to be in the presence of a full-fledged evil genius.

"Yes," the Don acknowledged. "It is perfection, I suppose."

"It seems too coincidental," Jimmy suggested.

"Not when you consider the context. Given her past, it's not unusual that she would choose to work in the FDLE's witness protection program. The world of witness protection is very small. With so few subjects to protect, it's not such a fluke that she would be assigned to the Johnston family. This gives us our lucky chance.

"If Don Domella approves, your mission will be two-fold," Brucci commanded, staring coolly at Jimmy Biggs. "You must kill the young boy and the FDLE agent, Janelle Hawkins. If you succeed, the payoff will be spectacular. If you fail, the risk is all yours. We will disavow any knowledge of your involvement, like Mission Impossible," he added a narrow grin. "Are you willing?"

"Do you have to ask?"

"We are agreed." The Don smiled and stood. "Now, gentlemen, you must excuse me. I must speak with our sponsor to see if he wants to add a new contract for the boy. If so, our plan is on."

"Excellent!" Jimmy exclaimed.

"One more thing. As you know, killing a law enforcement agent is completely outside of protocol. We must keep this close... very close, even within our families."

"Omerta," Jimmy Biggs whispered with a smile and a wink.

"Omerta," chimed in Sonny, deadly earnest.

With few exceptions, La Cosa Nostra strictly banned the murder of government authorities. Sonny did not wish to test these time-tempered values, for he dearly valued his own life. Omerta, in this instance, would protect them from their esteemed colleagues inside the other families of La Cosa Nostra.

"Capos DiAngelo and Biggliatello, you must excuse me," the Don said wryly with a mock bow. "I must set the table for our expensive little job." He smiled wickedly and left the room.

Like most men of vision, the Don had already moved on. Walking down the hall, he hummed tunelessly as he considered his plans and pondered the thrill of the Next Big Thing.

Concealed Weapon

"Where did you get that gun?" Drew asked. The car swiftly accelerated past the speed limit on the narrow, deserted country highway.

"Hey, I really like this car." Danny responded hopefully, trying to change the subject.

"It's illegal to carry an unsecured handgun on a public road in Florida without a permit."

"If I was a law-abiding citizen, we'd both be dead." *The kid has a point,* Drew considered with a frown.

"This is my father's gun. It's my dead father's gun, okay?"

"Then put it in the glove box, will you? I have a concealed weapons permit, and that'll make it legal for both of us."

"Since when did concealed weapons become stylish for Hollywood rock stars?"

"I keep a home in South Beach. A couple of years ago, a stalker threatened my life. After that, I jumped through the hoops and got a permit. What makes you think I'm a Hollywood type, anyway?"

"Oh, maybe just Entertainment Tonight, the tabloids, the cover of People magazine…"

"Okay, you've got me, kid. A few years ago, I served some time in Hollywood, sure. It's not so bad once your star fades a little and the paparazzi leave you alone. But I grew up in Wakulla County, Florida. Do you know where that is?"

"No."

"It's a rural county that borders the Gulf, just south of Tallahassee."

"You grew up in the boondocks?"

"Big time. I knew how to shoot before I could write. If my grandma had lived, I'd probably still be living in Wakulla County: huntin', workin' as a mechanic, and playin' music on weekends."

"No kiddin'?"

"Yeah. My grandfather owned a garage in Woodville. I guess I might've taken it over some day. But with my grandma gone, me and my granddaddy didn't see eye to eye. The night I turned 15, I grabbed my guitar and left. I hitchhiked to Atlanta to play rock and roll, and I never looked back." *I lied about my age like you, kid. It was three years before the guys in the band knew my real age.*

"Heavy metal would've dodged a real bullet if you'd stayed home." Danny smirked happily.

"You bet."

Danny put the gun in the glove box and slammed it shut. "There. We're legal now. Okay?"

"Okay. Now give me some directions. Where are we goin' in Tally?"

"Aunt Marcy lives on Monroe Street in a big condo. It's called 'The Tennyson', or something literary. Maybe The 'Longfellow'."

"That reminds me," Drew added. "Considering the situation, don't you think we should call your aunt?"

"Can't we just surprise her?"

"She might be at risk. Did you think of that?"

"No way! There's no way that Uncle Pete would hurt Aunt Marcy. He calls her his baby cousin. Daddy says she's his favorite." He paused for a moment, thinking. "She's a brainiac. She left after high school and we never saw much of her after that."

"Who's this Uncle Pete you keep talking about?" Drew asked, fumbling for a stick of gum. He offered one to Danny. In unison, they each un-wrapped a stick and popped it into their mouths.

"He's the guy who had my daddy and momma killed," Danny stated matter-of-factly. As he remembered his parents' murder, Danny showed no emotion. He felt curiously detached, as if the nerve linking his mind to his heart had been severed. *Something's wrong with me,* he reflected, but he did not care to know the details. He certainly did not want to reconnect with his feelings at this particular time and place.

"Don't worry," Danny added. "Our FDLE case worker told me

she'd call Aunt Marcy. She's probably sitting up, waiting for us to arrive." He turned and stared out the window. *Why don't I feel anything?*

"Okay, good."

"Do you want to hear something strange?" Danny asked, tilting his head.

"Sure."

"When the car was on fire and I ran up to it, I wanted to kill that guy. I wanted to put a bullet right in the middle of his head."

"I can understand that."

"When I saw that the roof was crushed down to the steering wheel, I was glad. I laughed out loud."

"Wow."

"Yeah," Danny agreed.

"Bummer."

"That ain't right."

"Cut yourself some slack, kid. You've been through a lot."

"I guess so." He paused, staring at the darkness outside the car. "Mama was a good woman. She became a Christian after Daddy went to prison. We were in the witness protection program for two years. Two whole years."

"I didn't know."

"I was in witness protection on the day of my first shave."

"Not many folks can say that." Drew sympathized.

"Yep."

"A guy shouldn't be in hiding on the day of his first shave,"

"It ain't right," Danny agreed.

"It's messed up."

"Anyway, Daddy became a Christian two weeks ago. Now he's dead. Just like that." Danny snapped his fingers. "Don't that seem strange to you?"

"I don't know."

"Daddy shouldn't have gone to prison in the first place. He said the devil meant it for bad, but God used it for good."

"No kiddin'?"

"That's what he said. Isn't that weird?"

"I don't know. A lot of people turn to God when they're in trouble. I saw plenty of that in rehab. We had all kinds."

"I used to be a good Christian," Danny speculated. "But I ain't been so good lately."

"Nobody's good but God." *Where did I hear that? It sounds right.*

"Maybe that's why my folks were killed. Do you think so? They weren't good enough. You think?"

"I don't think God's waiting for a chance to whack us with a hammer, kid. I don't know why… but I believe he wants the best for us." Hearing these words, Danny felt the tears rise and fought them back. *Not now; not here!*

"How do you know that?"

"I don't know… I just believe it." Drew shrugged. *Before rehab, I didn't believe it. Now, I do.*

"Well I don't believe it, okay? That may have worked for my parents, but it ain't workin' for me. You got that?"

"What's with the attitude, kid? That's between you and the big guy."

"Hmph." Finished with his commentary, Danny turned away and stared into the darkness.

JIMMY BIGGS TURNED OFF HIS CELL PHONE and threw it into the trash. *So much for that one.* When conducting family business – to minimize the chance of a trace – he used an encrypted telephone once before tossing it.

"Don Domella sends his regards," he said solemnly, addressing Don Brucci. He was glad to have finally spoken to his Don. "He has approved my participation."

"Excellent," replied Don Brucci. To celebrate their deal, he poured three small glasses full of unadulterated grappa, a raggedly distilled drink long on strength and short on refinement. He carefully passed the glasses around to his companions.

"To death and money." He winked. "Long may they prosper."

"Death and money," the men affirmed sarcastically, smirking at the Don's wry wit. They knocked the shots down and exhaled: eyes watering, faces tingling from the powerful kick of the grappa.

"That's'a some spicy meatball'a," Don Brucci blurted, imitating a stereotypical Italian accent from an old TV commercial. The men laughed heartily and clinked their glasses together.

Oh, well, Sonny DiAngelo reflected, warmed by the drink. *The kid was gonna die sooner or later, anyway. We might as well make money from it.*

"Is this the place?" Drew asked as he pulled the PT Cruiser into a well-lit asphalt lot. They had just arrived in downtown Tallahassee and turned into a parking lot among the trees behind a tall condominium.

"I think so. Let's see if she's here." They parked and climbed out of the car, stretching slowly, sore from the long ride.

"Things got pretty hairy back there," Drew said as they walked up to the building and stepped into a well-lit entry alcove. "You did okay, kid."

Under the bright lights, he could see his young companion more clearly. Danny's skin, tanned by the hot summer sun, showed the shadowy remnants of numerous faded freckles. The boy looked extremely thin: unhealthily skinny, or so it seemed.

Studying the list of names, Danny pressed a button beside the name of his aunt, Marcy Johnston. A young woman's voice answered almost immediately, shaky and tense.

"Who's there?"

"Hi, Aunt Marcy. It's me, your favorite nephew, along with my famous rock-and-roll sidekick." Danny winked mischievously at Drew. "Can we come up and play?"

Long-Distance Connection

Billy Tigerclaw, a Florida native, had lived in the heart of the Alaskan wilderness for five years. During those years, he had not tired of the land's tempestuous beauty. In daylight and darkness, through the long nights of winter and the unending days of summer, Billy had marveled at the power, fragility, and changeable resilience of the wilderness.

During the first four years he had worked with John Donley, a gregarious Inuit guide who had taught him how to survive in winter's cold and summer's swarms of stinging flies. They had hunted for pleasure and for their livelihood… during bow season, black-powder season, and every other imaginable season: fishing and hunting and living free under the unblinking sun.

Several months ago, he and Donley had parted on good terms. Since that time, Billy had worked alone as a guide in the Armand Waite Wilderness Area, on call as the local bad-bear contractor. As both a hunter and a lover of the wilderness, Billy held mixed emotions about his work. During the past years, he had found that the animals he hunted were more interesting – and more respectable – than many of the humans he guided. Polar and grizzly bears were the most fascinating wild creatures he had ever encountered.

Before moving to Alaska, Billy had given 20 years of his life to the United States government. After serving as a Long Range Reconnaissance expert, training and supporting various governments against guerilla threats, he had graduated to become one of the few Long Range Termination Specialists in the United States Army. Billy had eventually risen through government service and joined the CIA. For the love of country and the addictive rush of adrenaline, Billy had hunted some of the world's most dangerous men. Five years ago, he had retired from his trade to become a hunting guide. Now, he sought less dangerous prey.

Today's hunt would offer Billy a trip down memory lane. Today, he would track a man-killer.

The bush plane dropped Billy off far north of his usual haunts, deep within the artic circle along the coastline of the Arctic Ocean. The bear had begun his crime spree by killing an Inuit boy near one of the northernmost summer hunting camps in Alaska, lurching from the water to drag him out of his canoe. After the first bloody murder, the bear had snatched a young girl from the same encampment before fleeing north across the permafrost.

The Inuit men could not be reached, for they had traveled far into the ocean, seeking walrus among the pack ice. An elder had used his satellite phone to call for help, and the state wildlife agency had contacted Billy to track and kill the big bear.

Billy had to destroy the bear. Any predator that dined on human victims twice in rapid succession had demonstrated an unhealthy appetite for human flesh.

Tracking the bear from the site of the kill, Billy had traveled north on foot across the tundra for two grueling days before reaching the rocky barren flats of the far northern coast. By that point, the man-eater had sensed another predator on his trail.

Midsummer days could last more than 22 hours this far north. By July, the light at 10 o'clock in the evening resembled dusk in Billy's native state of Florida. To wanderers crossing the broken terrain in the fading half-light, the sun seemed to linger on the horizon like a mischievous spirit that taunted those yearning for sleep.

In the near-darkness after midnight on the third day, Billy sensed an ambush. Doubling back, he crouched low behind a stone outcrop and waited. After a while, out of his sightline, he heard a distant thumping, as if a snow giant pounded on a frozen drum. Ranging wide to his left, he struck the bear's trail atop a carpet of slick, frozen moss that plunged down a cliff within sight of the sea.

The bear's path disappeared on a rocky shore lining a narrow bay, sheltered on three sides by jagged rock walls. Inside the walls of the bay, the air had retained the bite of winter: dark and bitterly cold. A large ice floe remained frozen to the shore in the shade of the surrounding cliffs, defying the summer and the anemic rays of the reluctant sun.

The bear's trail led toward a hole in the ice that looked very fresh. At the edge of the hole, the bear sign disappeared into the water. Scratching his head, Billy put two and two together.

That must've been the thumping sound I heard before I got here. He was breakin' a seal hole in the ice.

Billy had seen polar bears do this many times. Choosing a patch of thin ice, the bear would jump up and down on their forepaws to break a hole, providing quick access to seals swimming in the frigid water below.

Billy possessed the power of endurance, and he could be a remarkably patient hunter. For more than an hour, he sat quietly on the shore within sight of the hole, waiting for the bear's return as he scanned the broken land in every direction. Periodically, he dozed upright, the nod of his head waking him. The wind, blowing in from the icy sea, whistled through the steep canyon.

Almost an hour elapsed before he stood stiffly, his hard clothing cracking in the cold. For hours, the sun had hidden just below the edge of the frozen horizon. Soon, it would rise. The permanent, half-lit dusk of this weary, midsummer night's dream would yield to a lengthy sunrise as the orb weakly crawled around the rim of the horizon.

Billy walked carefully onto the ice. He knew better than to approach this new hunting hole too closely. He had seen big bears suddenly surge out of holes like this, skidding onto the ice, soaking wet. He kept a wary distance.

Turning away, the hunter realized that he stood on a thinner part of the pack ice: a section swept clean of snow by a bitter wind that sluiced through the narrow, coastal canyon. The ice felt tenuous and untrustworthy. *I'd better get back to shore.* He paused for a moment. *The air is changing.* A breath of wind stirred his jet-black hair.

As Billy moved toward the shore, something strange happened, deep within. An instinctual alarm jangled his nerves. Something inexplicable – a primal fear – stood his hair on end. Electricity swept across his skin like a high-voltage brushfire.

He looked down. His spiked snow boots stood atop the glassy face of an older, iced-over seal hole. As he strained to see through the opaque ice, the sun peeked above the horizon and stretched a delicate finger deep into the bay, illuminating the ice and the clear, green water below his feet.

Billy understood immediately why he had been unable to locate the bear.

At least 30 feet straight down, in the waters of the rocky bay, the huge polar bear stroked upwards, slicing through the icy, pristine water. The bear swam powerfully, his massive arms and paws seizing the water and shoving it out of his way: his hungry eyes focused tightly on the human, Billy Tigerclaw.

Billy fled the scene with uninhibited abandon, running as only the terrified can. In five mighty leaps, he cleared the ice and reached the shore. Striking solid ground, he wheeled back toward the water and swung the rifle to his shoulder in a smooth, practiced motion.

In the bay, the ice blew up in his face.

The big bear exploded out of the frozen seal hole like a half-ton of dynamite blowing the lid off the whole affair. The white pack ice simply erupted, exploding upwards in a wild spray of air-borne snow mixed with flint-edged, icy shrapnel. It was as if a bomb had detonated in the belly of the bay, launching a cold, white, heat-seeking warhead.

The bear surged powerfully from the hole, floundering for traction at the edge. Robbed of his prey, he roared with deafening power.

Billy Tigerclaw could smell the brute's rancid breath as he squinted down the barrel of his .409 Alaskan. He saw the bear roaring, but he heard absolutely nothing.

A smothering silence surrounded the hunter. He watched as the great mouth opened. He saw the yellowed fangs, but he did not hear the battle cry. Instead of an angry roar, he heard his own tendons creaking as he steadied the rifle: his own breath pausing, his own heartbeat stopping as he slowly squeezed the trigger.

At the crack of the rifle and the heavy punch of recoil against his shoulder, Billy's senses returned with jarring clarity. He heard the roar as it echoed from the stony cliffs. He smelled the burnt powder, the stench of wet bear and the sour scent of his own, primal fear.

The shot blew through the beast's open mouth and hit the spine where it met the skull. Flesh and blood showered backwards in a grim, dark-red spray that stained the pristine green water and soiled the clean, white snow.

The bear collapsed like a rag doll at the edge of the hole: half in the water, half out. He exhaled slowly, and he did not breathe again. His limp paws extended outward, gently somehow, as he lay facedown and motionless in a crimson puddle that gradually grew, fouling the pristine snow.

Although Billy knew that no bear could survive such a shot, he kept his gun trained as he slowly counted to 60. Finally, seeing no motion, he began to back up. He stumbled as he tried to climb up the rocky bank backwards without looking, still aiming his gun in the direction of the bear. Losing his footing, he tripped and dropped indecorously onto his posterior atop a large, flinty rock: sharp-edged and bitterly cold. The solidity of the stone felt oddly comforting, in spite of its frigidity.

I'm alive, Billy remembered. He began to shake from head to foot, his heart racing.

What a bear. He pulled his wool cap off, allowing the cold breeze to painfully caress his face and ruffle his sweat-soaked hair. In the growing cold, the wind quickly turned his perspiration to ice. *What a bear! He almost got me.*

As he attempted to regain control, Billy felt the satellite phone vibrating inside his zippered coat pocket. *How long has that been goin' off?* He pulled it out and looked at the buttons, trying to remember how to answer it. He pushed a button and spoke, his voice breathing smoky vapor into the clear Alaska air.

"This is Billy."

"Billy, this is Rich." Billy almost dropped the phone in surprise. Rich Collins had once been his supervisor, but they had not spoken in years. Rich, older and wiser than Billy, had mentored him in the early days, when they had worked together in the field.

"Richie! What's up? Have you retired yet?"

"Yeah, I retired last year. Listen, Billy, I need a personal favor. It's a big one... and it's for me, not for our Uncle."

"Sure, Rich. What do you want?"

"Are you free to travel?"

"For you, I'm free as the breeze." Billy smiled broadly. "I'm retired, man. I served my 20 and moved on. Right now, I'm huntin' in the Alaskan bush."

"It sounds like you've made a good life."

"Yeah, I guess I have." *Not like the bear,* he considered philosophically. "What's the favor?"

"I need you to protect a civilian... a kid. It could be extremely dangerous."

"Just like old times, eh?"

"This will be deep cover, completely under the radar. I can't pay expenses, and I can only talk to you one more time. This is hot, Billy. Very hot."

"Long hours? No pay? Extreme danger? No respect from the locals? What's not to like?"

"Can you fly to Florida?"

"Sure. It's been three years since I visited my folks down there. They're both in their 80s, still livin' on the Big Cypress." He rubbed his eyes. "I'd love to see 'em." Billy waved his hand dismissively, staring at the bear. "Don't worry about the money. I'm doin' real good up here."

"How long would it take you to get to Tallahassee?"

"At least three days. I'm way north right now... I mean, way north. I have to fly out of the bush. That's what we call it up here, 'the bush,' even though there ain't no bushes where I'm at."

"Do you remember my old phone number... the one we used for special situations?"

"Sure."

"Call that number when you get to Tallahassee. Use a pay phone. I'll call you back."

"This is just like you, Rich. I'll be in Florida riskin' my neck, and you'll be sittin' pretty somewhere else, as cautious as an old man in a high-crime neighborhood."

"That's how I survived this long."

"True."

"Uh... listen, Billy... this could bring some heat. This job isn't approved."

"Good deeds don't have to be approved, eh? As long as I obey the law, I'm clean. Florida has great laws when it comes to protectin' the innocent. Outlaws aren't the only folks carryin' guns down there."

"Thanks, Billy. Call me when you get to Tallahassee, okay?"

"Sure."

Rich Collins paused for a moment, not yet ready to hang up. He ran his fingers through his hair and stared at the grandfather clock, ticking slowly in the dim light of the elegant sitting room. *After I tell the Agency that Sal called me, the heat'll be on.*

"Uh, Billy, there's one more thing."

"Yeah?"

"On this one, we'll be at risk from the bad guys and the good guys. No one would believe we're doing this just to help some kid free of charge, with nothin' in it for us."

"Same as always." Billy smiled, his face cracking in the cold. "We never had much backup, did we?"

"Isn't that the truth?" Rich paused awkwardly, unsure of what to say next. "Uh... Billy?"

"Yeah?"

"Thanks."

Deliverance

When Marcy Johnston heard Danny's voice, she dropped the phone and ran from the apartment without a backwards glance. Chesterfield Hamilton III followed closely behind her, momentarily pausing to return the phone to its receiver and place a coaster under her glass on the coffee table. By the time he reached the elevator, the door had shut in his face. An arrow blinked dolefully, marking Marcy's descent to the first floor. Shaking his head, Chesterfield pushed a button and waited, smoothing the wrinkles from his clean gray polo shirt as he whistled tunelessly and looked around the empty 12th floor lobby.

Over the past two years, Chesterfield had acquired a healthy pessimism regarding his relationship with Marcia Johnston – or, to put it more plainly, about the absence of a relationship. 'Ches', as his friends called him, had long lived the good life in Tallahassee as a charming, shamelessly rich bachelor. Now in his early 50s, he ruled the courtroom: a famous attorney performing at the peak of his profession. Beautiful women had chased Ches up and down the Sunshine State for most of his adult life in spite of his perennial potbelly, unkempt curly hair, and modest height. Ches had a way with the ladies. Something about him – his radiant personality, lively wit, intellectual gravitas, casual drawl, sly poetic gifts – seemed simply irresistible. He had always been the rascal that single women wanted to fix... until he met Marcy.

Ches had never chased a woman before. But when he met Marcy, the chase began. To this date, after a two-year marathon of poems and roses, he still pursued her hopelessly, like a forlorn puppy panting after a Purina truck.

Chesterfield Hamilton truly loved Danny's aunt Marcy. *She's going through the wringer tonight. Her brother and wife murdered... how dreadful!*

After decades of practice, Ches had become a wildly successful trial attorney. He exuded trustworthiness and confidence: the juror's friend and the life of any party, caustically witty and perennially well dressed. Above all else, Ches wielded his marvelous silver tongue like a veritable magician of the English language. He could explain away almost anything with a well-reasoned turn of a phrase. *Members of the jury, as you have heard, my client picked up the murder weapon when he found it in the dumpster, cutting his finger in the process. Suspecting foul play, he scratched his hands and face while searching for additional evidence to provide to the authorities. Because the police showed up at that very moment, they thought the worst of him. It's not their fault. They didn't know what you now know. But you know the facts. My client is not the perpetrator. He is a victim, snared in a web of bad timing and misplaced suspicion made worse by overly zealous prosecution. My client is on trial for his life because he took out the garbage!*

Ches mashed the elevator button again and tapped his foot impatiently. He glanced at his watch and frowned.

On the first floor, Marcy burst from the elevator and raced to the front of the main lobby, slamming the door open with abandon. She flung herself into Danny's arms, weeping with joy and sorrow.

"Danny! Thank God you're okay!" She hugged him fiercely. "I was afraid you wouldn't make it." She smiled though her tears as they hugged one another. The front doors shut behind her as they lingered on the sidewalk in front of the building.

She squeezed him harder, fighting back tears. "I'm so sorry," she whispered. Danny hugged her, but said nothing. Slowly, Marcy mastered her emotions. She stepped back, wiping her eyes. "Come inside," she said, pulling on his hand.

Danny gestured toward his companion, and she stopped cold. She tried to force a smile, but the effort fell flat. She let go of Danny's hand and looked up at Drew, then turned to Danny, questioningly.

"This is my friend, Aunt Marcy. His name is Drew."

"Your friend?"

"Drew saved my life, Aunt Marcy."

"Oh."

"Drew, say hi to Aunt Marcy." She managed a smile and extended her hand.

"Hello, I'm Marcia Johnston," she said, uncertain of how to address the tall, dark-haired, and extremely good-looking man who stood before her. He seemed vaguely familiar, but she could not place his face.

Nonplussed by what he saw, Drew gaped at Danny's aunt in frank surprise. He stared at her unapologetically, stunned into silence. Aunt Marcy tended to do that to young, unmarried men like Drew.

Marcia Johnston could have worked as a model instead of reading for the law, but she had chosen the more practical, less glamorous alternative. As she stood in the brightly lit foyer, barefoot in casual denims, she seemed to Drew like a heavenly vision of pure, unaffected womanhood. With her dark blue tee shirt and horned-rimmed glasses framed by rumpled, pale blond hair, her sea-green eyes and perfectly proportioned face and figure, Marcy represented the post-modern equivalent of the 'Ideal Woman': unhealthily slim, highly intelligent, and utterly independent.

At first, Drew could not speak. After several seconds, he shut his mouth and took her hand, shaking it firmly.

"Drew Marks, at your service." To his own surprise, he bowed from the waist, almost kissing her hand. *What a loser! I'm acting like a butler in a B movie.* When he spoke, his Southern accent returned automatically in response to Marcy's refined inflection. It was as if his drawl had been summoned from the depths of his rocky past. Worse, his reconstituted Wakulla dialect lacked the subtlety of Marcy's inflection; his was as strong as uncut chewing tobacco, the kind that could scarcely be understood by those not from the South. Encoded into his marrow during his childhood, it had long awaited its chance to return. Now the accent emerged without his bidding, startling and dismaying him.

Unable to restrain himself, Danny interrupted Drew.

"Some guy tried to kill us on the highway." He stated it matter-of-factly, as if he were discussing a fender-bender on Main Street in downtown Cutlerville, Florida. "Drew saved my life."

Now it was Aunt Marcy's turn to look nonplussed. She stared at Drew and shook her head swiftly, not quite believing what she had seen and heard.

"Somebody tried to kill you?" She looked at Danny uncertainly, then glanced at Drew. "This man saved your life?"

"Yes, ma'am," Drew said, looking over his shoulder at the parking lot. "Maybe we'd better go inside." He looked around nervously.

"Please, come in," Marcy offered hastily. She typed in a code, and the doors opened.

"Thanks," Drew mumbled as they entered the lobby and the doors shut behind them. He felt stupid, somehow... awkward in her presence. *'Thanks.' That's real eloquent!*

"It sounds like I should be thanking you," she blushed hotly as they crossed the lobby and stopped in front of the elevators. "Thanks for helping Danny."

The elevator doors opened to reveal Ches Hamilton. The sight of his would-be girlfriend talking to an unfamiliar and strikingly handsome young man instantly nonplussed Ches. The situation appeared critical, for the suspect of interest appeared to be – heaven forefend – not only handsome and charming, but close to Marcy's age.

"Is everything okay?" he asked squeamishly.

"Yes, thank you, Ches," she said, hugging Danny as they stepped into the elevator. "Danny and Drew, meet Chesterfield Hamilton the Third. Ches is the most famous criminal attorney in Tallahassee." She smiled at Ches. *That means so much to him.* Now it was Chesterfield's turn to blush.

"I suppose I am," he grumbled.

"Ches, this is my nephew Danny and his friend, Drew," she said to Ches. As the elevator opened and they stepped inside, Drew put out his hand.

"Pleased to meet you. I'm Drew Marks," he said automatically, reverting to the Southern manners of his youth. Hearing Drew's name, it was Chester's turn to be surprised.

"Are you *the* Drew Marks? The lead singer from Blunt Trauma? You look just like him."

"Guilty as charged," he replied as the door shut. The elevator began to move.

"Oh, my," Ches uttered, for once at a loss for words. When he began to speak, it became evident that he had been taken by surprise. His startled mind reeled, struggling to regain its scalpel-sharp edge. "I hate to admit it Mr. Marks..." he paused, unable to continue.

"Call me Drew."

"Okay, Drew. I mean, I hate to admit it, but I suppose I really don't hate to admit it," he babbled nervously. Drew looked at Ches wearily, resigned to his fate. He had been around the world three times. He knew what to expect.

"I hate to admit it, but I'm a huge fan of yours," Ches blurted. "I've followed Blunt Trauma since you guys were an Indy band. When you began to sell out – uh, I mean, to sell out stadiums – I still liked your sound. Awesome." He glanced at his intended girlfriend, wondering what her reaction would be.

Marcy did not appear to hear Ches. She hugged Danny around the shoulders with her left arm, keeping her eyes riveted on Drew, who stared at the floor, totally unaware of her gaze. As Marcy stared, her face shined expectantly with the glow of a woman fascinated by the man of her dreams.

Oh, no! She's completely smitten... out of the blue! Ches turned and saw Danny staring at him with a knowing gaze. *The boy... he can see what I'm thinking! He's reading me like a book.* As an able counselor accustomed to fielding grounders on the hop, Chesterfield Hamilton recovered almost immediately.

"Where are you staying tonight?" he asked Drew as the elevator doors opened on the 12th floor.

Profane Intervention

Just before dawn, the big tractor trailer delivered Pete Johnston and Paul Larson to a deserted airport bordered by orange groves in a sparsely developed area southwest of Kissimmee. Pete and his henchman silently climbed out of the cab and looked scornfully at the barren, weed-infested tarmac surrounded by scattered steel buildings.

"Small time," Pete said.

"That's good for us... no witnesses," Paul replied. He walked ahead of Pete, leading the way to a nearby hangar. They entered through a narrow side door.

As he entered through the darkened doorway, Pete Johnston noticed that they walked on a slick, slippery membrane. *Is that plastic? Why'd they spread plastic on the floor?*

He paused. Suddenly, his stomach sank as his mind answered the question. *To catch my blood!* He looked up into a blinding flash of light as Paul Larson pulled the trigger.

As he fell asleep, Pete Johnston awoke. *Uh, oh,* he thought as he searched the darkness in vain for a hint of light or a glimmer of hope. *What just happened?*

He began to sink into the abyss.

The darkness clung to him like a spider's web. He could not shake its sticky threads. The air seared his lungs: smoky and polluted with flames that ate into his flesh. The pain grew exponentially with an onrush of withering heat.

When he screamed, no sound came out of his mouth.

TWO HOURS LATER, in an airplane roaring high above the earth, Paul Larson smiled and hummed softly to himself. Events had unfolded swimmingly in his blood-soaked world.

By the time the sun topped the horizon, they had left the east coast of Florida far behind. Paul felt fantastic, glad that they would soon shed 220 pounds of dead redneck weight. The pilot had logged the flight as a fishing trip, but they would feed the fish before they caught any.

After an hour, the Cessna turned south and slowed, descending to a lower altitude. Larson looked up to see the pilot climb back into the cargo compartment.

They opened the side door, designed for dual use: loading cargo or skydiving. The roar of the wind, combined with the airplane's engines, hammered them with a chest-thumping rumble of bass vibrations. At their feet, inside a tightly taped roll of black plastic, Pete Johnston's body sloshed in its own blood, a pitiful end to an unmerciful tyrant.

"Let's unwrap him," Larson yelled. "Cut the tape so the fish can get to him."

"That's not a good idea," the pilot shouted, his mouth close to Larson's ear. The pilot, a wiry man with dark, curly hair, wore a nondescript, lightweight flight jacket and a pair of jeans. "The sharks won't mind the plastic wrap."

"You're sure?"

"Yeah. And if we unwrap him, the wind will blow blood all over the place." He spoke as one with experience.

They hauled the body to the edge of the door and rolled it out into the wind. Paul Larson leaned out to watch it fall, holding tightly to the cargo handle. The shiny black cocoon lazily twisted end over end before finally hitting the sunlit ocean below.

"Beautiful," he whispered as he stared at the rippling sea. "A redneck dumped by a Swede from a plane flown by a dago."

"Beautiful," echoed the pilot, pulling a pistol from underneath his loose cotton flight jacket. The first shot hit Paul Larson in the right kidney. The second entered the back of his neck and blew a red mist into the clean salt air through Larson's shattered larynx. Larson coughed twice, ejecting a narrow crimson spout each time, like the victim of a failed tracheotomy.

From sea level, if a sailor had searched the bright blue sky and caught sight of the distant plane, the view might have seemed almost peaceful. Like a falling leaf, Larson's miniature body floated out of the open cargo bay and descended slowly toward the restless waves below. At the end of its flight, the body slammed hard into the surface of the sea.

Back in the plane, the pilot experienced a deep satisfaction. His career path had taken him far, and the thrills had exceeded his sickest dreams. "Take that as a warning," he shouted, appreciating the irony of his words. "Don't sell out your boss."

Tommy Casaluto, a master mechanic on the staff of Chicago's premier Mafia family, put his gun away without a hint of regret. "Nothin' personal," he murmured. Closing the plane's jump door, he locked it tight and climbed back into the cockpit.

Tommy removed the autopilot and pulled back slightly on the wheel, pushing the throttle forward. The plane began to climb, accelerating as the pilot whistled happily. Checking his coordinates to confirm that he was within range of the cellular tower in Key West, he dialed a number and sent Sonny DiAngelo, the Brucci capo, a predetermined text message to indicate the success of his mission, "On vacation and loving it. T. C."

The message was accurate. To preserve the cover that had been filed with his flight plan, Tommy would hang out in the sunny Cayman Islands for two relaxing weeks. Diligence in the pursuit of death had its rewards.

Charnel House Rules

By 4:00 AM the wooden house had burned to its foundation, collapsing into an overwrought bed of super-sized, smoldering coals with a few twisted, red-hot beams that still stood upright like stunted trees preparing to wilt down into the wreckage. Jets of water from myriad fire hoses soaked the piles of fallen ash, roaring whenever they encountered a hidden pocket of heat.

Soon, the arson investigators would begin a detailed inspection of the crime scene. Amid the smoking coals, they would uncover a worse case scenario.

This was not just another burned house.

This was a charnel house.

Just after dawn, the investigators uncovered the charred bodies of four adults. The child's body could not be found. The discovery lent credence to the story told by Janelle "Jamie" Hawkins, the FDLE special agent who had reported a telephone call from the child shortly after the murders.

Federal agents arrived at 7:15 AM in two large, dark sedans. They emerged ominously from their cars and glided softly through the crime scene like undertakers working a high-priced wake. There had been no obvious violation of federal law, but that did not slow them. They sought out Jamie and drew her aside to a picnic table, ready to conduct an intense round of questioning. *My reputation precedes me,* Jamie reflected. Undoubtedly, they had heard of her past, when she had hidden in a witness protection program – and how she had been saved from an untimely death, by a man now wanted for questioning in the nation's most scandalous unsolved arson-murder.

In spite of her exhaustion, Jamie appeared more than willing to provide all the information they asked for. However, she planned to skip one detail: the fact that she had called an old friend, asking for help to protect Danny Johnston.

The federal agents bunched together like buzzards on a picket fence: a resolute cluster of dark-haired white males perched side-by-side on a long picnic bench, hunched expectantly over the table as they peppered Jamie with questions regarding the Johnston family and the early-morning phone call she had received from the surviving child. As she answered, they watched her reactions carefully, like carrion fowl eyeing a wounded soldier.

Less than two minutes after the interrogation began, they were interrupted by a tall, thin, clean-shaven man in his late 30s, dressed in a light blue long-sleeved shirt, striped tie, and dark gray slacks. An undisciplined shock of blond hair flopped about his forehead, unruly and damp in the July heat.

"Clay!" Jamie said, standing abruptly. "How wonderful to see you!"

"Hi, Jamie," he replied with a thin smile. "Delia caught me on vacation in Oree County. She told me I'd find you here." The lead agent, a short, heavy-set man, stood up and confronted Clay.

"Excuse me, sir. This is a crime scene. We're conducting an investigation," he stated, showing his badge. "You'll have to leave."

"No," Jamie said to the men, looking up at Clay and raising her eyebrows. "Please," she mouthed silently.

"Gentlemen, I know that you have a job to do," Clay responded politely, "but so do I. I'm an officer of the court, and I'm here at the request of Delia Rawlings, the Sheriff of Oree County. I'll be representing Mrs. Hawkins as her attorney."

When Clay uttered the word 'attorney,' the agents reacted as if he had claimed to be a monster cobbled from an amalgam of snakes, swamp gas, and untreated sewage. *First, kill all the lawyers,* Clay remembered, smiling generously.

"Mrs. Hawkins has already given one statement to the Florida Department of Law Enforcement and another to the Davis County Sheriff's Department. She loved this family, and she felt personally responsible for their safety. Although she seems to be holding up well, the extent of the tragedy has not yet sunk in. She's been awake all night, gentlemen. She's been under a tremendous strain. She needs to get some rest."

"Mr., uh..." the lead agent replied.

"Calhoun. Clay Calhoun."

"Mr. Calhoun," he stopped, scratching his chin. Then, he surrendered to the reality of the situation at hand. *She's been up all night, and she's an FDLE special agent. He's right. We'd better cut her some slack.* "We'd like to question your client as soon as possible."

"Here's my card." He said, signaling for Jamie to stand. "Please call my office next week." He took her arm. "Now, my client needs to go home."

Leaving Montana

Wally Hamilton sat at a rough-hewn wooden table in the kitchen of his family's aged wooden ranch house, enjoying breakfast. With the windows wide open, he savored the cool breeze. In the majestic Montana silence, the slightest stir of air pressed loudly against his eardrums.

He heard the horse approaching long before the rider topped the last rise. At the sound, Wally stood stiffly, stretching against the pain of sore morning muscles. Pouring two mugs of steaming black coffee, he carefully carried them through the living room and onto the front porch, shouldering open the unlatched door. By the time Salvatore Benuto had dismounted and tied his horse to the rail, Wally had been sitting almost motionless for several minutes. He thoughtfully sipped his coffee in his favorite rocking chair, looking like a short, lean statue of a cowboy, complete with waxed moustache, checkered shirt, worn leather boots, and a tanned face with deep cracks from the dry Western heat.

Wally raised his mug to salute his friend as he clumped up the front steps. Sal's elderly, ever-present cat dangled loosely across his left shoulder as the tall, wide-shouldered man knocked the dust of the trail off of his pants with heavy blows from his cowboy hat.

"Long time no see, old bud," Wally drawled. "I thought you'd be stayin' in the high country all summer."

"That was the plan." Sal Benuto took the cat in his hands and collapsed into the rocking chair beside his friend. He hungrily slurped a mouthful from the steaming mug and grimaced, gritting his teeth. *Now, that's what I call coffee.* "The plan's changed," he added after a long pause.

"What's up?"

"I need a favor. A big one."

"Whatever it is, you've got it."

"I need you to groom and stable the horse. I have to leave Montana right away. I mean, like, right now."

"You can't stay here long enough to enjoy a cup of fine Western coffee?"

"One cup? Sure."

"Good."

"I have another request."

"Shoot."

"It's a doozy."

"Fire away."

"I need to borrow your Cessna for a long hop."

"Hmm. You've never soloed."

"You told me that I'm ready for it."

"Well, yeah. That's true." He rubbed his chin, scratching half-grown whiskers.

"I want to fly the Cessna to your hunting camp. I'm gonna take a vacation. I might not be back for years… maybe never. That means your plane will be stranded in the hangar at your camp with nobody to fly it back."

"Which camp?"

"Georgia." In southwest Georgia, on the banks of the Chattahoochee River, Wally owned 160 acres. The site, which included a landing strip, hangar and cabin, lay within a mile of Wally's hunting lease: 4,000 acres of undeveloped Georgia wilderness. In the depths of late winter, when the snow turned Montana into a big-sky facsimile of the North Pole, Wally would sometimes fly south to Georgia to hunt whitetail deer, turkeys, and hogs. Salvatore Benuto had accompanied him more than once.

"Bill Evans has been talkin' about visitin' me," Wally replied, squinting at the jagged horizon. "You don't know Bill. He's a Montana boy and a top-notch pilot. He lives in Atlanta now. He'll fly the plane back, no problem."

"Uh… one more thing, Wally… when I get to Georgia, I'll need to borrow your Jeep. I don't know when I'll be able to return it."

"Go ahead and keep the dad-blamed thing," he offered with a

dismissive wave of his hand. "I was fixin' to get rid of it. It's a wreck."

"Thanks, Wally. You've been real good to me."

"Now, don't start with that kind of talk." He frowned sourly. "I won't hear it."

"No, really. I wanna say it. Hear me out." He took a long sip of hot coffee and leaned back in the chair. The sun had risen in the thin blue sky, illuminating the painfully green, providentially wide valley that sprawled in every direction from the front steps of Wally's house. The morning light led Sal's eye across the valley to the west, over the rolling hills to the jagged, pale purple wall of white-capped mountain peaks. He stroked the cat in his lap, and the big tom began to purr.

"You've been the best friend I could've hoped for, Wally. You gave me a place to stay. When I wanted to work here for free, you went along with it. Each year at Christmas, you gave me a gift of ten thousand dollars, no strings attached. When I asked you not to tell anybody I was here, you went along with that, too. You never asked any questions. You trusted me, and I appreciate it."

"What did you expect? You saved my life twice in 'Nam. I wouldn't be here otherwise."

"A lot of folks would've moved on. They would've found an excuse, no matter how many times I saved their lives. But you're different. You came through in the crunch, and I'll never forget it." Both men grew silent. They finished their coffee as a cool breeze stirred through the open porch.

"Where are you goin', Sal?"

"I can't say. Trust me, you don't want to know."

"All righty, then. There's no point in messin' around." Wally stood and stretched. "The plane's gassed up and ready to go. I was gonna fly to Helena tomorrow, but I can drive. Just remember what I taught you about flyin' and you'll do fine."

"Wally?"

"Yeah?"

"I have to tell you something. After I leave, trouble might be comin' your way." Wally raised his eyebrows and smiled.

"Who'd you tick off this time?"

"You'll find out soon enough. I'll give you a call after I get to Georgia. When I call, please do what I ask, okay?"

"I'll play along… as long as you don't ask me to do somethin' stupid."

"I've already asked you to do somethin' stupid."

"Did I do it?"

"Yep. You let me stay here for all these years. But when I call you from Georgia, I'll be askin' you to do somethin' smart for a change."

"How smart?"

"Smart enough so that maybe you'll look as clean as you really are." Streetcar looked at his friend with a sad, pensive smile. "And considerin' that you're my friend, that'll really take some doin'."

Big Fun in Little Tally

Since early Saturday morning, they had dutifully answered every question posed to them at the Tallahassee Police station. By 10:00 AM, Danny grew hungry. The experience had become unbelievably tedious for a child in a room full of adults. Marcy, Danny, Drew, and Ches sat on one side of the conference table, while Chief MacArthur, Detective Major Jennings, and two grim FDLE agents sat on the other.

To the officers of the law, the presence of Chesterfield Hamilton III – a famous criminal attorney – felt like a splinter that could not be removed. Marcy Johnston had just lost her brother and sister-in-law, and she had asked her attorney friend to stay by her side on this difficult day. Given those facts, who could pluck such a splinter… no matter how great the pain?

After hearing a second recitation of the night's events from Danny and Drew, the officers could only shake their heads. The eyewitness accounts sounded far-fetched, but they agreed with the evidence. The stories rang unbelievably true.

As strange as it seemed, this 13-year-old boy had coolly executed two professional killers before fleeing to Tallahassee. Along the way, he had hitched a ride with a surprisingly resourceful recovering rock-and-roller who had saved their lives when they were attacked on I-75.

Danny Johnston had offered his father's handgun to the FDLE as evidence, and the Highway Patrol had confirmed the presence of a fiery wreck off I-75 beside the exit ramp to Highway 54. So far, the stories had checked out in every detail.

The arsonist who torched Danny's home appeared to be the same man who had chased them on I-75. Lending credence to this theory, a man's fresh footprints had been discovered in the orange grove behind the arson site. The footprints followed the boy's smaller tracks through the sand all the way to the truck stop.

As Chief John McArthur rose to his feet, the other officers followed suit. He smiled sadly, bowing slightly at the waist.

"I appreciate your time," he offered. "That's it for now. We may have a few follow-up questions at a later time." The chief, a robust man of light-brown complexion and above-average height, radiated confidence and decency.

"Thank you, Chief," responded Marcy listlessly. They left the room in single file.

Thank God this is over, Marcy thought as they walked from the station. Awake all night, they had now entered the stultifying, dreamlike realm of utter exhaustion.

Outside of the station, they climbed into Chesterfield's Mercedes and quietly traveled the short distance to Marcy's apartment. They ignored the spectacular weather: the blue and cloudless sky, the pleasant westerly breeze.

As he disembarked from the car at his Aunt Marcy's towering apartment complex, Danny stood still for a moment and listened. *Songbirds.* He marveled that the birds could still sing. Two squirrels chased one another around the trunk of a large live oak, oblivious to the death of his parents.

It seemed to Danny that the jubilant wildlife behaved badly, violating the memory of his parents' lives and somehow trivializing their deaths. *It should be raining,* he considered miserably. *Those birds should shut their stinking yaps.*

In silence, they entered the apartment building and rode the elevator to Marcy's floor. They knew that the police would post a watch on Marcy's building 24 hours a day. Given recent events, this offered cold comfort. *Another killer may be coming in our direction,* Marcy thought glumly as they stepped out of the elevator. *If the FLDE failed, how can the Tallahassee Police protect us?* She would have entered a witness protection program with Danny, but the boy would never cooperate, and she would not try to force him. *Witness protection didn't work.*

"Aunt Marcy?" Danny asked as she unlocked her door.

"Yes?" She paused at the thresh hold.

"Are we going to sleep now?"

"Yes."

"Can we order a pizza later today?" She stared at him, surprised.

"Sure, Danny." She stepped inside, smiling in spite of her grief. *He's still Danny.*

"Can Drew stay with us?"

Marcy looked away from Danny as she walked into her apartment. She knew that the boy's request grew out of emotional trauma. His parents had just been killed, and now Drew, a surrogate, had saved Danny's life. Drew seemed to be decent enough, but the request unsettled Marcy. She scarcely knew the man, and she gathered that his reputation was less than spotless. Marcy stopped behind the kitchen counter, looking from Drew to Ches.

"I'd like it if both of you stayed with us for a few days, if you want to."

"Of course," said Ches hurriedly.

Drew paused uneasily. He had no prior commitments, but he did not feel ready to assume so much responsibility. *It's my 105th day as a sober man, folks. How much stress can I handle?*

"Sure," Drew finally replied with a tight, forced smile. "I'll stay." *One day at a time, God. Please help me make it.*

Drew had made the plunge. He would stand by this nervy kid and his curiously cohesive family.

As for his personal limitations, one thing would prove to be certain. He would soon discover how much stress he could stand. And if things went well – very well – he just might survive the act of discovery.

Old Friends

As Marcy brought out extra sheets for Ches and Drew, the telephone rang. She carefully placed the sheets on the couch and picked up the receiver, pushing a strand of hair out of her eyes.

"Hello?" As she listened, her eyes widened with surprise. She turned to Drew.

"It's for you," she said, handing him the receiver. Drew took it uncertainly. *Who knows I'm here?*

"Hello, Drew? This is Sister Conway."

"Sister Conway? I can't believe it!" *I thought you'd be dead by now.*

"It's me, alright," the elderly woman vouched. "Why can't you believe it?" Sister's voice, as powerful as ever, blasted through the receiver like an air horn in his ear. "I bet you thought I'd be dead by now." As always, Sister's scary insight was exceeded only by her lack of subtlety.

"How are you doing, Sister?" Drew asked delightedly. Miss Anna Mae Conway, a.k.a. 'Sister,' had been his grandmother's best friend. Sister had visited their house almost every day during Drew's youth, watching over him like a craggy old hawk that had adopted a wayward falcon. "Sister Conway!" Drew marveled. "I haven't seen you since I was, what… 14?"

"Yep. One week before your 15th birthday. That was when you told me you was runnin' away. You asked me not to tell your granddaddy."

"You've got a good memory."

"I didn't tell the old man, either. Just like you asked. Do you remember what you said?"

"I sure do." Drew rubbed his eyes and lowered his voice, embarrassed by his past. *She was a good old lady. I could always trust Sister.*

"I told you that I was afraid the old man would kill me. I meant it, too."

"Drew, can you come down to my house in Wakulla County? I've got some stuff to give to you."

"How did you know I was here, Sister?"

"Alton is a sergeant with the Tallahassee Police Department. He told me you were down at the station, and he gave me this number."

"Alton? He used to sell homebrew out of his trunk. I never thought he'd cross over to the legal side." Sister laughed loudly.

"A few years ago, Alton said it was time to play the odds, and he went straight. Surprised me, too."

"Maybe he's straighter than before," Drew observed skeptically. "But that wouldn't take much doin'." Sister laughed heartily.

"You're a mess, Drew. Like your daddy."

"I'll have to take your word on that."

"I hear that you ran into some trouble last night."

"Some."

"I want to see you, Drew. It's important. Can you come down here? I'm still living in the old house on Fox Squirrel Lane." Drew looked at Marcy, busy spreading the sheets on two oversized couches. Ches watched CNN with a blank expression, obviously fighting exhaustion. Danny sat in the corner playing Marcy's Nintendo Game Boy.

"Is tomorrow morning okay? I don't think I'll be up to driving today. I'm really beat."

"Sure."

"I can be there by 11:00 AM."

"Okay," she replied. "Stay safe until then." Her powerful voice trailed off. "I'll pray for you, son."

"I need it, Sister. I'll see you tomorrow." He hung up and rubbed his face. *Man, am I wired.* "I'm goin' to take a walk," he stated to his exhausted companions, who scarcely reacted to his words.

"Sure," Marcy acknowledged with a vague wave of her hand. "Here, take a key. My entry code is 1492. You can sleep on one of the couches." Marcy's bedroom silently beckoned to her weary body, and she had no time for formalities. After sleeping less than 30 minutes within the past 24 hours, she felt ready to collapse.

AS DREW WALKED OUT OF THE APARTMENT BUILDING, he noticed a squad car parked by the curb. Inside the car, a uniformed, middle-aged officer nodded at him and tipped his hat.

"Are you okay?" The officer asked. He had opened his windows to savor the breeze.

"I reckon," replied Drew, slipping easily into the vocal inflections and rhythms of his rural Florida roots. "Is it always this quiet on Saturday?"

"You've been gone too long. This is busy for mid-summer."

"Uh... do I know you?"

"Nah. But I know Sergeant Busby. He told me all about you." The officer smiled knowingly.

"I'm not the guy I used to be," Drew said, misconstruing the officer's comment. "I've been sober for 105 days and counting."

"No kidding? I can beat that. I've been sober for 18 years and counting." The officer leaned back in his seat and smiled.

"You're an alcoholic?" Drew asked, surprised by the comment.

"Some folks would say that. I prefer to think of myself as a former drunk. I've found a better way of living, and I'm not going back."

"No kiddin'?"

"Yep."

"18 years?"

"Yep."

"That's great," Drew said, meaning every word. "I hope I can say that someday."

"Trust me. If I can do it, anybody can."

"Who's your higher power?" Drew blurted, reverting to the language of his recent rehabilitation.

"God," the officer replied with a quizzical look. "Who else?"

"It was stupid question, I guess," Drew answered with a nervous laugh. "It's just that... well, a guy in rehab claimed that Pink Floyd was his higher power." He tried to remember the man's name, but he could only recall his face: sunburned and frozen into a perpetual smirk.

"How'd that work out for him?"

"Not so well. He got stoned and fell off the roof of the cafeteria. They kicked him out of rehab." *Why am I talking to a complete stranger about these things? Especially a cop!* Drew felt betrayed by his own, compulsive affability.

"You'd better get some sleep, buddy," the officer said. "I heard you were up all night. They say you saved a boy's life."

"Yep. I did something right for a change. It felt pretty good."

"I guess it would."

"I'm too excited to sleep. I'm gonna take a walk."

"Go that way," the officer suggested, pointing toward the southwest. "A couple of blocks over you'll find a bunch of white tents in the park. It's a nice, open market with artsy-crafty booths, authors, sculptors, ex-hippies selling hand-blown sun catchers, stuff like that. It's a regular Saturday event called the Downtown Marketplace. There's some great produce and vegetarian food."

"Great. I'll take a look."

"Take it easy, brother."

"I'll try." *Good luck,* he told himself bitterly as he walked away.

After all of his wasted years – and all the wasted nights spent basting his brain with illegal drugs – Drew Marks felt like Bilbo Baggins after too many spins with the magic ring. Unlike the hobbit, however, Drew had no hole to hide in. He felt stretched somehow, as if he had been scraped over a gigantic, burnt-out slab of Melba toast and left to dry until thoroughly baked: a helium-headed, semi-deep-dish, vacuum-packed space cadet with a mind congealing like slow-setting concrete – as dumb as a stick, and twice as thick.

On this particular morning, Drew did not need drugs to feel stoned out of his gourd. He was exhausted to the point of intoxication. He would have pinched himself, but he was afraid that he might wake up.

Take it easy? Yeah, right! In the foreseeable future, Drew could not anticipate when he might be able to take it easy.

In the surreal brightness of a hot summer morning in lovely downtown Tallahassee, he felt as if he had tripped over a mushroom and fallen down a rabbit hole. He seemed stuck in the twilight, lost between last night's carnage and the neat little world in front of him: a beautiful, sunlit Southern city with a façade that hid neither guile nor deceit. This small Southern world, on this quiet summer day, seemed orderly and quaint. His own inner world seemed out of joint, awry in a way that destabilized all he knew.

Drew hated how he felt, but he had to admit one thing. He felt much better than the man who had burned to death beside the exit ramp.

In spite of the heat, he shivered.

Telephonic Persuasion

Salvatore "Streetcar" Benuto arrived in Georgia on Saturday afternoon flush with more than $50,000 in cash. On the outskirts of Atlanta, he hid his pickup truck in a storage room and paid the rental fee for one year in advance. He took the commuter train, arriving in downtown Atlanta just after dark. There, using fake IDs, he bought an anonymous, low-priced Honda sedan at a used car lot in a less-than-stylish neighborhood.

Salvatore had already destroyed the cell phone that Jamie had called. He had to move quickly.

By now, Rich had gone to the federal authorities. They would try to turn up the heat, seeking to intercept his every call.

Using his last cell phone, he had called Wally briefly during the flight south to Georgia. The conversation had been difficult. Wally had not known of his friend's outlaw status, and the revelation had stirred concern.

By this time, Wally had contacted the local sheriff. Soon he would have to deal with the fallout.

Streetcar destroyed his second cell phone in Atlanta and paid cash for two prepaid phone cards before placing a call from a phone booth to a number he had memorized years ago. A recorded message answered the phone.

"The offices of Diversified Industries are closed. Please call back during regular business hours. If you are calling to report a power outage or a similar emergency, please enter 12, followed by the pound sign." Streetcar punched in the numbers and waited.

"Diversified Industries."

"I'm a friend of Ace Feldmann. I'm calling to report a serious breach of security."

"You're a friend of whom?"

"Ace Feldmann. You'd know him as Mr. James Provencenti, the

owner of your company. I need to talk to him right away. It's urgent."

"I'm afraid that's impossible. This is the answering service. Please contact the office during regular business hours."

"I could do that, but I know for a fact that Mr. Provencenti would want you to contact him right now. If you don't, I think you'll lose your job."

"I seriously doubt that, sir."

"I don't doubt it. I know the man! Do you? He'll fry your fritters, son. Go ahead, check it out; call your supervisor if you have to. Just tell him that an old friend called about a vital security matter. Let *him* decide if he wants to call back. He'll know what to do."

"Who are you?"

"Tell him I'm an old friend who used to say 'hi' every morning when he walked to the 21st Street Market to get his coffee and rolling papers. He'll know who I am."

"What's your name?"

"He'll know my name."

"What's your number?" Streetcar glanced up and down the street. A light drizzle had begun to sift from the sky, and the city streets were streaked with flickering rays of ambient light from scattered streetlights. Multicolored waves of light glimmered above the roadway, fluttering gently as cars hissed swiftly past his phone booth.

"Don't you have a display that shows my number?"

"Well... yes."

"For the next 15 minutes, I can be reached at the number on your display. If he doesn't call me by then, I guess I'll have to call back tomorrow – to get you fired." He hung up the pay phone and waited.

When the phone rang, Streetcar picked up on the second ring.

"Ace."

"Streetcar. Why did you call?"

"Is the line safe?"

"Are you kidding?" *We own Tampa, dude.*

"Good."

"Wait a minute." Don Provencenti hit the mute button and put his feet on his coffee table. Taking out a cigar, he groped around his desk for a lighter. He did not feel dread or panic, for he had grown accustomed to life and death situations. To the Don, a call from a 'person of interest' – wanted for questioning in a domestic terrorism case – amounted to no big deal.

The door to the Don's study slammed open, and light streamed in from the hall. Two squealing children chased the light into the room, frantically engaged in an impromptu game of catch and release. The smaller child, running a half step in front of his sister, charged up to his father and vaulted into his lap.

"Daddy, daddy… help!" he cried, pointing toward his little sister. The girl, all of eight years old, smiled at her father, proudly displaying plastic Vampire fangs. "She's a monster!" the boy cried.

"She's just a vampire. Put a stake through her heart."

"Oh, boy!" the little boy cried, wiggling in glee.

"I'm kidding!" The Don laughed, lightly swatting his posterior. "Go on, get out'a here. Daddy's busy." He looked up and saw his wife, Amy, standing in the doorway. The Don pointed toward the telephone, winked and held up one finger. Smiling and rolling her eyes, she hustled the kids out and shut the door.

Don Provencenti leaned forward and released the mute button. He held a lit wooden match to his cigar and drew hard, savoring the rich Cuban smoke.

"Salvatore."

"Ace."

"It's been a long time, my Sicilian friend." Always the ham, Ace rasped the words slowly, like a young Vito Corleone. He spiced his accent with a hint of standard Ybor City drawl for effect.

"You're still a joker."

"Yup."

"I hope it hasn't gone to your head that you're such a big shot."

"I'm still just a regular guy."

"Uh... right." *As in not.*

"So Street', why'd you call?"

"On Friday night, somebody made a big mess in your back yard. Or was it early Saturday morning?"

"I watch the news," he replied disingenuously. "It was Saturday morning, sometime after midnight." Ace had followed the news with intense interest, and had managed to piece together the shards of the story. By now, he knew more about the execution of Dan and Sarah Johnston than all of Florida's law enforcement agencies combined.

"It's bad." Streetcar stated without adornment.

"I know. They say that some crazy redneck drug dealer went after two protected witnesses. He escaped from jail, then he brutally murdered his brother and sister-in-law."

"Do you really think a redneck drug dealer did this?" Streetcar queried. "Could an unconnected thug kill protected witnesses? When the crime involved a cop? I'm not buyin' it."

"CNN's buyin' it."

"They don't know Florida like we know Florida. These were FDLE witnesses. That means that somebody penetrated the FDLE. The person behind these murders was hooked up, big time."

"Ya think?"

"Oh, yeah."

"Maybe you're right. I think it's rotten. But it's over now," Don Provencenti suggested.

"It ain't over, Ace. They didn't get the whole family. One guy got away... a boy, just 13 years old. He smoked the killers like a pro, and he got away clean."

"Who told you that?" The networks had not broadcast the details of the boy's escape.

"I've got connections too, Ace. And I'm tellin' you: whoever did this won't stop until they run the table. They're gonna find that kid, and they're gonna take him out."

"How do you know that?" the Don asked, sitting up.

"Call it an instinct."

"An instinct?"

"Yeah. It's an instinct that's never failed me once since I was a kid in Hell's Kitchen."

"I'm not involved in this. What's it to me?" he asked, testing Streetcar.

"No games, Ace. I knew you back before you was big."

"True."

"I know you didn't do this. You're too smart to make a mess like this in your own back yard."

"I appreciate that vote of confidence," Ace replied dryly.

"My point is, it don't matter if somebody else did it; you'll take the heat. Especially if they get the kid... and they're gonna try, Ace."

The Don glanced out the window, deep in thought. *Those stupid, knuckle-draggin' apes. I agreed to let Brucci get his vengeance for the murder of Billy Bones. Just one redneck drug dealer... not a family of innocent bystanders protected by the FDLE! I'll bet Streetcar's right. They're gonna chase down the kid and finish the job.*

"Okay; so, what if you're right? What can I do about it?"

"I like you, Ace. I'm just layin' out the facts. You're a smart guy. You'll figure it out."

"You're not comin' down here, are you?"

"No way! I promised I'd stay out of Florida. A deal's a deal."

You promised me, all right, Don Provencenti reflected. *I've kept my promise, and you've kept yours.*

"Ace, can you give me a number where I can reach you?"

"Sure. But if you have to call, be very careful. If this heats up, I can't vouch for the privacy of my lines." After he gave Streetcar his number, the Don thoughtfully hung up the phone.

The doorknob turned, and he heard the sound of his wife hushing the children. The Don's face grew grim as he considered his options. *Streetcar's right. Brucci will continue to encroach on our turf. He's put us on the hot seat. He's testing our strength.*

A sickening thought hit him. *Did Don Domella in New York know about Brucci's plan to whack protected witnesses on my turf?*

The idea staggered him. Over the past decades, the Domellas had forged a close alliance with the Bruccis. A Brucci-Domella incursion would offer a direct challenge to Provencenti rule in the Sunshine State.

The Provencenti's empire, built on connections, surgical violence, financial success and fear, could crumble if outside families insulted their honor without retribution. If the killings went no further, they would be blamed on Peter Johnston, an unconnected gunslinger who had fired a lucky shot in the dark. But if Chicago continued to meddle in Florida – especially if they managed to kill the boy – the involvement of organized crime would become obvious to the public at large, threatening Provencenti dominion.

In Florida, with the exception of the independent southeastern coast, the Provencenti family had ruled supreme since the days of Prohibition. If the Bruccis killed again without his permission, Don Provencenti would be forced to punish Chicago publicly, risking open war. To do otherwise would display dangerous weakness. *I don't have the power to take on Chicago... not unless Atlanta or New York stand with me. New Orleans might weigh in on our side, but Memphis will stay out of it. Who knows about Kansas City and Little Rock?*

He drew deeply on his cigar, staring blankly at a bookshelf. *What if Domella is behind this mess? If that's true, I'll have to give him a way out. I can't fight New York openly. I'll have to checkmate him in private, without fanfare. If he loses respect, he'll go to war... I'd have to fight the five families. Nobody would help me with that.*

To avoid these troubles, the solution appeared obvious. His family would have to protect the boy, Danny Johnston.

Against the Provencentis, a perfect storm of bad publicity had begun to gather strength. Newspaper hounds, unleashed by their editors, had begun to bay up the family tree: writing inky, somber stories of the Provencenti's storied past.

Local reporters had already implied that his family could have perpetrated the recent Independence Day Massacre of Dan and Sarah Johnston. They had begun to question how an unconnected hick like Pete Johnston could have penetrated a sealed gauntlet of witness protection

Don Provencenti's reputation could absorb a few hits. Tampa loved him. They had publicized his philanthropies for years. Regardless of public support, however, his reputation with other crime families remained vitally important. Any hint, any shadow of weakness could endanger his domain… not to mention his life.

If the Bruccis killed the child in open defiance of his authority, the word would get out. Trouble would enter his well-fed fiefdom. Those in the know – like the FBI – would suppose that the Provencentis had backed the bloody murders. Pinned beneath their spyglass, he would have to choose between capitulation to Brucci or outright war. He could not abide such a risk.

His enemies had placed his wife and children at risk. He did not deceive himself. His crime family held power due to alliances of convenience. Mafia life, based upon time-tested protocols, endured as a cold-eyed business that mimicked a family in name only. If he died or went to prison, he could not rely on his soldiers to protect his wife and children. They might become easy prey in a merciless world.

Whether Brucci planned to defy him or not, the solution appeared obvious. He had to minimize further damage.

He had to protect the boy.

Grinderswitch

"Minnie Pearle was a genius," Jimmy stated dismissively. "You can say whatever you want. Facts are facts."

"She was as dumb as a fence post."

"Dumb like a fox."

"You're serious, aren't you, Biggs?"

"Sure. I'm tellin' you the truth. They should take Minnie Pearl's home town of Grinderswitch, Tennessee, and make it a national monument."

"Grinderswitch? It don't even exist, Biggy. She invented the place."

"So what?"

"It can't be a national monument if it don't exist!"

"Says who?"

"Says me, that's who."

"Nuts," Jimmy Biggs responded emphatically, gritting his teeth as he adjusted his shades. "Nuts to you, bird-brain."

"Grinderswitch was a figment of Minnie Pearl's imagination."

"Did you ever consider that maybe the guys in Grinderswitch are sayin' the same thing? Maybe they think *you're* the figment."

"Oh yeah, that really makes sense."

"Why not?"

"You're unbelievable!"

"Unbelievably on target, my little friend. I'm givin' you the straight dope. Minnie Pearle was a national treasure. Her story was buried in the back pages during her lifetime, but she deserved to be splattered across the headlines."

"Splattered? I'll grant you that."

"Nuts."

"She was lucky to make the back pages. She deserved to be wrapped in a newspaper and buried in somebody's back yard. That'd be a headline worth reading."

"Hey! Watch it!"

"What's to watch?"

"Minnie Pearl was a star for the ages. Her face belongs on Mount Rushmore beside Cole Porter and Bill Gates. She was a wonder to behold."

"I'm wonderin' about your sanity."

"Nuts. She was the greatest... greater even than Grandpa Jones."

"That's nothin'. Bozo the Clown was greater than Grandpa Jones." At this they paused, resting before another round.

"Ha!"

"Now *that* would be a face-off," Dom the Pill added enthusiastically. "Minnie Pearle versus Grandpa Jones. The Japanese could make a monster movie. Minnie and Grandpa could trash the skyscrapers and wrestle in the bay while fighter planes buzz around their heads like mosquitoes."

"Minnie Pearle was a genius." Jimmy Biggs stated stoutly. He would not yield a single, silly millimeter.

"A genius?" The smaller man moaned. "Who could say such things?"

"I can." Perceiving the extreme certainty of his cohort, Dom the Pill decided to try mockery.

"Oh, Mr. Biggs, you're so impressive," Dom spouted, imitating a star-smitten gangster groupie. "You know everything."

"I guess I know a little bit about entertainment. I can tell the good stuff from the stinky stuff."

"Bet you can't!"

"Try me."

"What about the Beatles?"

"Good stuff."

"That was too easy."

"You asked the question, bird-brain!"

"What about Eminem?"

"He's stinky," guffawed Jimmy.

"Why?"

"Too much nasal. He should quit singin' and work with his hands."

"Like us?"

"Yeah, like us." They both laughed.

"How about Jay-Z?"

"He stinks because he's so brilliant. What a waste! He could'a been a contender, but instead he trots out that same old fakazoid gangster act."

"Pavarotti?"

"Good stuff. You know he's my favorite."

"The Stones?"

"Stinky stuff. Ruby Tuesday was their last decent song."

"How about Usher?"

"Good stuff. Needs a tailor."

"Elvis Costello?"

"Good and stinky, like a fine French cheese. Just like you."

"You're quite the critic."

"I suppose."

"So what are you: gangster or critic?"

"Both," Jimmy asserted glibly.

"How so?"

"Gangsters and critics share the same profession. Whether it's character assassination or the assassination of characters, it's pretty much the same thing."

"I'll buy that. What's the difference between 'em?"

"Gangsters kill to eat. Critics kill for fun."

"Ha!"

"I thought up that one myself," Biggs added proudly.

"But Biggsy, you kill for both reasons."

"That's why I *am* both, you nitwit!"

They laughed uproariously.

To all appearances, life had dealt them a royal flush. For the two killers, these were the best of times. For their victims, these were the worst of times.

Since their teenage years, Jimmy Biggliatello and Domingo

Pillicilatta had served time as an unmatched pair of old-school gangsters who knew how to have a good time. They had spent the past decades together, shamelessly slumming through the seamier side of life as they destroyed lives for the love of money. In almost any environment, they managed to fit in swimmingly. The world was their oyster, and if it smelled a little gamy, that was okay with them. They enjoyed recycling the world's moving parts, contributing to the overarching reek of high society. They loved their lives, and delighted in their self-chosen role as rotten apples in the cosmic barrel.

Life, in their eyes, seemed like a sleazy, comic strip club: a cash-green globe packed with winners and losers, ruled by sharks and crooked bouncers. They saw themselves as canny predators taking a walk on the wise side. Like Great Whites, they slowly cruised through that swinging club, Chez Earth, sniffing for blood and savaging the booty with carnivorous abandon.

At this particular moment, the two gangsters were cruising down the interstate at a high rate of speed in Jimmy's mechanically enhanced 2006 Toyota Avalon convertible, a family car designed to blend in with the traffic. Hurtling down I-95 with the top down, just after sunrise on a fair Sunday morning, the two men looked relaxed and happy as they sped south on a mission of mercilessness. They had dressed to kill: dark slacks, pastel knit shirts, and dark, stylish shades. Their well-tanned skin glistened in the early morning sunlight, and their short, jet-black hair whipped wildly in the wind.

"I hate convertibles," Dom whined. "All of this sunshine and fresh air is makin' me sick. Can we put up the top, Biggy? Should I push the button right now?" He asked his questions with a sly grin, living up to his nickname, Dom the Pill. Always annoying, Dom worked as a powerful stimulant on listeners who had a low tolerance for pain.

"Dom, I swear, if you don't stop whining, you'll spend the rest of the trip in the trunk."

"No, please! Anything but the trunk!" Dom laughed. "It still smells like that little greaser who skimmed the books on Hank!"

"You are one sick poppy. Not a bagel poppy, either. You're the kind of sick poppy that puts people to sleep forever."

"Same to ya, Biggs." They smiled at one another, savoring the moment. As friends who had grown up on the same city block, Jimmy Biggs and Dom the Pill had stuck together since childhood, when as unruly toddlers they had terrorized daycare workers at the Mother of Mercy Nursery School.

"Hey, Jimmy, check this out. Do you remember this?" Dom changed his voice to a raspy, low pitch, imitating a character from their past. "Come on, fellas, gimme a break. I knew you boys back when you was pinchin' pennies from old lady Stasko." He sounded exactly like Carmine Lepps, a small-time hood they had killed several years before.

"Don't do that!" Jimmy said abruptly. "It gives me the willies when you imitate Carmine. I really liked that old guy."

"Sure, Jimmy. I liked him, too."

"That's the only job we ever did that I hated. I really hated it."

"Carmine was one cool gangster. Old school."

"Tell me about it. He helped me get my first break. Instead of saying thanks, I whacked him in the alley behind Hannigan's."

"It wasn't your finest hour."

"No kiddin'?"

"Yeah. And we whacked him for something he didn't even do."

Biggs remembered it well… too well. Somebody had killed a small-time grifter named Max Diamond without Don Domella's permission. At the time, a local punk claimed that he saw Carmine Lepps doing the job on Max Diamond. The unauthorized murder in Domella territory – a death penalty offense in the Mob – sealed Carmine's fate. To uphold family values, Carmine Lepps had to die.

Two days after Carmine's execution, they had learned that Louie Stracco, a made man in the Fallachi Family, had whacked Max Diamond. The famously absent-minded Don Fallachi, the Domella's closest ally, had forgotten to mention it to Don Domella. This meant that Carmine Lepps had died an innocent crook.

The news had shocked Jimmy Biggs, and the murder of Carmine

still troubled him. Dom knew this, but he could not understand why. Lacking anything resembling a conscience, Dom felt completely indifferent toward murder and mayhem. He slept like a log at night. Biggs was subject to occasional – if rare – twinges of conscience. Dom's atrophied conscience, dry and shriveled from a lifetime of disuse, never even twitched.

"Enough about Carmine!" Biggs shouted at his partner, angry and dismayed. He turned on the radio and cranked up the volume. To his surprise, 'Whip It' by the band Devo blasted from his speakers. In spite of his funk, he could not resist the song's cheerful allure.

Biggs began to sing, murdering the song, free of charge. With his booming, off-key voice, he did not actually sing. He brayed tunelessly, like a donkey stuck in a peat bog.

> When a good time turns around,
> You must whip it!
> You will never live it down,
> Unless you whip it!
> No one gets their way
> Until they whip it!
> I say, whip it!
> Whip it good!

"That's so stinky, it's good," shouted Dom above the tone-deaf racket. "Like the movie, *Raising Helen*. Whip it, Biggs!"

As the car rocketed down the road, the two gangsters happily anticipated what lay ahead: the sweet scent of blood, the acrid taste of burnt gunpowder, and the rank stench of fear. *It doesn't get any better than this,* Jimmy reflected.

They had entered unfriendly territory, but they would not be deterred. The Domellas had a man on the inside of the FDLE, and Jimmy and Dom felt confidant that they would succeed, with or without his help. They always performed under pressure. They could become deadly creative in a pinch.

The two killers dreamed that somewhere, beyond the horizon, a young boy cowered in fear. Their entry into his pathetic world would be like the rising of an evil, atomic sun... like the ascension of a fire-breathing Hiroshima express that would blast the trembling teenaged bunny into oblivion. Surely, he would shake before their god-like radiance, quaking to behold the mighty power of death that they held in their bloody hands. Surely, he would beg wretchedly for his miserable, worthless teenaged life.

This was bad... way bad... bad beyond measure, a fact that they savored like a fine wine. They loved to kill, for hate or money.

Who could call them to account? Who could dare to try? Who could condemn them as they killed at will, living as they wished on the globe they owned: lock, stock, and smoking barrel? Who could match their power as they tore a fresh path through the spinning, earthy sphere of cosmic coincidence? In their barren inner world – a blasted landscape lacking truth or beauty – the strong prevailed, and nothing else mattered. They slaughtered the weak like sheep, fodder to feed their greedy feasts.

They planned to continue as the slaughterers and not the slaughtered. They had it all figured out.

Sure, they were killers. Sure, they were merciless.

Who cared?

Posing the Question

At 7:00 the next morning, Marcy awoke to a throbbing blast of brutally loud, window-rattling hard rock music. Temporarily disoriented, she thought for a moment that an earthquake had struck. As she came to herself, she realized that the sound came from Danny's room. She stumbled out of bed, threw on a robe, and walked to his door.

"Danny!" she called loudly, banging on the door. "What are you doing?"

The door burst open and Danny confronted her, grinning at her early morning disarray. *You look terrible,* he thought, but knowing his aunt, he did not dare to say the words aloud. Marcy's hair pointed in several directions, like bundles of standing wheat beaten down by the hail. One shoulder of her robe rode higher than the other, and the fabric bunched beneath the robe's belt, loops askew.

"Good morning, Aunt Marcy," Danny cried happily. "This is your 7:00 AM wake up call." She strode inside the room and snatched an electric plug from the wall, unceremoniously silencing the tsunami of sound.

"You keep that up and I'll send you to a military school," she grunted half-heartedly. As her nephew smirked and glanced over her shoulder, his eyes widened.

"Aunt Marcy! Get your camera! It's a famous rock star." He pointed to Drew Marks, who stood in the open doorway. Drew had dressed to the nines in black jeans, a velvet coat, and a white silk shirt. On his stylishly-coiffed head, not a hair looked out of place.

"Are y'all ready for breakfast?" he asked hopefully.

"Aagh!" Marcy screamed, slamming the door in his face.

"Ha, ha, ha!" crowed Danny happily. "Marcy likes Drew! Marcy likes Drew!" In response to his taunts, Aunt Marcy squared off and stared her nephew down, gritting her teeth.

"Listen, Junior," she said evenly. "This is my apartment, and while you're staying here, you play by my rules."

"Sure, Aunt Marcy. What are they?"

"Number one: no loud music. Number two: do what I say. Number three: obey rules one and two."

"What about number four?"

"I'm reserving jurisdiction on that one," she said with a tight smile.

"Okay."

"Good. Now, let's work on the second rule," she stated emphatically. "We're both going to get dressed and go to church. After that, we're packing for the trip."

"Trip?"

"We're driving south tomorrow to attend the funeral."

Danny looked into her eyes, stunned by the word, 'funeral.' All morning, until this very moment, he had managed to repress the memory of his parent's horrific murder. Taken by surprise, his defenses suddenly failed.

In an agonizing instant, he recalled a brutal image indelibly burned into his brain: two lifeless bodies on blood-soaked sheets in a wretched, moonlit bedroom… two cooling corpses that no longer held the sacred souls of his murdered parents. He would never see them again, for the remainder of his days on earth.

The pain hit like a thunderbolt, taking his breath away. Marcy saw it in his eyes, felt it pierce like a lance through her soul. *How could I be so cold? I lost my brother, but he lost his entire world.*

"Oh, Danny, I'm so sorry," she breathed, reaching out and pulling him close. That was the final straw. The boy began to sob freely, collapsing in her arms. His knees gave way, and he lost control of his emotions.

Drew and Ches stood in the hall outside the closed door, exchanging glances of awkward dismay. The sound of sobbing intensified inside the room as both nephew and aunt wept in utter abandon, consoling one another as only family members can.

Danny and Marcy clung together as they wept, propping one

another up. Their grief seemed to intensify by the second.

"God help us," Marcy cried with soul-wrenching sincerity. "Lord Jesus, help us." For a moment she felt Danny's muscles stiffen as he resisted her prayer; but then he relaxed, yielding to her plea.

At the sound of Aunt Marcy's prayers, Danny remembered his mother. Each morning, before dawn, she had shut herself in the spare bedroom next to his and prayed fervently for her family. Sometimes he had awakened and listened to her muffled pleas and hymns of thanksgiving. He would wonder about her faith, but the sound had comforted him with the knowledge that she was close enough to touch... if he could only reach through the wall. *Is that what heaven is like? Like she's right here, praying for me, but I can't reach through the wall?* The thought surprised and intrigued him.

Fascinated by the idea of his mother alive and well in another dimension, Danny decided to pray. *God, if you're real, please let me know. And if Jesus really is your Son, please show me that too. Mama would want me to know it.* To his surprise, a wave of peace washed over him. He knew that his prayer would be answered.

In the hall, Drew and Ches lingered, filled with dismay. They wanted to help, but had no idea how.

"What they've endured is unspeakable," Ches whispered. "I can't imagine."

"Horrible," Drew agreed.

Looking at Ches, Drew noticed that the attorney – like himself – had dressed impeccably in spite of the early hour. *Why is he dressed like that at 7:00 AM on Sunday morning? Is he trying to impress Marcy?* For some reason, the thought troubled him.

The astute counselor, a canny student of human nature, immediately discerned the meaning behind the younger man's dismayed expression. *He's finally noticed me. Until now, Marcy had distracted him completely.* Ches sighed from the bottom of his heart, watching with morose fascination as his plans for the future melted before his eyes like late-morning frost.

"Drew?" he asked impulsively.

"Yeah?"

"Are you a Christian?" The question shocked Drew. He paused before answering.

"I'm not sure. I've been thinking about that lately. In the 12-step plan you're supposed to ask your higher power for help, so I asked God to help me stay sober. And while I was at it, I asked Him to help me – to show me what to do with my life, and to show me who He is. I grew up in the Church, but I rejected it as a teenager."

"Has He showed you who He is yet?"

"I don't know. I guess you could say I'm a work in progress."

"That's an honest answer. Refreshingly well thought-out. So many people don't even think about these things, or go straight to hostility. Or worse, they're unpleasant fanatics."

"Why do you ask?"

"Because Marcy's a Christian. She's real. Not a phony. She won't marry a nonbeliever. She puts her faith first, and that's that."

"Interesting," Drew replied politely. *What does that have to do with me.* "Are you a Christian?"

"Yes. I wasn't one when I first met Marcy two years ago. But knowing her has changed me." His face grew pale, and he looked older than his years. "She's the real deal."

"I see," Drew answered. *But why should I care?*

"You love her, don't you?" Chesterfield asked quietly.

"What?" Drew was shocked by the question.

"You love her, don't you?" Ches repeated, resigned to his fate. The question reflected the characteristic insight and bluntness that had long been his trademark.

"I just met her," Drew bluffed uncertainly.

Ignoring the disclaimer, Ches grasped the younger man's shoulder and stared into his eyes. After a moment, he released his grasp and shook his head knowingly. Drew Marks had gone down for the count, but he remained blissfully unaware of the fact.

Chesterfield Hamilton sighed and walked toward the kitchen, beckoning for Drew to follow. A man of vision, he could see the writing on the wall. This young man had already supplanted him. Marcy would remain to Ches as she had always been: an alluring vision of feminine grace, forever beyond his reach.

"Do you want coffee?" Chesterfield asked politely. Now that his hopes had hopelessly collapsed, he mellowed by the second. "It's fresh. I made it when you were primping in front of the living room mirror." He poured two cups, smiling crookedly in spite of himself. *I like this guy. I wish I hated him, but I don't.*

"Thanks," Drew replied, smoothing back his hair. Nonplussed, he tried to remain calm. *How can I be in love with a woman I just met? That's crazy. I mean, she looks great, but so what?*

"What do you think about love?" Ches asked.

"I'm not a believer."

"Love transcends belief."

"How so?"

"Love predated belief and will endure after belief has passed away. Its depths exceed our comprehension."

"Why don't you write this stuff down? Call it Romance for Dummies."

"Maybe I will."

"I'm not totally ignorant on the topic. Some people consider me an expert."

"Really?"

"Love is an excuse for people who can't deal with reality. It's a marketing tool run amok."

"Sometimes you have to experience something before you believe it exists," Ches continued, undeterred by his companion's skepticism. "Love is like that."

"So, you admit you can't prove it exists?"

"I know it exists. I don't have to prove it."

"Then define it. What is love?"

"It's a mystery… like a riddle."

"A riddle?"

"It can be found and lost, given or taken. It can be acknowledged, defied, ignored… but it can't be dummied up. If you fake it, you can't fool yourself. When it's real, you can't deny it. Kings give their kingdoms for it. Only fools ignore it."

"Juries must eat that stuff up."

"You're in love with Marcy." Ches added. "Why not admit it?" To Drew, the sad smugness of Chesterfield Hamilton had become insufferable.

"With all due respect, you're crazy, counselor. Shouldn't I get to know the person first?" *Take that, sad sack!*

"It takes decades to really know someone," Ches suggested, subdued and lachrymose. "Without love, knowledge lacks value. Curiosity evaporates, and it leads to boredom."

"Bah!" Drew spluttered skeptically, annoyed at the prospect of being out-argued on the nature of love – a subject that he considered his own, to deny at will. "This is weird."

"Undoubtedly."

"Aren't you supposed to be Marcy's boyfriend?"

"I was, almost. Until last night," Ches replied wistfully.

"I mean," Drew sputtered, "give me a break, okay?" He tried to reject Chesterfield's logic out of hand, but the harder he evaded it, the more believable it seemed.

How could I love a woman I just met? Quite understandably, he did not wish to know the answer.

ON THE SAME SUNDAY MORNING, in an emergency veterinary clinic in south Atlanta, Salvatore Benuto stood beside the examination table and fidgeted nervously. The veterinarian, a petite young woman with dark brown hair, finished her examination and then gazed up at him myopically through thick, black-framed glasses.

"Just how old is this cat?" she asked. As she spoke, she self-consciously adjusted the collar of her officious, long white coat. In her second week on the job, she still felt unsure and somewhat nervous. The presence of the tall, lean stranger, so roughhewn and lacking in the finer social graces, somehow unsettled her.

"I don't know. He was a feral cat when I first met him a few years ago."

"Well, I can tell you that he is quite old," she replied, all business. "I would guess that he's at least 14 years old, maybe older."

"That's pretty old for a cat, eh?"

"Yes. This cat has lived a long life, and I'm afraid he won't live much longer." As soon as she said the words, she regretted them. *Stupid, stupid, stupid! Where's your bedside manner?*

Streetcar's mouth fell open, and he paused without breathing as the blood drained from his face. Haggard and haunted, he looked as if he had just been told about the death of his only child.

"But," he suggested, hesitating. "He'll be okay, right?" She looked at him, filled with pity and unanticipated insight into the heart of this craggy stranger. *He loves this cat.* If she could have, at that moment, she would have emptied her bank account to restore the health of the raggedy, tufted old Maine Coon. She reached out and placed her hand on his.

"Mr. Freeman, I hate to tell you this, but I'm afraid that your cat is too old to live much longer. His health appears to be faltering. He can't hold down his food. He could leave us any day."

"But," he whispered. "He'll be okay?"

"There's an outside chance. He might rally. He could come back from this and live for years. But I think it's unlikely."

"What should we do?"

"The shot will ease his discomfort," she said brusquely, donning the armor of professional concern. "I'm prescribing pain medication. We can try the latest treatments. They're expensive."

"Not a problem. I can pay in advance."

"For now, he needs to be medicated four times a day." She knew that it was hopeless to suggest euthanasia. She scribbled on a pad. "They'll give you this prescription at the front desk."

"He's my best friend," Streetcar murmured. He stopped and cleared his throat, wiping his eyes. Gently picking up the frail, aging cat, he cradled him in his arms. For a moment he held him close, then he turned to the young veterinarian.

"Thanks, doc."

"You're welcome, Mr. Freeman."

Will-Kill-Ya County

When Drew saw the bumper sticker, he had to laugh. The mud-encrusted sticker on the faded blue pickup truck declared in vivid black and yellow, 'Welcome to Will-Kill-Ya County.' *I guess we know his position on gun control.*

He turned off of Wakulla Springs Highway and began the long drive down the deserted country road leading to Sister's place. The trees had grown larger, but the scenery otherwise remained unchanged. Savoring the natural beauty of his long-lost home turf, he rolled down his windows and slowed the car's speed to a crawl.

He passed three small, well-kept wooden houses on the right side of the road one-half mile before Sister's house. As he watched, a black Lincoln Town Car disgorged its lively contents into the yard of the largest house: a mixed-age group of children returning from church. The glee of the joyous family brightened the peaceful Sunday morning with a pleasing confusion of shouts and shoves, colorful clothes and shiny black shoes. Stepping out of the driver-side door, a short, elderly, dark-skinned woman in a purple dress and resplendently red-feathered hat stepped toward the street. She shaded her eyes and stared at Drew, frowning skeptically as she waved warily with an elegant white-gloved hand. In response, Drew waved and smiled. With his car almost past her house, she abruptly smiled in recognition.

"Well, I'll be," she whispered softly. She turned back toward the car.

"Elder Cromartie," she said sternly to an elegant, elderly gentleman still sitting in the front seat.

"Yes, Mother Cromartie?"

"You'll never guess who just drove by."

"Then you'd better tell me." The elder had been daydreaming, reflecting upon today's sermon.

"Little Drew Marks. He's a grown man now. I almost didn't recognize him."

"Glory to God!" said the elder. "Wouldn't you know? I dreamed about that boy last night." Elder Cromartie opened the door and pushed himself to his feet, retrieving two aluminum walking sticks from inside the car.

"What kind of dream?" she asked warily. "You didn't tell me."

"I didn't remember it until now, Mother."

"I guess he's come to visit Sister Conway."

"It's about time."

"Mmm hmm," Mother Cromartie agreed, shaking her head disapprovingly. "I know that's right."

SISTER CONWAY WAS SWEEPING THE DUST out of her house through her open front door when the PT Cruiser pulled up in her yard. She put one hand over her eyes and squinted, casually nudging a curious chicken out of the way.

"Get, you little hussy," she murmured at the small red hen. Bantam roosters and hens filled her yard, busily searching for insects. The chickens roosted in her trees at night, protected from itinerate bobcats by her geriatric blue-tick, Bull.

Hearing the car's arrival, the big hound limped out from under the steps and began to bay at the top of his lungs. An eager redbone puppy popped out behind him, attempting to emulate his grizzled hero. The puppy bayed frantically with its shrill puppy voice, extending his skinny, trembling neck as he trumpeted a warning with all of his heart, as if his very life depended on it.

"Drew!" the old woman shouted. "Come on down, boy!" She boomed the words with authority and not a little humor.

Drew climbed out of his car and eyed Bull cautiously, offering a hand. The big dog smelled him delicately, sensing familiarity with the tall stranger who had just invaded his space.

A jolt of recognition hit the big dog like a bolt of lightning from the depths of his clouded memory. His ears perked up, and his mouth popped open. With a loud whine of painfully exquisite canine joy, Bull jumped on Drew, battering him with his paws and almost knocking him to the ground.

"Sit, Bull. Sit!" Sister cried in dismay, hobbling down the rickety front steps.

"It's okay, Sister. He remembers me... I can't believe it!" Drew knelt beside Bull in the clay. "Hello, buddy. I love you too." The dappled blue-and-white dog shivered in delight, eagerly licking his face.

"Well, I'll be," Sister mused. "He *does* remember you, Drew. It's been almost 15 years."

"He's still my buddy." Drew gave the barrel-chested hound a bear hug. The redbone puppy leaped up, desperate for any crumb of affection that he might vacuum up with his damp, snuffling nose... or slobber upon with his floppy red mouth.

Drew rubbed the puppy's head, squeezed his ears, and stood, signaling palms out for them to calm down. Both dogs regained control of their glee and sat expectantly at his feet. Bull stared in his face, panting with his mouth open wide. The puppy copied his mentor, lost in the throes of love.

Drew sighed and looked around. The place looked just as he remembered.

Weathered pecan trees towered overhead, as tall and lovely as ever. Unseasonably cool morning sunlight slashed through the high branches of the trees in the grove surrounding Sister's house, splashing the grass with pools of bright green light. The scattered trees seemed to rejoice, basking in the breeze and the sunlight: alive and hale as they flexed arboreal muscles in the clear morning air. Swimming amid the currents of air, against the backdrop of the deep blue sky, the riotous mix of luminous, pale-green pecan leaves waved in unsullied clarity from the highest branches. Each stem, each twig, each fiery green leaf seemed vividly alive.

Sister's front door faced east. Behind her house, in the western distance beyond the farthest pasture, loomed the ominous border of the Big Nasty Swamp. The morning sunlight brilliantly lit the edge of the swamp, illuminating a glorious tangle of fallen logs and ancient bald cypress: the disorganized, ambient greenery of the snake-filled sump in all of its steaming glory.

High above the Big Nasty, drafting in a breath of heat, a bald eagle circled watchfully. Drew heard its cry as Sister hustled up and clamped him with a hug that took his breath away.

"Whoa," he sputtered. "You're strong!"

"I'm 91 years young and still fit as a fiddle. I have to be, living next to the Big Nasty." She shoved him to arm's length and studied him closely. "You don't look half bad for a city boy." Sister stated as if she sized up beef on the hoof. "Skinny, but solid."

"Thanks for the compliment, Sister."

She waved her hand dismissively. "Let's go inside. The coffee's fresh, even if I'm not." She took his hand in hers and squeezed tightly. "I missed church for you this morning."

"I'm worth it," he responded with a grin. At this, she pulled up short and stared into his eyes.

"Are you jokin' about church? I'll hide you with my razor strap, boy." To Drew's dismay, she did not smile.

Sister Conway had been bowed but not broken by age. Her skin had grown tight and dry, like old leather that cried out for saddle soap. Seeing the fire in her eyes, he did not doubt the seriousness of her threat.

"I'm kidding, Sister," he added quickly. "You don't have to whip me."

"Good." They walked into the kitchen and sat at a worn oak table. In spite of his age, Drew felt like a small child who had narrowly escaped an ominous punishment. Sister Conway had never touched him with her legendary razor strap, but its symbolic presence had lost none of its power.

He had to admit the unflattering truth.

After all of these years, Sister Conway still scared him silly.

Torque Wrench

"I like the way you talk," Drew claimed happily, rasping the words with a strong southern accent. Relaxed and rested, he found himself enjoying his time with Sister as if the intervening years had been stripped away.

"I like the way you talk," Sister Conway drawled, slapping him on the shoulder so hard he almost coughed a mouthful of biscuit across the kitchen. They had been laughing for more than an hour, catching up on one another's lives. "When you talk like that, you sound like that crazy guy in the movie, Sling Blade. I have the DVD."

"No kiddin'?"

"No kiddin'. That was Billy Bob Thornton's best work. His character in that movie reminds me of Timmy Ray Milton."

"Timmy Ray Milton?"

"You remember Timmy Ray?" She pushed back a strand of hair, waiting for Drew's reply.

"How could I forget. He courted you after Grover died."

"That's him."

"I called him Torque Wrench. I like the comparison, Sister. Torque Wrench, father of Sling Blade."

"You tormented that old man," she replied with a disapproving frown.

"He deserved it for trying to date my granny's best friend!"

"I can't believe I almost married that old man. He acted like he loved me to death."

"It was an act, all right."

"Maybe."

"I was afraid that he'd work me to death," Drew added. Timmy Ray Milton had run his grandfather's garage like Ahab stomping across the poop: the most hard-edged, monomaniacal master mechanic imaginable. As an apprentice in the shop, Drew had chafed beneath his jurisdiction, dreading the inevitable harpoon. "I can still hear him saying, 'The next time, you'd better hand me the right tool, or I'll brain ya'!'" Hearing Drew's dead-on imitation, Sister Conway had to laugh.

"I reckon you're right. He was a hard man. Every time I get sentimental about Timmy, I watch that Sling Blade movie. It helps me remember why I moved on."

Drew looked at Sister with admiration. In his youth, she had loomed large, almost six feet tall and as wide-shouldered as a professional wrestler. Now, she looked bowed beneath the weight of her age as if permanently ducking to dodge a low doorjamb. Her skin, the hue of well-tanned calfskin, bore white splotches like leather upholstery that had been randomly splashed with bleach. A prominent nose and two elephantine ears dominated her facial landscape: monolithic slabs, remarkable for their size and more venerable than Stonehenge. A faint mustache lingered like a late-morning dew on her upper lip. As he stared, two long, grey hairs waved at him whimsically from a large mole on her chin.

"Was Timmy Ray as bad as the character in Sling Blade?" Drew asked.

"Timmy Ray weren't as *good* as that feller." She laughed loudly, running her right hand through her hair. "Well, that's enough fun for now. I reckon I'd better give you your stuff."

"Stuff? What stuff?" She stood up and stretched her legs painfully, bending over with her hands upon her thighs. Slowly standing upright, she shuffled into a darkened, windowless bedroom and turned on a light. Drew followed her into the room.

Stacked on a clean piece of canvas in the middle of an iron bed were several worn cardboard boxes, covered with dust. As if reading his mind, she offered a disclaimer.

"I fetched 'em out of the shed this morning. They're from your granddaddy. He asked me to give 'em to you if you ever showed up." Drew gulped loudly, embarrassed.

"I should have come home to visit," he began to apologize.

"Shoot, boy, I don't blame you. I saw what happened back then. I loved your granddaddy like a brother. He was my best friend's husband, after all. But somethin' happened to him after Edna died. He turned as mean as a snake." Her words affected Drew deeply. She could see it on his face.

"The old man came to his senses about five years after you left. He knew he'd done you wrong." She cleared her throat. "He died sudden. He didn't get feeble first. One day, he was strong and full of vinegar; the next day, he just up and died."

"I should have visited," he protested again, but she waved him off.

"Maybe, but don't beat yourself up. This needs to be said." She rubbed her hands together nervously, as if she felt cold. "For years, he blamed you for Edna's death, the old fool... as if your shenanigans gave her cancer." She sighed deeply, staring blankly at the floor as she recalled a distant, evil memory. "He was cruel to you, boy." She raised her head and looked him in the eye. "I should have called the state. I should have reported that old fool. I'm the one who should be sorry."

"I... I've moved on, Sister. It wasn't your fault. You were good to me."

"Thanks. You're right. It's over." She sighed and looked at the boxes on the bed.

"Take your time. I'll be knittin' in the living room. Call me if you need anything." She turned to leave and paused, looking down at the ground. Drew could see that her lip trembled. *Don't go soft on me now, Sister.*

Sister turned back and threw her arms around him, hugging him tightly. Then she turned and shuffled from the room.

As the door clicked shut, Drew stared hopelessly at the dusty stack of boxes on top of the bed. Broken and disheveled, they sagged dishearteningly on the box springs under the bright overhead light. *Where should I start?*

"Thanks, old man," he said through gritted teeth. "Why'd you give me all this stuff?" Tears tried to form in his eyes, but he battled to suppress them. Emotional repression had led to some of his best work as a songwriter, and he would not change his ways because of one sentimental encounter with a kindly old lady from his past.

Pulling a box off of the stack, he opened it. Inside, he saw a jumble of long-forgotten mementos: report cards from Spring Creek Elementary, baseball cards, class pictures, cub scout badges.

In another box, he saw a manila envelope perched atop a stack of documents. Inside the envelope, he found a document related to his grandfather's hunting tract: 100 acres of old-growth hardwood forest on Cedar Creek, a spring-fed coastal tributary that wound through a fertile estuary before emptying into the Gulf of Mexico. His grandfather had signed the deed with a shaky signature, properly notarized and witnessed. The deed gave the tract to Drew.

He frowned as he read the hand-written note. 'Hi, Drew. I gived Sister enough money to pay the tax on the huntin land. Its yers if you want it. Best times of my life was spent there. You fished real good.' Drew blinked, thinking about long-lost weekends spent hunting and fishing at Cedar Creek. His grandmother had loved the place. He shut the box abruptly.

Drew pulled another box off the tallest stack and looked inside. His mouth fell open, and he exhaled slowly in the dusty silence.

Inside the box, poised as if ready to strike from a discreet, maroon shoulder holster, lay his grandfather's stainless steel Smith & Wesson .357 Model 15 Combat Masterpiece. Beneath the stainless revolver, like a well-tanned snake, someone had coiled a belt that matched the fancy leather holster.

In the bottom of the box he found row after row of hollow-point magnum cartridges packed in a transparent plastic case. Beneath the case's crystal-clear cover, the bullets shone as if new: round and smooth and harmless until prodded in the right place by the proper firing pin. The pointed heads glistened neatly, all in a row: shiny brass rockets, primed and ready for launch. Surprised and dismayed, he spoke aloud.

"I can't believe Granddaddy gave me his Combat Masterpiece." He said the words bitterly, disappointed by the act of generosity. *I thought he'd give it to one of his good ol' drinking buddies.* Drew's grandfather had bought the gun in 1977 from a retired Chicago cop who had moved south to fish the Gulf of Mexico in his golden years. After the purchase, he had cared for the gun with an unhealthy degree of diligence that bordered on idolatry. Drew picked the gun up gingerly, pointing it toward the ground.

The revolver, a compact weapon with a durable design, had been years ahead of its time. He flipped open the empty cylinder and gazed down the pristine, stainless steel barrel.

"Still clean as a whistle," he said aloud. He tested the safety and sat down on the bed. The safety felt tight: difficult to switch on and off, but in good working condition. *The way I like it.* Opening the ammunition case, he carefully loaded the pistol, keeping an empty chamber below the hammer. He slipped it under his belt and gazed into the mirror. Under his oversized shirt and baggy, pleated pants, the gun's outline could scarcely be seen.

"Thanks, Granddaddy," he said with a grimace, remembering the terror on Interstate 75. "This just might come in handy."

A Word from Elder Cromartie

Hearing voices in the living room, Drew put the covers back on the boxes and opened the door. What he saw surprised him.

Beside Sister Conway's worn couch, in a state-of-the-art wheelchair, sat a distinguished, ebony-hued, bone-skinny elderly gentleman in a dark suit, white shirt, and black bowtie. He held a dark gray hat loosely in his hands, and he tilted his head slightly when the door opened. His dark sunglasses effectively hid his aged eyes. The impenetrable shades added an edge to his ensemble, as if he were a blues musician ready to step onto a smoky stage.

"Drew, you remember Elder Cromartie, don't you?"

"How could I forget?" In Drew's youth, the elder had terrified Drew by virtue of his uncanny intuition. The elder had read souls like Drew's peers read comic books. His unsparing gaze had illuminated every dark corner and pierced every veil, leaving no secret hidden in the shadows. "Hello, Elder Cromartie," Drew said respectfully. The old man offered his hand, and Drew shook it heartily.

"Hello, Drew." The elder's voice had grown rough and breathy with age. "Sit down, won't you?"

"Of course. It's good to see you, sir. How's little Eric doing?"

"Little Eric's bigger than you now, Drew. He's finishing up this year at FAMU." In the local manner, he pronounced FAMU – the acronym for the Florida Agricultural and Mechanical University – as 'fam-you'.

"He's studying to be a pharmacist."

"Unbelievable! He was just a squirt when I left." Eric had been like a little brother to Drew. The two misfit country boys had often hunted together in the woods near the edge of the Big Nasty Swamp.

"Elder Cromartie wants to speak with you," Sister informed him.

"He wheeled down here all by hisself, and he has somethin' important to say." She straightened in her chair, brushing a stray piece of lint off her faded skirt.

"We're takin' care of the grandkids this weekend," the elder offered by way of explanation. "Mother couldn't come down with me."

"What is it, Elder?"

"I had a dream last night," the elder began, tilting his head slightly.

"Yes, sir," Drew replied politely, unsure of what to say. The elder held up his hands, palms out, and began to explain.

"Now listen, Drew. I usually don't take no truck with dreams. Any ol' false prophet can claim a dream, and anyone can lie through his teeth about the interpretation of a dream. You know what I mean."

"Yes, sir." Drew had heard a fire-breathing sermon on this subject in his childhood. It had made quite an impression.

"Dreams can lead fools astray," Elder Cromartie continued, pausing thoughtfully. "On the other hand, only a fool would claim that every dream is foolishness."

"Yes, sir."

"The good book shows that some dreams come from God. Think of Joseph in Egypt, and you'll know what I'm talkin' about. And Saint Peter preached that in these latter days the young men will see visions and the old men will dream dreams. He wasn't talkin' about no fakey old dreams. He was talkin' about the real deal." He paused and turned toward Sister, then back to Drew.

"Yes, sir."

"Well, now, I had a dream last night, and that's why I'm here." He stopped again. He appeared to be waiting for a response.

"What was it?" Drew asked, afraid of the answer.

The old man put his cane firmly on the floor and leaned forward with both hands on its broad brass top. He turned his head sideways and began to speak slowly and clearly.

"I dreamed that I saw a young man. He was standing and

looking at a tree. It was an oak sapling, you see, all hale and hearty. While I watched, flowers grew out of the branches." His face lifted toward the ceiling, as if he stared at a far-off vision. "It was a beautiful day." His tightly closed mouth worked soundlessly as they waited. He turned to Drew's aunt.

"They was pretty little lavender flowers, Sister Conway. Like purple day lilies, but just as pale as hydrangea blooms, covered with dew. They looked like they had just opened.

"Well, as you can see, everything was beautiful, but I could see that the man was in danger. Then I looked at his side, and I seen that he was wearing a sword. It was a big sword, but dirty. That's when somethin' glorious happened."

"What?"

"I heard the Lord speakin', soft and sweet." Elder Cromartie's voice tightened, and tears began to squeeze from his eyes. "It was the Lord all right. His voice sounded so humble and sweet."

"Glory!" Sister Conway whispered fervently.

"What did he say?" Drew asked, transfixed by the elder's mysterious story.

"He said, 'Tell him to put his sword away, for all of those who take up the sword will die by the sword'." As Elder Cromartie finished saying these words, Drew experienced a sinking sensation. The elder straightened up. "That's what he said."

"Who was the man with the sword, Elder Cromartie?" He dreaded the answer, but felt compelled to ask.

"Why, you know who it was," the elder replied softly.

"Who was it, Elder?"

"It was you, Drew. You! Why do you think I rolled down here in this wheelchair?"

"I don't know," he stammered in reply.

"I've come down here to warn you, son."

"About what?"

"Put your sword away," the Elder declared with Biblical authority, "for all those who take up the sword will die by the sword."

Slumming with Sharks

The big Hammerhead went nuts, slathering and snapping in desperate rage as he swung his tail with leg-breaking abandon. Precariously perched around the edge of the boat, the three fishermen stared at each other, fear contorting their faces. Their gaze swung to the captain: the only expert on the boat.

"Shoot him," shouted the lobster-red novice in the yellow Hawaiian shirt. "Shoot him before he eats us!"

"Stop it, you idiot!" the captain barked as the youngest man prepared to duck into the cabin to retrieve a rifle. "You'll put a hole in my boat."

"He's gonna eat us alive!" shrieked the yellow shirt, his panic showing as vividly as his atrocious sunburn.

"Shut up," growled the captain, standing on the pilot's seat in the middle of his big sport-fishing boat. "He's dying as we speak." Disgusted at the bald-faced cowardice of these city slickers, he frowned and glowered at each of them in turn. "I told you not to drag him into the boat with that gaff. Didn't I tell you to wait?"

"What do we do?" shrieked the gray-haired man leader of the group.

"Wait him out," the captain said. "He'll die eventually." As he spoke, the shark slowed down. He thrashed once and stopped, his gills slowly sucking for water, hopelessly drowning in a sea of air. "That'll do." The captain reached beneath the steering wheel, retrieved a large aluminum baseball bat, and gingerly slipped up behind the inert fish. "I told you guys to wait, but you just wouldn't listen." He raised the bat above his head and swung down with all of his might, smashing the hammerhead between his dull, evil eyes. "That's a kindness," he whispered to the shark. "I'm delivering you from these idiots." *But who will deliver me?*.

The big shark shivered, quivering from stem to stern as he began his final throes. It was a pitiful end to a voracious life.

"Cool," oozed the yellow-shirt.

Cool? thought the captain. *What an idiot!*

The shark swung his tail one last time – as if in response to the novice's comment – and smacked the dude's dangling foot. "Ow!" he squealed.

As if on cue, the big shark began to vomit.

"Ewww," groaned the yellow shirt.

I wish he'd broken your leg, the captain reflected, deeply regretting that he had guided such foolish men to catch such a spectacular fish. The shark shuddered and vomited one last time. Then, his movement ceased.

"No, way," the captain breathed staring at the mess on the deck. His heart seemed to stop, and his eyes widened with dread.

"Aaagh!" the yellow shirt shrieked, scrambling backwards and almost knocking a companion into the water.

"Aagh!" the other men cried, their faces contorted with panic and dismay. They stared transfixed at a pool of viscous matter in front of the dead shark's mouth.

Glistening in the middle of the red-brown slurry, palm-upward as if beckoning for help, they beheld a dreadful sight. As the realization hit them, the big, manly dudes shrieked like little boys on a roller coaster. Even the captain felt sick to his stomach.

The Hammerhead had puked up a human hand.

Southern-Med Style

At 8:00 PM Eastern Standard Time, a cellular phone rang on an exclusive Mediterranean beach.

"Hello?" A fit, thin, red haired, and thoroughly freckled man in his early 30s answered the phone. He lounged on his stomach, soaking in the morning sun. A handsome man of medium height with a straight, thin nose and wholesome appearance, he had no features that made him stand out in the crowd. He lolled on the white beach near the outrageously clear, blue-green water, clad in nylon trunks. With nowhere to go and no one to see, he roasted slowly in the hot sun, loving every minute.

As long as you did not notice the homicidal intensity of his gaze, his face bore no hint of his profession. Square and pale, with large blue eyes and delicate lines, he had the face of a naïve teenager.

Except for his youthful face, the man did not stand out in any particular way from the other souls scattered across the white sands. He blended in perfectly among the pale-skinned hordes.

A stylish pair of sunglasses hid his intense blue eyes. Using the dark lenses as a shield, he observed the beachgoers as a hawk might study a flock of plump chickens. As he watched, he listened carefully to his cell phone.

"Right," he answered. He listened intently for several more seconds, then sat up and scratched his beard. "No problem," he concluded, snapping the phone shut and looking around impatiently. *I'd better shower.* He stood and began to walk toward his villa. In his mind he began to run through a checklist to ensure that he would not miss any details.

The call had come from the top of his criminal organization. His wait had ended.

He would go to the airport and take a jet to Florida. There, he would provide backup for the local talent. This did not insult him.

They would pay his exorbitant fee in advance, and that satisfied his ego and his ravenous wallet.

He felt great. As he turned a final, longing gaze on the sun-lovers, his face revealed an incongruous mix of expressions: fallen choirboy mingled with hungry lion casing a savannah packed with loafing gazelles.

He considered himself an artist of death: a craftsman who produced performance art rich with deadly brilliance. He saw himself as a savant in the flower of his prime: the Vincent Van Gogh of contract murder. *I am like Vincent,* he reasoned, *but much wiser. The ears I cut off are not my own.*

Like a shining star, he savored his moment in the sun. And like certain stars of stage and screen, he shared the spotlight when it suited his pathology. For the right paycheck, he would do anything. He smiled and pushed back a thick cluster of healthy red hair, thinking about the job that lay ahead of him. As he thought about it, he just had to smile.

I love working with children.

A Big Pill to Swallow

The South Florida sun dropped swiftly at dusk, plunging below the horizon like a millstone tossed off the deep end of the peninsula. As soon as the sun hid its face, the sunburned partygoers of South Florida crawled off the beaches and crept into the stylish restaurants and bars.

Over the past 50 years, the bars and eateries of coastal Florida had flourished like cankers at the water's edge. They festered like sand fleas, sucking the marrow from the wallets of tourists and locals alike, replacing the dunes with oil-stained asphalt perfumed with sour beer. From Jacksonville Beach to Key West, a Pandora's panoply of air-conditioned restaurants and bars had spawned like poisonous algae, hiding the beach beneath the weight of their lucrative glory.

In one such crowded bar, located on Hallandale Beach, Jimmy Biggs and Dom the Pill busily polished off a platter of steak and eggs in a private booth they shared with Harpo Benvialligimo, an up-and-coming soldier in the Domella family. Harpo, posted to Fort Lauderdale for the past decade, served as a Domella ambassador to the Gold Coast. Day in and day out, he cultivated connections with a wide variety of South Florida gangsters and politicians. Today, his connections would prove invaluable.

"So, Harpo, tell me about our guy." As Jimmy spoke, he stuffed a piece of steak smothered in ketchup into his huge, gaping mouth.

"He's a weird looking redneck named James Herrington. We call him Bug Eyes, but not to his face."

"Bug Eyes?" interjected Dom. "Sounds like a cartoon character."

"He ain't that. Not by a long shot. He's like a redneck terminator."

"Tell us about him," Jimmy directed.

"Bug is from an old southern family."

"Gangsters?"

"Moonshiners. Most of his people had gotten out of the business by the '80s, but Bug was just gettin' started. He switched to dope, and he never looked back."

"A wise move."

"He's nothin' if not wise. He started makin' real money out there in the boonies... good, honest drug money. He was livin' the American dream."

"A self-made punk."

"Exactly. So one night, a couple of small-time operators gave him some mouth in a bar. You know the type. Nobodies. Anyway, within a week, Bug shut their big mouths forever. The way he did it was funny." Harpo bit the head off a jumbo shrimp and sloppily slurped it down the hatch.

"What was so funny?"

"Do you guys know what a citron is?" Dom the Pill stirred uneasily.

"It's car from France, right?"

"Right, but wrong. It's a melon that grows wild in the boondocks of South Central Florida. They grow about the size of a honeydew melon. Striped like watermelons. Really weird."

"Who cares?" Biggs asked.

"Those punks should'a cared, that's who, but it was too late. After Bug Eyes whacked 'em, he stuffed a couple of half-grown citrons into their mouths and wrote 'dumb' and 'dumberer' on their foreheads with a black marker. He dumped the bodies in back of the bar where they had mouthed off."

"Nice touch."

"The local news took a picture that made the National Enquirer."

"The Enquirer?" Dom asked respectfully. "No kiddin'?" *Why don't we ever make the Enquirer?*

"I must'a missed that issue," Biggs sneered.

"The two punks were unconnected, so nobody cared. The law had nothin' on old Bug. Then, somethin' happened that caused the Facciamellis to notice him." Harpo adjusted the buttons on his faux casual shirt. He looked every bit the dark-haired, brown-eyed, toothily handsome type-A hood. He had tried but failed to blend in with the laid-back South Florida beach crowd. His slacks looked too spotless, his shoes too shiny to blend.

"Why should the Faccis care about a punk from the boonies?"

"After he killed the local punks, he whacked a big-time player who had set up shop in Oree County."

"Who?"

"Do you remember Art Bungellio?"

"Artie Bungles? Who could forget old Artie?"

"Yeah, but did you hear how he got it?"

"I heard that he was whacked by the Polentas because he dumped Don Polenta's daughter."

"Nah. The Polentas didn't whack Artie. He made them a ton of money with the unions. It would'a been bad for morale."

"That's why the Polenta's are losin' their pull."

"Right. So anyway, it's Provencenti territory in the boondocks, so Artie Bungles asked the Provencentis if he could live in Oree County. They said okay, as long as he kept things quiet. He and his partner wanted to build a resort."

"Who was the partner?"

"Emilio Rigio." Hearing the name, Dom the Pill whistled between his teeth.

"I served time with Rigio at Riker's," Dom said. "I wouldn't want'a cross him… not unless there was real money in it."

"Well shucky darn, it's a small, small world," Biggs hissed. "You knew Rigio at Riker's. Let's all hold hands and sing!"

"It's a small world if you're in with the in crowd, like me," Dom agreed with a wink. "But you wouldn't know about that, would you?"

"So anyway," Harpo continued, "when Rigio went out drinkin', he would mess with the local punks for laughs. One night he jerked Bug Eye's chain in a local bar, and Bug pulled a Vito Corleone on him. He suggested that Rigio be reasonable, just back off, cool his jets. Rigio wouldn't listen. He made fun of his big, buggy eyes."

"That takes real comedic genius."

"Yeah, well, Rigio wasn't the sharpest guy around. When he kept hammering away, old Bug just shut his mouth and left the bar. He went straight to Rigio's house, broke in, and waited. He shot him as he came in through the front door. For good measure, he killed Artie Bungles two weeks later. The cops had no evidence, so Bug walked."

"Hmm."

"After that, the Faccis recruited Bug. They could see that he had talent. They paid him some major bucks to move down here. Since then, he's been the best independent hitter on the Gold Coast."

"For how long?"

"Ten years."

"Ten years?" Dom whistled softly. "He must be good," he said, glancing at Jimmy Biggs, who stared back without smiling. "It ain't easy to live that long as an independent hitter."

"He's that good," Harpo added. "Plus, he knows Oree County like the back of his hand. He grew up there. He's perfect for this job."

"Do we have to talk to the Faccis?" Jimmy asked.

"That's the beauty of it," Harpo said, waving his hand expressively. "These are open cities. The Faccis give him business, but they don't own him. He's not a made man in their organization. Before he takes a contract, he runs the names past 'em. That's all. If they give him the green light, it's a go. It's good for him, good for them. Win, win."

"Will the Faccis know we're messin' with the Provencentis?" Jimmy interjected.

"They already know. Don Domella set this up at the highest level."

"Have you talked to this guy yet… this Bug Eyes?"

"Yes, we have. He's on the road already."

"Already? He ain't goin' after the kid, is he?" Dom asked, disappointment showing on his face. *I thought we were gonna get the kid.*

"You guys have the contract on the kid. Bug has the contract on the FDLE broad. Her names Jemima, Janey, Jenny… something like that. She lives in the boonies in his old stompin' grounds: Oree County, Florida. The armpit of the state."

"Good. The kid's the important one. That's why we came down from New York City." Jimmy flexed his shoulders under his jacket. "The Don gave me the job himself."

"I know. But there's something else I have to tell you, from the top." Harpo paused, steeling his nerve. He was more of a racketeer than a gangster, better with money than blood. The temper of Biggs was legendary, and he did not wish to bear its brunt.

"Go ahead," Biggs interjected harshly. "What is it?"

"Don Brucci and Don Domella have decided that they can't afford to miss the hit on the kid. For the time being, the cops don't know anybody will be goin' after him. Protection will be slack."

"Maybe."

"Right. But if we miss, that'll all be history. They'll lock the kid down tighter than Capone at Alcatraz." Harpo tried to smile, but the frown on Biggs' face successfully stalled his effort.

"The bottom line is that you guys have to hit the kid at the same time the FDLE agent is killed. After she's whacked, the heat will go through the roof. It'll be like cracking Fort Knox to get another whack at the kid."

"When do we do the job?"

"Tomorrow morning."

"Tomorrow morning?" Dom blurted. "We haven't scoped it out!"

"Our best guys have set it up. The kid's staying with his aunt in Tallahassee. They'll be going south to Cutler County for the funeral. Our man in Tallahassee is watching, and he'll give us their route after they leave. The funeral is on Tuesday afternoon."

"Who's our guy in Tallahassee?"

"You don't need to know. We ain't supposed to have anybody there. Even the Provencentis don't have anybody in Tally, just mouthpieces and lobbyists. You know the rules. It's a state capitol."

Jimmy Biggs felt a surge of fury. Who was this mere button man to give him instructions? Yet he recognized that the plan had come from his don. Swallowing his pride, he straightened up and delicately wiped the egg yolk from his lips.

"When do we leave?"

"Right away. You have to drive."

"Drive? Are you nuts? We just drove straight through from New York City!"

"All the airports have cameras. We don't want the feds involved."

"Whatever," Jimmy grunted angrily. Harpo had a point, but he did not care to acknowledge it.

"They want you on the ground in Gainesville before dawn."

"Gainesville? Why Gainesville?"

"It's centrally located. From there you can intercept their car no matter which route they take. Our guys will meet you with the plan. Here are the directions to the house and the phone numbers." He handed him a folded piece of paper. "We're doing all the planning for you: maps, getaway, everything. Don't worry; we'll be thorough. Our best guys are on it."

"Who?"

"Tony Nickles and Gimp Giancoli."

"Good." Tony and Gimp were the best tacticians in the Domella organization. "How are we doin' the job?"

"Since you're a marksman, they decided to let you use your rifle. You'll hit 'em as they drive by. Dom will be your spotter."

"Excellent." His finest rifle was in his trunk, ready for the fun.

"For a job this important, we don't do many long-distance hits. We haven't done one like this since Bugsy Siegel in Beverly Hills. Your reputation precedes you."

"What about cops?" He ignored the compliment.

"They'll have a police escort: one, maybe two cars. Two of the most likely routes that go to Cutler County involve I-75, and we've identified a couple of overpasses with minimal traffic and no exit ramps. You should have plenty of time for a getaway."

"What if they take another route... not the interstate?"

"There's one other route. If they go that way, it'll be dicey. If you can shoot out their tires, you'll get away. Otherwise, you're dead."

"Great."

"We're pretty sure they'll take the interstate route. The other routes are too slow, with a lot of traffic lights and hinky little towns."

"What if they take a plane?"

"That's unlikely. It's a six-hour drive from Tallahassee to Cutler County. If they fly by commercial jet, the nearest commercial airport is Orlando. That's a good two hours away from their destination, so they won't save any time by flying. They have to hook up with the cops, go through security, check luggage, yadda yadda yadda. We figure they'll drive. But if they fly into Orlando, you'll have to hit 'em as they drive from there to Cutler County. We have a couple of sites selected for each route."

"Sounds like fun."

"You'll have plenty of time to intercept them unless they take a private plane into the Oree County Airport. It's a small airport with no commercial flights."

"What if they take a private plane into the local airport?"

"Then we'll cancel everything and reschedule."

"Anything else?" Biggs asked. At this question, Harpo blanched, turning as pale as a young punk with a gun jammed in his mouth. *Great,* Jimmy thought. *Whatever he's gonna say next, I ain't gonna like.*

"There's something else. Don Domella has hired a closer."

"What?" Jimmy almost shouted the word.

"He's bringin' in a closer," he repeated. This news enraged Jimmy Biggs.

"A closer?" he hissed angrily. "Unbelievable! Does he think we can't handle the job?" As soon as he said the words, he regretted it. He hoped that Harpo would prove to be discreet and would not repeat his words to Don Domella. If Harpo ran his mouth, Jimmy's anger could cost him dearly.

"Who's the closer?" Dom asked, trying to defuse the infamous temper of his friend.

"Chucky." When he heard the name, Dom dropped his fork. The clatter caused heads to turn toward their enclosed booth.

"No!"

"Unfortunately, yes."

Dom the Pill turned to Jimmy Biggs. "Do you think we'll get a chance to meet him?" In response, Jimmy's hand flashed out and seized Dom's oversized ear.

"If we fumble this hit, we'll meet him, all right. Not that we'll survive the experience!" He barked the words tersely, twisting Dom's ear and then releasing it with a shove. "Do you think he'll leave witnesses if he has to clean up our mess?" Jimmy recognized the bitter truth. At this point, a successful hit offered their best hope of survival.

"Oh, right," Dom replied stupidly. His face segued from glee to glower. "That ain't good."

The Chicago Mob had given the irreverent nickname of Chucky to a meek-looking, unfailingly polite Canadian who lived a secret life as the most effective hit man in North America. They brought Chucky in only for the biggest of jobs. As the child of a prominent Russian gangster and a nice Canadian wife, Chucky's fresh-faced looks gave him an edge with the locals wherever he went. His impeccable manners never failed to open doors, and his skills as a killer inevitably closed the deal.

Jimmy Biggs pushed his chair away from the table. "Chucky," he murmured. "What does that make me, Chucky's bride?"

"I want'a be Pinocchio," Dom interjected joyfully. "Where's the Land of the Boobies? Let's shoot pool and knock down a few brewskies."

"Stop clownin', Dom. I've gotta think."

"You've met him, right, Biggs?" inquired Harpo. He felt a morbid fascination – shared by most guys in the know – regarding the legend of Chucky, the doll-eyed messenger of death.

"Yeah, I've met him."

"What's he look like?"

"Like Opey. Like innocence personified," Biggs complained. "He's got big ears and a smile that makes little old ladies offer him cookies. He's so scrawny, he makes Snoop Dog look like Tupac. He's a killer who don't look like it. So what? Big deal."

"Wow!"

"He's got dead eyes," Biggs added quietly, his mind wandering. "There's no life in 'em. It ain't a pretty sight." As he considered the changed playing field, Jimmy Biggs felt a surge of dismay. Taking on the Provencentis would be no small matter, even with the Brucci and Domella families assisting. The decision to bring in a closer seemed inevitable. In such a high-stakes gambit, even a capo could become expendable.

"How's he so good at it?" Harpo continued.

"He's a fitness freak," Biggs replied. "A control freak, too. He's sharp as a razor, but he doesn't look it." He shook his head as if awakening from a bad dream. "Hey, can we talk about our job?" he added irritably. "Who cares about Chucky?" *Domella don't care if we live or die.*

After their dinner with Harpo, Jimmy Biggs and Dom the Pill left the bar without their usual happy-go-lucky banter. They glumly climbed into their convertible and fired it up for the long trip to Gainesville. At the other end of the parking lot, a small, dark, slender man with short black hair sat up inside of a nondescript Nissan Titan. As their car pulled out of the lot, he turned on a GPS positioning device. It flashed once, twice, and then locked into the signal, displaying a detailed map on a high-resolution video screen. On the map, a bright red light slowly moved down a long, narrow street. *There they are,* he reflected. *Two little Pac Men gobbling up everything in sight. They don't know a ghost is chasing them through the maze.*

Flipping out his cellular phone, he pushed a button and let it ring. He left a voice mail message that had been prearranged to indicate the success of his mission. "Johnny, this is O. The beaches are incredible. Wish you could be here. Later." The speaker's distinctively southern, Latin-flavored accent identified him as a native of Ybor City.

He had left the voice mail for John Dicella, the consigliere of the Provencenti family. Guessing correctly that the Bruccis would not act without Domella's direct involvement, John had ordered a stakeout of Harpo, the most prominent Domella contact in South Florida. Tonight, the Provencentis had identified Jimmy Biggs and Dom the Pill as the gangsters sent to kill the boy.

The killer leaned back in his seat and lit a cigarette, taking a sharp drag. Exhaling slowly through his nose, he turned on the stereo and pumped up the volume. With ear-crunching abandon, the speakers blasted out an oldie by Linkin Park.

He started the truck and slammed it into reverse, burning rubber. *Oops! Don't foul the air.* Pollution offended his environmental sensibilities. As a homegrown Floridian and a native of Hillsborough County, he respected Florida's fragile environment. In a manner of speaking, he could be called a naturalist, and in keeping with the naturalistic ethos, he had evolved into an avid hunter – albeit, an unnatural one.

As a hunter, he had long ago identified his favorite prey. Some Floridians hunted deer. Others hunted turkeys. Ovido Santiago, an adrenalin addict and respected Provencenti specialist, preferred to hunt predators. Over the years, the murder of man-killers had become his greatest glee. Ovido's remarkable success at such a coveted calling had cemented his claim to infamy among the blood-spattered bullies haunting his fallen world.

Because he worked for a civilized family – a model of old-school Mafia decorum – Ovido would never be allowed to stuff the heads of his victims and hang them in his den. When he reflected on this limitation, it provoked him to rage, and one thing would lead to another. Angry and frustrated, he would ask for another contract, eager to vent his wrath on another unwitting killer.

Anger had paid Ovido well. Loaned out to other families, he had worked all over the nation. His career had been profitable but corrosive, like dealing hot batteries out of the trunk of a car. His soul had become so twisted, so contorted by evil fantasies, that he had lost all sense of right or wrong. His moral up was down. He swam in a sea of blood and money, richly rewarded for his misanthropy.

Ovido hunted man-killers because it earned him respect. He hunted them because, for him, the thrill of the hunt intensified exponentially with the deadliness of the prey.

He loved to hunt predators.

Sometimes, just for fun, he did them for free.

Monday Morning Coming Down

Jamie took a sip from her cup and closed her eyes, savoring the sweet taste of Delia Rawlings' hot chocolate. Delia had concocted the creamy brew from an old family recipe, and the cup brimmed with good taste, a rich legacy from the days before butterfat became a bad word.

"Merely divine," Jamie murmured, leaning back in her chair. "As always, Miss Delia."

"Miss Delia? You sound like Ellen," she replied, leaning back in her chair as she took her first sip. "How is Ellen doing nowadays?"

"As outlandish as ever, as you might imagine." Jamie smiled shyly at Delia, glad to have the pleasure of her company.

"It's too bad she couldn't come to your party."

"I know."

"It feels like it's been a month since the party, doesn't it?"

"Yes. But it's been less than three days."

"Three very long days. Especially for the Johnston family."

"What's left of them," Jamie replied, leaning forward to place her mug carefully on the coffee table.

"How are you holding up, Jamie?"

"I'm okay. It's the Johnstons that I'm worried about. They lost two out of five family members in a single night."

"You're not counting the fugitive."

"Pete Johnston? I don't think they'd count him as a family member after all of this."

"You never know," the sheriff mused sadly. "I heard that Winston raised him for years when he was just a boy, back when Dean Ray was in prison. It's hard to hate someone you raised or grew up with. You remember the child, not the man."

"Do you think they still hold out hope that Pete can change?"

"Yes, I do. For a close family like theirs, it can be hard to give up on hope." She raised her brows. "I've seen it with plenty of families. They love the criminal, even when they hate the crime."

"How can Pete Johnston be related to them? They're so good, and he's so bad."

"I know. He's a poster child for Sheldon's Somatotype Theory of criminal behavior: a Neanderthal with atavistic tendencies."

"Do you really believe that?"

"It's rubbish. But he sure looks the part."

"I'll say."

"Don't ask me about criminology, Jamie. You're the one earning the doctorate."

"If I survive my internship," she replied with a frown.

"Right. Seriously, though, how are you holding up?"

"I'm not sure. My boss suggested counseling, but I'm not going. I don't need to talk about how I feel."

"No?"

"No. I know how I feel. I feel angry. I feel terrible. If I felt okay, then I'd be worried."

"How's your husband handling this?"

"He's accustomed to the risk, but we don't think that Pete will bother with me. By now, he probably wants to give me a medal."

"Don't blame yourself, Jamie. You didn't reveal the family's location."

"Somebody did."

"You were tight-lipped, even with me. Don't you remember?"

"Yes." Jamie sighed heavily.

"There must be a mole inside the FDLE. I told them as much."

"I'll bet they didn't want to hear that."

"If they have a leak, they'd better deal with it. Somebody gave them Dan Johnston's address."

"I know."

"Keep your head up, kid." They exchanged a weary smile.

"I'm glad you decided to visit, Delia."

"It's the least I can do."

"Thanks."

"I had to get away from the station, Jamie. My deputies have been hovering around like a bunch of mother hens now that Pete Johnston's on the loose. They want to keep me locked up like the crown jewels."

"You *are* the crown jewel of Oree County. Didn't you know?"

"Yeah, right," she laughed. "That'd be me. The crown jewel."

"Tell me, Delia." Jamie paused reflectively. "Uh, never mind."

"Never mind? Since when do you hold back?"

"I don't know. Since now."

"Speak. As your older sister, I command you."

"Okay, but this is way off subject."

"Spill!"

"Do you ever think about Tommy Durrance?" Over the past few years, they had seldom mentioned his name.

Sheriff Durrance had given his life in the line of duty six years before. He had been close – very close – to Delia Rawlings. He had been her mentor, and had become her best friend.

"I think about him every time I put on the uniform." Delia paused after saying this, as if she had run out of words.

"Sometimes," Jamie agreed, "I think that except for Donny, Sheriff Durrance was the only good man I've ever met."

"Sometimes I *know* he was the only good man I ever met," Delia said. "Then I remember my little brother, and your man Donny. Then I think about old Alibi Albritton down at the station. There are still a few good men."

"If you say so," Jamie replied. "Since you're my best friend, I'll take your word for it."

"Good."

"It's good to know there are a few good men out there."

"A few, little sister," Delia replied softly. "A few."

The M-Class Blues

Marcy felt incensed. Who was this guy to tell her what she could or could not do? She stood in front of the elevator, tapping her foot and scowling. A small suitcase teetered precariously on the carpet next to her, threatening to fall at any moment.

She watched Drew's reflection in the brass elevator door as he hurried to catch up. She turned and frowned, punching the button. *Hurry up, elevator!*

"I'm sorry, Marcy. You're right," Drew blurted as the doors opened on cue. She ignored him and stepped inside, waving her hand dismissively. He followed and reached out, lightly touching her arm. She pulled away and stared at the wall as he pressed the 'open' button.

"You're admitting that I'm right?"

"Yes. If you want to drive, we'll drive. I shouldn't have argued. You've been through a lot." *I don't think it's safe to drive. I think we should fly a private plane to Oree County, but I don't want you to leave without me.*

She glanced at him from the corner of her eye and realized again how astonishingly good-looking he was. *Hmmm. He saved Danny's life.* She sighed deeply.

"Marcy, will you forgive me? Please?" he added humbly. He really liked this woman.

"Yeah, sure," she answered brusquely. "But if you're going with us, would you please help Danny with the suitcases?" She pointed through the open elevator doors. "We shouldn't make Ches wait."

IN THE PARKING LOT, CHES TAPPED HIS FINGERTIPS on the steering wheel and closed his eyes. He loved to drive his big Mercedes M-class sedan, and he looked forward to the trip. When Marcy climbed in, he felt a twinge of regret. *I wonder if she realizes that she's already left me behind?* Ches had become ancient history, and he knew it.

Drew and Danny walked out of the building and paused, squinting in the sunlight. Surprised, Marcy noticed how similarly they behaved: their walk and gestures, their mannerisms. The similarity seemed strange considering the fact that they were not related and had only just met. Ches pointed at them.

"They act like brothers," he drawled. "That's rather unusual."

"Yes," Marcy said as she put on her sunglasses. "I suppose." They waited as Drew and Danny loaded their suitcases into the trunk, slammed it shut, and climbed in: Danny on the right, Drew on the left.

"Go south, young man," Danny ordered imperiously as he fastened the seat belt. "Let's see what this baby can do."

"I'm afraid we won't be seeing that," Ches responded with asperity.

"Why not?" Danny asked.

"This car was designed for the Autobahn. Its top speed is way too fast. Even if I wanted to go that fast, we can't. We'll have a police escort."

"How fast will it go?" Danny asked.

"More than 180 miles per hour."

"Whoa!" He turned to his left. "Hey, Drew, have you ever driven that fast?" The question embarrassed Drew.

"Does anyone want a Butterfinger?" Drew asked, trying to distract Danny from his line of questioning. Predictably, the effort failed.

"Have you ever driven more than 180 miles per hour?"

"Yeah. I guess so."

"What's the fastest you've driven?"

"I drove a car 220 miles per hour once, on a racetrack." He slipped on his shades, trying to sink into the seat and hide. He felt extremely self-conscious.

"Whoa! That's fast. What kind of car was that?"

"I was driving my Testarossa," Drew mumbled softly. He liked Ches and did not wish to steal his thunder.

"Your what? I couldn't understand you," Danny persisted, annoying Drew to no end. *He knows I don't want to say it, the little creep!*

"It was my Ferrari, kid," Drew finally sighed, giving up the fight. "I went 220 miles per hour on a test track in my Ferrari Testarossa." *I hope your happy, you little monster. I probably just shredded Chesterfield's ego like a turnip in a stump grinder.*

"Wow!" Danny gloated. "A Ferrari Testarossa! Now, *that's* what I call a car!"

A Wicked Cough

At 9:35 AM, in a sedate suburban house in downtown Gainesville, Jimmy Biggs got the call. He stood up spontaneously, unconsciously slicking his hair back as he spoke briefly into his cell phone. By the time he had snapped the phone shut, Dom stood on his feet, reaching for the keys to their rented Ford Explorer.

"Let's beat it," Biggs growled. They left the house without looking back. In the SUV, Dom asked the burning question.

"Which route are they taking?"

"I-10 to I-75. Best case scenario." They smiled at one another.

"Sweet."

"We have more good news. Tommy just told me that Chucky's flight was delayed. He won't be there to back us up."

"We don't have to worry about him, Biggs. We've never missed a hit yet. Why would we miss this one?"

Their support team had identified an ideal site for the hit. Within forty minutes after leaving Gainesville, they turned onto a deserted, two-lane country highway. Both men wore sunglasses, defending their eyes from the dazzling onslaught of summer sunlight. The lonely country highway paralleled the interstate, turning right to cross at an overpass on top of the next hill.

"We'll be laying up in those trees," Biggs said, pointing across the busy interstate to the woods at the edge of the overpass.

"Cool."

"Let's rehearse it one more time. What do we do?"

"We go to our spot just past the bridge on the right. It's perfect: sheltered from both highways, but with a clear view of the interstate through the trees. I'll set up our spotting scope and keep an eye on the southbound traffic.

"When I see a dark blue Mercedes with a good-looking blond in the front seat, I let you know. You shoot the kid, then we beat it."

"What else?"

"I tell you where the kid's sittin'."

"What else?"

"As soon as I tell you, I pack up the scope and get behind the wheel of the Explorer. I don't wait for the hit. You'll come to the truck as soon as you do the job. We drive south for one mile, then we turn right on a dirt road beside a Purina Cow Chow billboard."

"Cow Chow?"

"Yeah, Cow Chow. Cattle food."

"Right." As their SUV turned right and began to cross the interstate, Jimmy craned his neck, looking for the right place to set up on the other side of the bridge. "What else?"

"At the end of the dirt road after I turn, there's an air strip. Our guys will be waiting. We fly off into the sunset, rich and happy."

"Right," he said, pulling off the side of the road just past the bridge. "Let's do it."

CHES HAMILTON'S MERCEDES passed the last Gainesville exit at 10:15 AM and continued south without stopping. Drew looked at the Archer Road exit sign and frowned. Jim Kent, the bass player in his band, had grown up in Gainesville. Drew had once visited Jim's parents' house, a huge brick estate off Archer Road. As they passed, he remembered the years he had invested in his band.

Blunt Trauma had felt like a band of brothers. Drew had joined young, and had stuck with them for almost 14 years. He had invented the band's name, sung most of their songs, and written most of their hits. But when he fell down and couldn't get up, his band of brothers had treated him like a stranger.

He felt like a chump. *I was offered gigs with better bands,* he remembered, *but I stayed with them. Now it's over. They couldn't care less that I've changed. They probably think less of me because I couldn't handle the dope they're still shoving up their noses.*

He reached into his coat and pulled out his sunglasses. Slipping them on, he slumped low in the seat and wearily closed his eyes.

DOM THE PILL STARED through the large lens of the spotting scope, fully absorbed in the task at hand. A cigarette dangled carelessly from his lips. He intermittently puffed away, coughing wickedly. Jimmy did not understand how Dom could smoke and cough while focusing through a scope, but he did not question his methods after a lifetime of experience. He had no doubt that Dom would spot their target as soon as the car topped the horizon.

Jimmy Biggs chambered a shell and swept his rifle up, panning the scope across the highway. He randomly placed the crosshairs on a truck driver and followed his approach. The southbound cars came almost straight at them down a long downhill run. He could see for miles in the clean Central Florida air. He would be able to take out the kid before they knew what hit them.

They had a perfect setup: well hidden, but with a great view. Trees towered overhead. The undergrowth offered cover, but the line of fire ran straight and true, unhindered by leaf or branch.

"Come on down," Dom whispered as he scanned the highway. "Come to Daddy Dom."

"Hey, Biggs, I have a question."

"What?"

"Do you ever regret our line of work?" The question took Jimmy Biggs by surprise.

"Why should I regret it?"

"I was just wonderin'."

"No! I don't regret a day. We've got a dream job. We make big bucks for easy work. We get respect. Strangers give us their seats at the bar. Guys are afraid of us. We steal their girls, and they don't utter a peep. Why should I regret that?"

"You're right, Biggs."

"Sure I'm right."

"Do you ever think about God?"

"Dom, are you crazy?"

"No, I mean it. Do you ever wonder whether God likes what we do?"

"Who cares?"

"I guess you're right. Who cares, huh, Biggsy?"
"Absolutely. Who gives a flip?"
"We're the cream of society."
"We're the sharks. At the top of the food chain."
"Hey, Biggs," he blurted excitedly. "I see 'em! They're comin'!"
"Great!" he grunted, swinging up his gun. He picked the car up in his scope just as they topped the horizon, almost a mile away. He would have all the time in the world to take his shot.

INSIDE THE BIG MERCEDES, Drew put down his magazine. The green countryside showed Florida at her best: large live oaks draped with Spanish moss and scattered pines overlooking broad, grassy plains.

"What do you think about this land, kid?" Hearing Drew's question, Danny looked up from the book he was reading and gazed out the window.

"It's nice."

"Yeah. It reminds me of the land around Lake Wassahachee." Drew stared at the trees, unaware that his face was being tracked by a spotting scope.

JIMMY BIGGS CAREFULLY SETTLED into firing position: belly down in the dry leaves with his rifle locked into his tripod. Finding the Mercedes in his scope, he whistled tunelessly, raising his thumb to trip the safety. He could see the boy in the back seat, looking out the window. *Beautiful.* He gradually lowered the barrel until the cross hairs met in the middle of the boy's studious face. He took a deep breath and exhaled slowly, preparing to squeeze the trigger.

A cough to his right distracted him. To his great annoyance, a large spot of moisture hit his cheek. Wiping away the drop with his thumb, he barked gruffly at Dom without looking in his direction.

"Hey, cover your mouth! Get in the truck, you schlub." Growling like an enraged bear, he glanced at his wet thumb and froze. A splash of bright red blood quivered on his thumb, glistening in the summer sunlight. *Oh, no!*

He rolled over frantically, floundering for the handgun in his belt. He had always been fast... remarkably, shockingly fast. But time had run out in his neck of the woods. The storied speed of Jimmy Biggs could not save the day.

Biggs drew his weapon with a curse as the stranger's silencer spit fire. The gun coughed softly, deliberately, right in his face: rude – to be certain – but deadly effective.

A nine-millimeter bullet punched a discreet hole in the center of Jimmy Biggs' forehead. It was an efficient hit, as neat as a surgical incision. His eyes rolled upwards as the back of his skull exploded, raining a gusher of gore down the wooded slope overlooking the highway. The sickening shower rattled loudly onto the leaves below as Biggs fell onto his back to stare blankly at the hot Florida sky.

Ovido Santiago smiled with grim satisfaction. Holstering his weapon, he carefully studied the dirt and leaves until he found both of his spent shell casings. He put them in an envelope and tucked them into his shirt pocket.

Except for the shell casings, Ovido left the crime scene undisturbed. He hummed as he climbed up the bank toward his pickup truck, looking up and down the deserted rural highway.

Opening the chrome toolbox behind the cab, he sealed his gun and casings inside a plastic bag and stuffed them beneath a jumbled pile of hand tools. He closed the box, snapped on the padlock, and climbed into the cab, donning a John Deere cap and a pair of cheap sunglasses.

As slow as a sightseer on Sunday afternoon, Ovido drove away from the scene of the crime.

AT ABOUT THE SAME TIME, APPROXIMATELY 50 MILES SOUTH of Ovido Santiago's crime scene, Sheriff Delia Rawlings reached into the sunglass case behind her driver-side sun visor and came up empty-handed. Her sunglasses could not be found. *Shoot! I must have left them on the counter in Jamie's kitchen.* She turned down her CD player and pushed the button on her collar. "Lettie, forward my calls to Alibi. I'm going back to Jamie's house to get my sunglasses. I might stay there 'til Donny gets home."

"Will do, Sheriff," a voice answered over the radio. Delia made a U-turn and rolled down her windows. After a minute, she turned right and began to navigate the bumpy road to Jamie's ranch. The sun shone brightly as she hummed and rapped her fingers on the door of her squad car. *What a beautiful day.*

Home Alone

Jamie had never fully recovered from the trauma. Six years after the violent assault that almost killed her, she still kept her house locked tight, curtains drawn, whenever she stayed home alone. After Delia left, Jamie locked the front door and returned to her work in the back yard.

Potting an azalea, she heard the big engine of a car idling through the patriarch oaks that lined the road leading to her farmhouse. With her acute sense of hearing, she never failed to notice the sound of a visitor's car long before it came into sight. Out of habit, she washed her hands and stepped into the house, locking the door behind her.

The air conditioning felt great. She opened the refrigerator and pulled out a fresh pitcher of lemonade.

After Delia had left her house, Jamie found her sunglasses. She expected her return, and the approaching vehicle sounded just like her squad car.

She was pouring lemonade into a glass when a loud knock rattled the front door. *That's not Delia,* she thought, rubbing her hands on her jeans as she walked into the living room. She stopped at the front door.

"Yes?" She spoke loudly, so she could be heard through the door.

"I have flowers for Mrs. Janelle James Hawkins."

"Please leave them on the porch," she said. "Here's a tip." Reaching in a purse in her desk, she retrieved a five-dollar bill and slid it under the door. *If I'm paranoid, it's based on experience.*

"Thanks, ma'am." The voice sounded like that of a middle-aged man with a hard-core Oree County accent. But somehow, something didn't feel right. *I'm being paranoid,* she told herself.

Out of the blue, a tragic memory returned. *Paranoid? That's what I told myself on the night Johnny was killed.* At the thought, she paused. On that dreadful night, her instincts had saved her life.

Jamie began to back away from the door. She felt electricity sweep across her skin, and her hair seemed to stand on end. *Surely, lightning won't strike twice.* The thought unsettled her. She had suffered in the past from random violence, but surely the odds argued against a recurrence.

Through the pale, gauzy curtain in the window to the left of the door, Jamie noticed motion. As she gazed intently, a shadow approached the window with surprising speed.

Swift as a wildcat, she wheeled away from the window as a rocking chair from her porch blasted through the glass. The force blew brittle shards into her living room as the heavy chair skidded across the floor and smashed into the coffee table, missing her by inches. Instinctively, she sprinted toward the back of the house.

In the jagged window, another shadow appeared. With startling quickness a balding, heavily muscled man in a blue jump suit leaped inside the room, ignoring the broken glass. Catlike, he landed on his feet, hard boots crunching the splintered shards.

JAMIE RAN HARD AND FAST like an impala fleeing a lion. Her speed, propelled by instinct, was a marvel to behold.

She burst into the kitchen before the man's boots could gain traction. By the time he careened into the kitchen behind her, she had unlocked and opened the back door. She managed to slam it shut in his face, but her effort was futile. He was a large man, accustomed to creative thinking in stressful situations.

Without slowing down he lowered his shoulder and slammed full-force into the old pine boards of the farmhouse door. The brittle door blew off its hinges, dumping him helter-skelter down the concrete steps. At the foot of the steps, as he rolled to his feet in a smooth, practiced motion, he seized a clay brick from the dirt and flung it at Jamie with all of his might.

Jamie had speed.

She might have outrun the man, but she could not outrun the brick.

The heavy brick smacked solidly into the back of her head, knocking her to the ground as it dropped her universe into a tailspin. Before she could gather her wits, he pounced onto her back.

The killer smashed Jamie's face into the dirt and punched her twice in the back of head. Savoring the moment, he rolled his stunned victim over and straddled her, pinning her arms with his legs.

He began to punch Jamie's face with thunderous, ham-handed blows. With extreme strength and unmerciful cruelty, he packed power in every punch: crushing her flesh and crunching her bones.

Help, me, sweet Jesus, she prayed, bewildered. *What's happening to me?* The blow from the brick had caused a severe concussion, and she could not fight back. She stared at the man curiously: detached somehow, as if she were viewing the brutal assault through a telescope, backwards.

As each punch fell, reality would return for one cruel instant. She would feel the crunch, suffer the jagged stab of pain, taste the salty blood in her mouth, now smeared like an open wound across her shattered face. *Lord, help me! He's killing me,* she reflected dully. Her eyes rolled upwards, and her consciousness began a strategic retreat.

The killer's anger grew with each heavy punch. Deep in the throes of an evil trance, his mental state segued from blood lust to frenzy. Staggering to his feet, he groped for the pistol in his belt.

His knuckles dripped with Jamie's rich, crimson life. Thin streams of blood cascaded down his face from a stray piece of glass that had cut him as he leaped through the shattered window.

He did not care about the cut.

He did not care one whit.

This much he cared about; he cared about death. Death was what he lived for, loved for, longed for. He revered death almost as much as he hated life.

Staggering slightly, he stood with one foot on each side of Jamie's limp body and pulled a handgun out of his waistband. A grimace – the cruel parody of a smile – twisted across his face: red with lust, contorted with sadistic glee.

"Loser," he spat as he placed his left hand on top of the pistol to jack a around into the chamber.

Suddenly, without warning, his world changed forever.

"Drop the gun, or I'll shoot!" a strange voice shouted. He heard the words dimly, as if through cotton earplugs. This was a strong voice, robust and distinctly feminine: authoritative and powerful. He heard the distant echo of the words, but for the moment, he could not conceive of their meaning.

"Drop the gun, or I'll shoot!" the voice cried again. This time he heard the words clearly. It felt to him as if the voice drilled deep within him, unleashing a flood of adrenalin that rushed coldly through his brain. As if from a trance, he emerged from his blood-frenzy with the abrupt realization that he was not alone. His eyes flashed to his right, and he glimpsed the source of the sound at the edge of his field of vision.

Delia Rawlings, the Sheriff of Oree County, stood 20 feet away: knees slightly bent, feet set wide apart in a classic firing stance. She held a .12 gauge riot shotgun at her shoulder: safety off, shell chambered, and ready to shoot. She sighted down the barrel, calm and unblinking.

He failed to drop the gun.

That was his first mistake.

Without further adieu, Sheriff Rawlings squeezed the slack from the trigger. The big gun bucked hard against her shoulder as it released a magnum blast of buckshot that smacked into the killer like a sledgehammer straight from bloody hell. The impact spun him around like a top and knocked him down hard onto the dusty earth. She pumped another round into the chamber and inched cautiously forward.

Bug Eyes lay on his back with the automatic pistol still held in his hand. He appeared to be dead, but she did not take a chance.

"Let go of the gun and put your hands on your head! Slowly!" As she stared, she noticed that his right eye showed signs of life. Behind the slit of an eyelid, the light gleamed in wait. He watched her closely, studying her like a wounded serpent eying a hungry hawk.

"Let go of the gun!" she cried.

Refusing to let go, he coiled his strength for a lightning-quick shot.

That was his second mistake.

The shotgun boomed, and his body jerked spasmodically as another load of buckshot slammed home. His eyes opened wide, glassy and lifeless, as he exhaled his final breath.

Cautious to the end, the sheriff kicked his pistol away before kneeling beside Jamie. As she touched the broken face of her dearest friend, the shock almost overwhelmed her.

"Oh, no!" The words came from deep within her: at once a moan and a plea. "Jamie, no!"

The attack had brutalized Jamie's beautiful face. Mutilated and bloodied beyond recognition, it seemed to swell by the second. "Baby, no!" she groaned. Sitting in the dust, she cradled her friend's broken head. "No!"

She began to weep as against her will, pictures emerged from her memory: Jamie smiling as they shared hot cocoa… the two of them laughing as they painted the farmhouse, beginning to heal after the death of Tommy Durrance. The images felt weighted with sorrow, as if Jamie were about to die.

"God, let her live," she moaned, lifting her eyes toward the heavens. "Lord Jesus, have mercy!" She punched the transmitter on her right shoulder. "Officer down! Officer down! This is Sheriff Rawlings at the Hawkins ranch. Special Agent Hawkins has been severely injured. Send an ambulance, now!" There was a pause before the dispatcher answered.

"An ambulance is on its way. Deputies are responding."

Gazing upwards, the sheriff closed her eyes and gritted her teeth. "God help me," she whispered grimly. She rubbed her tears away with bloody hands, inadvertently smearing her face with Jamie's blood. Remembering her prayers, she took courage. Her will began to harden, tempered deep within her pilgrim soul. *Whoever set this up will not escape,* she vowed, suddenly filled with fiery faith in inescapable, inerrant judgment.

She cradled Jamie's head and kissed her on the cheek, rocking in pain and sorrow. *Somehow... some way... somebody's gonna pay!*

Backpressure

Win Johnston, ill-tempered and obdurate, lay propped against a stack of pillows in the Cardiac Care unit at the Oree County General Hospital. Impatiently, he pressed the button to call for a nurse.

"Lunch is late," he barked into the speaker. Marcy frowned at him. They had come to the hospital as soon as they arrived in town, and by the end of a five-minute chat, her father's attention had turned to his next meal. *I could set my clock by his stomach,* she mused. *It's probably as accurate as the atomic clock at Greenwich.*

"Give them a break, Daddy. It's barely past noon."

"Gotta keep 'em on their toes, little girl," he replied with a wink. "Besides, they won't give me a straight answer around here. I need to know when I'm goin' home!"

"You've been sick. Very sick," Marcy replied, pursing her lips. "They want to play it safe."

"I'm ready to walk out, I tell you. I don't care what they say."

"Your doctor hasn't okayed it."

"I'm ready to split the scene of this accident, with or without her permission."

"You'd better not try," she replied ominously.

"What's got you so all fired up, little girl?" He raised his eyebrows and gazed innocently at the others in the room, recruiting their support. Lips pursed, Marcy sternly followed his glance as it traveled from face to face.

Danny and Ches smiled at Win, but Drew stared pensively out the window. The story of the Johnston family troubled him deeply. He reflected morosely on the apparently random madness of their lives: the years of personal damage wrought by Marcy's cousin, Pete Johnston, followed by the death of Marcy's mother, her father's heart attack, and the murder of Dan and Sarah.

In spite of these things, the family strove for normalcy. They persevered as world-class optimists, experts in the art of denial. They had gathered at Win's bedside in an attempt to forget their latest tragedy, hopeful that somehow, in some way, things would change for the better.

Drew eyed them skeptically. This family's ability to jettison the past may have served them well over the years, but he reasoned that it had to cause problems when taken to such an extreme. He sensed an angry reservoir of emotional backpressure lurking in the recesses of their collective psyche, building up steam and burning for a chance to vent.

"I'll leave this place when I want to," Win grunted. "The last I heard, I was still a free man."

"You'd better not test that theory," Marcy repeated sternly.

"I declare, you sound just like your mother, God rest her soul!" A smile flashed across his face. "Alright, I'll wait for the doctor's okay." He winked at Drew. "I'm afraid of what she might do. She's a lawyer, you know." Marcy gently pushed Win's shoulder.

"Daddy," She blushed. "I don't sue patients in hospitals."

"Oh, yeah, I forgot, you stick it to the hospitals, not the patients. You tilt at the giants on behalf of the squirts."

"That's not the way I'd put it."

"Okay, then, let's test the accuracy of my statement. Do you advocate for the poor?"

"Yes," she admitted.

"Free of charge?" he added hopefully.

"If our clients can't afford to pay."

"Do you ever sue large organizations, such as hospitals?"

"Yes."

"On behalf of the little guy... the average Jane or Joe?"

"Yes."

"Then I was correct. You tilt at giants on behalf of squirts."

"I give up."

"Help me! I'm poor. Sue this hospital and get me out of here!" He laughed loudly, ending with a bitter, body-wracking cough.

"What do you think?" he whispered to those in the room, struggling to regain his breath.

"You do beat all, Win," said Donny Hawkins. He stood beside the door, dressed in civilian clothes.

After working the morning shift, Donny had taken annual leave for the rest of the week so he could spend time with Jamie and attend the Johnston funeral. He had visited Winston at the hospital more than once during the past few weeks.

He thought of Jamie and smiled. *I love to surprise that girl*, he thought, anticipating the expression on her face as she opened the door of their farmhouse.

AT THAT MOMENT, A FAINT SOUND caught Donny's attention. It sounded wild and delirious, like the far-away wail of feral cats. Tantalizing and distant – and just beyond the threshold of apprehension – the sound drifted in and out of focus, like a cosmic radio tuned by an unseen hand. *What is that?* he wondered.

With a start, he recognized the sound. *Sirens.* He stirred and nodded. "Excuse me," he interjected politely. "I've gotta go."

"Sure thing, Donny," replied Win with a wave. "Kiss your pretty wife for me, okay?"

"Yes, sir," Donny replied shyly as he turned to leave the room.

Outside the door, he saw an orderly rushing toward the emergency room. He fell in step beside a nurse pushing a cart down the hallway.

"Do you know the reason for those sirens?" he asked. The nurse, a short young woman with fine black hair, stared at him blankly. "Are you a cop?"

"Yes."

"You haven't heard? A cop was shot," she repeated the rumor she had heard. "They're bringing her in."

"Her?"

"Yeah. It's a lady cop."

To the nurse's surprise, her audience rushed away mid-sentence. Donny ran blindly toward the emergency room, driven by instinctive dread. He felt unmoored, as if his head trailed behind his body like a balloon. His body, in the throes of panic, did not wait for his head to catch up. He rushed headlong past the elevator and past a nurse's workstation, dodging white-clad professionals, leaving startled glances behind him.

In a county with such a small population, Donny had to know the victim. Worse, given Jamie's painful past, he had a sick, sinking feeling that the victim would turn out to be the one true love of his life.

Emergency Ethics

Donny burst into the sterile, brightly-lit waiting room. Reacting without thinking, he showed his badge to a short, startled orderly and looked around, scanning the area, frayed and nonplussed.

"Where do the ambulances unload?" he asked brusquely. In response, the orderly pointed to his left.

By the time the first green squad car raced past the dock and squealed to a halt, Donny stood waiting on the loading dock, nervously awaiting bad news. Delia Rawlings climbed out of the cruiser, her pale green uniform smeared with dried blood. She placed her hands on the dock and jumped up, climbing to her feet and dusting herself off. Looking around, she noticed him.

"Donny," she blurted with a start. She paused, unsure of what to say. "I'm glad that you're here."

"Who's been shot?" he asked, straining to see the approaching ambulance. "Is it Jamie?" Delia grasped him firmly by the arm.

"Nobody's been shot. Come with me," she ordered gently. Like a small child, the big man complied, meekly allowing her to lead him down the steep steps into the harsh summer sunlight. They followed a landscaped path that wound away from the emergency room, stopping in a small clearing past the edge of the building. The summer heat pressed hard on their shoulders.

"Jamie has been hurt," she said bluntly. "She's been seriously injured, but her life is not in danger. Do you understand what I'm saying?" His eyes wandered.

"I understand." His gaze settled on Delia's face. He looked like a man who had been stunned by a body blow.

Donny had long dreaded this moment. Since the day he met her, Jamie had always faced danger: stalked and threatened, it seemed, by evil forces beyond her control. "How did it happen?" he whispered hoarsely. He cleared his throat and blinked, trying to focus.

"Someone tried to kill her, but I was able to rescue her. I killed the perpetrator," she added.

"What should I do?" He asked the question feebly, suddenly disoriented. He was at a loss, not wanting to interfere with the health care professionals. "How can I help?"

Delia glanced over his shoulder. "The ambulance is arriving. Stay with me. We'll watch over her. I'll ask someone at the station to bring you a uniform. Do you have your weapon?"

"It's in my glove box."

"Get your weapon and keep it with you. You can live in Jamie's room for as long as she's here." He turned to watch as the medical vehicle rolled into the loading area and swung wide to back up.

"What are you going to do, Sheriff?"

"I'm staying here until the deputies arrive to guard her room. I'll be calling the FDLE as soon as I get a chance. Between the FDLE and our deputies, we'll make this hospital one of the safest places in Florida." As the ambulance backed up to the dock, Donny put his hand out and gently touched Delia Rawling's shoulder.

"Thanks, Sheriff." They hurried back toward the dock. The ambulance opened and two men jumped out. Without wasted time or effort, they opened the back doors, unlatched the gurney, and lifted it onto the dock.

Donny gasped. A thin blanket covered his wife's body. Woven straps secured her to the stretcher like a bruised side of beef lashed to a meat packer's cart.

Jamie's face, swollen to the point of absurdity, resembled a Mardi Gras fright mask: a grotesque study in purple and blue. In spite of it all, she appeared to be conscious. Responding instinctively to Donny's presence, her open eye turned toward him and struggled to focus beneath a swollen lid as the medics began to roll the gurney into the emergency room.

"Mmmph," she grunted. Her jaw would not open. When she tried to speak, her jawbone – broken into fragments – grated against itself without managing to part her swollen lips.

To Jamie, the grating of bone against bone sounded uncannily loud. Like a solar storm from an evil sun, the unspeakable pain danced across her head, her eyes, and her bruised and battered soul.

Attuned to his wife's every grimace, Donny watched as her jaws flexed in vain. Astonished and dismayed, he heard the faint, ghoulish sound of bone painfully grinding against fragmented bone.

"Don't try to speak. Please, baby, don't even try," he said as he followed the gurney through the glass doors into the building. They traveled swiftly down the hallway together, Donny staring into her face. To Jamie, it seemed as if they floated down the hall. "You're going to be okay," he said. Her good eye shut, and she tried to wiggle a finger weakly in response. As the pain raced down her arm, she grimaced involuntarily, and her contracting facial muscles drove shards of agony into the core of her fractured head.

"God, please help her!" Donny whispered as they rolled through the double doors that led to the surgical center. Once again, evil men had dealt Jamie a bitter blow.

Recently, he and Jamie had discussed taking a vacation. They had hoped to spend quality time together.

This was not exactly what they had in mind.

A View from the Hill

It was not much of a hill, but it was the only one around. If Drew, Ches, Marcy, and Danny had not felt so wired, so completely awake, their protectors could have browbeaten them into staying home. Instead, they had all left the Johnston farmhouse at midnight, speeding off in Chesterfield's car, with Drew following close behind in the Thunderbird coupe he had rented in beautiful downtown Pezner. They were on a mission, determined to catch the view from the top of Overlook Hill.

When they had tried to rest, a cruel confluence of evil events had swirled haphazardly through their minds, keeping them awake. They would attend a double funeral tomorrow, and they had heard about the assault on Jamie Hawkins. They desperately needed a break... a few moments of normalcy in which they could find rest.

A contingent of four FDLE special agents followed in unmarked cars, complaining bitterly about their hard luck. Of the four souls they guarded, two were lawyers. Marcy and Ches had insisted that their little group could and would travel freely: wherever, whenever, and with whomever they wished.

Chesterfield parked his car in the small grassy clearing on top of the low, rounded hill. They climbed out slowly, stretching in the warm evening breeze. In the utter darkness of this remote area, with the moon hidden by a cumulous cloud, the ethereal clouds of quivering stars dominated the night sky, magnificently bright.

They had parked atop a stunted rural overlook. The hill would scarcely have qualified as a hump in a more mountainous locale, but here in Cutler County, it practically scraped the sky. Standing a whopping 100 feet high, Overlook Hill towered above the hard-baked, sugar-sand tableau of pan-flat Florida terrain that stretched in every directly: an ocean of scrub oaks spotted by splashes of snow-white sand and dry palmettos rattling in the breeze.

"What's that?" Chesterfield asked, pointing east toward a faint glow at the edge of the sky.

"That's the bustling metropolis of Pezner," Marcy said.

"They must have more streetlights than people," Drew observed.

"Are you sure that's Pezner? " Ches asked.

"Well, that's due south, and Pezner is the first town south of here," Danny informed him. "Duh! We drove through it today on the way to the hospital."

"It looks different at night," Ches suggested. "It's like a small, faint sunrise… suitable for a small child… like you, Danny." The boy smirked at him.

"If you say so, it must be true," Danny suggested, slicking back his dark red hair. *The smart-alecky brat,* Ches reflected. *I'd hate to face him in court.*

"The breeze feels good," Drew observed. "Real good." He spoke to no one in particular, which was just as well since no one listened.

Drew had the sweats.

In the throes of a nicotine withdrawal, he felt jittery and unsettled. Sweat beaded on his forehead, reminding him that he was in his third day of a full-blown, cigarette-free cold turkey.

On the outside, he seemed calm. On the inside, he suffered a firestorm of angst. His stomach surged like a blender stuck on puree. He felt like he would blow sky-high at the least provocation.

Drew did not merely crave a smoke. He yearned for a smoke like a parched wanderer yearns for water in the desert. He desired it… no, he ached for it. He longed to caress the rich, hot tobacco haze, to take in his mouth and painfully drag it down, suck it deep: burning his aching lungs, damaging cells piecemeal as he gobbled the smoke deep into his innermost being.

Drew smoldered for a smoke. He shivered at the thought, sick from the absence of toxic tobacco.

"Are you okay?" Danny asked, studying him closely. "You look terrible."

"I'm great, kid. Just great."

"I am, too. But I guess I'm the only one who thinks so."

Below the hill, they saw a car approaching on the two-lane highway. It stopped at the intersection, and the door opened.

The FDLE agents snapped to attention. The driver stepped out, emptied the ashtray, and drove away.

"False alarm," Danny said. "Unless you guys want to bust a litterbug."

"Not a bad idea," answered agent Tom Moynahan, the youngest of the four agents shadowing them tonight. "It's a slow night. Let's write him up."

"Ha!" his partner scoffed.

"I could stand some action. I'm from Miami. There's nothing to do out here."

"Dude," Drew replied. "I grew up in the country, and it was a lot like this. You're dissin' my roots."

"But you left the country for the city, right?"

"Yeah. But I still love the country."

"Do you mean to tell us that after selling out stadiums all around the world, you still like the boondocks?" asked Tom.

"Yeah, I guess I do," answered Drew, glancing at Marcy. Her distinctive blond hair seemed to glow in the starlight. *How does she do that?* "That's what I'm talkin' about," he whispered softly.

As Marcy leaned against the front of the Mercedes, the moon emerged from behind its cloud. In the moonlight, he could see her face clearly. Dressed in a clean white shirt, dark blue jeans and pale blue sandals, Marcy turned her face toward the sky, savoring the night like a child, immersed in the experience. She closed her eyes, drifting sweetly in the ambient lift of warm summer breeze.

"Boring?" Drew replied, wondering whether the law enforcement professional had gone mad. *With her around?* "I don't think so." He put his hand into his pocket, and his keys rattled. *Eureka!*

Drew approached Marcy hesitantly. He cleared his throat. *Great... I'm so accustomed to groupies, I've forgotten how to talk to a woman.* He stopped in front of her and paused.

"What?" She spoke, and then opened her eyes. He had not

spoken, but she had sensed his presence.

"Would you like to take a ride?"

"I don't think so," she answered warily. "I've heard bad things about you."

"Oh."

"Are they true?"

"I don't know what things you've heard, but if they're bad they're probably true. At least they were until a few weeks ago."

"What's changed?"

"I've been sober for more than three months."

"That's nice," she said politely. "It's a start." *I've been sober all my life,* she did not add.

"It's different being sober. I don't know how to describe it. Sobriety is… well… intense. It's unfiltered, you might say." He stared into the distance, searching for the words. "For the first time in years, I can smell the dew in the morning. I notice the color of the sky. I hear kids laughing."

"Really?"

"Yeah, really. I'm totally over my old way of life. Even if my new life goes downhill, I'm not going back."

"How do you know you'll be able to stay sober?"

"During rehab, I asked for help from a higher power." He cleared his throat. "It sounds stupid, I guess... but it works."

"It doesn't sound stupid to me."

"Really?"

"Really," she said softly, pushing herself away from the hood of the car and dusting off her jeans.

"Cool," he whispered.

"Well?" she asked.

"Well, what?"

"How about that ride?"

Not in Front of the Hand

John Dawes, forensic pathologist in charge of the night shift at the Dade County morgue, looked like one of his subjects. He presented the perfect picture of forensic decay: dour and long-faced, with a yellowing complexion stained and stretched paper-thin by years of painful drags on hot cigarettes. As gaunt and hollow as a South Beach supermodel, Dr. Dawes towered above his colleagues, a Caucasian authority figure crowned with white hair and wrapped in a clean white coat. When wielding a cigarette, he resembled the iconic doctor from the infamous Elvis-era advertising campaign... the physician who boasted that 'more doctors smoke Camels than any other cigarette.'

Some faces have character. John Dawes' face had outgrown the character phase. Sordidly unique, his countenance looked as tumbled and tortured as a topographical map of the Missouri Breaks: pale beige terrain scarred by intense vertical rifts. The deep declivities running the length of his face resembled nothing so much as the folds in a pockmarked leather bagpipe.

To John Dawes, death had paid off in spades. Over the course of a lengthy career, Dawes had looked at, carved up, sniffed, probed, and otherwise examined so many corpses that by now, almost nothing shocked him.

Dr. Dawes unceremoniously opened an autopsy drawer and slid out a stainless steel slab. He gazed at its grim contents without blinking, unfazed by the carnage: another day, another death: another honest dollar.

The oversized autopsy slab dwarfed the grisly remains upon it. In the middle of the stainless slab – tiny and out of place – lay a severed human hand: palm open as if petitioning for mercy. The fingers showed signs of savage mutilation, and much of the skin was missing, but otherwise it appeared to be well preserved.

"So this is the famous 'hand across the water' they're all talking about?" Dr. Dawes observed dryly. "Wasn't that a song?"

"Yep. And this is the bitter end of the lovely song," replied his companion, Ethan Braden. "Here lies the 'hand across the water'… fresh from the stinking belly of a dead Hammerhead shark."

Dr. Braden, a recently minted medical school graduate, served as second in command on the night shift. A stocky young black man with a goatee, thick glasses, and a clean-shaved head, Ethan admired the graveyard humor of Dr. Dawes and dearly loved his job in the morgue.

"What do you make of it?" Ethan asked. Glancing at Dawes, he watched as the old man flipped through paperwork, buried in the minutia of the case.

"It says here that they haven't received any reports of missing boaters," John Dawes observed, reading through the chart. "No reports of missing persons on the entire East Coast." He put down the chart and rubbed his eyes. "As for what to make of it, I don't have a clue. Yesterday afternoon, about 20 miles east of Hallandale, a shark vomited this hand onto the deck of a fishing boat. The boat docked in Miami, so we got the case. That's all I know."

"Was the day shift able to get fingerprints?"

"Nah. It's too degraded. Just look at it!" He stared intensely at the hand, leaning closer. Mumbling something unintelligible, he straightened up and turned back to the chart.

"How about DNA?" Ethan persisted.

"Romer ordered a workup. They sent the sample out this morning." The older man almost spat the words out, filled with disgust. Staff at the morgue hated Dr. Brent Romer, the Deputy Coroner for Dade County. An annoying bean counter, Romer had earned the disrespect of every employee in the department.

"Did he request expedited testing?"

"Nah," Dawes replied, flipping through the chart again. "He's too cheap."

"No surprise there."

"Hey… that gives me an idea."

"What?" In response to Ethan's question, John picked up the phone and dialed a number. "Romer, this is Dawes. Yeah, I know it's late." He rolled his eyes and moved his hand in a rolling motion. *Blah, blah, blah.* "Listen, I think we ought to expedite the DNA testing for the John Doe in Locker 12." He paused for a moment. "Yeah, the infamous hand." He held the receiver away from his ear and banged it on the table. "What did you say, Dr. Romer? You're breakin' up. What'd you say? Go ahead? Sure thing!" He hung up abruptly, snickering softly.

"What'd he say?"

"He hit the roof. He says that I spend the county's money like it's made out of paper. He thinks I'm a complete idiot."

"Is he right?"

"Not completely," he answered with a wink. "I'm an incomplete idiot."

"Don't take it too hard. Maybe you'll be a complete one someday."

"Maybe."

"What are you gonna do?"

"What do you think? I'm gonna drop a bee in his bonnet."

"An expedited DNA test?"

"Yep. It'll drive him crazy."

"Excellent."

"Where's the fax machine?"

"How would I know?"

"Find it, would you? I'm gonna do it. When he comes in tomorrow, he'll hit the roof. 300 bucks, but you'd think it was his money the way he acts."

"He'll freak," Ethan agreed. "I wish I could be here."

"Really?"

"No," he admitted. Dawes laughed and drummed his fingers on the shiny steel table.

"Well," Dawes stated with satisfaction, "*I* wish I could be here."

"Really?"

"Oh, yeah. But listen, I need a favor."

"Shoot."

"Let's see if we can get a good palm print. That'd really get Romer going. He'll be sick with jealousy if we ID the John Doe before he does." Walking to the sterile operating table, he turned on the powerful operating spotlight and began to don a pair of rubber gloves, humming tunelessly. As he readied the table, Ethan returned to the autopsy drawer and raised a magnifying glass to inspect the hand more carefully.

"A readable print? From that palm?"

"It's worth a shot."

"Hmm," Ethan mused, studying it closely.

"Would you mind stoppin' your yappin' and give me a hand?"

"Hey, watch it! I'm not yappin'," Ethan replied defensively.

"I said, could you give me a hand?"

Getting the joke, Ethan straightened up, adjusted his glasses, and grinned broadly. Dawes smiled back, nodding toward the grisly souvenir on the autopsy tray. To lifelong twerps passing as nerds with careers in forensic medicine, Dawes' wisecrack was sophisticated workplace humor.

"If I give you a hand, it might go to your head."

"Ha, ha; funny!" Dawes' grunted, chuckling with a curious dry croak. The sound was unnerving. Dawes laughed like a ghoul mocking the custom of human laughter.

"I could slam a Dew right about now," Ethan replied, licking his lips. Both men loved Mountain Dew, the official soft drink of night shifts.

"I could slam a jammin' Dew myself."

"I'd like a Snickers with my Dew. How about you?"

"Not in front of The Hand," John smirked. Health Department regulations forbade the consumption of food and beverages in autopsy areas.

Ethan and John laughed aloud. If it had been legal to crack open a soft drink in the presence of The Hand, they would have fetched their drinks and toasted their stupidity, right on the spot.

Word Hits the Street

On Tuesday morning, in a dirty bed on the outskirts of Atlanta, Streetcar awoke. He squinted at the clock. *Ten in the morning. I slept late.* He rolled out of bed, fully clothed in wrinkled jeans and a pale blue tee shirt. Rubbing his fingers through his long gray hair, he slipped on a pair of shoes and pushed the switch on a chipped black coffeepot before stepping out the front door.

On the street corner, he bought a copy of the Atlanta Constitution and beat a hasty retreat back down the block to his fleabag apartment. The place was filthy, but for now, it was home.

His elderly Maine Coon slept fitfully on the bed, twitching occasionally. His chest barely moved as he breathed. As Streetcar gazed at the sleeping cat, he felt a twinge of profound emptiness. The words of the veterinarian returned like the voice of doom. His cat might not live much longer. *We had a good run,* he told himself, but the thought did not cheer him.

Pouring a cup of coffee, he sat at the small, tottering breakfast table and opened the newspaper. As he began to read, his eyes widened and his mouth fell open.

"No!" he cried aloud, leaping to his feet. His thigh struck the table, scattering newspaper and coffee as he stared at the paper in his hands. A bolded heading midway down page one stunned and sickened him.

"Florida Officer Critical after Brutal Assault," the words cried. Below the heading he saw a photograph of the victim, Janelle "Jamie" Hawkins.

"No!" he shouted, waking the cat. He kicked the table and sent it crashing into the refrigerator. "Somebody's gonna pay!" He grabbed his keys and slammed open the front door.

In spite of his rage, his mind began to calculate the most logical path to revenge. *I've gotta call Ace. His line will be tapped by now, for sure.* He drove for several miles before parking in front of a busy Laundromat beside a deserted gas station. A lone phone booth stood among the weeds at the edge of the parking lot, and another pay telephone graced the filthy stucco walls outside the Laundromat. After writing down the numbers of both telephones and testing the receivers, he jumped into his car and drove several blocks to another pay phone, where he dialed a Tampa number. Hearing thunder, he looked up and squinted at the sky. *Rain. That figures.*

Alone in his office, Don Provencenti immediately picked up the phone. "James Provencenti," he said brusquely.

"Mr. Provencenti?" As a former musician with an exquisitely attuned ear, James "Ace" Provencenti immediately recognized Streetcar's distinctive voice. Given the circumstances, however, he decided to play dumb.

"Who is this?"

"I'm John Block. I'm a reporter for the Tampa Tribune."

"What do you want?" *John Block? That's a good one.*

"I'd like to request a confidential interview."

"That may not be so easy to arrange."

"The Tribune would greatly appreciate it."

"I must warn you, Mr. Block. Our conversation may not be confidential. My name has been in the papers recently. Some false accusations have been made. Who knows what's going on? It's been crazy."

"I understand, Mr. Provencenti. But don't you think the public has a right to know the truth?"

"Of course."

"Then we agree."

"What do you propose?"

"Can you give me your cell phone number?"

"Sure. It's 813-555-6487."

"Get into your car and drive. Bring your cell phone and plenty of change."

"Change?"

"Just do it. I'll call you back." Streetcar hung up and climbed into his car to return to the Laundromat.

Ace hurriedly left the room and called his bodyguards, who were playing gin rummy in the game room. They left his office in his armor-plated Ford Excursion with Rolando Micci, an old friend from King High School, behind the wheel. By the time they turned onto Dale Mabry Boulevard, the Don's phone emitted an annoying chirp.

"Provencenti here."

"This is John Block." Streetcar leaned against the wall of the Laundromat as he spoke.

"Mr. Block, I can't guarantee the confidentiality of this conversation."

"Stop at a gas station," Streetcar said. "I'll stay on the line."

"Rollo," Ace said, pointing ahead. "Pull into that Shell station."

"Sure thing." The big vehicle wheeled into the station and rolled up to the pump.

"Now what?" Don Provencenti asked into the telephone.

"Go to the pay phone." The Don hung up and quickly walked to the telephone.

"What now?"

"Hang up your cell and dial 863-555-4682." A few seconds later, the telephone at the Laundromat rang, echoing through the deserted parking lot. Streetcar slowly picked up the receiver.

"Mr. Provencenti?"

"Yes."

"Go to another pay phone and call me at 863-555-7466," Streetcar hung up the receiver and trudged across the parking lot toward the other pay phone booth. He picked up after the second ring.

"Ace?" he asked.

"Make it quick."

"Who tried to kill Jamie?" There was a brief pause on the other end of the line.

"The biggest Don in Chicago," Ace replied.

"What's his name?"

"Antonio Brucci."

"What's his address?"

"He works from the top floor of the Kefauver Tower. It's the old federal building, downtown." The irony did not escape either of them.

"Give me the name of somebody who works for this guy. I need an in."

"Try Gabor's Sports Bar on SW 47th. There's a bookie there named Bronco Everett."

"The wrestler?"

"Not anymore. He runs the biggest sports book on the south side."

"What's his security?"

"He's a made man. He doesn't need security."

"Good."

"If they find out what you're up to, some folks will think you've been workin' for me all along."

"That won't hurt your reputation, will it?"

"No."

"But we know better. I never worked for you." In a flash, Ace remembered Streetcar's persona when he had lived in Ybor City: like just another street person, more friendly than most, and a little loopy, but as harmless as a bunny. Who could have guessed that he would prove to be a stone killer… better than the best?

"What can I do for you, Street?"

"You can pay for my funeral if I don't make it back. I don't want to be buried in an unmarked grave." They paused.

"Anything else?"

"Yeah. Take care of my cat. Okay?"

"Sure."

"I'll board him at the Lowery Animal Hospital in south Atlanta, under the name Ira Freeman."

"What's his name?"

"Cat."

"That's logical."

"I'll pay the bill in advance, and I'll tell 'em that my cousin Ace will be comin' by to pick him up."

"I'll keep him safe."

"Good. Take care of him if I die, okay?"

"I'll find a good home for him, Street."

"Thanks, Ace."

"De nada."

"Uh... Ace..."

"Yeah?"

"He likes tuna."

"All cats like tuna, Street." Ace felt a chuckle coming on.

"Oh, yeah."

Ace guffawed spontaneously, and his infectious humor spread to Sal. They began to laugh heartily in spite of themselves, surprised by the passing ray of humor. After a moment, they caught their breaths. Neither of them wanted the conversation to end.

"You've always been straight with me, Ace." Streetcar paused uneasily. "You should've stayed away from this kind of life."

"You too, Street." Ace lowered his head and rubbed his eyes with his right hand. "Look, we've gotta wrap it up, okay?"

"Yeah."

"Listen, Street. If you survive, do me a favor."

"What?"

"Call the La Bamba Grill in Dade City, north of Tampa. Ask for a guy named Troutman. Les Troutman. Tell him your name is Monty Green. Can you remember that?"

"He's Les Troutman. I'm Monty Green."

"Right. He'll get you anything you need. Anything."

"The La Bamba Grill in Dade City?"

"Right. Les Troutman."

"What a name."

"Les is more, Street. And listen, about that promise you made to stay away from Florida?"

"Yeah?"

"Forget about it. We're square."

"Thanks, Ace."

"Adios." Reluctantly, they hung up.

Thinking about his new mission, Streetcar's head began to swim. Word of the assault on Jamie had wrenched his emotions out of joint. He felt chain-sawed down the middle of his soul. He could scarcely bear it. His mind struggled to stay afloat as his spirit spiraled downwards.

He longed to converse with someone: anyone. He wanted to call Ace again, but he knew better. He would have to proceed without the luxury of human companionship.

Within him, the anger grew by the minute. He battled in vain, struggling to retain a shred of self-control. *Don't lose it!* He felt empty and useless, whipsawed between wrath and grief.

Years ago, in Ybor City, Streetcar had taken vengeance after the murder of Jumbo Poindexter, his only friend. Knife work had led to gun work, then to flaming, bloody fireworks. His grand finale had been, quite literally, the bomb. He had detonated Mob headquarters in the heart of Ybor City, killing seven men while demolishing most of a city block.

Although revenge had satisfied him temporarily, it had seared his conscience and bitterly scorched his soul. Revenge had cast a pall across his lonely, miserable life. The memories plagued him. Warped dreams vexed his sleep like smoke twisting upwards from the mouth of a gun. When the nightmares came, he would wake in a sweat, revisiting the fatal carnage.

Vengeance had come too easily on that grim and fateful night. The bright, shiny packs of high-tech ordinance had served him well, lined up for battle like well-drilled GIs in neat little green plastic rows. Looking back, it seemed inconceivable that the compact, obedient blocks of malleable C4 had destroyed an entire city block.

In his nightmares, he still saw the fear, smelled the gun oil mingled with the tang of burnt powder, and sniffed the stench of fresh-spilled blood. He saw their surprised faces as the hot pain seized their souls: men once so hard, now pitifully soft… rendered squishy and weak by the terrifying onrush of their own, sudden demise.

Streetcar understood that his revenge had been wrong... inescapably wrong. The act of murder was a crime against God and humanity. He knew it intellectually, he knew it viscerally, but now, he did not care. News of the attack on Jamie had cut him to the quick. His mended ways were unraveling before his eyes.

He lifted his eyes and remembered the vows of a former life. *I should have followed you, Lord. I should've, but I didn't.*

Now, he made up his mind. Once again, he would make a wrong turn. He would follow the path of vengeance.

Streetcar would force Jamie's attackers to pay bitterly. He would confiscate their lives to repay their debt. He knew it was wrong, but he simply did not care.

He would go to Chicago and find the famous Don Brucci. He would visit the great man in his towering skyscraper. Up close and in person, he would make this devil pay his dues.

If Streetcar had his way, Don Brucci would be leaving Chicago soon, bound for a famous destination. He would not need to pack.

At Streetcar's expense, the famous gangster would descend to the ultimate Sin City: a come-as-you-are resort where the souls of its revelers burned at both ends. The infamous locale invariably exceeded the expectations of its guests. In season and out, the weather remained famously warm. Every room allowed smoking, and the Don would never again have to shovel snow.

There was only one little problem.

It would be hot as hell.

Dead Serious

"Thank you for agreeing to speak with us on such short notice, and at such a difficult time." The tall senior agent leaned forward as he spoke: packed with nervous energy, but hiding it well.

"I don't know if we can help you," Marcy replied. "None of us know where Peter is." She spoke the words tersely, staring at the table. "He's betrayed our family. He killed…" she stopped speaking, unwilling to say the words in front of Danny. *He killed Dan and Sarah… my brother and his precious, perfect wife.*

"We're sorry about your loss," the agent offered.

"Thank you. It's hard to talk about it."

"Of course."

"We're a determined family. We don't dwell on the past."

"Your brother Dan was a hero."

"Sarah was a hero, too."

"Of course."

"How can we help you?" She gazed up at them inquisitively.

Four federal agents sat on the other side of a large mahogany table. Across from the agents sat Ches, Marcy, Drew, and Danny… recently returned from the double funeral of Dan and Sarah Johnston.

They had agreed to meet with the agents due to the urgency of the request. Pale and shaken, Marcy and Danny sat rigidly upright in their chairs. She bore the world-weary expression of an experienced Legal Aid attorney, but Danny stared with naive curiosity somewhat stunted by exhaustion.

The day had been brutally hot. In a concession to the South Central Florida heat, the Florida-based feds wore short-sleeved white shirts fronted by the obligatory black tie. Despite their prima facie respectability, they looked guilty somehow, like perpetrators from a white-collar criminal lineup. The lead agent, a square block of a man with a five-o'clock shadow and a graying flattop, looked vaguely displeased for no apparent reason.

To the right of the lead agent sat a petite, dark-haired Caucasian female with a red ribbon in her hair and a small scar above her lip. To her right sat a dark Hispanic male, about six feet tall and 35 years old with thick eyebrows, heavy chin, and the faded tattoo of an arrow on his right forearm. At the left of the lead agent, a slim, dapper, dark blond Caucasian male could scarcely restrain his boredom. He reclined in stylish insouciance, rapping his manicured nails lightly against the table as he pretended to listen.

At the head of the table sat Delia Rawlings. During the past few days, she had spent considerable time in the sun, and as a result, she looked particularly black and beautiful. Her smooth, dark skin contrasted sharply against the richly dyed resonance of her hunter green uniform.

The lead agent cleared his throat and paused. Gazing into Marcy's eyes, he popped a question that none of them expected.

"Do you know what has happened to your cousin, Peter Johnston?"

"What do you mean?" she asked, puzzled.

"Do you know anyone who wanted to kill him?"

"Kill him?" she echoed, too shocked to comprehend his question. She gaped at the agent incredulously.

"Did something happen to Uncle Pete?" Danny blurted. "Is he dead?" Delia Rawlings sat up, glancing sharply at the four federal officers. She knew nothing about this line of questioning. Predictably, the agents avoided her gaze as the sheriff raised her hand, palm out.

"What are you doing? This is not the way to deliver bad news," Delia growled ominously. "This family just came from a double funeral."

"You're kidding!" Danny interjected, standing so abruptly he knocked his chair to the ground. "Are you saying that Uncle Pete is dead? This is how you tell us?" The agent ignored Danny and leaned closely forward, staring across the table into Marcy's eyes.

"Are you saying that you know nothing about the death of Peter Johnston?"

"Know? How could we know?" She asked in amazement. "What are we, a crime family? Do you think we had something to do with it?"

"Are you saying this is the first you've heard of his death?" the agent asked stubbornly, unwilling to abandon his original line of inquiry.

Drew, experienced with moral corruption in high places, recovered quickly. He straightened his back and stared carefully at the agent.

"You, sir, are way out of bounds."

"I'm not talking to you," the agent replied sharply. *Druggie scum.*

Still on his feet, Danny shook with anger. He pointed his finger toward the agent's face.

"You're just like Uncle Pete! You're a big, fat bully!"

"Danny, please," Marcy whispered, still in shock from the news of her cousin's death.

"Bully!" Danny shouted in disgust. "Just like Uncle Pete, you big ol', block-headed bully!"

"Danny!" Marcy interjected sharply, standing and shaking his arm. "Stop that! Sit down." He looked at Marcy, saw the pain in her eyes, and shut his mouth. Meekly, Danny sat. Slumping forward with his elbows on the table, he cradled his burning face in his hands.

"Danny, apologize to the man," Marcy persisted with tears in her eyes. Chesterfield, Drew, and Delia stared at her in disbelief, not knowing how it would turn out. *He's 13 years old*, Delia remembered.

"Why?" Danny asked, weakened but defiant.

"You called him names." She eyed Danny with the jaded gaze of experienced authority. "You were raised better than that." In spite of his anger, Danny perceived an overpowering parental logic behind her reasoning. *What would Mama want?*

"Can't we pretend I didn't say it?" he asked hopefully.

"No. Apologize."

"For sure?"

"Danny..." her tone changed. He took a deep breath and puckered his face like a swimmer about to plunge into a sewer.

"I'm sorry," he said. "I was mad. Angry mad, not crazy mad." He smiled coyly and winked at Marcy. She did not smile back.

Now, it was Delia's turn. She arose majestically, rising from her chair like a queen from the ancient past. She towered over the agents: grim, solemn, imperious, and deadly serious.

"Now listen up, boys and girls." As she spoke, she strafed the agents with an elegant black finger. "This is my room, and this is my building." She stated the facts flatly, without a smile to soften the blow. In her anger, she reverted to the schoolyard vernacular of her Tampa childhood. "I allowed y'all folks to interview the family, here in my station, as a favor. This interview took place by my good graces. Get it? But now, I'm fresh out of good graces."

"We should have told you, Sheriff..." the senior agent began, but Delia waved him to silence.

"Stop! Not another word." Her nostrils flared, and her eyes narrowed. "This is not about me, officers," she frowned and pointed at each in turn, taking her sweet time. "Believe it or not, this is not about you, either. This is about the Johnston family. *This* family. This is the family of a hero who saved my life... a hero who was murdered only four days ago. Believe you me, I am not ungrateful to him, or to his family." Her anger had built slowly, like the flame in a brick kiln. Now, it ignited. "These people, officers, are the law-abiding citizens we are supposed to serve. But you – with your moral superiority – you have kicked them while they're down."

"Yes, ma'am," the agent replied softly. The truth of her statement chastened him. He could see which way the wind blew. These people, including the sheriff, loved one another. In his zeal to discover whether the family had a criminal connection with Peter Johnston, he had breached the bounds of common decency.

"So, spit it out. Is Peter Johnston dead?" Delia pinned the lead agent with a laser gaze from narrowed eyes.

"We think so," he replied.

Hearing this, Delia turned to Marcy and Danny. She spoke to them softly, with profound sensitivity.

"Marcy, do you want to hear about it?"

"Yes," Marcy nodded.

"Then go ahead," she snarled, waving her hand dismissively. "Tell them everything you know." The lead agent nudged the man who lounged distractedly in the chair to his left.

"McNair, tell them everything," he ordered.

"Everything?" McNair asked. He could deliver an encyclopedic treatise upon demand. The lead agent sighed and rolled his eyes.

"Summarize, McNair. Summarize everything we know." *We don't want to be here all day.*

"Okay." The younger man sat up self-consciously and straightened his tie. He was a slim scholar in his late 30s topped with oily blond hair, clad in tanned skin manufactured from chemical goop, death rays from tanning booths, and organic colorants. On the surface, agent McNair looked handsome. He seemed vaguely hungry: superficially intense, like a tuxedo model yearning for a solid meal.

"This morning, we received a call from the Dade County Coroner's office," he began. "They identified a palm print belonging to Peter Johnston. Based on their evidence, it appears likely that he is dead. We are not 100% certain, but I believe it's obvious." In the quiet room, Chesterfield Hamilton cleared his throat.

"What's the evidence?" Ches asked.

McNair glanced uncomfortably at his boss. "The palm print, which matches Peter Johnston's, was lifted from a severed hand," he mumbled. At this, Danny's eyes opened wide, alight with morbid curiosity.

"Uncle Pete's hand was cut off?"

"Yes... uh, well, they think it was bitten, not cut."

"Where did they find it?" Danny asked.

"On Sunday afternoon, the hand was regurgitated from the belly of a hammerhead shark onto the deck of a party boat, somewhere off the east coast of Florida."

"No!" Danny gasped. He felt simultaneously fascinated and repulsed.

"I'm afraid so."

"What happened to the rest of Uncle Pete?" Danny asked, unable to shut his mouth. For a teen-aged boy, the story held dreadful appeal. *Uncle Pete, dead?* The thought of his uncle's death created an odd mixture of emotions, at once comforting and cutting.

"We can only speculate, but it doesn't look good for your uncle," the analyst replied dryly, staring distractedly in their direction. He looked, but did not really see the family.

"Police in South Florida have interviewed witnesses and confirmed the facts. Shear patterns on the wrist indicate the hand was severed by a bite: most likely from the shark that... uh... delivered the hand to our attention." He spoke dispassionately, as if dictating a memo. "The coroner estimates the time of death as early Saturday morning, within hours of the fugitive's escape from the Broward County Jail. Based on these facts, we believe that Peter Johnston was murdered early Saturday morning, just after his escape, and that his body was dumped in the Atlantic Ocean. The hand appears to have been ingested just before the shark was caught."

Marcy, Danny, Drew and Ches stared at one another. The story seemed surreal. After the tumult of the past few days and the outpouring of grief at today's funeral, they could scarcely absorb the news.

Danny suddenly lost interest in the details of his uncle's death. "Can we go now?" he asked, looking at his Aunt Marcy. "Please?"

"Of course," Marcy replied. She stood. "We'll talk to you later," she said to the agents. "Thanks, Delia," she added with a smile in the sheriff's direction. A tear trembled at the edge of her eye, but she blinked, refusing to let it fall.

Marcy looked around at her companions and gestured gently, like a farmer directing a small flock of sheep. "Let's go." Without a word, Ches, Drew, and Danny stood up and followed her out the door. Delia followed close behind.

"Marcy," Delia said gently, touching her arm. "I didn't know about your cousin Pete. Are you okay?"

"Sure," she replied with an unconvincing smile, continuing to walk down the hall. Delia squeezed her shoulder.

"I'll be by the hospital later to visit your daddy."

"Thanks for everything, Sheriff."

"No, please; it's your family that deserves the thanks."

"I have a question," Marcy asked, pausing as the others continued into the foyer. "If Peter is dead, does that put us out of danger?"

"I think so. But honey, I'm so sorry you had to learn this way."

"It's not your fault."

"You'll have to excuse me," Delia added. "I need to share some choice words with our friends from the FBI."

"Thanks," Marcy smiled sadly. "We'll see you at the hospital."

Marcy followed her companions out of the cool building, into a blast of late afternoon heat. The sun had dipped low in the pink-singed sky, announcing the onslaught of another humid night. Drew stopped, waiting for Marcy to catch up.

Last night, Marcy and Drew had driven in the convertible for hours through the rural countryside with the top down, talking beneath the dark summer sky. Arriving at the Johnston farmhouse at dawn, they had staggered to their respective beds, bone-weary but happy, their troubles momentarily forgotten. Four hours later, they awoke to get dressed for the funeral.

The double funeral had hurt them deeply. Their emotions throbbed with a dull, overwhelming ache, like the pain from a cracked bone: as unrelenting as the summer sun that had pounded them at the graveside. Drew had weathered the ceremony uneasily, out of place and unsettled. He could only imagine the misery that Marcy and Danny had endured.

As the sun sank below the horizon to mark an end to another doleful day, Drew and Marcy watched Danny and Ches hastening down the sidewalk ahead of them. The boy and the aging attorney rushed toward the car, as if to flee from the waning day. As Marcy walked beside Drew without seeing him, she hung her head, wrapped in sorrow. Watching her, he felt a surge of pity.

"Uh, Marcy," he said uncertainly as he fell into step beside her. After the trauma of the past few days, their emotions throbbed: jagged and raw like stripped wires, highly charged and dangerous to the touch.

He lightly placed his hand on her arm. "Hey, Marcy."

"What do you want?" she asked sharply, pulling her elbow away.

"I... I just want to say that I'm sorry. I'm so very sorry about everything." His face bore a curious expression of perplexity mingled with pain. Marcy stopped and stared at Drew as Danny and Ches continued to hurry toward the parking lot.

"I mean," Drew repeated uncertainly. "I just wanted to say it." *You are so beautiful,* he thought but could not say. Complicating his attempt to communicate, Drew's voice had constricted as if an unknown force clutched him by the throat.

"We'll make it," she replied. "As a family, we've been through a lot. Nothing like this, but we'll survive anyway."

"What you're going through is just unbelievable. I wish I could help."

"Look, I know that you care," she replied, looking up into his eyes. "It shows." He stared down at her, at a loss for words.

Marcy's smoothly tanned face stood out as if it had been deliberately lit by the sun's last beckoning rays: golden and fair, with light freckles that provided a faint overlay of appealing imperfection. Her eyes, so green and piercing, seemed to cut to the chase, stirring his soul. Her gaze felt almost painful, her beauty overwhelming... pale blond hair glimmering in the breeze, sea-green gaze so straight, sincere. Her face reflected innocence, yet looked fully informed: pure in sincerity, but wise to the world. Marcy lacked naiveté without suffering for the loss.

"Look," she said. "You've been a real help to our family. If you want to move on, that's okay. We appreciate all you've done."

In response to her words, he felt a surge of blood stir deep in his heart. *She has no idea.* He rested his hand lightly on her arm. This time, she did not push away.

"You have no idea, do you?"

"What?" she asked, afraid of what she might hear.

"It's just..." he tried to speak, but could not overcome the pressure against his throat.

"What?"

"I think I love you, Marcy," he forced the words out. "I can't breathe without you." Marcy shook her head.

"That's crazy."

"It's true."

"You can't mean that. We met three days ago!"

"I mean it."

"You're on the rebound... you're bouncing back from a traumatic period in your life."

"That's true, but so is this. I love you, Marcy." His own words shocked him, but he plowed ahead. "I know it's crazy, but it's true."

"You can't," she breathed, shaking her head. "I thought that you just liked our family." Her voice trailed off. Her head felt light.

"I do. Your family is terrific. But that's not what I'm talking about." He faced her with both hands on her arms.

"I'm in love with you, Marcy," he said. He shook his head, trying to clear the cobwebs. *She is so beautiful.* She blinked at him, stunned.

"You're going through a lot," she began. "Maybe it's..."

"Please," he whispered. She stopped, interrupted by his hand as he touched her face. "I didn't know that something like this could happen." He stared into her eyes as tears began to pour down her face. "God help me, I'm a living cliché," he groaned. "I didn't even believe in love. Now I've fallen like a chain-sawed tree."

"Stop saying that," Marcy protested, shoving him weakly in the chest. And yet, despite her grief – despite everything – she felt a tidal pull against her soul: the thrill of blossoming love, the ebb and flow of its mystical, intoxicating pulse.

"My timing is wrong, but I can't help it. I love you, Marcy: your heart, your face, your soul: everything I can see and hear and touch about you. It hurts me to think about you, but I don't want to stop." He paused, not knowing whether or how to continue.

"Shut up," she whispered. Her knees weakened along with her will. The exoskeleton of Johnston family toughness, so hard and formidable, melted like smoke in the wind.

Drew wrapped his arms around her and held her tightly. Tears streamed down his face, wetting her hair.

"What are we going to do?" she asked. She was a good Christian girl, levelheaded and studious: assiduously unaccustomed to the unpredictable gyrations of a heart in the throes of love.

A loud sound from the parking lot shattered their reverie. Ches had finally cracked. He was shaking his fist at Danny and yelling at the top of his voice.

"Let me in that car, you little rascal!" They looked up to see Ches with his back to them, pounding loudly on the window of his car. Safely locked inside, Danny twirled the keys insouciantly.

"Help!" the boy cried, his voice muffled by tightly shut windows. "I'm being attacked by a madman! Help, police!" Attempting to gather their wits, Marcy and Drew reluctantly released one another and stared at the spectacle. He cleared his throat, and she wiped her eyes discreetly.

"That boy is a danger to himself and to others," Drew stated matter-of-factly. Turning, he wiped the tears from his face with his open hand.

"I hate how he teases Chesterfield," Marcy said disapprovingly. Gathering her wits, she stalked past Drew and bore down on the car, embarrassed and nonplussed.

"Danny Johnston!" she called. "Open that car and give Ches his keys!" She shouted with authority, but her tone did not convince Danny, smugly ensconced in the luxurious car. Marcy had never served time as a parent, and her voice lacked the proper edge.

"Lord, please help us," Drew sighed, looking upward. "This is what I've stepped in the middle of!" In spite of it all, he smiled.

Face to Face

At 5:00 that afternoon, two agents from the FBI visited the downtown headquarters of Worldwide Financial Services. After a short wait, the receptionist escorted them to a small conference room with a large oval desk and several well-padded leather chairs. In the room waited James Provencenti and Brad Johnston, the ancient, sun-scalded attorney who served as his consigliore. Both men stood when the agents entered.

"You must be agents McLain and Ebbes," the Don said softly. "This is my attorney, Bradley Johnston."

The men nodded at the tanned octogenarian, as handsome and dapper as a fit man in his 50s. Decades of workaholic excess, liquor, tobacco, hard partying, and intemperate sunbathing had preserved Brad Johnston like a mummy pickled in a tomb of vice.

"To what do I owe this dubious honor?" The Don inquired humorously. The agents did not smile as he gestured for them to sit. Don Provencenti was a good-looking, tallish, fit man in his 40s with long dark hair just beginning to turn gray. He did not resemble his Italian father, but favored his handsome Jewish mother. In the Don, nature had fused Semitic good looks with the bravery, cunning, tactical skills, and political savvy of a Sicilian chess master.

Todd McLain and Wolfgang Ebbes, two of the best interrogators at the Tampa branch of the FBI, had not come to play. They had come to rattle the cage of Tampa's Don of Dons, hoping to shake loose some information. They did not bear gifts, but freshly inked court orders, and they wore wires beneath their buttoned-down white shirts.

They had a plan, and they had backup. But for all of that, as they sat across from the Don, they uneasily suspected that they would be outclassed. After all, they were facing off against the most powerful gangster in the southeastern United States, not to mention his legendarily slippery mouthpiece, Brad Johnston.

The paneled room in which they sat spoke volumes about the discreet application of power: dark wood, lush fabrics, and richly appointed decorations both meticulous and tasteful. The target of their investigation wore a fine silk suit that fit like a kid glove. Don Provencenti and his lawyer seemed as cool as a pair of home-brewed Ybor beers reclining in a bucket of ice. *They knew we were coming,* Wolfgang realized with a start. *Do they have a mole in our office?*

"We're here to ask a few questions," he began with alacrity.

"Before you begin, my client wants it on the record that he is willing to cooperate," the attorney replied. "But first, I have a question of my own. Is Mr. Provencenti a person of interest in your investigation?" Wolfgang Ebbes cleared his throat and straightened his tie, buying time to consider a reply. Agent Ebbes, a tall, thin man, played Mutt to his partner's feisty Jeff. For years, they had parlayed their act into success, worrying their prey to distraction: comical, but remarkably effective professionals.

"We can't address that question," he stated. "If your client were under investigation, it would be confidential."

"Fair enough," Brad Johnston replied. "However, you realize that, absent your assurance, I may advise him not to reply to some questions."

"Fine," Wolfgang snapped. *Lawyers.* Getting a grip, he turned toward the Don without offering a smile. "Mr. Provencenti, do you know anything about the recent crimes against state witnesses in South Central Florida?"

"Of course I do; that's big news. I know what I read in the papers and see on TV. A racist drug dealer killed his cousin, right? That's what the papers say. His name is Peter Johnston. No relation to Brad." His attorney smiled at the mention of his name.

"Are you saying that you don't know anything about these crimes beyond what's been mentioned in the news?"

"Sure. What else would I know?" he asked in surprise. "I'm a financier."

Until this moment, agent Todd McLain had bided his time

impatiently. The last glib response irked him, and he decided to jump in.

"Don't play us for fools," agent McLain hissed. "Everybody knows who you are."

"Who am I?" Don Provencenti asked innocently.

"You're a scumbag gangster, that's who. You're the boss of bosses. No hood in Florida would dare kill someone this important in your territory without your okay."

"Please, calm down, Mr. McLain. You're unattractive when you're angry." He shot a glance at agent Ebbes and smiled. "He turns purple," he whispered with a wink. In spite of himself, Ebbes fought back a smile.

Leaning back in his chair, the Don waved his hand dismissively. "You've got a bad attitude, Mr. McLain. But I want to help you anyway." As his attorney started to protest, the Don shook his head. "Please, Brad, I might be able to help them. It's not about me. It's about the victims."

Hearing the Don's reply, his attorney smiled inwardly. *The Don could charm a lamb from a hungry wolf.*

"What do you know?" Wolfgang continued.

"I know that I hope you catch the racist pig who did this crime, and I hope that you give him the needle. Or better yet, bring back the electric chair just for him," the Don stated emphatically. "I'll throw the switch myself."

"Peter Johnston has escaped from state custody."

"I know that. It's in the papers," the Don replied. *Don't worry, boys,* he reflected jovially. *The Bruccis did the job on that idiot. They saved the taxpayers a bundle.*

"A funny thing about that escape," Wolfgang continued. "Do you think he got away unharmed?"

"Didn't he?"

"Do you think he's still alive, Mr. Provencenti?" Both agents watched the Don's face closely. To their disappointment, his face showed nothing but heartfelt concern.

"What do you mean?"

"On Sunday, a party of fishermen in a chartered boat found one of Peter Johnston's hands inside a shark's belly."

"What?"

"How do you think that happened?"

"That's incredible!" the Don responded with genuine surprise. To all appearances, he looked like a clueless civilian fascinated by a grisly news report. "How did it happen?"

"That's what we're asking you. What happened?"

"Did the shark eat him, or did it just bite off his hand?" the Don asked. "Maybe Peter Johnston had his hand amputated and fed to a shark, just to throw you guys off the trail. Unlikely, but possible. I'd take a hard look at that fishing party if I were you." Sickened by the Don's irreverent tone, McClain had heard enough.

"Is that the best you've got?" he interjected bitterly. *He's playin' us.*

"That's what came to mind," the Don replied glibly. At his reply, McLain jumped to his feet.

"Maybe Pete Johnston was killed by a puke like you and dumped in the Atlantic," he blurted angrily. "Maybe you did it!" In response, Brad Johnston stood up: indignantly, dramatically shocked. He stared angrily at the agent.

"Mr. McLain, your accusation is completely inappropriate. This interview is over." Responding to Brad's well-engineered wrath, Don Provencenti raised his hand in a conciliatory gesture.

"It's okay, Brad. Let me have my say. Then, we can all go home."

"Well... all right, Mr. Provencenti," Brad replied, sitting down in a huff. "But this is outrageous." The Don smiled at his attorney and looked at the two agents, raising his eyebrows. He gestured with one hand to McLain, who warily took a seat.

"Gentlemen, let's finish this, once and for all," he whispered softly. The two agents moved uneasily in their chairs. *Finish this, once and for all?* They eyed the door warily, wondering what he meant.

"All right," McClain replied, clearing his throat nervously. "We have one more question," McLain continued. "Yesterday, two bodies were found in the woods beside an overpass at Interstate 75. The victims were gangsters from New York City. There is some indication that they may have planned to murder state witnesses. It looks to us like they were stopped in the very act. Do you know anything about that murder?"

"You're asking me about another murder? Please, officers, I'm a businessman, not a punk… or a puke." The Don locked his gaze on Wolfgang. "As I said, let's finish this. I'll make a statement, and then our interview is over."

The Don eyed the two officers critically. Shaking his head, he opened a humidor on his desk. Giving a fine Cuban cigar to Brad, he offered one to each of his visitors, who sourly waved him off. He shrugged and smiled at his attorney, leaning back with a happy sigh. They clipped the ends off their aromatic Havanas in perfect tandem, like synchronized swimmers. Striking a kitchen match against a rough granite paperweight, the Don lit Brad Johnston's cigar, followed by his own, shaking out the fading flame just before it burned his fingers. They puffed deeply, ignoring the discomfort of their visitors.

"That's good," the Don murmured.

"Mighty fine," Brad agreed. The hot hiss of burning leaf, interrupted by satisfied puffs, tantalized the agents almost as much as the rich smell of illicit Cuban smoke.

The Don turned to the agents and smiled, wreathed in fumes. He looked like an evil, hip Saint Nick offering naughty presents to good little boys. The two feds squinted skeptically as he began to speak.

"Crimes against witnesses… crimes against visitors, crimes against law officers: such acts are stupid and senseless. They generate bad press. They're bad for business in the Sunshine State. These types of crimes hurt innocent civilians and scare tourists. You know that we Floridians live and die by the tourist trade. We share that in common, even with you."

Don Provencenti glanced at agent McLain and pointed his

index finger like a gun. "Boom, boom," he said with a crooked smile. "The path of the gun is a bloody awful path. It's a slippery slope for fools to slip on, and fall on, and die. Not to mention that it's bad for business."

"You're saying you had nothing to do with these crimes?"

"Yes, that's what I'm saying," the Don lied brusquely. "I'm not the criminal scum that you think. But if I *were* a criminal, be assured that I would not attack an officer of the law." He looked at Brad, who nodded knowingly. "That would be madness, not business. No private citizen in his right mind would openly defy the power of the state." He paused, weighing his words. "As for the two men killed near I-75, they sound like very bad men who met a very bad end. I can't speak to that."

Wolfgang listened intently, parsing every word. *Can't, as in won't?* he wondered. *He's choosing his words like a lawyer. He had those men killed, and he wants us to know it!*

"What do you know about the attack on the FDLE agent?" Wolfgang interjected.

"You know the answer to that," the Don replied. "Do I look crazy to you?"

"Not quite," Ebbes replied.

"I know nothing about that terrible crime," the Don replied blandly, "but I can offer a guess as a concerned citizen who follows the news. I would guess that the assault was arranged by the redneck Peter Johnston before his escape. Obviously, he did not plan to wind up in the belly of a shark. Surely a man like him might choose to kill an officer who protected someone he hated. For him, such a thing might be personal. If the attack was not arranged by him, however, I think it would have to be someone with no roots in our state." The two federal agents stared at him, shocked by the Don's openness.

"What do you mean?" McLain inquired suspiciously.

"I love Florida. I respect her citizens. I respect honest cops. Whoever attacked the FDLE agent doesn't care about our state. The brave agents of the FDLE defend our lives every day. I've got no bone to pick with them. They fight the worst of the worst:

pedophiles, rapists, you name it."

"Then who was behind the attack on the FDLE agent?" Wolfgang asked.

"How would I know?"

"Do you have a name?"

"How could I? I'm a financier, for goodness sake! You asked for my opinion, and I gave you my best guess." At this, Brad Johnston took his cue and stood, politely nodding to the two lawmen.

"It's after five. You must excuse us. We have families waiting for us at home."

"Just a few more questions," Wolfgang blurted. The attorney smiled knowingly and shook his head. *Of course. Just a few more minutes with our mouths open, so you can set the hook.*

"Gentlemen, I'm sorry. This interview is over."

Three Days Later

Head Case

Night fell like a pestilential cloud over the streets of the Windy City. From his palatial suite atop the former Kefauver Federal Building, Don Brucci gazed through a heavy picture window and surveyed the lights of Chicago. The city lights twinkled like fallen stars cast out of heaven, scattered across the earth to lay prostrate at his feet.

At 9:00 PM, Don Brucci spoke on the telephone with a United States senator in the self-serving grip of angst-ridden regret. "I'm sorry, that's not possible," he stated emphatically into the telephone. "Our project cannot be cancelled. I've tried; believe me. The contractor is old-fashioned. He was paid in advance, and he intends to deliver."

Don Brucci winced and covered the receiver, winking at Capo Sonny DiAngelo. "This guy's falling to pieces," he whispered philosophically. "Some big shot."

The Don returned his attention to the telephone and clucked sympathetically. "Sometimes," he told the senator, "you can't force a dedicated professional to abandon a job. Too much pride." As the voice raged on the other end of the line, the Don looked at Sonny and shrugged. "It's the risk of doing business," he stated bluntly into the receiver. "These things are unpredictable."

As he hung up, the Don began to smile. He tried to suppress it, but failed.

"Can you believe it? Our friend wants to call off the deal."

"All show and no go," Sonny replied. "No guts in the clutch."

"You know that our Canadian contractor is a traditionalist. He will kill or die trying. Ce la vie."

"A real pro," Sonny stated admiringly. "Old school."

"Indeed. One must respect that level of professionalism."

"Even a garbage man can take pride in a job well done."

"Garbage man?" asked the Don.

Sonny's words reminded him of events long past, when they were up-and-coming hoods. In those days, Sonny had been the Don's most reliable muscle when push came to shovels of dirt on shallow graves.

Noticing Don Brucci's smirk, Sonny could practically read his mind. He grinned knowingly as the Don smiled at him and tapped his head with his index finger.

"You're reading my mind again, eh, Sonny boy?"

"Primo Butarosso," Sonny said slyly. "The Prime Butt Roast."

Remembering Primo, they could fight the feeling no longer. Their mirth overflowed like water from a poisonous well.

They did not simply laugh. They howled with laughter until they wept, rocking in their chairs, grasping their knees with both hands for support.

"Primo the clown!" the Don gasped. "Where did that guy come from?"

"From the bad side of Calumet City."

"I thought both sides were bad."

"You're right, of course," Sonny chortled. "And Primo was the livin' proof." Tears moistened his eyes as he struggled to regain his composure.

"What a clown. Didn't he run numbers for Lenny K?"

"Yep, he worked on Boo Boo's crew until he made the dumbest mistake in the history of Chicago."

"Tell me the story," the Don ordered. "How did it happen?" The Don had lived the tale, but he loved hearing it again from Sonny, the gifted clown prince of his family.

"It was the perfect storm in a nutshell," Sonny began. "It all began when Boo Boo Tomolianza heard a knock on the door. It was Primo Butarosso, askin' for some work so he could move up in the organization. To give him a chance to earn his bones, Boo Boo gave Primo the contract for Dimonio Lucci. But Primo, bein' half deaf, thought the contract was on a certain Antonio Brucci."

"Idiota!"

"He had no idea who you were."

"He should've asked. Who could confuse Lucci with Brucci?"

"A bonehead. A Prime Butt Roast."

"He should'a worn a hearing aid."

"No kiddin'. Do you remember Johnny Stassa?"

"Sure. Stassa was a funny guy."

"Stassa said that Primo died from a case of terminal earwax."

"Ha!" The Don scratched his chin and popped half of a biscotti into his mouth. "Who was this Lucci… the intended target? I don't remember this stuff like you." The Don chewed voraciously as he spoke, firing crumbs in every direction.

"Lucci was a garbage collector who'd got elected to the local union hall. Boo Boo was havin' labor trouble, but he couldn't buy Lucci. He was a sap… as straight as they come."

"So Boo Boo gave Lucci the choice? Silver or lead?"

"Yep. When Lucci refused the silver, Boo Boo sent Primo to deliver the lead."

"Primo was a virgin, right?" The Don loved hearing the bloody tale.

"Yep. It was his very first job."

"First and last," the Don observed.

Sonny tapped his head. "Terminal ear wax." They chortled like decrepit wolves worrying a rotten bone.

"Do you remember what he said when he pulled out his gun?" Sonny asked.

"Who could forget?" the Don snorted. "'Goodbye, paisan. The Hammer of Sicily is about to fall!'"

"The Hammer of Sicily!"

"About to fall!"

"What a schlub!"

"Idiota!"

They laughed loud and long, howling with glee until their rheumy eyes watered and their mouths got sore from unaccustomed smiles. They savored the memory of Primo's demise like hellhounds savaging a trembling bunny.

"He should'a run his mouth *after* he pulled the trigger," Sonny wheezed happily.

"But you gotta admit," the Don giggled. "From his perspective, it made perfect sense. He thought we were garbage men."

"Remember the sound he made when you shot him in the face?" Sonny asked.

"He bleated like a goat... like a poor little goat that had lost his way."

"Baa, baa, baa," Sonny bleated, his voice filled with pathos.

"Good times," the Don chuckled as they paused to dry their eyes.

A LONE SECURITY GUARD, manning his post in the middle of the empty marble lobby, daydreamed sleepily behind the information desk. At 9:17 PM, a messenger rapped on the glass at the grand entrance of the Kefauver Building. Groaning, the guard stood and began to cross the extravagantly decorated lobby. After clacking across 200 feet of glistening marble, he reached the door, pulled his flashlight from its holster, and wearily shined it in the messenger's face. He could not see the man's face clearly, but he acted as if he could; due to an eye irritation, the guard had removed his contact lenses during his dinner break.

The tall, rangy, broad-shouldered man lifted one hand to shield his eyes from the guard's flashlight. The bike messenger had a short grey beard, a hawk's-beak nose, and olive skin turned leathery from long summer days under the dry western sun. His pale blue coveralls bore the familiar logo of the Windy City Messenger Service. He had jammed a White Sox cap low over his forehead, a fruitless buffer against the summer heat.

"You can't come in. We're closed," the guard shouted through the door. The deliveryman hung his head and stared at his feet, nonplussed by the development.

In the rear of the vast lobby, four men stepped out of an elevator. They began to cross the marble floor with focus and purpose: short, dark, purposeful men in expensive silk suits who spoke discreetly to one another, laughing occasionally. They walked swiftly... as if they earned their livelihoods based on distance traversed versus time elapsed.

"I have a delivery for Mr. Antonio Brucci," the messenger shouted from the other side of the big glass door. He obviously suffered from laryngitis, for his shout amounted to a raspy wheeze that could scarcely be heard through the glass. "Gimme a break!"

The messenger spoke with a curious Southern European accent, an anonymous amalgam of various Mediterranean inflections. *What is that accent?* the guard wondered casually.

"It's too late. Come back tomorrow."

By now, the fast-walking businessmen had reached a discreet private exit. Pausing, their leader glanced across the lobby and noticed the bike messenger's plight. Alberto "Big Al" Tattaliamo, a lieutenant in Sonny DiAngelo's crew, loved to rummage through the mail: especially mail addressed to their infamous boss of bosses, Don Antonio Brucci. Signaling to his men, he slowly crossed the lobby and stepped up to the towering glass doorway, followed by his well-dressed crew. As the bike messenger stared dejectedly at the ground, Big Al rapped on the glass to get his attention.

"Who sent the package?" he asked the messenger. In response, the lanky man held up the box and squinted to read the return address. The old-fashioned package resembled a square hatbox wrapped in brown paper, tightly taped and crisscrossed with string. The messenger took his time, apparently struggling to read the obscure handwriting.

"It's from a Mrs. Bunco Everest," he wheezed. He looked away, apparently befuddled and weary after a long day delivering packages in the summer heat.

"That'd be Bronco Everest," answered Big Al Tattaliamo with a smirk.

"The wrestler?" the messenger asked.

"Let him in," Big Al directed.

Bronco Everett, one of the most successful bookies in Chicago, had disappeared two days before. His weekly payment was overdue, and it appeared likely that this messenger carried the cash along with an apology. Bronco, a semi-reformed drunk known to go on the occasional bender, occasionally dropped out of touch, but always returned, cash in hand.

The door buzzed loudly. The messenger entered the lobby and ambled up to the high-tech security gate, peeling off his gloves and stuffing them into the top pocket of his lightweight coveralls. The man looked as scruffy, disheveled and sunburned as one might expect of someone pedaling Chicago's busy streets in the middle of a heat wave.

"Stand over here," Big Al ordered, taking the heavy package from his hand and turning to the security guard. "I'll take care of it," he said, pushing the guard off to the side. "Go ahead, Louie, run it through the scanner," he ordered, handing the box to a short man who stood beside him.

Little Louie Bianco, Big Al's second-in-command, turned on the machine and put the box on the belt. "Take a break, pal," he said to the security officer. The officer complied without question, knowing these men to be high-ranking executives in the employ of the building's owner.

When Little Louie saw the image on the screen, he gasped. Inside the box he saw a solid mass the size of a misshapen soccer ball. Along the left edge of the mass, clearly visible against the grey background, he could discern the unmistakable profile of a grotesquely contorted human face.

"Mr. Brucci, the priest is waiting to see you." The high-pitched, nasal voice cackled over the old-fashioned intercom like angry chicken ready to fly the coop. Hearing her voice, the Don frowned.

"That crazy priest has been waiting for three hours," he complained.

"Why don't you get rid of him?" Sonny asked.

"Get rid of him?" The Don lifted his eyebrows quizzically, pointing his index finger and cocking his thumb.

"Ha! I saw that movie, too. I mean send him away."

"That won't work. He'll get on local TV again. I don't want a bunch of tree-huggers picketing my job site."

"It's too bad he's a priest, or we could solve it the old-fashioned way."

"Yeah." The Don leaned forward and pressed the buzzer to answer his receptionist. "Give me a minute, then let him in."

"Yes, Mr. Brucci," the tinny voice replied, rife with annoyance. Esther Lemme, his antique, flame-haired secretary, hated to work late.

The Don looked at Sonny and smiled wanly. "I'd better handle this alone. Go on. Get outta here. Don't you have a girlfriend?"

"What makes you think that?"

"I know everything. Go, take her some Chinese," he advised, shooing him away. "She likes the orange duck." Seeing Sonny's shocked expression, he smiled. "Imogene Pallazi told me."

"That old biddy knows everything."

"Imogene's my eyes and ears in the old neighborhood."

"She's right. I have a new girlfriend." Sonny blushed.

"Go on, get out'a here."

The capo slipped out of the room by way of a discreet foyer located at the back right corner of the office. He entered the Don's private elevator and pushed the button to descend to the secluded private exit.

The priest opened the door and entered slowly, tapping his cane on the floor. The Don stared, surprised by his red cane. *He's blind,* he thought, grinning cruelly, *yet Ester let him find his own way into my office. She can be nasty when she has to work late.*

"Thank you for seeing me, Mr. Brucci," the priest began.

"Not at all." The Don stepped up, took him by the elbow, and directed him to a chair. "Thanks for waiting, Father... uh..."

"MacIntyre."

"Of course. Father Frank MacIntyre, right?"

"Correct. I'm Episcopalian, not Catholic," the priest added nervously. "Not that there's anything wrong with that."

"Of course not."

"I just don't want to make a false impression."

"Thanks, but I know a little bit about you already. Your protests have gotten a lot of attention."

"Uh, yes. Of course."

"You raised quite a stink when we tore up that illegal garden and all of that unsafe playground equipment on my land."

"Yes, Mr. Brucci," the priest began. He sweated profusely, terrified at the thought of resisting the will of the infamous Antonio Brucci: Don of Dons, Capo di Capos, and reputed leader of the infernally renowned Brucci family.

"Do you approve of people using land without the owner's permission?" the Don asked. "Isn't that wrong?"

"Mr. Brucci, we're hoping that you'll reconsider your plans to develop that parcel. It's very important to the neighborhood."

"It's my land, Father. Those people are trespassing."

"That's true. But your land provides the only garden space in the neighborhood."

"Those people need jobs, not gardens. It's a blighted area. We're planning an upscale office park. My development will pump millions into the neighborhood."

"Maybe, or maybe not. The office park will be located right beside the station. We think that people will just commute… pop in and out on the El. They won't spend much money in the neighborhood. The project will take away the only green space without adding much value to the lives of local people."

"Father, we'll hire those local people in our building. We'll give them jobs."

"You're right. You'll need service staff, but that's the only benefit I can see."

"That's nothing to sneeze at. It means jobs."

"Yes… I'll grant you that."

"Property values will go up."

"Sir, with all respect, almost all the people living in the area are renters. Higher property values will hurt them."

"Okay," he said, leaning back in his chair. "What are you proposing?"

"Uh, well, sir, I'm proposing a compromise. I'd like to suggest that part of the space be retained and enhanced as a neighborhood park... perhaps one third of the site. It would be good for business and good for your image."

"You think?"

"Yes, I do. I'm asking that you set aside just one third of that site for a proper public park. That's all I'm asking."

"That's all?" the Don asked skeptically. "Why don't you ask for stock in Brucci Enterprises? Maybe a new Cadillac that you can use when you visit the park?"

"Really... that's not what I'm after, sir," the priest blushed. "I know you're a businessman. If you donate a public park, it will be good for your image, good for your business, and good for my parishioners. That's my argument, and I think it holds up. What do you think?"

In spite of himself, the Don smiled.

This guys an Episcopalian? He reasons like a Jesuit.

IN THE LOBBY, EVENTS UNFOLDED LESS PROSAICALLY. Stunned at the X-ray image of a severed human head in the messenger's cardboard box, Big Al gaped in disbelief. The package continued through the machine and stopped in front of him.

Noticing an envelope taped to the top, he hastily tore it open. On a piece of paper inside the envelope he found words cut from a magazine. They carried a grim message. *You are next.*

Big Al Tattaliamo made a snap decision. He straightened abruptly and pointed at the clueless security guard, who had not seen the X-ray image. If the truth were known, the guard could see little without his contact lenses.

"Sit over there." Big Al pointed to a bench in the center of the lobby. He picked up the box by its string binding, flipped his cell phone open and dialed the head of building security. As it rang, he began to walk swiftly toward a quiet, curtained corner of the lobby. After the fifth ring, a subordinate answered the phone.

"Joey," Big Al hissed. "Where are you?" He paused. "Good. Stay there, okay?" He stared blankly at the wall, formulating a plan. "Listen up. Today's your birthday." He listened for a moment. "Well it is now, okay? I want you to clear your guys out of the building. That's right. Send 'em to Nick's on East 2nd. The Greek joint. Tell 'em you'll meet 'em there in a few minutes. Tell 'em you're all gonna have a big birthday dinner." Al laughed grimly. "And take the security guy at the front desk with you. We'll handle the security while you're gone." He shook his head. "Just do it." He smiled. "Right. Tell them to go on ahead, but you wait for me. I'll be right up." Hanging up and walking back to the center of the lobby, Big Al pointed at the lanky deliveryman.

"You," he barked sharply, "come with us." Leaving the security guard behind, they took the elevator to the second floor.

As they stepped out of the elevator, they encountered a jovial group: three security flunkies anticipating a free dinner at a great Greek restaurant. The men joked as they entered the elevator, completely ignoring the dapper gangsters and their prey. Big Al and company waited in the hall until the elevator doors closed on the laughing group.

"Wait here," he ordered his men as he swiped his security card at the control room door and punched in a security code. The door slid open and he ambled inside.

"Mr. Tattaliamo, how can I help you?" Joseph Fradiavala asked. The head of security for the Kefauver Building, Joseph sat at a large computer console facing the door.

"Don't 'Mister' me, Joey. I knew you when you were boosting newspapers."

"Okay, Big Al, wha'd'ya want?"

"Is the building empty?"

"Sure. Everyone's out'a here but Mr. Brucci and a visitor in his office."

"What about the cleaning crew?"

"They arrive after midnight."

"Good. Here's the deal. I want you to erase the past 30 minutes of security film: everything, for the whole building. After that, I want you to shut down the cameras and get out'a here. Go eat dinner with those ugly jamokes." He peeled a few 100-dollar bills off a roll and stuck them into the younger man's shirt pocket. "That ought'a cover it." In response, Joey typed busily, making the keyboard rattle.

"Erase everything?" he asked innocently.

"For the past 30 minutes, for every camera in the building. Then, shut it all down. Do you think you can you handle that?"

Joey tapped a key, moved the mouse, and tapped again. "Done!" he answered blandly. "Anything else?"

"Yeah. Forget I asked."

"Forget what?"

"Exactly. Now go eat dinner, wise guy."

Al opened the door and signaled with a sweeping motion for Joey to leave. The younger man walked through the door and down the hallway without glancing at the bike messenger or the other men. *Joey's a smart kid,* Al ruminated. *He minds his business and keeps his mouth shut.*

As soon as the elevator door closed, Big Al turned to the messenger. Smiling congenially and without any warning, Al drew back his fist and delivered a body blow. As his victim collapsed, Al kicked him hard in the ribs, effectively punting him down the hall. The tall, thin deliveryman tumbled across the shiny tiles like a skeleton dumped from a rucksack.

"Pick him up," Al ordered his men. "We're goin' to the Red Room." Obediently, Little Louie bent down and helped the stranger to his feet.

"Please." Their victim wheezed, struggling to his feet. "Why are you doin' this?" he gasped pathetically, his whispery voice leaking air like a worn accordion. "What'd I do?"

"We're just gonna ask a few questions," Little Louie said tersely as they entered the elevator. He pushed the button for the top floor. "If you cooperate, you'll be okay." He lied quite naturally, experienced in the arcane art of deceit. *Poor schlub,* Louie mused. *He has no idea that he's a dead man.*

Blood Red

Because their soundproof workout room occasionally doubled as a torture chamber, the Brucci soldiers had cleverly named it the "Red Room." The Red Room inhabited a discreet area in the windowless center of the top floor, a dark spot embedded in the heart of the family business.

Although the Red Room brimmed with workout equipment, the flabby hoods preferred to exercise guns and garrotes, leaving workouts for health nuts and other losers. Brucci muscle men burned smokes instead of calories. Their power drinks reeked of alcohol, and they remained defiantly free from any taint of good health.

For the Bruccis, the Red Room served as a silent haven for some of their bloodiest business. Symmetrical sheets of soundproofed tiles covered the ceiling: arrays of conical pyramids like those in state-of-the-art recording studios. The Bruccis had chosen an extremely expensive ceramic wall covering that absorbed sound, but did not absorb liquid. Blood might spray, but it would not stain their hard, cold walls.

An outer door led to an entry alcove. A second, inner door sealed the room in a cone of silence that Maxwell Smart might envy. Trapped in the Red Room, sound waves could abandon all hope of escape.

As he opened the inner door to the Red Room, Big Al Tattaliamo lifted his right leg, pressed a slick Italian loafer against the messenger's bony posterior, and delivered a hearty shove. The hapless worker bee tumbled into the room face-first, hitting the floor hard and rolling twice before tumbling to a halt.

Al rolled up his sleeves and winked at his companions. "Hold him up, Danny. Shut the door, Tommy." He pointed at Little Louie, then at the box. "Open that thing up. I want to see Bronco's head. Maybe there's a note in there. We need to find answers."

"Cool," whispered Tommy Canto.

The fourth gangster in the room, a strong-arm specialist named Gino Genari, pulled the victim to his feet. The hapless deliveryman tried to focus, coughing and spitting blood in a fine spray that misted the mobsters and drooled down the front of his heavy coveralls.

"Help'a me, boss," he whispered hoarsely.

"Who sent the package?" Al asked. "Who sent the head case?"

"I can'a hear you," the victim sputtered in a thick European accent of indeterminate origin. He began to weep, his chin trembling visibly as thick tears coursed down his brown cheeks. "I don' hear so good, boss. Please!" In thoughtful response to his victim's plea, Big Al balled a hammy fist and smashed his blubbering mouth.

The messenger went limp and slid from the grasp of Gino Genari, collapsing to the floor like a limp strand of spaghetti. On his back, he groaned loudly, rolled over, and forced himself to his hands and knees. He moaned pitifully, drooling spittle and blood in a foot-long strand that descended from his mouth to the cold beige tile. A tooth dropped from his mouth and slid down the slime like a fireman hurrying down a bloody pole. The tooth clicked against porcelain to swim in an evil puddle – clean white enamel winking from a pool of bright red slime.

At the back of the room, Louie placed the box on a table, cut the string and tape, unwrapped the outer paper, and lifted the lid. Inside, he saw an irregular sphere wrapped in smeared reddish brown paper, tied with thin wire. *Here lies the head of good ol' Bronco. What a way to go.* He slid his knife beneath the wire, then paused and looked up when he heard the slap of a heavy punch: flesh against flesh, the way it sounds in the real world. Al was doing what he loved best: damaging somebody's face. To a hardened criminal like Louie, watching Al work was like watching a slow-motion train wreck: nasty and grim, but curiously fascinating.

In the middle of the room, Big Al focused on the task at hand. A husky bruiser, he loved to hurt people deeply. He felt a surge of perverted glee at the sight of his wounded victim.

On his hands and knees, swaying slightly, the bike messenger groveled at the big man's feet. He shook his battered head, spattering delicate red drops across the floor in a wild spray pattern, a tiled canvas that resembled a crazed crimson oil painting fired from the brush of Jackson Pollack. The messenger begged for his life, crawling toward his tormentor: face down and sniveling like a witless worm.

"Please, don'a kill me, boss," he moaned pathetically.

Hearing these words, Al recognized the accent. The realization chilled him. *He's Sicilian.*

For an instant, it seemed to Al as if the groveling messenger mocked him. "Please, don'a kill me, boss… you so big and bad!"

The stranger looked up and met Al's eyes. Big Al stared intently at the stranger's bloody face: lean and hawk-like, with a piercing gaze that belied his feeble groveling. The light in the messenger's eyes seemed eerily powerful and remarkably clear – dramatically unlike his trembling words.

As the messenger spread his arms to beg for mercy, Big Al drew back a thick leg and kicked with all of his might. Yet somehow, for some reason, he missed his approaching target.

The slobbering victim shifted seamlessly to his left, as subtly as a drifting breeze. The victim's sideways motion transformed Big Al's kick from a brutal blow into a miss that slipped harmlessly past as Big Al stumbled and almost fell down. *How'd he do that?*

At the other side of the room, Little Louie turned back to the grisly bundle, ready to unwrap the final layers. He paused for a moment as a chill swept down his spine. *Why the chill?* He heard a noise, and looked up again.

"Don'a kill me, boss!" the bike messenger squealed. "Please, don'a kill me!" He collapsed against Big Al, wrapping his arms around the big man's waist as he tried to struggle to his feet. He sobbed wildly, turning his head away from the grisly hatbox.

In the back of Big Al's mind, an alarm went off as the messenger clung to his expensive silk jacket, weeping inconsolably. *I'm ending this,* the gangster thought, thrusting his victim away.

With his knife beneath the wire, Little Louie sneered at the shenanigans. *Al is such a gorilla.*

As the bike messenger stumbled backwards and Louie turned back to the package, Big Al tried to close the deal. But when he reached into his shoulder holster, he came up empty. He groped under his jacket, but found no gun.

Totally unprepared for such an event, Al watched in surprise as his open hand emerged from his jacket. He gaped in dismay and pointed the empty hand at the messenger like a child with an imaginary weapon.

Having turned away from the action, Little Louie leaned in close to the package. With a smile, he studiously severed the wire. That was a big mistake.

The head case blew up in Louie's face.

The sudden blast simply blew Little Louie away. The force threw him backwards, slamming his body against a concrete column and whipping his head against the unforgiving surface like a smashing pumpkin at the end of a rope.

Little Louie had triggered a powerful stun bomb. Because of his close proximity, the device had acted as an anti-personnel weapon, ending his criminal career with impressive finality.

The blast ripped through the open room, dissipating by the millisecond. The force did not knock Big Al off his feet, but stunned him completely, shattering his eardrums in the process. His universe rang like a bell, with his head serving as the clapper.

Al squinted through a vivid grid of jumbled colors and tasted hot gunpowder, marveling at the beauty of the kaleidoscopic haze. The right side of his face felt as if he had been sucker-smacked by a cast iron skillet. But given his suddenly semi-comatose state, he did not particularly care.

What's happening? He wondered stupidly. Through the smoke, he noticed his own empty hand. *Gee, look at that.* His outstretched index finger pointed at a stranger with a bruised face and bloody mouth. *That guy looks familiar,* Al reflected. *Somebody whipped him good.* The stranger's hand did not appear to be empty.

Big Al slowly noticed that the stranger held a pistol, pointed in his direction. He recognized the gold finish and expensive detailing of his prized Glock presentation piece. *What's my best gun doin' in that guy's hand?* The stranger showed no ill effects from the blast.

In a sputtering moment of blurred cognition, Big Al recognized the man. *That's the bike messenger.*

The messenger's countenance had changed. He no longer wore the fearful fright mask of a hapless working drone. Instead, his expression revealed wrath tempered by hard experience.

"How did I get your gun?" the stranger asked innocently. Quite incongruously, he smiled.

STREETCAR'S PLAN HAD WORKED TO PERFECTION. His ears rang and his head throbbed, but the blast had not stunned him. His high-tech earplugs had done double duty. They had lent authenticity to his protestations of deafness, and they had protected his eardrums from the concussive shock of his homemade flash-bang device.

The Brucci gangsters had made a fatal mistake. This was no hapless worker bee smoked out of the swarming metropolitan hive. This man had come to kill, not to play.

The effect of the explosion exceeded Streetcar's expectations. The bomb blasted the room into total disarray, with one gangster dead, two groaning on the floor, and Big Al Tattaliamo teetering at the outer limits of consciousness, blinking at Streetcar in splendid stupidity.

As Streetcar paused, an unexpected idea flashed through his mind. *I shouldn't kill them.* Surprised by the innate power of the thought, he almost lowered his weapon. In spite of the cruelty of these men, he recognized the truth. Bloody murder – by any other name – still smelled as foul.

Long ago, the act of murder had earned a place on God's short list of forbidden acts. It remained a fundamental sin to this day: inhumane, ungodly, and cruel. He knew it, and he felt it, but he resisted the voice of his conscience. Remembering the Brucci's vicious assault on Jamie, he steeled himself to finish the job.

"Bloody scum," he growled with earthy intensity.

The gun bucked in his hand, punching a neat hole in Big Al's forehead. The dull light in the gangster's eyes winked out as his legs forsook him like rubber bands. He collapsed to the floor with surprising speed, as if pulled by a magnet.

Behind and above the fallen hood, a thick spray of bright red blood lofted slowly upward into the smoke-stained air. Among the vapor trails, the gore lingered momentarily: a gruesome cloud preparing to unleash a plague of bloody hail.

As the grisly rain began to fall, Streetcar wheeled to his right. The hood named Dan opened his eyes just in time to watch the muzzle flash as two bullets sent him to his eternal unrest. Both slugs blasted into Dan's open mouth, blowing out the top of his unrepentant head.

Gino Genari, tougher and more resilient than his peers, almost managed to draw his weapon before a bullet ripped through his heart, bounced off a vertebrae and fragmented, escaping through his back and the front of his neck. He wilted backwards, warm breath leaking out like a balloon that lacked the lift needed to ascend.

Squinting through clouds of burnt gunpowder, Streetcar surveyed the wreckage. He stepped up to a concrete beam, bent over Little Louie, and put a foot on his chest, checking for life. As expected, the heart did not twitch. *Four down, one to go.*

"Infamnia," he murmured without pity.

Straightening and stepping away from the bodies, he stripped off his water-resistant coveralls to reveal a tan silk shirt with an open collar and non-descript pleated navy slacks: typical clothing for a Chicagoan out for a walk on a warm summer evening. Bending over, he retrieved his missing tooth from the hard tile floor, wrapped it in a Kleenex, and secured it in his right pocket. Straightening up, he slowly wiped his face with a handkerchief. Slipping on clean cotton gloves, he carefully rubbed his fingerprints from Big Al's handgun.

Streetcar dropped the pistol on the floor, walked up to Gino

Genari, and wrestled a Beretta semi-automatic from the dead gangster's grip. Checking the clip, he saw that it was full and slammed it back in place. Slipping the gun beneath his shirt, he patted it and took a deep breath, looking around at the remains of the Red Room. He surveyed a scene of carnage strewn with the remains of wasted lives... violent lives ended violently, now hopelessly lost.

As he prepared to leave the room, Streetcar placed a compact incendiary device on the floor and set the timer for 20 minutes. *That ought'a burn up my DNA.* He looked around one last time and noticed a latex Halloween mask lying on the floor. The rubber mask stared at the ceiling with eyeless sockets, as lifeless as the dead gangsters scattered around the room. *There's old Bronco. Still in one piece,* he reflected. *Go figure.*

Streetcar had not killed Bronco Everett. He had sedated and bound the bookie, leaving him in a flophouse on the South Side to further his deadly plans. To get inside the Kefauver Building, he had hid a stun bomb inside a faux head wrapped in lead foil and faced with a rubber mask. The gangsters had taken his bait like serpents charmed by a mongoose.

What a bloody mess, he reflected.

Against his will, the pungent scent of burnt gunpowder unlocked long-buried memories. The smell reminded him of friends long forgotten: good men who had died too young, too hard. Some had even died in his arms. *Stop it!* he reminded himself. *This is not a time for mourning.* To fortify his repentant willpower, he said the words aloud.

"This is a time to kill."

THE ATMOSPHERE IN DON BRUCCI'S OFFICE felt lofty and serene. The lights of Chicago glimmered below his window, paving the city like fallen stars. As the Don stood with his hands behind his back, gazing at the gorgeous cityscape, it seemed as if the lights twinkled gaily... like the gleaming eyes of crooked cops taking bribes from natty Evanston motorists. The glamorous city streets glowed in dutiful obeisance, reminding him that he ruled a glorious domain.

For a moment, the Don stared out of the window distractedly, his gaze lingering on the luminous beauty below. Then, with a happy sigh, he crossed the room to sit behind his desk.

"All right, Father MacIntyre," Don Brucci jovially asserted, settling into the rich leather chair. "You drive a hard bargain, but we have a deal." Leaning forward, he extended his hand to shake before recalling the priest's blindness.

"We have a deal," Father MacIntyre replied, pleasantly surprised. As he spoke, he felt an unexpected breeze against his cheek. *What's that?* The Father paused, listening intently.

"Is someone there?" the Father called. Both men turned toward the doorway.

The door swung open to reveal a tall, thin, neatly dressed man wearing clean white gloves. In his right hand, he held a gun.

With remarkable speed, the Don reached beneath his desk and pulled out a handgun, swearing loudly.

Streetcar's gun erupted, echoing inside the huge office.

The bullet blasted an unseemly hole just below Don Brucci's heart. The old man coughed and lunged to his feet, spraying hot blood over his desk, the carpet, and the stunned Episcopalian. The Don fired his handgun wildly, fighting against the agony. In vain, he pressed one hand against the spewing fountain that had so recently been his left lung.

Streetcar fired again, hitting the Don in the neck. Don Brucci's legs began to fail. He stumbled backwards and attempted to regain his balance before falling heavily onto his back. When he hit the ground, the blow to the back of his head completely disoriented him.

Mortally wounded, the old man tried to speak. His gaze wandered aimlessly as he fought to gather his strength.

"Mama," Don Brucci whispered before coughing up a fountain of blood.

Streetcar carefully stepped past the priest, past the desk. As he closed in on the fallen Don, the gangster's eyes lingered on the face of the advancing killer. He struggled to breathe, watching death draw close. With each inhalation, Don Brucci sucked air through the hole in his chest only to see it erupt upwards in a volcanic blowout with each exhalation.

"Mama," he whispered desperately to no one in particular. Watching the grisly scene, Streetcar suppressed all pity.

"Sonno eterno con diavolo," he rasped, his voice scarcely audible. "Ciao, Brucci." The Don's eyes focused. For a moment, the light of recognition flashed in his eyes, and he sneered angrily.

"No," he gasped. As if on cue, the flow of blood increased, and his life force gushed from his chest in a pell-mell rush, as if yearning to be free.

One more time, Streetcar aimed and slowly squeezed the trigger. The gun spat fire, punching a neat, precise hole between the gangster's eyes. The eyes locked into place with the glassy gaze of a dead doll, released from decades of service as windows to the Don's fallen soul.

For several seconds, it seemed to Streetcar as if his spirit had left his body and entered a dark place. He heard nothing. He knew nothing. He saw nothing except the flickering image of Brucci's face gaping in surprise as he witnessed his own, sudden death. Then, in the silence, Streetcar heard a quavering voice.

"My God, what have you done? What have you done?"

He turned toward the voice. Slowly, mechanically, he raised his gun.

"Why have you done this monstrous thing?" The priest literally shook with fear, yet he refused to bow before whomever – or whatever – had entered the room. "Who are you?" he asked plaintively. "What is your name?"

Streetcar studied the pale, shaking priest, noticing the dark sunglasses and the red-tipped cane. *He's as blind as a bat*, he realized, lowering his weapon.

"Who are you?" Streetcar rasped. He coughed deeply: a painful, wracking spasm that continued for several seconds. Pausing to catch his breath, he blinked his watering eyes. When he swallowed, it felt as if he had quaffed a shot of whiskey filled with tiny razors. *I guess the Motrin has just about worn off.*

"I'm Father MacIntyre," the priest stammered. "I'm an Episcopalian," he added, as if that held relevance at the moment.

"Why are you here, Father?"

"I came to talk with Mr. Brucci. I was asking him to donate land for a park."

"Well, you hit the lotto, Father Mac. You get to live." His voice, stricken by laryngitis, scarcely rose above a whisper.

"Who are you?"

"A killer," Streetcar whispered. His voice had begun to fade fast, and he could scarcely rasp out a response.

"Why have you done this terrible thing?" the priest pleaded.

"I just executed judgment." Streetcar replied. Noticing an alcove at the back of the huge office, he turned and approached it, stopping in front of the elevator. *A private exit. Very good.*

"His judgment was not yours to give," the priest said, finding the courage to continue. "We have laws."

"The system failed us. He beat the law every day of his life."

"His judgment was with God."

"Yes. I know that I've sinned, Father. I guess I'll pay with my soul."

"Your soul is not yours to condemn or redeem. There's still hope… even for one such as you."

"I gave up on hope a long time ago." For a moment, they paused. The room had grown eerily quiet.

"Yet hope has not given up on you."

"No? Then where is it, Father? Can you see it? Can you touch it?" He tried to yell, but could barely wheeze.

"Hope is alive in Jesus of Nazareth, the risen Son of God."

"Are you crazy, old man? I could kill you! I could kill you right now."

"Hope has not given up on you."

"This ain't Sunday school," Streetcar hissed, raising his gun as he walked toward him. *He's the only witness.* The unexpected thought sent shivers down his spine. *What am I thinking?* He had never slain an innocent bystander since his earliest days as a soldier in Vietnam. The idea deeply dismayed him. *What kind of monster have I become?*

"Your life is not over, my son."

"Shut up!" Streetcar whispered weakly. Taking a handful of Kleenex from a dispenser on the desk, he studiously wiped down the gun and laid it on the carpet before tucking the tissues into his pocket. He looked up at the priest with a face devoid of emotion. "You have a lot of faith," Streetcar stated. He said the words enviously, bitterly.

"I believe in hope," the priest replied.

"Give up, Father! I had my chance, and I threw it away." As he glanced away from the priest, he noticed the lights of Chicago though the large picture window. The beauty of the sight somehow pained him. *What a lovely city.*

"Father?" He rasped the words painfully, forcing them through his laryngitic throat.

"Yes, my son?"

"I killed many men tonight." He stated it flatly, without emotion. "I sent them straight to hell. I enjoyed it… and I hated it. I knew it was wrong, but I did it anyway."

"Call upon Jesus, my son. He will show you the Way."

"Why should I waste His time?"

"I'll pray for you."

"Pray for the living, Father," Streetcar whispered. "I'm already dead."

Turning away, he returned to the elevator and pressed the button. The door opened silently.

"I will pray for you, my son," the priest repeated as he turned his sightless eyes toward the alcove at the rear of the office and moved his head slightly, listening intently for the killer's reply. "Can we pray together?" In spite of his acute hearing, he had not noticed the fact that the elevator's doors had closed.

Waiting for a reply, the priest stood patiently in silence. He could not see that the body on the floor was his sole companion.

Streetcar had left the building.

Bad News Makes Good Copy

After his birthday dinner, Joseph Fradiavala returned to the Kefauver Building in high spirits. He and his well-fed security crew joked as they entered the control room, full of good food and high spirits.

Joseph sat down at the main desk and reactivated the security system, whistling tunelessly and tapping the keyboard. When the cameras came online, he glanced at the live feed from Don Brucci's office and gasped in unbelief.

Like a crushed spider, the Don's body lay sprawled on the carpet. A bloody stain surrounded the corpse, dominating the view inside the Don's palatial penthouse suite. The size of the bloodstain dwarfed the broken body. It filled the screen like a crude outtake from a cheesy crime drama: a pond of darkness surrounding a cold island of pale flesh.

At the edge of the flickering picture, with his lips moving in silent prayer, sat the blind Episcopalian. The priest had finally fallen apart. As soon as the killer left, he had groped through the darkness until he found the Don's body. Hopelessly attempting to revive the fallen Don, he had compressed his chest and blown into his mouth until his hand sank deep into the open wound.

As Joseph stared, not quite believing what he saw, a deep thump rattled the huge building as Streetcar's incendiary device ignited inside the Red Room. Immediately, a fire alarm sounded loudly throughout the deserted hallways. Joseph continued to stare at the flickering screen as a sprinkler began to spray water on the carnage in the Don's office. Thinned by the falling water, the Don's blood cooled and stiffened on the priest's clothes. Father MacIntyre shivered and whispered inaudibly: alone with his trauma, scarcely noticing the shriek of the alarm.

The priest would not be able to think clearly for several hours. By then, the jig would be up, and the fire-swept Red Room would reveal its sordid history of violence to a titillated world.

Morning newspapers across the nation would carry headlines leaking the foul essence of the grisly tale. As in its gangland past, a brutal Mafia slaying had stained the streets of Chicago. Judging from the body count, the City of Broad Shoulders would need a big shovel with which to bury its infamous dead.

Five gangsters had been murdered in the heart of the city, and the killer had escaped without a trace. The discriminate slaughter lent new meaning to Carl Sandburg's beefy description of Chicago: Meat Packer of the World.

EARLY THE FOLLOWING MORNING, Don James 'Ace' Provencenti received an unpleasant wake-up call. Hearing the ring, he gasped and rolled over in bed, eliciting a sour moan from Amy, his long-suffering wife.

"What on earth?" she groaned. Ace picked up the cordless receiver and crept quietly from the room, shutting the door behind him. "This had better be good," he whispered angrily. Amy did not respond well to early calls, and he expected to hear from her later.

"Ace, this is Johnny. Turn on CNN. You won't believe it." John Dicella had served for years as his devious, yet stoutly loyal consigliere. "You'd better come in today. This is big... and who knows? The kooks out there might try to use it against you."

"Okay, I'll take a look," he mumbled. "See you at the office." He staggered into the family room and flopped into an overstuffed leather chair. Picking up the remote, he turned on the television and changed the channel to CNN.

"I'm standing at Number One Kefauver Plaza in the heart of downtown Chicago," a dark-haired male reporter stated. "Last night, a fire damaged the top floor of the Kefauver Tower. The blaze was quickly put out, but the entire building has become a crime scene." The reporter stood in front of the barricades, lit by flashing lights from an army of patrol cars. "News of a mass murder at this exclusive address has stunned the city of Chicago. We've received reports that several people were killed here last night, and that there may be witnesses to the crime. A press conference will be held soon, and we expect more information at that time."

"Do we know anything else?" asked the anchor, a polished female of indeterminate age and inscrutable, proto-occidental face.

"We have heard that most of the bodies were badly burned in the fire. However, police have confirmed that one of the victims is Antonio Brucci, a prominent Chicago businessman."

"Wasn't Mr. Brucci charged with racketeering several years ago?"

"That is correct. In 1999, Mr. Brucci was charged by a federal grand jury under the RICO act. The government's chief witness at that time was Arturo Demaduisi. The jury could not reach a verdict, and a mistrial was declared."

"Didn't the chief witness disappear before he could testify?"

"Yes, that's also true. Mr. Demaduisi disappeared under suspicious circumstances. Authorities considered Mr. Brucci a person of interest, but no charges were filed."

"We'll be looking forward to that press conference. "

"One more thing. We've heard an unconfirmed rumor that someone disabled the security system just before the crime. If that's true, the police may face a real challenge. Back to you, Diane."

Completely stunned, Ace turned off the television and stared at the screen. *I can't believe it! Streetcar actually pulled it off!* His cell phone chirped on the kitchen counter, and he picked it up.

"Have you heard the news?" asked his attorney, Brad Johnston.

"I just saw it on CNN."

"Unbelievable. Who could have done such a thing?"

"Who knows?" Ace replied. "Who could even consider such a horrible crime?" Ace asked innocently.

Brad immediately recognized Ace's tone. *He knows who did it. Unbelievable!*

"Yes, it's unthinkable," Brad agreed glibly, hiding his amusement. *That Ace.... he's the best Don ever!* Needless to say, Brad realized that Ace had just solved the Brucci problem.

"This kind of thing could lead to public hysteria," Ace stated brusquely. "John and I will meet you at the office at 9:00.

"This could raise questions in the minds of the uninformed. We have to get out in front of it: on message, and spot on."

"Spot on."

"The way the media has accused me of being some kind of Mafia kingpin, they might latch onto this like a pack of hungry lemmings, chewing us up with the same old stereotypes."

"I'll bet you're right."

"It's a terrible crime," Ace added for the benefit of the many law enforcement professionals who happened to be listening in. "What's worse, I think my father had business dealings several years ago with some fellow named Brucci in Chicago. The victim might be the same guy… who knows? It's not a common name. If this is the same guy, the press will launch an inquisition."

"My thoughts exactly," replied Brad with a subtle smirk, realizing that honesty served his purpose for the moment. "That's why I called. And speaking of inquisitors, let's not forget the FBI. They've been hounding you since the redneck killed those state witnesses, and there's no telling what they'll try to make of this."

"Thanks for understanding, Brad."

"It's just not right. They want to punish you for the youthful indiscretions of your father."

"I know."

"9:00 in your office?"

"Right."

"See you then."

As he hung up, Ace smiled at the attorney's choice of words. Brad Johnston had made it sound as if Ace's father, the Don of Dons for the entire southeastern United States, had merely stolen a few hubcaps in his youth… ignoring the fact that, for decades, he had run one of the most powerful crime families in the world.

As they knew, the FBI shared their phone line, busily recording their every word while impatiently biding their time. If the feds could generate some friction, they just might strike a match. Whether the feds gained traction or not, however, one fact appeared evident to the Don and his attorney. Things had begun to heat up exponentially, and the sizzle had hit the pan in their dear old Cigar City.

Go West, Old Man

Streetcar drove west. He ran from Chicago instinctively, bereft of hope. He harbored no illusions.

He left the city like a dog fleeing a cruel master he had just bitten to death. He could not imagine how he might somehow escape, how he might elude Chicago's brawny shoulders and its hot, hammy hands.

The rumble of his car lingered listlessly at the periphery of his awareness. The engine emitted a dull, hypnotic drone, offering small comfort during his long drive through the darkest hours of the night.

At dawn, the sun topped the eastern horizon with tactless authority. The light of the sun smote the stars with unabashed vigor, like a bronze war hammer smacking the daylight into the sky. Streetcar squinted past the long shadow of his truck and stared listlessly at in the flat farmland of Minnesota as it rolled relentlessly past his windshield. His head throbbed mercilessly.

Thirty years ago, when he had first moved to Tampa, Streetcar had established four sets of false identities, searching obituaries and public records. During the past ten years, he had used three of the identities to purchase traceable items such as cellular phones. One by one, he had destroyed the IDs before each aroused suspicion. On his way to Chicago, he had purchased a 10-year-old Camry in Memphis using his last false identity. Soon, he would have no need for subterfuge.

Turning south, he drove all day, beginning a voyage across the great ocean of earth called the Great Plains. Sometime after dark, he paid cash and checked into a small roadside motel under the name of Elliot Rosen. After unpacking, he drove 20 miles to the nearest city, parked at a busy convenience store, and used a pre-paid phone card to call directory assistance.

AT 10:23 PM ON A BUSY SATURDAY NIGHT, the business line rang at the food counter in the La Bamba Grill in Dade City, Florida. A waitress picked up and shouted into the phone above the thundering din of live country music and the reveling crowd.

"You want Lester? Who's calling?" She paused. "Okay."

"Les!" she screamed with a voice that drowned out the entire band, "you have a call."

"Who is it?" Les shouted back.

"Monty Green." Les signaled that he would take the call in his office. "He'll pick up in a second," the waitress informed the caller.

Les shut the door of his office and wiped his brow. He was a large, pink-skinned man in his 40s who loved life and took his role as tavern-keeper seriously. Sitting behind the desk, he picked up the line and put his feet on the desk.

"I've got it, Elaine," he said into the receiver. "You can hang up now." He heard a loud click, and the background noise disappeared. *Nosy broad.* "This is Les," he boomed jovially. "What can I do you for?"

"This is Monty Green." Streetcar paused to cough, loud and long. *Ouch!*

"Speak, Mr. Green. I'm here to help."

"Can I talk?"

"On this line? I think so."

"You're not being watched?" He rasped the words. His bad case of laryngitis had begun to ebb, but still affected him when he tried to carry on a conversation.

"I'm a law-abiding citizen, Mr. Green. I haven't so much as jaywalked in the past 20 years." Les paused and grimaced. "I know, you're probably wondering why I'm doing a favor for our mutual friend, Ace Feldmann Provencenti." He picked up a dart from his desk and tossed it at a board on the back of his door. It stuck inside the bull's eye.

"I went to school with Ace back in Tampa. We were best friends. When he started out in music, his band used to play here. My uncle owned the joint back then. I just bought him out last year.

"When our bar burned down in '93, Ace organized a benefit to raise money. I know the press says that he's a bad guy, but I don't buy it. I love him like a brother. When he asked me to take care of your cat and give you a hand, I said, 'Sure, Ace, your friend is my friend.'"

"Did the cat die yet?" Streetcar asked. He cleared his throat, ignoring the pain.

"What makes you think your cat's gonna die?"

"The vet told me in Atlanta."

"The vet was wrong. I had him scanned the day I got him, and they found a benign tumor wrapped around his esophagus. He couldn't swallow. They operated this morning and took it out."

"He ain't gonna die?"

"Not any time soon."

"No kiddin'?" He whispered in response, completely stunned.

"The doc said he might live for several more years."

"Several more years?" Streetcar asked weakly.

"Yep. You can pick him up anytime you want. But I'll keep him as long as you want. I like that cat."

"Unbelievable," he rasped. His head whirled. He tried to speak again but his voice, which had been failing, chose this moment to give out altogether. He could barely whisper a reply. "Ah… I'll call you back later. Okay?"

"Sure." Les smacked his forehead with his hand. "Oh, I almost forgot. Ace gave me a bunch of stuff for you. I've got a pile of cash… a whole suitcase full, believe it or not. He's even arranged a private flight out of the country, if you want it. One of his friends has a house in St. Lucia. He said you can stay there as long as you want. Don't tell me why you'd want to leave the country; I don't wanna know. Ace likes you. That's good enough for me."

"Okay, thanks," he whispered. "Keep the cat for now, okay?"

"Sure."

"I'll be in touch." Streetcar hung his head, biting his lip as he slowly returned the phone to its cradle. *My cat's gonna live.* Wiping away a tear, he turned and walked back to his car.

Long Distance

On Sunday morning, Jamie awoke after six days in a medically induced coma. Her eyes wandered aimlessly around the room as she tried to remember where she was and how she had gotten there. Her husband Donny, who had lived in the room for the past several days, had just left to eat lunch downstairs in the cafeteria. The room appeared empty except for the I.V. and several monitors that chirped and hummed beside her bed.

A telephone rang loudly. As tenacious and independent as ever, Jamie reached with her good arm and tried to pick it up. Wincing in pain, she managed to snag the cord, reel it in, and place the receiver against her ear.

"Huh?" She grunted through jaws wired shut. The vibrations from her voice made her head throb, but she ignored the pain. "Hello?"

"Is this Jamie?" a voice whispered, faint and scarcely audible. Although she did not recognize the voice right away, an instinct filled her with pity.

"Who is this?"

"A friend… just a friend," he grunted. "Don't say too much. Somebody may be listening."

"You," she whispered, shutting her eyes. "It's you." *Streetcar*.

"Yep."

"I'm sorry," she whispered through the pain. Jamie struggled to pronounce her words with her jaws wired shut. "I shouldn't…" she forced out, scarcely able to speak. *I shouldn't have asked for your help.*

"Don't worry about me, Jamie. I'm doin' okay." Jamie began to weep, sick with regret.

"I'm turnin' myself in," he added simply. "I'm through runnin'."

"Please, go to Clay first," she whispered loudly. Her head throbbed, spinning with painkillers, pounded by jagged shards of pain and a sickening rush of anticipation. "Call Clay Calhoun… Clay Calhoun in Tallahassee. He's an attorney. A friend. He'll help you. Please!" Her head fell back onto the pillow. *Ow! That hurts.*

"Okay," he replied. Jamie heard steps in the hall and looked up to see the familiar face of Danny Johnston. The boy paused in the doorway, speaking to someone behind him.

"Danny's here," she whispered into the receiver. "Speak to him, please! He's killed three men. I'm afraid for him."

"Danny Johnston?" Streetcar recognized the name from the newspaper accounts.

"Yes."

"Put him on."

Danny entered the room, trailed by Drew and Marcy. In spite of their forced good cheer, their faces bore the distracted expressions of fish stunned by dynamite. Considering all that they had endured inside a fish bowl of unwanted publicity, Jamie almost expected their tormented souls to turn sideways and float to the surface. Fortunately, there was no chance of this happening. As they had proven time and again, the Johnstons were survivors in the algae-encrusted aquarium of life.

"You're awake!" Danny exclaimed. "She's awake, Aunt Marcy!"

"Danny," Jamie whispered, suddenly exhausted, "take the phone." Danny glanced quizzically at Jamie, then back at Marcy and Drew. He took the receiver and smiled.

"Alien here," he smirked. "Is this Predator?"

"Are you Danny Johnston?" The voice on the telephone had segued from a whisper to a poly-harmonic wheeze that sounded like someone softly exhaling through a train whistle.

"That's me."

"I hear that you killed three men. Three pros." Danny stopped smiling.

"Who are you?" he asked suspiciously.

"A friend. Someone who knows how it feels."

"How what feels?" Danny's face flushed, and he looked at Jamie as if she had betrayed him.

"I know how it feels to kill the bad guys."

"Are you a shrink?" Surprised by the question, Streetcar chuckled.

"No."

Danny looked at Drew, who watched him closely. Marcy looked away.

"Who are you?"

"I'm a killer. When I was 16, I lied my way into the Army. I rose to the top of the dog pile. I was America's best killer. First they gave me medals, then they spit and waved signs in my face."

"That stinks."

"Vietnam."

"Oh."

"I'm still one of the best, even though I'm an old man. And do you know what I've finally figured out?"

"What?"

"Murder is never right. Never."

"I know that," Danny bluffed, but he knew the voice on the phone had called him out. He had begun to feel proud of the fact that he had killed three professional hit men. He had felt proud and powerful and more than a little dangerous.

"Don't do like I did, please," Streetcar pleaded. "Don't waste your life." From a hidden source, emotion welled up deep within Streetcar and threatened to choke back his words. He remembered Vietnam: the smoldering hot rice paddies, the black-clad peasants rooted hand and foot in the rich, dark earth.

He remembered one day when a mortar round struck them out of a clear blue sky with no hostiles in sight. It had been a lovely day, with the ubiquitous Vietnamese peasants hard at work in the rice and mud, bowing their slight forms beneath huge straw hats like little human mushrooms: innocent mushroom people who blew up in a bloody cloud of smoke and sound that knocked him into the rich brown earth. In the eerie silence after the blast, he had realized that his eardrums were ruptured because they did not ring from the concussion.

His ears had healed with time, but his memory had refused to cooperate. The remembrance remained... a bitter splinter buried deep within his mind.

He recalled three nights spent alone on a comfortless stalk: miserable nights sunk deep in a mire of squirming bugs and warm, creamy mud: sweltering days buried under bushes and leaves. He had suffered from titanic itches that he could not scratch, enduring it all for the love of country. For two days and three nights he had edged forward, crawling like a poisonous creeper vine that grew toward the enemy's encampment. After he ended the stalk with a high value kill, he had received a shiny medal.

Faces returned against his will, the beloved and the lost: the same faces he tried to push away each night when he tossed alone in his bed. Like a perverse kinescope, hellish memories flashed before him. He saw Vickers, brave Vickers knocked flat at the foot of a tiny hill with his face blanched white, mouth agape, his shredded chest filled with warm blood like a punch bowl for a passing vampire. He saw Gary on a footpath in the steaming heat of a rice paddy, twisted like a contortionist with his head jammed under one arm, as limp and hopeless as a marionette bereft of its human dummy. Far away, against a heat-warped horizon, he saw a baby, dripping and blue: murdered at birth by a Vietnamese elder offended by its gross deformity.

He shook his head and the images fled as quickly as they had arrived. He blinked and looked around. *I'm in a parking lot in the boondocks of the Midwest, and I just killed the biggest don in Chicago.* Reality had merged with the surreal. Present events seemed mundane and out of place, as if he had parachuted into another life. Surely, he could not have murdered those men in Chicago. Could he have done such a thing?

"Why are you telling me these things?" Danny asked. The child's voice woke Streetcar up, returning him to the matter at hand.

"Killin' ain't no way to live. Quit now, before it's too late. Put down the gun. Just be a kid, okay"

"I saved Drew's life with a gun. My life, too."

"You did what you had to. I read about it in the paper. But it's over now. You gotta move on. Live a normal life."

"You think I'm not normal?" Danny asked, but he received no answer. The man's sadness pulled at him, tugging him into his orbit. His sorrow seemed tangible, atmospheric, like an evil fog. It pressed against Danny like the specter of intuition. *I could become just like him,* he realized. "How do you know so much?" he asked.

"I've lived a long time. I've learned something."

"What?"

"I'm thinkin' that maybe we're the guys who have to quit. We've got to rise above the killin', no matter what the bad guys do. Otherwise, it's tit for tat, and they're setting the agenda."

"Okay, I'll make a deal. If you change, I'll change," Danny blurted impulsively. "Otherwise, no deal."

"I'm too old to change."

"If you don't change, I won't."

"Okay then, how about this. I've been wanted by the law for a long time."

"So?"

"What if I turn myself in? Is that good enough?"

"Sure. You give up the gun, and I'll give up the gun."

"Okay. Deal?"

"Deal."

"That's it, then."

"I guess so." They paused.

"See you later."

"Later."

Streetcar hung up the phone and hurried to his car. He would turn himself in… but if possible, he would do it on his own terms. *The kid's right. I can't ask him to give up the gun if I won't.*

STREETCAR DID NOT KNOW IT, but the FDLE and FBI had not bothered to place a wiretap on Jamie's telephone. To a man – and to a woman - they believed that Pete Johnston had financed the attack on Jamie. As a result, they believed that the threat against Jamie had died with Pete. Don Brucci's brilliant gambit had failed miserably. The authorities felt certain that Don Provencenti, cagy and discreet, would never have authorized an assault against a law enforcement officer.

When Jamie had asked Streetcar to call Clay Calhoun before turning himself in, he had immediately developed a plan. He would return to Florida, his adopted home state. He could drive to Tallahassee in less than two days, allowing time for the occasional catnap.

In spite of his guilt, he began to see a glimmer of hope. The conversation with Danny had given him a new mission, unpolluted by murder or mayhem. *If I can keep him from makin' the choices I made, maybe my whole life won't be wasted.*

Streetcar could not foresee one fatal fact. For Danny Johnston, the trials of life would soon multiply. The result would not be pretty.

Danny had a stalker: a deadly hunter who had already locked on his target. The stalker loved the thought of Danny, but not of the living child. He had fallen deeply in love with the thought of Danny, dead. As the best mechanic in the business, he had meticulously prepared for the moment of truth.

Soon, the killer would make his move.

Open Invitational

Two days later, the surviving members of the Johnston family left Winston with his live-in nurse and drove to Oree County to visit Jamie again in the hospital. Soon, she would go home. She seemed to gain strength by the hour.

The arrival of Danny, Marcy, Drew, and Ches greatly cheered Jamie and Donny. After a 30-minute visit, they left to visit Delia Rawlings at the Oree County Sheriff's Department.

Pezner had changed during the past five years. A medical group had constructed the hospital, two fast-food restaurants had expanded the commercial palate, and rumor had it that a Super Wal-Mart would soon arise from the asphalt of a brighter tomorrow. The day had dawned hot but clear, with low humidity diminishing the brute force of mid-summer heat. They decided to walk from the hospital for an up-close tour of the new and improved Pezner.

As they passed in front of the Hoggly Woggly grocery, less than a block from the sheriff's department, they heard a shout from the parking lot. "Hey, Danny," a high voice called. "Over here!"

The group turned to see a boy Danny's age waving beside a corroded door at the front of the store. The boy jumped up and down. "Hey, Danny!" He was thin and tall for his age like Danny, with dark black skin and a thousand-watt smile. He wore the obligatory summer uniform of all Pezner males: blue jeans and a faded T-shirt. To the standard attire, he had added his own touch: a towering Afro embellished by a dark blue hair pick. The massive head of hair towered above a face adorned by bright yellow, mirrored, wrap-around shades.

"It's Mikey Goodenough," Danny said jubilantly. "What's he doing here? He's from Cutlerville. Hey, Mikey," he shouted with ear-numbing volume. "Hey!" He turned to Marcy with a pleading expression. "Aunt Marcy, do you mind if I hang out with Mikey?"

"Of course not," she said with a worried smile. *You need a distraction,* she did not add.

"Here, take my cell phone," Drew offered. "We can give you a call when we're ready to leave town." Glancing at Marcy, Drew noticed a frown on her face. "If that's okay with your aunt, I mean," he added apologetically.

"Of course," Marcy replied. *He steps in with solutions whether I want him to or not,* she thought disapprovingly. *I always wanted to meet a good-looking guy who's not afraid to take charge. Now that I've found him, I'm not so sure.* "Be careful about what you ask for. You just might get it," she mumbled.

"What?" Drew asked.

"Just talking to myself," Marcy replied tartly. Hearing her response, Danny brightened.

"Do you listen to yourself?" Danny inquired.

"Not often enough," she answered with a wry smile.

"Do you ever answer yourself?"

"No, I don't think so."

"Well, then, you're not *that* crazy," Danny replied. "Just slightly cracked." Marcy laughed.

"Go on. Get out of here, you little skink." She hugged him impulsively.

"Hey! You're squeezing too hard!"

"Go!" She shoved him away. "Have fun." He turned and ran away from the adults, who anxiously watched him depart. He had suffered too much, too soon. They felt his pain, even if he could not.

"Hey, Mikey!" he shouted as he ran. "What's for supper?"

AT FIVE O'CLOCK, AFTER A LENGTHY VISIT WITH DELIA RAWLINGS, Drew, Marcy, and Ches left the chilly confines of her office and stepped out with her into the late afternoon heat. She had thoroughly enjoyed their company. As Chesterfield finished their discussion with the sheriff regarding fascinating past events involving the infamous Provencenti crime family, Marcy called Drew's number. Danny picked up on the third ring.

"Hi, Danny."

"Aunt Marcy," he blurted, without so much as a hello. "Can I stay with Mikey tonight?"

"I don't know, Danny."

"Please? Please?"

"Where are you right now?"

"We're at Mikey's uncle's house. He's a high-school teacher. Mikey's granddaddy is preaching a revival here in Pezner, and I want to go tonight. Can I go? Please?"

"A revival? That doesn't sound like you. What's the catch?"

"There ain't no catch, Aunt Marcy. It's an old-timey revival, with a Gospel band from out of town, people singing and clapping, and some old-school preaching. That good old, fiery bring-stone type of preaching."

"Brimstone. It's fire and brimstone, not fiery bring-stone."

"Yeah, that. And that ain't all, Aunt Marcy," he added, lowering his voice. "His granddaddy has white hair and a beard that looks like Moses. He has this big ol' jaggedy white scar that runs right down his face, with a gray eyeball and a wooden leg to boot. It'll be cool."

"Now, *that* sounds like my Danny," she replied, rolling her eyes. "What's his uncle's name?"

"Uncle Ivory. Ivory Goodenough. He's right here in the kitchen making French fries from scratch. He cut 'em from potatoes with a kitchen knife. They ain't the frozen kind in a bag. He's fryin' 'em in hog lard. Man, do they taste good!"

"Okay, wait a minute." Marcy placed the phone on mute. "Sheriff, I'm sorry to interrupt, but could you help me out?"

"Sure," she said, turning from Chesterfield. "What's up?"

"Danny wants to stay overnight in the house of a man named Ivory Goodenough. We don't know the folks around here. Do you know Mr. Goodenough?"

"Ivory? Sure."

"Is he a good man? Can I leave Danny with him?"

"Certainly. He's a prince among men. Here, honey," she offered. "Let me talk to the boy." Marcy handed her the phone.

"Danny?"

"This is Mikey. Danny asked me to talk to his aunt."

"Hi, Mikey. This is Sheriff Rawlings."

"Oh. Hello, Miss Delia," Mikey breathed, awed by the famous sheriff.

"Would you please put your Uncle Ivory on the phone?"

"Yes, ma'am." He handed the phone to his uncle, who busily stirred sliced potatoes, frying in a large iron skillet.

"This is Ivory," he said, passing the spatula to his nephew and signaling for him to stir. "How can I help you?"

"Ivory, this is Delia Rawlings."

"Hello, Miss Delia. How are you?"

"Never better. I have a question."

"Fire away."

"Do you mind if Danny Johnston stays at your house tonight?" Hers was a question loaded with unspoken meaning. The Johnston family had garnered great controversy in this part of the state. Peter Johnston and his evil father had stirred bad blood throughout their lives with their in-your-face racism. Some citizens blamed the entire Johnston family for the sins of the few.

"Of course it's all right for the boy to stay here. He's promised to mind his Ps and Qs," he added, glancing at Danny skeptically. Uncle Ivory wagged a finger, and Danny smiled.

By profession, Ivory had spent most of his career dealing with teenagers. Hard experience had tempered his enthusiasm without dulling his love of children. Danny nodded jubilantly, aware that Ivory could not be conned, but happy in spite of that fact.

"The boy's been through a lot, Ivory. Y'all take care of him, okay?" Delia paused uneasily. *Why am I worried about Ivory's family?* she wondered. *The threat's over. Peter Johnston is dead.*

"Mikey loves Danny like a brother," Ivory replied. "We'll take good care of him."

"Thank you. And please tell Mother Goodenough that I said hi."

"Yes, ma'am. And you can tell his Aunt Marcy that I'll drive him home tomorrow. I haven't been in Cutler County in years. I hear they've got a new bowling alley on Highway 34."

"Here's his Aunt Marcy," Delia added. "Hold on just a minute." She covered the receiver and addressed her.

"Ivory said it'll be fine. He's offered to drive Danny back to your ranch tomorrow." She handed Marcy the phone.

"Mr. Goodenough?" Marcy asked.

"Yes, ma'am?"

"Thanks for letting Danny stay at your house."

"I don't mind. I kind'a like the little rascal," he smiled at Danny, who feigned innocence.

"Well, thanks anyway. After all he's been through, he needs a chance to just be a normal kid."

"We'll give him that. Don't you worry."

"We'll see you tomorrow." She ended the call, relieved and anxious at the same time. *Why am I so worried?*

Marcy had no logical reason for concern. And yet, for some reason, anxiety caused butterflies to swarm in her stomach. *What's that about?* she asked herself. She seriously considered that perhaps the past few days had driven her slightly mad.

THEY SCARCELY SPOKE DURING THE DRIVE back to the Johnston's ranch. After dinner, Marcy and Drew took a walk down to the wooden dock that jutted awkwardly out into the middle of the small lake behind the house. They sat on the bench at the end, far from shore, and stared out across the still waters. The sun had begun to set, and the light gloriously filled the sky, shooting red and gold rays in every direction from the midst of a thunderhead that hovered in the distance above the western horizon.

"Beautiful," Drew said quietly.

"Yes, it is," Marcy affirmed. "God is good."

"Marcy?" he asked reluctantly.

"Yes?"

"After all that your family's been through, how can you still say that God is good?" He gazed at her from the corner of his eye, curious about her reply.

She looked at him, slightly surprised.

"Well… I just believe it, Drew. I believe that God was in Jesus, giving his own life for us. He took our place and suffered our condemnation so that we can live with Him. That proves his love."

"What about the evil in the world? How could a good God allow it?"

"God gives people free will. People either trust Him, or they follow something else… money, fame, their egos, whatever."

"So, God is totally good?"

"As innocent as a lamb."

"Do people have to believe in Jesus Christ to be saved?"

"That's what I believe."

"Why?"

"Well… it's like we were drowning, and He threw us one perfect lifeline. To be saved, we have to believe that it's a lifeline."

"But what about people who have never heard the truth?"

"They can't be held responsible, can they?"

"Okay, then… what if they've heard it, but they're not sure?"

"Anyone who doubts the gospel can ask God to show him the truth. If a person asks, they'll see. If not, it's not God's fault."

"So, we're all guilty, and it's not God's fault?"

"Not quite. We're all guilty unless we let God pay our debt."

"How do we do that, Marcy?"

"Believe in Jesus Christ. If you really believe, you'll follow Him."

"I believe that Jesus is the Son of God," Drew said, surprised to hear the words emerging from his mouth. *It's true. I do believe it.* He marveled at the fact.

"Really?" Marcy asked, taken aback.

"Well, yes, I do. I believe that Jesus is the Messiah. But what do I do about it?" Shocked to silence, Marcy stared at Drew intently. As he looked at her face, he noticed tears in her eyes.

"What do I do about it?" he repeated quietly, as if to himself. In response, Marcy felt powerful joy arise, deep in her heart. She laid her hand lightly upon his.

"Hold on for dear life," she said, with a smile that rivaled the sun. "It's gonna be a bumpy ride."

Stalking Horse

Dusk descended like a cold, wet blanket on the quiet streets of Pezner. For 30 minutes, hard rain pummeled the little town, but by nine o'clock, the rain had stopped and the revival had begun.

The worshippers gathered beneath a huge tent in a vacant lot at the edge of downtown. The tent had no walls. The sides, tied up after the rain ended, allowed the moist summer breeze to bless the gathered faithful. A warm wind slipped between the grateful souls, as if searching for a seat.

Danny and Mikey sat down near the right rear of the tent, at the edge of the aisle. Behind them, in the center section, sat the killer.

Now and again he glanced at the boy. To blend into the mass of humanity, he stood when the congregation stood and he clapped when they clapped, pretending to focus on the music. A tall, fair-skinned white male in his mid-30s, the killer did not stand out in the crowd. He had dressed in local casual dress: clean, faded jeans and a thin, checkered shirt. He blended easily into the packed audience.

The tent offered a mixed bag of cultures and backgrounds: blue collar laborers and sedate office workers, reformed criminals and lifelong believers: the black and the brown, red and tan, rich, poor, sinners, saints, and one well-disguised killer stalking his prey from close quarters.

After a series of upbeat songs, the crowd began to move more slowly, swaying as they worshipped with all of their hearts. As they hungered for righteousness, the killer hungered for the life of his quarry. He wanted nothing to do with their vain superstition, or so he told himself.

He wanted Danny Johnston. He wanted to see him dead.

As the music paused, an elder of great age, seated at the edge of the stage, struggled to his feet and slowly approached the microphone. He limped as he walked but did not display pain or sorrow: to the contrary, his face seemed alight with serenity and joy. Even the killer took note, impressed by the man's formidable dignity.

The prophet Isaiah Goodenough, a thin, wide-shouldered, dark brown man burnt black by the hot Florida sun, stood tall and walked gracefully across the stage. Dressed in a plain black suit that hung loosely on his lanky frame, he resembled nothing so much as a seer of the old days, recently returned from a desert place. He had buttoned his rigidly starched white shirt at the neck, but he wore neither tie nor hat.

An ethereal crown of flowing white hair surrounded Isaiah's head like a diaphanous, ivory halo. The white cloud hovered around his ebony face as if it prepared to discharge a bolt of righteousness to enliven the faithful and scorch the scornful where they sat. A pure, white beard cascaded down from his face to his chest, as vast and significant as the snowy crown atop his head.

Isaiah Goodenough reached the lectern and stood sternly behind it, clutching the weathered brown wood with hard, knobby hands as he scanned the crowd with unflinching ardor. He turned his head aside and shook it as if to clear the cobwebs, then looked again at the crowd.

Even from the back of the tent, the killer could see the pale, jagged scar that ran down from the preacher's forehead, across his left eye, through his cheek, and down into a cloven upper lip. His left eye, lifeless and gray, glistened like a steel ball beneath the bright lights.

Long ago, during his wayward youth, the preacher had suffered a nasty slash wound. The faded remnants of that evil encounter had left an indelible tattoo across his face, severing half of his earthly vision forever. For some reason, the thought unnerved the killer. An unexpected sense of revulsion – out of the clear, black sky – caused him to shiver with disgust. *That old man is eerie,* he thought. *This whole show is eerie... even the music.* He knew nothing of tent revivals, nor did he care to learn. He had simply followed his prey to this unlikely event, watching and waiting for a chance to strike.

"The Lord is good," the old man began with a low and fervent voice. In the quiet after he spoke, scattered 'amens' could be heard. "The Lord our God is mighty!" he thundered suddenly. The crowd responded with heart-felt 'amens' and loud shouts of assent.

"Man is not good," he stated. "Men are evil, indeed. If you have come to mock my words, you would be well advised to turn away. Shut the book! Turn the page! Run away before your mockery cuts you like a sword!"

"Amen!" a voice cried from the back row.

"Jesus is the Mighty God!" the preacher cried in full voice, filled with invisible power. It seemed as if the sound of his voice might cause the glass of water to vibrate off his lectern, but it somehow stayed in its place.

"God alone is our Holy Father."

"Amen!" several voices shouted in unison.

"The Holy Spirit is our Strength."

"Amen!"

"The Lord, the God of Israel, is one Lord."

"Glory!" a deep voice cried in response.

"God has come to live within us. He has bought us with his own blood." The preacher looked around slowly. "The Gospel is no myth. The words of life hold the power of salvation." He paused again. The tent remained silent.

"The Gospel is simple." He looked around the assembly. "Jesus died for the sins of the world. He was resurrected for our justification. In Jesus of Nazareth, God visited his people Israel, and now, He has visited us. He lives within us. Our Gospel declares the mystery: Christ in us, the hope of glory!" Together as one, the crowd stood on its feet and responded with cries of joy. The killer stood with them, staring curiously at his prey. The boy appeared to be fascinated by the tall preacher with his message of eternal love.

"There's somebody here who's wonderin' if God exists. You've been through hell. Well, so has God. Think about how He suffered when He walked in human flesh. He was hung on a cross by the very folks he loved best. He was hung up in shame, for the whole world to see. You're wonderin' whether God is alive? Well, maybe God is wonderin' whether you're alive!" He quieted the laughter with a large, calloused hand. "I'm asking you a question. Are you alive to God? Are you alive to His Word?" The audience hushed.

"Haven't you seen His power? Didn't he forgive a murderer who taunted Him… even as He hung on the cross?" The preacher stopped. The crowd remained silent. "I'm talkin' to you. You know who you are. Your daddy became a believer just before he died. Didn't he tell your mama about it? Weren't you hidin' in that attic when you heard him share the good news?"

"Lord, have mercy," a female voice moaned, redolent with sympathy.

"You know who you are. God has nothin' to prove. But you haven't told anybody these things, so you know down deep inside that my message is from God. I don't know who you are, but I do know this." He paused, and then smiled. "Tonight is your night."

"Oh, yes," a soft voice murmured fervently.

"This is your moment!" He cried the words with power. "This is when it all comes together. This is the night when it all makes sense."

"Glory!" cried a voice. The rest of the crowd stood silently without moving, rapt faces focused on the wise old preacher.

"My son, you ain't a child no more!" he cried. "Your childhood has been stolen by the devil. Now, he's tryin' to steal your soul! Well, there's no need foolin' around with it. You gots t'listen to what your mama and your daddy tol' you.

"You gots to stand on your own two feet. You gots to stand like your mama tol' you, the last time you two talked."

The blood drained from Danny's face. *How does he know what Mama said the last time we talked? How does he know what I heard Daddy say when I was hiding in the attic? I haven't told a soul.*

"You gots to stand up now, son. You gots to become a man."

"Mercy," a voice said softly.

"God loves you, son. He hasn't given up on you. Don't you give up on him." He wiped his face, looking frail and faded. "You know who you is," he added wearily. Then, his eyes flashed upwards, and power clothed him again, like a mantle.

"This is your night!" he cried. "Cry out to the Lord in the Name of Jesus! He will pour out a blessing beyond your wildest dreams."

The preacher halted abruptly. His countenance seemed to darken, turning angry: like a storm cloud about to unleash hail upon the land.

"Now, I'm goin' to change the subject." He paused and took a sip of water. "I'm gonna talk to someone else. I'm talkin' to you… you hunter of men. You know who you are!" He pointed toward the back of the tent. "How does it feel to earn your 30 pieces of silver? You lust for blood, you child of the devil, but God knows your evil works! The blood of your brother cries out against you!"

The preacher's words stunned the killer. *Do they always preach like this?* He had the uncanny sense that the preacher had pointed directly at him, but the idea seemed illogical, so he rejected it out of hand. *They must preach like this all the time.*

"Turn from your wickedness while you still have a chance," the preacher cried. "If you do not hear me – if you do not repent – your end will come suddenly, and there will be no deliverance." He paused and slowed, catching his breath.

The sweltering worshippers, focusing on the sermon, did not notice when a visitor slipped out the rear of the tent. After leaving, he paused in the darkness and looked back at the bright lights and the colorful crowd inside the tent.

"Freaks," he spat angrily. On the way to his car, he took out his keys. Whistling tunelessly as he passed a new Cadillac, he raked a key down the side for good luck.

The killer reassured himself that he lived within the realm of logic, dwelling high above the cowardly superstitions of religion… especially the primitive religion practiced in that tent. His was a rational universe in which he planned to live, kill, and thrive on his own terms. For him, the math seemed straightforward: one gun plus one child equals one night of fun.

A song came into his mind. He could imagine it clearly, as if he heard a tape rolling. In the song, Mark Knopfler had played one of the greatest guitar riffs of all time. His own version of the lyrics made him smile. *I got the moves... 'cause I'm the lion. Money for killin', and the lambs are free.*

He had resolved the matter. Time was on his side. He would wait for the perfect opportunity. And then, like a serpent, he would strike.

Alter Call

For 30 minutes, the preacher continued his sermon, offering hope to villain and victim alike. He exhorted them to strive for the faith of the saints, to follow the example of holy men and women of ages past. The band began to play. The choir started to sing, and the voices took wing.

Danny heard a celestial refrain: the uncut music of the angels. For some reason beyond coincidence, they began to sing his mother's favorite songs: devotional offerings with gorgeous melodies, full-throated and lush. He felt stunned. He had not expected this. He had come for entertainment, not for miracles.

The anticipation felt palpable. The worshippers had come in faith, expecting to experience holiness. They waited, hushed and reverent like the crowds at Lourdes, expecting a miracle.

Danny had come to see a scar-faced preacher who spoke like Moses and walked on a wooden leg. He had joined the singing skeptically, because his mother would have wanted him to.

He remained for a better reason.

The preaching and the singing began to touch the core of his soul. Somehow, as he listened, he started to feel alive for the first time, stirred deep inside by a clean breath of fresh air.

During the singing, something awakened his deadened emotions. With their return came stunning pain – the memory of bereavement. And yet, the pain seemed bearable in the presence of holiness. The hope of heaven, which had sustained his parents, came alive within him. *They're living with Jesus*. At the thought, he wept.

Softly at first, the congregation began to sing a classic hymn. The lyrics – written centuries ago by Sir Isaac Watts at the advent of America's Great Awakening – comforted his grieving soul.

> When I remember the wondrous cross
> On which the Lord of Glory died,

> My richest gain I count as loss
> And pour contempt on all my pride.

Somehow, through the agony of bereavement, Danny caught a glimpse of the depths of love poured out through the broken body of the Jewish Messiah, Jesus of Nazareth. This one man, of his own, free choice, had shed his blood to save the world from death. After suffering at the hands of evil men, he had risen from the grave.

> See from His head, His hands, His feet,
> Sorrow and love flow mingled down:
> Did e'er such love and sorrow meet,
> Or thorns compose so rich a crown?

As he sang the hymn, Danny experienced a revelation.

For love, God had laid aside the honors of heaven. Out of love, He had taken on flesh through the body of Christ. For love, the Lord had suffered unspeakable agonies on a shameful cross. He had endured death at the hands of those he loved, to free those who loved him from death, forever. By His life, His death, and His resurrection, Jesus gave life to all who believed.

How could Danny repay such love? The last verse sung by the congregation expressed his feelings in full.

> Were the whole realm of nature mine,
> That were an offering far too small.
> Love so amazing, so divine,
> Deserves my soul, my life, my all.

He made up his mind. He had doubted the New Testament for years, but he would doubt it no more. Deep within his heart, Danny made a life-altering commitment to answer the call. *I will follow you, Jesus,* he prayed with all his heart. The God of Israel – the God of his mother and father – would now be his God. He would begin to read the New Testament, and he would follow the teachings of Christ. In Christ alone he would hope and trust.

Danny had come to see the spectacle. He had sung hymns to honor the memory of his mother.

He would stay for better reasons.

DANNY WOULD NEED ALL OF HIS NEWFOUND FAITH to weather the impending storm. A killer had entered Danny's world, intent upon snuffing out his tender life, determined to savor the experience.

The killer longed to crush, to break, and to twist his victim like a psychotic child might torment an unsuspecting puppy. He yearned to take – no, to taste – his pound of bloody flesh from Danny's throbbing, teenaged heart.

As a type-A perfectionist who planned his work impeccably, this man had never failed to get his man, woman, or child. He had fixed his sites on the latest prize, and had locked down on his target.

Soon – too soon – he would smash into Danny's life, intent upon destruction. And deep within him – down, deep inside – the killer felt certain that it would all end badly.

The thought made him almost giddy with glee.

Lakeside Manners

Beneath the stars, they rested without speaking, flat on their backs at the end of the long wooden dock. The distant drone of shore-bound mosquitoes sounded a dirge of futility, for the length of the dock had conspired with the evening breeze to thwart their bloody insect dreams.

Drew and Marcy lay side-by-side and silently observed the dazzling night sky. The stars filled the void above them with indescribable beauty: untouchable, remote, unfathomable, and profound. Each star glimmered in masterful splendor, as if glad of the moon's departure. After a long silence, Marcy spoke.

"How about those stars?" she asked.

"Awesome," Drew replied softly.

"That about says it," Marcy agreed.

"Yep."

They quit speaking, taking a clue from the heavens. The darkened night wrapped them in a mysterious mantle of unutterable, ineffable beauty. The silent sky, inscrutably serene, bore the hallmark of creative genius. The earth had once born the same, spotless stamp, but men had shamelessly soiled it.

For the two young souls on the dock, a jaded world held little interest. They lay quietly, side-by-side, staring up at the unmeasured heavens. The peace of the night settled in like a fog.

For a long time they lay without moving, silently watching the sky. Then, lost among star-clouds and shimmering lights, they fell sweetly – and softly – asleep.

Powering Up

At a truck stop just outside of Tallahassee, on a lazy Wednesday morning, Streetcar used a pre-paid phone card to call the downtown law offices of Calhoun, Portnoy, and Schmetzengraf. To his considerable surprise, a person – not a machine – picked up.

"C P & S," spoke a youngish male voice with a slow southern drawl. "Can I help you?"

"Uh, yeah. I promised a friend that I would call Clay Calhoun. He's listed in the phone book under your firm. I guess I need a lawyer." At the sound of the raspy voice on the other end of the line, the attorney slowly swung his feet off his desk and scrounged for a piece of paper. He was a tall, thin criminal attorney in his late 30s with an unruly shock of blond hair and a handsome, boyish appearance.

"This is Clay. Who referred you?"

"Jamie James. I mean, she's Jamie Hawkins now. She got hurt last week, but the newspapers say that she's okay." He waited for a reply.

"Jamie referred you?"

"I'm her friend, Streetcar." Clay Calhoun gasped inadvertently, then slowly exhaled. He recognized the name and knew immediately that he was speaking to a man wanted for questioning in the nation's largest unsolved domestic terrorism case.

"You'll have to turn yourself in immediately," he said.

"I know. I'm ready."

"Where are you right now?"

"I'm west of Tallahassee on Highway 20, a few miles from the city limits. I'm driving towards town."

"Okay. I'll get in my car and head your way. Call my cell phone in ten minutes." He gave him his number and hung up. Exactly ten minutes later, the phone rang as Clay drove west on Tennessee

Street. "Where are you now?" he asked.

"I've stopped at a McDonald's near an auto parts store."

"Okay, perfect, I know where you are. I'll be there soon." He shut his telephone. In a few minutes, just past the Capital Circle intersection, he turned right into the old Tax World complex that had once housed offices of the Florida Department of Revenue. At the McDonald's beside the entrance, he parked his car and walked inside.

Clay recognized Jamie's friend immediately from the picture on the FBI's Website. He felt a surge of pity, for it appeared obvious that someone had beaten Streetcar within an inch of his life. His face showed evidence of brutal treatment: two black eyes, a split upper lip, and ugly splotches of purple slashed from forehead to cheek like morbid tattoos. A three-day growth of salt-and-pepper beard pocked his olive skin, and a dirty white shirt hung on his broad, thin shoulders like a worn-out flag of surrender.

Clay saw a broken, aged remnant of the outsized boy who had enlisted in the Army at age 16 after successfully lying about his age. Somewhere between Vietnam and the States, Streetcar had lost his way.

After the war, Streetcar had ached with loneliness as he tried to start over. America had changed beyond recognition. During the war, he had made his home back in the jungle of Vietnam. There, his heart remained. Years after Saigon fell, when he worked as a cop in San Francisco, he still felt like a lone soldier manning a forgotten outpost.

Theoretically, Streetcar's tour of duty had ended long ago. In fact, it had not ended. His men had come in from the cold, but he still lived at the fringe of society, mistrusting its cold comforts. During his tour, America had changed into something hard and new... a place, it seemed, with no place for lost souls.

When Streetcar saw Clay walking into McDonald's, he recognized immediately that he had to be the attorney mentioned by Jamie, and he suddenly felt even more out of place. His dirty clothes contrasted completely with Clay's suspenders and tie, impeccable hair, and glossy black shoes. He stood up in dismay, suddenly ashamed, slicking his hair with his left hand as he extended his right.

"Hey," he uttered. Dismayed by his own rough appearance, Streetcar froze like a bunny in a spotlight.

"Hello. I'm Clay Calhoun," the attorney said, shaking Streetcar's greasy hand. "You must be Jamie's friend." Clay directed him to a corner where they could talk without interruption.

"Yeah, I'm the guy," Streetcar mumbled, ducking his head. "Jamie told me to call you. Not that I need help, or anything like that. If Jumbo was here, he'd tell you I'm independent. But Jumbo can't be here, because he's dead. But if he was here, he'd tell you I do things on my own. You know?"

"I'm afraid I do."

"I want to turn myself in."

"Good. But first, I need to know something." Clay leaned close to Streetcar, his eyes narrowing. "I need your word on something."

"About what?"

"If I become your lawyer, will you follow my advice?"

"What advice?" Streetcar asked. Clay lowered his voice and glanced surreptitiously around the room.

"I know you're wanted for questioning, but I suspect that they don't have much evidence. I'm asking that no matter what, you do not talk to anyone but me. Don't speak to anyone unless I'm present, and don't volunteer anything. If there's any doubt, wait for my okay. We can discuss it before you answer. Do you understand?"

"Yeah."

"We need to see the government's case. They have to prove their case beyond a reasonable doubt."

"Whatever they say, I probably did it."

"That's exactly what I mean. You can tell me that in private. But you have to promise me that you don't say a thing to anyone else.

"Don't get me wrong; I'm not asking you to lie. I'm asking you to guard what you say. Just run it by me first, and listen to my advice. Do you understand?"

"Well… yeah, sure. I guess that's why Jamie asked me to talk to you."

"Good. Then, just to confirm, do you promise that you won't speak to anyone but me… about any crimes that you may or may not have committed?"

"You talk like a lawyer."

"I am a lawyer," Clay replied with a slight smile. "Do you promise?"

"I guess so."

"You won't allow yourself to be interviewed if I'm not present, right?"

"Right."

"All right, I'll take your case." Clay leaned back in the colorful yellow McDonald's bench and sighed.

"That's it?"

"That's it."

"No cash needed? Do you take checks?"

"Not necessary. You've got some wealthy friends who believe in you. You need to let them help you."

"What? I don't have any rich friends."

"Janelle Hawkins and Sheriff Rawlings are your friends. Let them pick up the tab."

"Jamie and Delia, rich?"

"Yep."

"No kiddin'?"

"No kiddin'." Clay raised one eyebrow.

"Wow! Who'd'a thunk it? Jamie and Delia?" Streetcar looked around the room and spotted a group of polite Tallahassee teenagers who had just entered the restaurant. "Hey, guess what?" he called. "My friends are rich." They looked at him in surprise, shocked into silence by his bruised, broken appearance.

"You can start listening to me right now," Clay interrupted, embarrassed by Streetcar's social ineptitude.

"Sure."

"Let me drive you downtown. I've got a friend who works for

the FBI, and I'll call him on the way. We'll meet him at the Sheriff's Department. You'll be voluntarily surrendering for questioning, but only when I'm present. Do you understand?"

"Sure." They left the McDonald's and climbed into Clay's Lexus coupe.

"Nice car," Streetcar commented. "But it's not nearly as nice as a Lamborghini. Jamie took me for a ride in a Lamborghini once."

"You're just in time, Mr. Benuto," Clay interjected. "I learned online that America's Most Wanted will be featuring you this week on national TV. They don't often feature an uncharged suspect, but you're the principle person of interest in the country's largest unsolved domestic terrorism case." The car wheeled out of the parking lot and sped into eastbound traffic.

"I'm just in time," Streetcar echoed happily, slicking back his hair. After days of tension, he began to experience an emotional release accompanied by a disjointed burst of glee. "Just in time to go in the old slammer-jammer. Into the big house. We're goin' to lockup, boys. Down the river to the joint."

"Funny."

"Thanks."

"Did anyone ever tell you that you look like Sam Elliot?"

"Are you gay?" Streetcar asked out of innocent curiosity. "Not that I'd judge you for it."

"No," Clay replied defensively. "Not that I'm afraid of your judgment. I'm married, thank you. Straight as an arrow."

"Keep tellin' yourself that, pal." The comment irritated Clay. *The nerve!*

"I'll have you know..." he began testily.

"Gotcha!" Streetcar interjected. "Ha ha ha!"

"Very funny."

"I really had you goin', huh?" Clay stared at him with an expression matching the teenagers' at McDonald's.

"Yep," Clay conceded with grudging respect. "You really had me goin'."

"Not that I'd judge you for it!"

Clay laughed aloud, glad that his new acquaintance could enjoy his final moments of freedom. A few blocks ahead, the county jail awaited his improbable cargo. In that cage of lost souls, bound by concrete and steel, the laughter would quickly die away.

A Return to the Scene

Danny called Aunt Marcy just after noon. When he learned that she would be cleaning the house all day, preparing for Win's homecoming, he asked to speak to Drew.

"Do you feel like takin' a drive in the country?" he asked Drew, coming immediately to the point.

"Takin' a drive?" he asked, raising his eyebrows at Marcy. "I don't know. Is it okay with your aunt?"

"I don't believe you!" Danny sputtered. "What are you turning into, man? Listen to yourself! You're a rocker... you're supposed to be a rebel!"

"Hey, kid, I don't have the authority to approve what you do. And to tell you the truth, I'm not in a hurry to die at the hands of the beautiful young woman who happens to be your aunt."

"You wimp," Danny said in disgust, rolling his eyes. "He's a wimp," he said to his friend Mikey, who was playing a video game.

"Rock and roll," Mikey replied with a sarcastic smirk. "What's it coming to?"

"Just cooperate, okay?" Drew suggested. "Talk to your aunt and get her approval. Can't we all just get along?" Drew looked at Marcy, who frowned and took the phone from his hand.

"You make me sound like an ogre," she muttered, putting the phone to her ear.

"Sorry about that," Drew replied wisely.

"Okay, Danny. What do you want?"

"I heard you guys fussin' with each other, Aunt Marcy!" Danny said happily. "Y'all sound like an old married couple."

"And?"

"Can Drew pick me up? I want to take a ride in the country."

"I thought Mr. Ivory was going to give you a ride home," she answered skeptically.

"He's ready, but I asked if I could call you first." Danny adopted his most innocent tone. "I was just wonderin'... you know, now that it's safe... if I could go by the place where we used to live. They say the house burned down, but I heard that the old barn is still standin'. There might be some things there I can save."

"Of course. You can go there if Drew will drive you. But don't stay past sundown, okay? It's an hour away." *The poor boy... Dan and Sarah dead... it's unspeakable.*

"Sure, Aunt Marcy. Can you put Drew back on?" She handed the phone to Drew and turned to wipe away a tear.

"What's up, junior?"

"Do you mind drivin' me to Davis County? I want to visit our old house. It's okay with Aunt Marcy." When Drew looked at her, Marcy nodded and waved her handkerchief, still fighting the tears.

"Okay, sure. Where are we going?"

"It's about an hour's drive from Pezner on Highway 67, through some real pretty countryside. No, make that a half hour the way you drive."

"No problem."

"Aunt Marcy wants us to leave before dark to come back home, but that's okay with me. I don't want to stay after dark. It would be too spooky."

"At your service, kid." He took directions, hung up the phone, and shrugged. "Well, I guess I'll be hittin' the road then."

"Thanks so much," Marcy offered.

"I like to drive. It'll be fun."

"Really, thanks for everything you've done for Danny," she persisted. They paused awkwardly.

"Okay, I'm out of here. You can reach me on my cell... once I get it back from the kid, that is." He retrieved a can of Pepsi from the refrigerator, cracked the top, and walked out just as Ches began to enter the room. They squeezed past one another awkwardly. *He's a good guy,* Drew reflected as he walked down the front steps of the clean white cracker homestead. Back in the kitchen, Chesterfield watched Marcy as she carefully tucked away her handkerchief.

"Are you okay?" he asked.

"I'm surviving." She considered the truth of her answer. *I'm barely surviving.* As she considered the events of the past several days, she wondered whether her world, knocked so badly askew, would ever again be righted.

Kicking Back

Drew's rented Thunderbird coupe rocked down the unpaved country lane and rounded a sharp bend. Directly ahead, at the end of a long, dusty driveway, they could see the ruins of what had once been Danny Johnston's safe house. *Safe house,* Drew reflected. *What a cruel joke for Danny's parents.*

Consumed by arson, the two-story farmhouse had morphed into a charred mess, fused with the melted, glassy earth. Looming above the ruin, a few feeble black sticks, lacking the strength to stand, leaned against one another for support. Only a soot-covered chimney remained unbowed, blasted and gaunt, but otherwise unchanged by the fervent heat. On the carbonized earth, shards of broken glass twinkled in the afternoon sun, scattered across the clearing like diamonds in the rough black sand.

"That's nasty," Danny observed sadly. "This house was so nice." As numb as he had been for the past few days, the extent of his sorrow surprised Danny. "I'm glad Mama and Daddy died before it burned."

"That building's still standing," Drew observed, pointing toward an oversized barn that towered among the oaks to their left.

"That's the workshop. I was hopin' it would be okay. Daddy used to work there. He was a sculptor. A metal sculptor."

"I didn't know that."

Drew parked the car, and they stepped into the clear heat of a July afternoon in Davis County. "Go ahead," Drew suggested. "I'll catch up." *This place gives me the creeps,* he thought.

As Danny ducked beneath the yellow crime scene tape that ringed the yard, Drew fished in the glove compartment and retrieved his revolver. *I've got a permit, so I might as well take advantage of it. After all of the craziness we've been through, I'll feel safer if I carry this thing.* For an instant, the warning of Elder Cromartie flashed through his memory. Then he pushed it out of his mind and tucked the gun in his jeans behind his back, stepping away from the car with the weapon concealed beneath his loose cotton shirt. Hurrying to catch up, he ducked beneath the yellow tape and trotted after Danny. Drew stepped into the barn just as Danny turned on the lights.

What he saw amazed him. He felt too surprised to gasp.

The huge old barn, with rusty nails protruding from unfinished walls and a sand-covered wooden floor, showcased an astonishing collection of metallurgical art. To an art lover such as Drew, the sight possessed overwhelming impact.

A contorted forest of art objects dully reflected the incandescent light: works small and great, abstract and realistic: masterworks in carved wood, welded steel, wrought iron, and bronze. The artist had chosen to represent almost every known school of sculpture. Like the stars in last night's sky, the stellar array of stunning works declared the inarguable brilliance of an ingenious creator.

"Your father did all of this?" he whispered, scarcely willing to believe it.

"Yep. We lived here for almost two years. He stayed pretty busy."

"Where'd he learn how to weld like this? Or to cast bronze?"

"He learned welding in prison. He learned about the bronze work on his own after we moved here. He read a bunch of books."

"In prison?" Drew mouthed incredulously, moving his lips without uttering the words. "They taught him how to weld like this?"

"They had a metal shop. Daddy said the teacher used to let him do stuff on his own. I don't think they taught this kind of welding." He looked at Drew and noticed the distant look on his face. "Hello? Are you listening to me?"

"I… uh…"

"Cat got your tongue?"

"I don't know what to say."

"That's a first."

Drew attempted to regain his equilibrium. The thought of such genius, unknown and unheralded – creating dazzling masterworks in an old barn in the middle of nowhere – simply stupefied him.

"Daddy learned how to make bronzes from the books. He made the molds, then he shipped 'em up north to get 'em cast."

"The level of detail is amazing."

"Daddy called it the 'lost ass' technique. He meant jackass."

"Oh."

"He said he was like a poor little jackass who'd lost his way, and that Mama'd come along just in time to save him from his own bad self."

"It's the 'lost wax' technique," Drew replied.

"I know. He told me. Daddy was a big joker."

"I have to tell you something."

"What?"

"This work is incredible. Unbelievable."

"I know. Mama used to say that Daddy was a bona fide genius. He worked out here all day, hammering and welding and going at it like crazy. Even all night, sometimes." Danny began to walk, picking his way through the familiar objects of art. He found what he was looking for in a cleared area beside a large steel table and a cluster of welding tanks.

"Mama used to send me out here to get him when supper was ready," he added half-heartedly. "I stayed away most of the time. I'd rather read books or go fishin'.

"This is it," Danny cried suddenly. "This is why we came here." He stopped in front of a remarkably realistic bronze bust of a beautiful young woman. "They delivered this in a big blue truck, on the last day we lived here. Special delivery all the way from Buffalo, New York," Danny grimaced, suddenly beginning to feel the pain. "I helped him unpack it."

"She's beautiful. Who is she?"

"That's my mama, Drew," Danny replied. He smiled through his tears. "Wasn't she purty?"

"She was beautiful." He felt overwhelmed by the sudden reminder of all that Danny had lost.

"Will you help me load this one in your car so we can take it home? I want to surprise Aunt Marcy."

"Sure. But it looks heavy."

"Don't worry about that. Daddy has… uh, he had… a cart and some moving stuff. It's around here somewhere."

Twenty minutes later, they had wrapped the bronze statue in blankets and strapped it to a heavy handcart. They carefully pushed the statue through the room, wending their way past other elegant works.

At the door, Danny paused. A bronze cross, rough and knotted, hung from a thin steel chain on a nail beside the door. Someone had affixed a small piece of tape to the chain. On the tape, in his father's hand, he read a single word: "Danny."

"Whoa! Cool!" Danny said. "It's got my name on it." He had not shared the story of last night's conversion, unsure of how Drew would take it. Now, he decided to speak. "Hey, Drew; guess what?"

"What?"

"Last night, I became one of those Christian fanatics."

"No kiddin'?"

"No kiddin'. I got saved last night. At the revival."

"Wow. That's quite a coincidence. Do you know why?"

"Why?"

"Last night, I finally realized that I'm a believer, too. That makes me a bona fide Christian, kid. Just like you, only nicer."

"No kiddin'?"

"No kiddin'."

"You, too? Last night?"

"Yep."

"That's unbelievable! It's… it's like we're twins, or something."

"Evil twins, maybe."

"Ha! Evil twins, saved by grace." Danny slipped the necklace over his head. "I think I'm gonna wear this thing."

"Come on, let's load up the statue and get out of here. It's getting close to sundown, and I don't want to get your aunt mad at me by bein' late." Drew leaned on the handcart and balanced the weight on the wheels, preparing to push it in front of him.

"Okay, let's move it."

When Danny opened the door, he saw a glint of light in the meadow beyond their parked car. Grabbing Drew's shoulder, he pulled him swiftly back into the barn. Drew almost dropped the handcart, but managed to back through the doorway and set it down inside.

"What's wrong with you?" he asked. "Man, are you strong!"

"Shh!" Danny hissed. He crept to the window and peeked through in time to see movement at the edge of the woods, behind the Thunderbird coupe. "Do you have your cell phone on you?"

"It's in the car. What's up?"

"Let's get out of here the back way. And I mean now!"

"What's wrong?"

"It's too quiet. No birds, no squirrels, nothin'."

"Oh, yeah," Drew breathed, remembering the hunting trips of his youth. *He's right.*

"There's a predator out there." Danny pointed at the window. "And considering our recent history, are you willing to bet your life that it's a bobcat or a fox?

"No way!"

"Way!"

"I can't believe it!"

"Me neither, but we don't have any choice. Remember the interstate?"

"Yes." Drew took a deep breath. "What should we do?"

"He's a hunter. That makes him predictable. We can use that against him."

"How?"

"Follow me," Danny whispered. "I know the way."

When it came to hunting, Danny had become a real pro.

People Who Read People

After she put the vacuum cleaner in the closet, Marcy collapsed in an overstuffed chair in the living room. On the other side of the room, Chesterfield had temporary forsaken his law books for more mundane pursuits. He leaned back in a recliner and flipped through the pages of People magazine.

"What are you reading?" she asked, half-interested in the answer to her question.

"Some article about Florida's whiz-kid senator, Howard Bedford. He's been appointed as the U.S. rep to the International Parliament in Belgium. Quite an honor."

"Howard Bedford is a pig." Marcy stated the words emphatically, without elaboration.

"Oh?" Ches asked, putting down the magazine. "Do you know him?"

"Yes."

"Really? You're full of secrets."

"Howard attended Cutler High School for two years. He was older than me... older and stronger. That's how I know he's a pig. Or at least, he was back then. He was the second-worst bully in school. My cousin Pete was the worst. But Pete always liked me for some reason. He treated me like a little sister."

"How old were you?"

"I was ten years old when Howie met Pete. After that, they hung out together all the time. They were like two peas in a pod, as thick as thieves. Pete never learned what Howard tried to do to me. If he had ever found out, I think he would have killed Howard."

"What did he do?"

"He tried to rape me, but he didn't succeed. I saw him coming through the trees. After he threw me down, I broke his nose with a rock, and I almost gouged his eye out. He never tried it again."

"Wow."

"Pete was my older cousin. He had been teaching me how to fight since I was a toddler. I never knew why until Howard came along."

"Did you ever tell anybody?"

"Only you. Only today."

"You didn't tell your cousin Peter? He was his friend, right?"

"Are you kidding? Pete would have murdered him, Ches. Do you think I'm exaggerating?"

"No… I guess not."

"Pete would have killed Howie. I didn't want that to happen."

"That was a terrible burden to carry around."

"You're telling me? I lived it. But I've moved on. Howie Bedford hasn't been back to this part of Florida since high school. I say, good riddance. He's a true sociopath."

"If he hasn't been back, how does Danny know him?"

"Danny?"

"Danny's met him."

"Danny's never met Howie Bedford." She stated the words carefully, staring at Chesterfield with doubt in her eyes.

"I think he has. He told me so himself." Marcy stared at him for several seconds.

"Danny said *what?*" she asked incredulously.

"He saw me flipping through this magazine yesterday. He told me that he met Senator Bedford back when the Senator visited Carson Creek Road."

"Danny met Howard Bedford… where?"

"At Carson Creek Road. That's what Danny said. Why?"

"Pete's house is on Carson Creek Road," Marcy replied.

"But why would a United States senator visit Peter Johnston?"

"I told you Howie was a sociopath. Why would an ambitious politician visit the house of a rich drug dealer?"

"Of course. Money, the mother's milk of politics."

"Exactly. Pete must have been bankrolling Howie from the beginning. The news reports say that Pete was a kingpin. If that's true, he had to be doing something with his money. He sure wasn't spending it on clothes. We didn't know that he had a penny."

"I see."

"Why else would Howie visit Pete? They were friends in high school, but friendship only goes so far for a person like Howie." Her mind wandered for a moment as she remembered Howard Bedford. *He was pure evil.*

"I wonder what the Senator thought, seeing your nephew at Pete's house."

"What?" she asked sharply.

"I just wonder."

"Say it again. What do you wonder?"

"I wonder what the Senator thought when he saw Danny at Pete's house. After all, Danny was witnessing a visit that could ruin the Senator's career."

"No!" she cried.

"What?"

"No!"

"No what, already?"

"It wasn't Pete!" she cried, standing on her feet. "Pete didn't have Dan and Sarah killed!"

"Then who did?"

"Howard Bedford." The fullness of the concept hit her with the force of an emotional pile driver. She stood and floundered like a blind woman in a panic, reaching around uncertainly. "It wasn't Pete who killed Dan and Sarah, it was Howie. He had them killed, and then he went after Danny!"

She scrambled for her telephone and pressed speed dial.

"I'm calling Danny," she stated abruptly. "You dial 911. Do it now!" She put the phone to her ear and turned away, biting her lip. "Pick up. Please, please, pick up." The phone began to ring.

Road Kill

As they slipped through a forest of heavy metal sculptures, hurrying to the back of the barn, Drew's cell phone began to ring inside his locked car. It rang several times before falling silent.

At the back of the barn, Danny opened a small back door. He looked both ways and began to run swiftly across a weed-strewn meadow, making for the orange grove less than 200 feet away. Drew followed hard on his heels: head down and running, hard and fast. They reached the trees and did not slow, dodging left and running north for a full mile before they paused at the edge of a lake. The sun had declined beneath the horizon, and the light had begun to fade.

"Let's split up," Danny said, breathing heavily.

As they paused to catch their breath, Drew remembered the words of Elder Cromartie. *Don't take up the sword.* "Here, take the gun," he panted, pulling the stainless steel revolver from behind his back. "I'll lead him away from you."

"Can you shoot?" Danny asked, not taking the gun.

"Not so good with a handgun," Drew replied. They could scarcely talk as they panted heavily with sweat pouring down their faces, soaking their shirts.

"There's a housing development that way," Danny said, pointing north. "Go there. I'll head south towards the truck stop. That way, at least one of us should make it."

Although the boy's logic was irrefutable, Drew did not feel comforted. "No way."

"Way!"

"Take this," Drew ordered, shoving the gun at Danny, who refused to take it.

"Keep it." Danny blurted impulsively.

Without further adieu, he dashed to his right and ran swiftly out of sight.

Drew turned and began to run north, trusting Danny's instincts.

For the moment, Chucky had failed to get his man. Hidden by weeds in the meadow behind Drew's parked Thunderbird, he had mounted his rifle, awaiting their return to the car. He had glanced up from his gun just in time to see his targets slip back into the barn and close the door. Realizing that they had spotted him, he had freed the rifle from its tripod and started his stalk.

The sun had begun to set, but this did not dismay him. He was ever creative, always ready to improvise.

Rounding the barn, he saw their tracks in the soft sand at the edge of the orange grove. He would have no difficulty following such a trail, even in the dark.

After talkng with Danny, Drew ran north for 200 yards before circling back to a bush at the edge of the lake within eyeshot of where they had separated. He quietly checked the chamber for a bullet and switched off the safety, waiting for the killer to arrive. *God, forgive me,* he prayed. *I tried to give this gun to Danny. I don't want to kill anyone. Please help me not to kill ... but most of all, please help us survive.* As he prayed, a weight lifted from his shoulders.

He had reached a decision. He would not shoot to kill, but to distract the man. He would buy time for Danny.

Drew crouched without moving behind a large bush, ready to die in Danny's place. A single strand of sweat trickled down his backbone as raw fear ran roughshod over his soul. Waves of terror swept across his skin, like swarms of voltage from a Van de Graaff generator. His stomach churned, convulsing anxiously.

When Chucky arrived at the lake and saw the diverging footprints, he grimly appreciated the logic of his prey. *The kid must have split them up,* he reflected, carefully scratching his chin. *That little creep has talent.* He literally tightened his belt at this point, taking a notch out of the shiny black leather.

The Canadian hit man had dressed in khaki Dockers and a patterned, moss green shirt, the better to blend into the brush. He wore cross-trainers that resembled boat shoes, perfect for those pesky chases in rural locales. He felt like a million dollars, bursting with rude good health.

He guessed correctly that the child had run south, for he understood the need for consistency in a time of trouble. The boy had followed a similar path through these same orange groves on the night of his parents' murder, navigating the sugary sand until he reached the distant truck stop. Like any animal of prey, he would follow the most familiar route.

WITH HIS SENSES FINELY ATTUNED FOR THE HUNT, the killer felt his hairs stand up on his neck. *That means danger.* He heard a bullet whine loudly past his ear and dropped instantly to the ground. A pistol cracked five more times, somewhere nearby. All five shots whizzed over his head. In the silence that followed, a large puff of smoke drifted lazily from the brush at the edge of the lake.

The killer fired three quick shots into the brush and heard a sharp moan as a bullet struck home. The outcry sounded like that of a man, not a boy. *That isn't him,* he reasoned. *Lucky me. The boy wouldn't have missed.* He heard a splash in the lake, and considered whether he should pause to dispatch the wounded man. *Why not?*

Gambling that the amateur had emptied a revolver, he charged directly toward the shoreline. When he reached it, he saw nothing but a broad, flat pond of bright green hyacinths and lily pads. The surface rippled slightly, as if disturbed by an alligator swimming underwater. Looking down, he saw a single, bloody footprint at the edge of the water. The print bore evidence of an oversized shoe, impressed deeply into the mud.

Oh well, no money here. Passing up an opportunity to kill the wounded man in the water, the killer turned and began to run south. Within two minutes, he had picked up the boy's trail in the sugary sand.

He loped like a leopard, fast and low to the ground, and as he ran he fantasized about the upcoming kill. He felt a deep elation.

"Hey, Bungalow Bill?" he sang softly. "What did you kill, Bungalow Bill?" He laughed at himself. "Hey, king of the kill, what did you kill, king of the hill?" His voice sounded weak, his pitch wandered all over the map, and his vibrato quavered like a cheap Farfisa organ. But in spite of these facts, he grinned.

Chucky could not hold a tune in a body bag, but that did not bother him one whit. He had no aspirations to be a singer. He lived his dream every day. He aspired to be the best hit man around, and he had to admit it: he had reached the top of the mountain.

He was one incredible killer.

AT THE TREE-LINED BORDER between two adjoining orange groves, Danny climbed a small oak to see if he could glimpse the man on his trail. He saw him less then one-half mile away, running at a startlingly fast pace. *I can't stay ahead for long,* Danny realized as he dropped to the ground. He veered to his left, panting hard as he ran. He covered ground furiously, giving his all, fighting to survive. *If I don't make it, Aunt Marcy will kill me.*

The stainless steel towers of the Alcon Citrus Processing Plant loomed ahead of him. At the sight, he redoubled his pace.

Danny almost flew across the unlit, two-lane highway that traversed the front of the plant. He slammed into the locked gates of the plant and climbed the chain link helter-skelter, ten feet straight up, like a human squirrel. He rolled over the top without pausing and dropped down into the loose sand as a bullet struck steel from the gate above his head, kicking up a shower of sparks before whistling sideways into the growing darkness. Immediately after the noisy ricochet, Danny heard the distant crack of a high-velocity rifle. The sound echoed through the orange grove and reverberated between the empty buildings of the deserted concentrate plant.

Danny ducked behind the cooling towers and used them as cover to run across the empty parking lot, sheltered by their concrete eminence. He ran for his life, not knowing his destination, unfamiliar with the layout of the exotic citrus concentrate plant. This was foreign territory to the boy: an alien industrial hardscape filled with man-made mists and the pungent smell of molasses mingled with orange peels: rotted fruit and sour acid, sickly-sweet cattle feed, raw lye and fermented citrus sugar.

THE KILLER PAUSED BEFORE CROSSING the empty highway. As he paused, he turned right and glanced toward the western horizon. A few streaks of light clung to the fringe of the western sky, fading by the minute.

At that moment, for an unknown reason, the hair on the back of his arms stood up. *Is that danger... again? I don't think so.* Nevertheless, an instinctive fear played across the surface of his skin like static electricity. He did not understand such instincts, but as a hunter, he had long ago learned to heed them.

When he turned to look east, down the darkened road to his left, he saw a sight that he could scarcely fathom, standing among the low bushes near the southern shoulder of the road. *What in the world is that? A gigantic house cat?*

To his inestimable surprise, he realized that he was staring at a mature Florida panther. In the gathering darkness, the cat looked coal black: huge and ominous and burning with hidden energy. The panther paused in the low bushes, partially hidden by palmetto fronds.

Without warning, the big male sprung into motion, leaping as if he had been launched from a missile tube. He soared high above a stack of empty barrels at the edge of the road and landed in the middle of the asphalt, swishing a long, heavy tail. At that very moment, he turned and stared at Chucky.

The Canadian, an urbanite by birth and choice, trembled in the road less than 50 yards away. He held his rifle tightly: his eyes wide open as he stared with unfamiliar fear.

The panther opened his mouth and screamed at the armed man. At the sound, he quailed in terror.

This was not the roar of a Western cougar, nor was it the

unforgettable shriek of a bobcat. This was a sound unique in the animal kingdom: the scream of a wild Florida panther. The big cat screamed ethereally, like an otherworldly human and feline hybrid hitting a high note at the end of a Wagnerian aria. The tone was hyper-naturally piercing and intense.

In the heat of his panic, the killer dropped his rifle on the ground. The cat continued to scream.

The man bent his knees and cowered low, covering his ears. Then – remembering its deadly power – he snatched up the rifle, stepped back, and swung it to his shoulder.

Before he could squeeze off a shot, the panther left the road just as he had come. With a single bound, he cleared the bushes beyond the pavement and blended completely into the stunted blackjack oaks at the edge of the orange grove. To the killer, it seemed as if he had vanished into thin air.

BY THE TIME THE PANTHER DISAPPEARED, Danny had run across the fruit yard and clambered up the steel steps leading to the orange bins. When he heard the panther's scream, it thrilled him, somehow filling his heart with hope.

Above the boy loomed the tall steel bins that, in season, fed fruit onto a conveyor belt leading into the concentrate plant. Danny climbed, ignoring the sound of a shot when his pursuer blew the padlock off the gate.

The gunshot at the gate woke up an elderly security guard. Thinking that he had heard a backfire on the highway, he opened the door of his small, air-conditioned office. "Is anybody there?" he asked plaintively.

Without missing a stride, Chucky raised his rifle and shot the old man between the eyes. As he walked past the quivering body, he did not spare it a glance.

Danny had not noticed the guard shack, and now it was too late to help the guard. He scrambled up a steel ladder and climbed atop the huge bins, racing down the catwalk. He reached the end just in time. As he dove into the top floor of the main building, a bullet blasted past his shoulder and punched through the steel wall.

CHUCKY FOLLOWED DANNY up the narrow steel ladder and angrily stalked along the catwalk on top of the bins. He felt utterly annoyed by the level of effort required to bag one wayward youth.

Steam had gathered at the top of the catwalk. The smoke swirled between the glaring lights like vapors from a grave, ominous and haunting. Feeling someone behind him, the killer glanced over his shoulder

In a flash, he saw a man walking toward him through the steam. Acting on instinct, he whirled and fired two shots.

Expecting to see the body drop, he saw nothing but a beckoning cloud. Fingers of steam writhed in the darkness... as if imploring him to leave the plant. *That was creepy!* He checked his rifle. *It's empty, and I left the shells in that stinking meadow along with my best tripod.* Cursing, he threw the rifle away and pulled a handgun from his belt. *Now, I'm mad!*

Inside the plant, Danny jumped down a flight of steel stairs and ran into the sorting room. There, in the darkness, he paused before sneaking down another staircase to the bottom floor. The room echoed his quiet footfalls: vast and dark, denuded of life. He decided to hide inside a pulp tank about four feet high, with a narrow neck. He could scarcely fit into the tank, and once inside he instantly regretted his decision. He panted quietly, desperate to disappear into the darkness.

The Canadian stopped at the top of the stairs that led down into the huge room. Looking to his left, he saw a light switch and smiled broadly.

"Nice evening, eh?" he asked conversationally, flicking on the switch. The plant lit up sequentially as the powerful overhead bulbs flicked on with loud clacks, one by one. The lights awoke, pop-by-pop, until every inch of the plant basked under the garish blast of unforgiving argon light. Chucky smiled contentedly, deciding to speak in hopes of startling his prey into revealing his hiding place.

"I'll bet you like it when I say, 'eh.' Eh?" As he spoke, he stepped down the stairs. "You Americans think it's quaint. It fits the stereotype, eh?" He reached to his left and popped the cover off a large steel box on the wall, then pushed the button inside.

The entire row of machinery leapt into life, from automatic fruit sorters to the long conveyer belts that carried fresh fruit during the time of harvest. Chucky relaxed, certain that he would soon discover his prey.

"Don't you agree with what I'm saying?" he asked. He stepped down the stairs to the next level of machinery and repeated the process, turning on the row of machinery. "I asked you a question."

Two levels of the juicing platform rattled and hummed with the raw mechanical power of machines designed to sort, ream, juice, and stir. The killer smiled, well pleased with his handiwork.

"I know you're in here," he said. "It was a perfect place for hiding when the lights were out. Eh?" He reached the bottom floor and pushed a large red button on the wall. Inside the gigantic blending tanks, massive blades began to turn.

Danny heard the sounds of machinery powering up and looked down at the blade beside his ankles. Soon, these blades might also start turning. He had to exit immediately.

The killer had just glanced away, but he heard the sound when Danny squeezed out of a pulp tank and dropped to the floor. Chucky whirled and raised his gun just in time to see a small steel handle heading his way, airborne at a high rate of speed.

The stubby piece of stainless steel had been hand-made to lock hatches on the mixing tanks. For an instant, the whirling handle appeared to be frozen in midair, but that was because of the heightened extent of the shooter's adrenaline-soaked awareness. As he watched it sail slowly end-over-end, it suddenly accelerated. To his surprise, the heavy steel handle smashed into his face.

He fell onto his back and stared at the bright lights in the ceiling, forty feet above. *Look at the lights. The pretty lights.*

Slowly, his wits coalesced, and he recalled his mission. With the return of full consciousness, the pain struck like a swarm of electric mosquitoes that bit into his face as he leaped dizzily to his feet.

"I'll kill you, you little freak!" he screamed, tasting warm blood as he spit out two teeth. Hearing the threat, in spite of his terror, Danny could not resist the temptation to offer a reply.

"You tried that already!" he cried loudly. "Not working!" He slammed the front door of the plant and ran for the pickup truck parked beside the guard shack. When he reached it, he found no keys in the ignition, and he had no time to search inside the shack.

He ran into the shadows, ducking out of sight as the killer barreled out of the plant and stopped on the landing, watching and listening. Danny paused, hidden in the shadows beneath the juice evaporators. Above his head, towering tubes of stainless steel thrust their bulk upwards into the starry sky. The contorted, surrealistic silhouette of the massive evaporator pipes resembled a nightmare from the Dr. Seuss school of industrial design.

The killer guessed correctly, and began to move in Danny's direction. Dismayed, the boy crept quietly through the darkness, sneaking past steel pumps that bristled with tubes as he searched for some way to escape.

Finding a steel ladder, he began to climb.

The Pinnacle

The steel ladder led straight into the sky, and Danny followed it without reservation. He knew he had entered a trap, but saw no other recourse. For some reason, the idea did not frighten him.

As he climbed, Danny remembered the revival last night: his friend Mikey, and the impressive preacher with the scarred face and glassy eye. Somehow, in spite of the terror of the past few days, his life finally made sense. *I'm ready, God. But please, whatever happens, don't let this man ever hurt anybody else!*

The darkness surrounded him like a concealing cloak. He climbed one level, found another ladder and climbed to the next level, then the next. After six heady levels, he reached the final platform, a pinnacle more than 100 feet above the parking lot.

Night had fallen, delirious and dark. Clouds hid the stars, but in spite of that, the view was spectacular. To the south he could see the distant lights of the truck stop where he first met Drew. *I guess Drew gets to live, and I get to die. Oh, well. If I die, I'll wake up in heaven,* he reasoned philosophically. *Not bad for a worst-case scenario.*

Hearing the killer climb up behind him, Danny turned. "Hello," he said simply.

"You've been a bad, bad boy," the killer spat, wiping thick blood from his mouth. Shocked, Danny recognized his accent.

"You really are a Canadian, aren't you?"

"Didn't I make that clear?"

"I thought that you guys were supposed to be nice."

"That's a negative stereotype!" Chucky retorted angrily. "How about those bloody little seal pups. We bash them in the head with sticks, don't we? Does that sound nice to you?"

"Not really."

"Thank you."

"You're right. I bought into the stereotype."

"You're a fearless little brat, aren't you?"

"Mama said I'm missing the fear gene."

"I would say that's interesting. But it's not." The killer looked around. "Not a bad view, eh?" He reached into his shirt pocket and pulled out a pack of cigarettes. "Smoke?" he asked.

"You're here to kill me, and you offer a smoke?" Danny gaped at him in surprise. In response, the killer merely shrugged.

"So what? You're about to be executed. All the more reason for a smoke, I'd say."

"I just quit smoking. Smoking is dangerous."

"Ha! That's a good one." Chucky squinted at the horizon, lit a cigarette, and took a deep draw before throwing away the spent match. Intrigued by the random motion, he watched it flutter down through the breeze.

"Well, all right, then. But it's a bad time to quit, little fella. You could use a smoke."

"No, thanks. Really."

"Whatever," the killer said. The wind began to swirl, bringing with it the smell of rain. "Is that rain?" he looked up. "I didn't see that coming."

"It whips up kind of quick in this part of Florida."

"Here," the killer said. He stepped closer to Danny, handing him his pistol. "Take this to defend yourself, okay?"

Lightning flashed from the darkened sky, revealing stark, glaring snapshots of the scenery below: the distant truck stop, the orange grove across the street, the concentrate plant, and the strange visitor from the Great White North. Illuminated by the flashes of light, the killer looked remarkably innocent in spite of his deadly mission. His behavior seemed delicately, painstakingly polite, like a murderous Pooh Bear apologetically preparing to brain Piglet with a bedtime book before smothering him with a soft, downy pillow.

Danny stared, curious and appalled at the same time. He did not admire villains, but this one drew his attention like an Eastern Diamondback rattling on an empty highway.

"Look over there," the man said. He pointed to the north, where distant glimmers of flashing blue lights could be seen below the horizon among a dark sea of trees. "That'd be the cops, looking for you. It's too bad they don't know you're here, miles away from their little blue lights."

"Take the pistol," the man repeated, thrusting it at him. "It seems unsporting to kill an unarmed child."

"Pretend that I'm a little white seal."

"Ha!" The man laughed, scratching his chin. "Another good one," he acknowledged. "Go ahead, take the gun."

"Okay." Danny reached out, took the gun, and stared at the killer. Chucky's eyes gleamed as a smile flickered across his lips.

"Oops!" Danny said, tossing the pistol over the edge. It banged twice against the pipes before smacking the asphalt below.

"Hey! That was a good pistol."

"Good and bent now." Danny smiled.

"How did you know it was empty?"

"I didn't. I just knew I wasn't going to shoot you."

"Why not?" the man asked as he pulled out another gun: a stubby .38 caliber revolver.

"I got saved last night," Danny replied. The man gaped at the child, astonished.

"What did you say?"

"I got saved at a revival last night," Danny repeated.

"You're kidding me. Right?"

"No, I'm not."

"You… got saved? You? The little deadeye who whacked three of the best mechanics in North America? You can't just walk away from talent like that. Come on!"

"Oh, I got saved all right. I went to a revival last night, and…"

"No!" the man yelled sharply. "Not another word! I attended that freak show. You fell for that?"

"Yeah, I fell, alright. I fell in love with the truth."

"Shut up!" the killer roared. He struck the child across the face with his handgun, knocking him off his feet.

"Shut up!" he repeated, greatly distressed.

From flat on his back on the hard steel platform, Danny stared up at Chucky. He felt neither fear nor pain. His nose poured blood and his eyes ran with water, but somehow, in spite of it all, he felt wrapped in peace. He felt no fear, no anger. Instead, he felt pity. *God forgive him,* he prayed.

As Danny prayed, he saw a man dressed in white, standing behind the killer on the platform. He pointed toward the man, and the killer followed his gaze.

"Look."

Chucky turned and saw the man standing beside him on the tower. He fired three quick shots into the stranger's gut. But as he shot, his target vanished before his eyes. He stopped, stupefied, and attempted to gather his wits.

"That was just an apparition," he mumbled softly to himself. "My mind's playing tricks." He turned to face the child.

"You saw him too, didn't you?" Danny asked. "He was an angel. I prayed that you would see him."

The boy's words enraged the killer, who drew back his leg. With all of his power, he kicked Danny in the side. Driven by the power of the kick, the boy rolled to the edge of the platform.

Teetering at the brink, stunned and unable to grab the railing, he slipped over the edge, and fell.

He hit the platform below, landing squarely on his back. Scarcely conscious, he looked up in time to see the killer leap over the edge. Chucky landed like a cat on the narrow steel platform beside him. Out of the blue – or in his case, out of the darkness – the Canadian began to laugh.

"What a view for a kill!" he exulted, methodically reloading his weapon. After Chucky reloaded, he paused for a moment and looked up into the dark storm clouds now stalking the tower. Unexpectedly, he caught his breath.

"What the...?" he breathed as the fire began to fall.

From the heart of the darkened heavens, St. Elmo's fire fell upon them. The tangled web of pulsating lightning skimmed across the top of the tower before pealing over the edge and pouring down to their level.

All around them, an ephemeral cascade of searing blue light danced across the steel structure. Curious flickers raced around them, pausing occasionally to spit out narrow threads that hovered, trembling, in space.

As Danny watched, a wild, electric halo crowned the killer with fluttering beams of high voltage electricity. Chucky tingled from head to toe as the lightning swept across his skin.

"What a rush!" he cried exultantly. "I've been struck by lightning. And, oh brother, I'm still here. And I like it! Check this out, my little friend."

Chucky raised his fist and shook it at the sky. "You can't touch me!" he howled at the God whose existence he had long denied. "I rule the heavens and the earth!"

The irony of his situation, as an atheist railing at God, entirely escaped him. "Ball lightning, indeed," he added with a sneer. "Is that all you've got?"

Turning back to Danny, he knelt and thrust the barrel of his pistol against the boy's head. Crouching low over the boy's fallen form, he bowed down, bit his ear, and whispered into it. Blood began to ooze, warm and salty, into the open gash of his hungry mouth.

"Do you believe in God?" he asked.

"Yes," Danny replied. The boy's entire universe rippled, squeezing smaller as his vision faded, and he began to pass out.

"Too bad," the killer whispered as he squeezed the slack out of the trigger.

DANNY DID NOT HEAR THE SHOT. He did not know what happened next, for he had drifted into unconsciousness.

He missed a bloody nightmare.

Like Danny, the killer did not hear the shot, but he felt the impact of the bullet.

In the last split second before Chucky collapsed, he experienced an incredible bolt of pain that lanced through the middle of his head. In that instant, he realized what had happened. Then, he began to seize.

Struck in the head by a high-velocity bullet, Chucky shrieked and flipped backwards onto the steel floor, completely out of control. This experience did not fit into his plans.

His seizure was profound. His eyes remained open, staring blankly at nothing as he mewed like a pitiful lost kitten, jerking spasmodically. It was a sight to make the devils dance: a sight to wring tears from the angels. The pulsating seizure caused the killer's entire body to spasm again and again, like a gaffed tarpon thrashing on the deck of a boat.

As if from a distance, he observed his own seizure, and in spite of the shock he sensed his body bowing backwards, again and again, as it jerked across the steel platform. He jolted across the hard surface until a final, cruel spasm blasted him over the edge.

No platform waited to catch his fall. He plummeted straight down, falling more than 90 feet before hitting the asphalt with a splat that broke almost every bone in his body.

For a moment, full consciousness returned as he lay on his back in a thick puddle of crimson ooze. *What just happened to me?* He opened his eyes and, to his surprise, he saw the same man, dressed in white, who had appeared to him on the top of the tower. The man shook his head slowly, looking down at him with profound sorrow. When the killer tried to raise his gun to shoot, however, his muscles tightened and sinews flexed in vain.

The killer's eyes wandered, then refocused.

When he looked up again, the first man had disappeared. Another stranger had taken his place: a tall man with a deep tan, dressed in lightweight camouflage clothing. A powerful sniper's rifle hung across his chest, the trigger at the ready.

STANDING AT THE FOOT OF THE TOWER, Billy Tigerclaw watched as Chucky's broken body tried to move. Hearing the faint, gruesome grinding of splintered bone against bone, he shuddered and felt a surprising wave of pity. Stepping back, he looked up at the top of the tower. *Is the boy still alive?*

For a moment, Billy paused. And then he spoke, pronouncing each word cautiously, as if it were a pearl carefully tied to a string.

"You should have listened to the tiger," he stated softly. Billy spat thoughtfully on the asphalt, deliberately missing the body. In spite of his disgust, he would not dishonor a human corpse.

"You preyed on your own kind," he told the fallen killer. "You wasted your life, like the worst kind of fool."

"Ahhhh…" Chucky breathed, exuding a final gasp at Billy's feet. From his harsh asphalt bed in the dirty parking lot, the killer slipped over the edge and fell, plunging downward once again.

This time, the earth would not break his fall.

Billy could breathe again. He had not said a word for the past six days as he had carefully stalked this man… this human disaster, now silenced forever. It felt good to speak, even to such a man as this.

Walking away from the body, he jumped onto the steel platform beneath the tall towers and found the ladder. Slinging his rifle, he climbed the steel ladder swiftly, proceeding from platform to platform until he neared the top. There, he found the boy.

He could see that Danny was alive but unconscious. Billy, a powerful man, lifted the child onto his shoulder and climbed back down, moving slowly and carefully. Reaching the bottom platform, he laid him carefully at the edge and jumped down to the parking lot. Moving swiftly now, he stepped over the body of the murdered guard and telephoned for help from the guard shack.

He had completed his mission.

The boy had survived.

At last, Billy Tigerclaw could go home.

Mercy Mission

9:11 operators in Davis County received a call at 9:05 PM. The caller claimed that Danny Johnston could be found beside the entrance to the Alcon Citrus Processing Plant on Weaver Road. A few minutes later, sheriff's deputies found him safely stowed beside the driveway near the front gate, covered by a bright orange blanket.

IN PHILADELPHIA, at 11:02 PM, Richard Collins heard the telephone ring as he lay in bed reading. He reached over and picked it up.

"Is this the Greyhound station?" a man asked. Immediately, Richard recognized the distinct voice.

"Sorry; wrong number." The caller hung up, and Richard smiled.

The call would undoubtedly be traced. A few days ago, when he had told the FBI about the phone call he had received from Sally Benuto, they had grilled him mercilessly in spite of his years of service and stellar reputation. None of that mattered now. The call from Billy meant that his mission had not merely succeeded: he had completed it without violating any laws. Richie Collins could sleep well again.

"What was that?" his long-suffering wife asked skeptically.

"A happy ending," he replied, thoughtfully returning the receiver to its cradle.

WHEN DANNY ARRIVED AT THE HOSPITAL, his biggest fans were there to greet him. Marcy, who had risen above her fears by virtue of emotional shock, seemed as calm and unruffled as an inland lake on a windless day. Drew Marks, wounded but unbowed, had survived in relatively good shape. The bullet had grazed the flesh of his calf without striking the bone, and surgery had not been necessary. He insisted on visiting Danny's room, much to the dismay of solicitous staff.

Danny, recovering from a concussion, wanted to leave as soon as they stitched him up, but Marcy convinced him to stay overnight for observation. He agreed, with one stipulation. She yielded, agreeing to buy him a puppy.

"Every boy needs a puppy," he argued convincingly. "Now that my folks are in heaven, I want'a give 'em something to smile down on."

"You dreadful little schemer," she had protested unconvincingly. "You're conning me." In spite of her protests, she folded.

EARLY THE NEXT MORNING, before she picked up Danny at the hospital, Marcy answered an ad in the paper and claimed a brown brindle puppy from a litter of eight-week old English bulldogs. Danny named him Stumpy.

The End of the Beginning

When they returned to the Johnston family ranch later that day, they found Win rocking on the porch. He arose and limped to the steps, clutching the rail as they got out of Chesterfield's Mercedes.

"Well, well," Win gloated. "I see that y'all have done bought Junior a little old poodle. Ain't it just as cute as a little ol' bunny!"

"He ain't a poodle, Big Daddy; he's a bulldog. Can't you see anymore? Shoot, I guess I shouldn't ask, you bein' so old and all."

"Come up here and say that to my face," the old man said. "I got somethin' for ya." Danny ran up the steps, and they hugged until the old man grew tired and had to return to his rocker.

Drew and Marcy turned aside and followed the path that led around the farmhouse, down to the lake. She looked troubled.

"What's wrong, Marcy?"

"We have to go back to Tallahassee tomorrow," she began. She spoke as if she had rehearsed the words. "I have to get to work."

"Let's stay here a while longer, Marcy. The work will still be there, later."

"Chesterfield has to get back. He has a trial."

"Let him go. He'll be okay."

"Look… Drew… it's been nice, okay? It's been very flattering, but you have a life to return to. Your fans will demand it."

"My life has changed," Drew replied haltingly. "*I've* changed. I've lost my faith in sex, drugs and rock 'n' roll. I have a different faith. I believe like you… that Jesus is the Messiah."

"I know."

"I almost would have faked it to get close to you. But I don't have to."

"I know."

"I'm not the man I used to be."

"I can see that."

"Then, what?"

"I'm a lawyer with a career in Tallahassee. I work for legal aid. My clients need me."

"I agree. I can move to Tallahassee." He placed his hand lightly on her arm. "I'll get a house. I'm from Wakulla; I'll blend right in."

"Drew, please." She turned away, her eyes wandering past the lake, along the horizon. "You've got your life, and I've got mine."

"You can't believe that."

"I… I just…"

"You *are* my life, Marcy." He heard himself say the words, but could scarcely believe it.

She turned back to him, and he touched her lightly. The next thing she knew, she was in his arms.

"Drew," she whispered. She wanted to push him away, but her will began to dissolve. She felt weak in the knees.

"Marry me," he whispered.

"What?" She pushed him partially away but still held tight, unconsciously digging her nails into his arms.

"Marcy," Drew repeated. "Will you marry me?" He blinked, staggered beneath the weight of his own words. *I just met the girl, and I'm proposing?* The very idea sounded outrageous, but he could see the irrefutable logic.

Drew had lived long enough to learn a few things. He knew the difference between up and down, and he knew what truly mattered in a world full of lost souls building mansions on the sand.

Undoubtedly, Marcy mattered. Her life exuded grandeur writ large… for many to look at, but few to see. In a fallen world, she presented a perfect picture of uncommon decency.

Drew had long lived with upheavals and nomadic travel, with abject hedonism and crippling addiction only recently broken. He did not consider himself to deserve the love of such a woman. He paused, uncertain of what to say.

"I don't blame you for thinking I'm crazy," he said hopelessly, resigned to his fate. His arms rested on hers, but he made no further move. *She'll walk away any minute,* he told himself. *She's too smart to wind up with a guy like me.*

Marcy mumbled something that Drew did not understand.

"What?" he asked hesitantly.

"Shut up," she whispered, pulling him back into her arms. She laid her head on his shoulder, smiling in spite of herself as she blinked through her tears. *I don't believe this,* she reflected.

In spite of it all, in defiance of the turmoil of the past few days, a profound sensation of peace welled up within her. *Thank you, God.*

"Yes," she whispered softly.

"What?"

"I said yes." He held her close, unable to believe what he heard.

"Yes?"

"To marriage, Drew. Hello?"

"Marcy, I…"

"Shut up," she said as the tears ran down her face. "Just shut up."

He squeezed her tightly as they leaned against one another, amazed by the power of their emotions. Somehow, the heat and pressure of the past few days had fused them together – completely and irrevocably.

"Marcy, I…"

"Shhh."

"I just…"

"Shut up and kiss me, you big lug," she murmured. "Didn't you see the movie?"

Epilogue

In his orange jumpsuit, the inmate hobbled down the hall, stooping low so he could walk in spite of the shackles that connected his ankles, belt, and wrists. He waddled slowly though an empty doorway, clanking all the way.

Salvatore "Streetcar" Benuto – in his current, fallen condition – offered an object lesson in why one should abide by the laws of the land. He shuffled slowly into the federal courtroom, the very picture of penitence. Two imposing deputy marshals flanked him, and a nervous bailiff trailed in his wake, obviously yearning to be somewhere else. By now, the reputation of Sally Benuto had been inscribed on the ink-stained pulp of legend. For two months, he had lived in this jail, awaiting the evidentiary hearing as the buzz increased and rumors multiplied in the press.

His friends stood when he entered the packed courtroom. Streetcar looked sideways at them, shocked by their appearance in court on his behalf.

Jamie's bruises had healed, and the worst of her scars had started to fade, but her right arm remained hidden in a large white cast. With makeup applied, she looked like the Jamie of old: innocent, fresh-faced, and painfully beautiful. At her side, uncomfortable in a stiff suit and crooked tie, towered her husband, on leave from the Sheriff's Department to attend the hearing. Behind them stood the Sheriff of Oree County, Delia Rawlings, flanked by a posse of Johnstons: Winston and Danny on one side, Marcy on the other with Drew at her side. Chesterfield, the odd man out, stood behind the table for the defense. The famous criminal defense attorney had offered to assist Clay's firm, and Clay had jumped at the opportunity to receive help from such renowned counsel.

The bailiff blared, "All rise," and the judge entered, walking swiftly to the bench. The judge was a stern, scholarly man of medium height, with a highly polished pate that harbored a wispy remnant of silver hair. As he sat down, he frowned at both teams of attorneys.

"This court is in session," Judge Larkin stated bluntly. "We will hear the defense's motion for dismissal." Clay stood. Facing the judge squarely, he nervously shuffled the papers in his hand before placing them on the table face down. Stepping in front of the bench, in the neutral zone between the defense and prosecutor's tables, he turned and pointed to Salvatore Benuto, who sat behind the defense's table, clad in an inmate's orange jumpsuit.

"Your honor, as you know, our defense team has given great deference to the prosecution in this case," Clay began. "When crimes of domestic terrorism are alleged, the matter deserves the gravest consideration." Clay turned and pointed to the constitution of the United States, framed on the wall to his left. "However, we know that descriptions of purported evidence – unsupported by evidence itself – must never deprive a citizen of precious liberty. Our system requires that evidence be produced before a man can be charged with a crime. The constitution demands it. No citizen can be held or charged on the basis of unfounded allegations.

"But exactly that, your honor, has happened to my client. He is a victim of prosecutorial speculation unsupported by solid evidence." Clay returned to the desk and waved some papers.

"He stands charged before this court with a bloody murder that took place in Tampa some time ago. Several gangsters were killed back then, and we're all sorry about that. None of us condone vigilantism, but that's not the issue before the court. The issue today is evidence… or in this case, the lack of evidence. The prosecution has not produced one concrete shred of evidence. They have only produced accusations based upon speculation. That, your honor, is indefensible.

"Mr. Benuto may appear to be a lowly street person, and indeed, a street person has the same rights as you and me. But Mr. Benuto has an honorable past. He served the public in San Francisco as a decorated policeman. He left the force with honor. He served our country as a Green Beret who won two Silver Stars and one Bronze Star in the jungles of Vietnam. As his reward, the government he once defended has jailed him without a single piece of solid evidence.

"The government has claimed that the explosives used in the infamous Ybor City bombing years ago matched explosives that my client had access to in Vietnam. The prosecution has referred to a report regarding a chemical analysis supposedly completed by the FBI several years ago. This is the only proof offered by the government to support its charges.

"Four weeks ago, we requested copies of that report. And to date, how many copies have been produced?" he asked dramatically. "Not one single copy."

The prosecutor rolled his eyes. The judge looked bored and stared out the window, tapping a pencil on his marble desktop.

"This week, we were informed that the alleged 'evidence' has vanished into thin air. How can we trust that it ever existed? How can we test its accuracy, even it if did exist? Simply put, we have nothing to affirm or dispute. The government has produced no evidence to support its claims.

"For all of these reasons, I respectfully request that this case be dismissed."

At the desk for the prosecution, federal prosecutor Robert Rothsberg stood up. The judge pointed at him with his pencil and the attorney paused with his mouth open, afraid to speak. The judge straightened up in his chair and began to address the court.

"The defense asserts that the prosecution has not produced evidence," the judge observed. "This is supported by the record."

"Your honor," the prosecutor blurted, only to be summarily interrupted by the pointing pencil and flinty eyes of a thoroughly annoyed judge.

"Does the prosecution have any evidence to present at this time?" The judge asked skeptically.

"No, your honor."

"This court is impressed by proven facts. It is not impressed by unsupported charges," the judge stated. He frowned at the prosecutor.

"Since no evidence has been offered to support the charges against the defendant, who has been held without bail at the request of the prosecution, I'm dismissing these charges… with prejudice." His hammer popped the wooden block with a resounding *thwack*. "So ordered," he stated tersely. He pointed his pencil at Streetcar. "Mr. Benuto, you're a free man."

Hearing the words, Jamie began to cry.

THREE MONTHS AFTER THE MURDER of Dan and Sarah Johnston, at five o'clock in the afternoon, Senator Howard Bedford received a telephone call from his favorite journalistic resource. The rasp of the reporter's gravelly voice provoked his tired lips into a grimace that slightly resembled a smile.

"This is Jessica Timberlane of the Washington Post," she stated brusquely.

"Why the formality, Jess?" he asked warmly, opening his emotional spigot to unleash a blast of boyish charm. "What's up?"

In the weeks since the demise of Chicago's infamous Don Brucci, Senator Bedford had quietly gone mad. Now, as he labored to suppress his dread, he took a deep breath. He felt terrified by the prospect that his inner turmoil might manifest itself through tension in his voice.

"I'm covering a breaking story," the reporter continued. "Are you willing to give me a statement?"

"Shoot," he replied carefully.

"A teenager named Danny Johnston just held a press conference in Tampa in front of the offices of the Tribune. He stated that he saw you in person three years ago, at the house of his uncle, Peter Wayne Johnston… a notorious drug dealer." She spoke mechanically, as if reading from notes. "Danny Johnston says that after your visit, his uncle boasted that he had bankrolled your political career. Do you have any comments?"

"What?" He practically spat the word out, terrified and enraged.

"Did anyone actually believe that nonsense?"

"Tell me what we should believe," Jessica replied wearily, jaded and cynical. "I'll relay your disclaimer to the credulous masses."

"Why would anyone listen to such foolishness?"

"Danny Johnston is the boy whose parents were murdered in a witness protection program in Florida a few months ago. He survived several attacks on his life. It was in the news."

"Yes. I remember hearing about that."

"Do you have any comments regarding the boy's claim?"

"I'm sorry about his parents, the poor boy. But to make such wild accusations out of the blue…" he paused. "Could you repeat what he said?" he asked, stalling for time.

"He claims that he saw you at the home of his uncle, Peter Wayne Johnston."

"Peter Wayne Johnston?" He stalled.

"The drug dealer who escaped from jail. You remember, the helicopter escape in South Florida? The hand in the shark's belly?" *What a story,* she recalled.

"Oh, yes, of course. He was a dreadful man."

"He was Danny Johnston's uncle. Is it true that you knew Peter Johnston in high school? That's what the boy's aunt claimed at the press conference today."

"High school? Which one? I attended two high schools."

"I'm referring to Cutler High School in Cutler County, Florida."

"Well, yes, I went to that school. What about it?"

"Danny Johnston claims that he saw you visiting an old classmate from that school… Peter Wayne Johnston, to be precise." Like a bulldog, she had clamped down upon her story. She would not readily release her prey. "Is it true?"

"Me? Visiting a racist drug dealer? The child is delusional."

"Can I quote you?"

"Quote me as saying that the poor child must have suffered terribly since the death of his parents. It's unfortunate that he would latch onto such a delusion… sad but understandable given the trauma that he's been through."

"So, that's your story and you're sticking to it?" she asked skeptically. *Now I know he's lying. He's too smooth. The snake!*

"That's my honest answer. Thanks for the information, but I have to go now. They're calling for a vote on the floor."

Senator Bedford hastily hung up the phone, muttering under his breath. He stood distractedly and turned to a huge, ornate mirror that hung on his wall. "Get your affairs in order," he instructed his handsome, well-tanned reflection. "Your political career is over."

TO RICHARD COLLINS' FRIENDS IN THE CIA, the violent deliverance of Danny Johnston read like an open book. They could see that Richie had pulled another fast one on the FBI, and the legality of his intervention made it all the sweeter. Because it had occurred in the state of Florida, and because Richard's shooter – anonymous to the end – had used the minimum force needed to defend a human life, it had all been as legal as a Sunday stroll.

Some staffers at the Washington headquarters of the FBI held the firm belief that Richard Collins remained guilty of something, but their theory could not transcend the proven facts. Collins had hidden behind lawyers from the beginning, stoking their suspicions while frustrating their game plan. The former Deputy Director of the CIA had tied their tails in a tight little knot.

They suspected that he had aided and abetted Sal "Streetcar" Benuto, but they could prove nothing – because, in fact, Richie had not aided him in any way, shape, or form. The deeper they dug, the cleaner he looked. Collins could not be charged. That fact dismayed them to no end.

The thought kept them awake at night. They turned in their beds, their restless minds hot on the trail of a crime that had not been a crime, searching the statutes in vain.

TWO WEEKS AFTER THEIR PRESS CONFERENCE, Marcy returned to her father's farm for an overnight visit with her fellow survivors in tow. They arrived late at night after a lengthy drive and quickly retired to their rooms.

During the night, Danny awoke. In a dream, he looked up through the thin branches of a tree swaying above him. Meandering past the lavender blossoms that blessed the branches, his gaze climbed upward into the clear sky.

The unclouded daytime sky seemed to shimmer, dramatically backlit by the fiery arc of an unseen sun. The sky was astonishingly blue, as beautiful and as clear as a flawless, fiery topaz.

The visible universe, alive with hidden energy, trembled in the thrall of remarkable luminance. The morning light poured across his field of vision like a benediction, adorning all visible objects with diffuse halos that shimmered with delicate clarity. His eyes lingered on the pale pink pavement and brick-red boxes bearing rangy oak trees. Everything looked bright and clean and free of dust: unblemished, uncorrupted and complete.

He slowly turned in a circle, savoring the beauty. The pale pink stones terraced the entire mountainside, step after broad step that marched down into the valley. He felt the kiss of a cool breeze on his cheek and inhaled the pale scent of unknown flowers. Looking up again, he marveled at the beauty of the trees. *Aren't those blackjack oaks? Why are they covered with flowers?* As if in answer, he heard a woman's voice.

"Danny?" He turned to the right and saw his mother. His father stood at her side.

"You're alive!" he shouted happily.

"Yeah," replied his father. "Go figure."

"Why'd you leave?" he asked, feeling the pain of bereavement deep within his chest.

"It wasn't our choice," his father said quietly. "It will all work out for you, Danny."

"Why did you leave?"

"Please don't be bitter. We were ready to go."

For the first time, Danny noticed a man standing behind them. *That's an angel,* he thought wonderingly as he began to weep. "Please don't leave me," he begged.

He hugged his parents with all of his might, weeping with

abandon. His mother and father gripped him tightly. As he held them, events from the past years returned in an emotional montage that tumbled through his consciousness lightly, like clouds passing before the sun.

He saw himself at the lake, his grandfather laughing at the miniscule size of the fish on his hook. They rode home together in Big Daddy's truck as the sun set, red and gold and unspeakably majestic.

He watched himself running into the last house he shared with his parents. His mother sat at the kitchen table, bent over a novel. The scent of cookies filled the room, hinting of the satiable desire that beckoned languorously from the hot stove. *Chocolate chips.*

After nightfall on a cold winter evening, he watched as his father entered the kitchen through the back door, clad in his welding leathers. The leathers smelled of heat from the blinding light of the welding arc: bitter smoke from scorched steel, the acrid stench of burnt welding rods.

Early one morning, on the very morning of the day they died, he had found his parents praying quietly at the kitchen table. Alone in the quiet of dawn, they had whispered like children sharing a delightful secret.

Tears soaked his face and his shirt, and he squeezed his parents tightly. He wept against his father's arm, unwilling to let him go. The clean sleeve smelled sweet, like the breeze after a rain: not smoky, as his father's clothes had smelled during the past two years – cruel days in hiding, consumed by hard, driven labor in his converted barn-studio.

"We have to go," his father whispered.

"No!" he cried. "Stay," he moaned. "Let me stay here with you."

"Baby," his mother murmured. "You can stay if you want."

"Danny," a gentle voice asked. "Do you want to stay here?" Danny looked up to see the man.

"I want to serve the Lord," he gasped, the tears falling from his eyes. "Wherever he wants."

"Then that's what you'll do," the man replied.

"Danny," another voice urged, "can you hear me?" *Whose voice is that?* He wondered. *It sounds familiar.* He hugged his parents tightly, burying his face against them.

"Danny?" the voice repeated. A hand tugged on his arm. "Danny, wake up."

"Oh," he moaned. "Oh," Danny sighed, rolling over and opening his eyes.

Aunt Marcy stood beside his bed in his grandfather's farmhouse, tugging on his arm. Light poured into the dark bedroom through an open doorway, slanting across the wooden floor and up the wall beside his bed.

"Wake up," she repeated. "You were talking in your sleep."

"Uhh…" he moaned softly.

"Were you having a nightmare?"

"No. I wanted to stay."

"Where?"

"In heaven."

"Heaven?"

"I saw Mama and Daddy. I wanted to stay, but then I changed my mind."

"You changed your mind?" she asked incredulously.

"Yep, I sure did," he replied, coming to himself. "So, here I am!" He stretched luxuriously. "Lucky you… huh, Aunt Marcy?" In response, she hugged him.

"That's for wanting to stay with your poor, old Aunt Marcy," she said. For good measure, she slapped the back of his head.

"Hey!"

"That's for scaring me silly," she added brusquely.

"With a little old dream?" Danny countered slyly. "You scare mighty easy for a Johnston."

"The dream didn't scare me. It's everything you've done in the past few months, you little monster," she replied with a crooked grin. "You shot up Florida like Ted Nugent, gone berserk."

"*Gone* berserk? Ted Nugent? Where's to go?"

"Good point."

"Is this a party?" rasped a deep voice from the hall. Win Johnston swayed sleepily in the harsh light, clad only in his baggy boxer shorts, thin tee shirt, and dispirited, drooping socks.

"Yuck, grandpa," Danny cried. "Can't you get dressed before you come out of your room?"

"This is my house, thank you," Winston observed dryly. "Or at least, it's my house while I'm still breathing, if you want to get all technical about it. I'll dress how I want to, Junior."

"Daddy, you're embarrassing Danny," Marcy interjected, averting her eyes. "What does that tell you?"

"That I raised a couple of whiny little babies, that's what. It tells me that Danny's as whiny as that little poodle he keeps for a pet."

"Big Daddy, you're too old to see a fig. Stumpy's a bulldog; we ain't got no stinkin' poodle!" Danny laughed uproariously.

"Are you guys awake?" Drew asked, shuffling down the hall and stopping behind Big Daddy. He scratched his head stupidly, and then looked at the old man in dismay, surprised by the unseemly view: faded boxers, drooping socks, sagging undershirt. "Uh, Mr. Johnston… shouldn't you be, like… dressed, or something?"

"Okay, okay," Win wheezed sourly. "I can take a hint." He stomped off, followed by their laughter.

"Thank you, Drew," Marcy said, unconsciously pulling her robe tight. "He wouldn't listen to us."

"It's five AM," intoned the somber voice of Chesterfield. "What on earth are you all doing awake at this miserable hour?" Drew turned around to look at Ches and gaped in shock at the sight of his refined silk smoking jacket and casual Italian slippers.

"What are you staring at?" Ches asked in a huff. "Don't you know style when you see it?"

"Is that what I'm seeing?"

"Without a doubt. Are you familiar with GQ?"

"The metal band?"

"The magazine!"

"Never read it," Drew replied. "Thought about it once, but I changed my mind."

"It shows." The two men, so different in background, shared a grin.

"*That's* stylish?" Drew asked.

"It's an acquired taste," Ches added.

"Like pickled pigs' feet?"

"I suppose."

"Well, gang, we're wide awake at five in the morning," Danny observed, climbing out of bed. "And we're all one big, happy family, so we might as well fix a whopping big breakfast before we hit the road to Orlando." He grabbed Marcy's hand and dragged her out of the room toward the kitchen. "I'll make the biscuits," he cried as they left the room. As they passed down the hall, Ches fell in step.

Drew paused and watched them walk away, wondering about the changes that had taken place during the past few months. *They're my family now*, he considered. As he stared, Winston returned to the hallway dressed in tattered overalls. In classic retro redneck style, he had fastened only one shoulder strap.

"So, y'all are goin' all the way to Orlando to see that stupid mouse," observed Winston. "You'll be the first Johnstons in history to get caught in a mousetrap. A billion-dollar mousetrap." He rubbed the stubble on his face and gazed at Drew thoughtfully. *So, this is the boy who's gonna marry my Marcy.*

"Yep. We're goin' to Disney World. Danny's never been."

"I reckon I ought'a know that fact. Danny's daddy hated Disney World. He called it 'The Mouse that Ate Florida.' He declared he'd never go there, and he kept his word."

"I wish I'd could've met Dan Johnston."

"Just keep the faith, kid. You'll get your chance." Winston slapped Drew on the shoulder and walked him down the hall. They entered the brightly lit kitchen to see Danny measuring flour and Chesterfield digging out the coffee as Marcy prepared the eggs.

"How far is it to Orlando?" Danny asked his grandfather, looking up from the measuring cup.

"About a million light years," the old man replied with a grimace.

"What's that in dog years?"

"A million times seven," his grandfather responded glibly.

Danny craned his neck and looked around the room. "Are we there yet? Huh? Huh? Are we there yet?"

"Well, *I'm* almost there," Win replied as he sat down at the head of the table. "But I reckon y'all have got a few decades to go."

ACE CLOSED THE BATHROOM DOOR and quietly locked the heavy steel bolt. He crept softly toward the occupied stall.

As Benny the Weasel opened the door to leave the stall, he looked up with a vacant stare. Then, as if roused from sleep, his eyes slowly opened wide. He recognized the face of his killer, and the blood drained from his face.

"Ace," he groaned.

"Put your hands up," Ace growled. "Kneel." In response to this command, Benny quaked visibly. "Kneel!" Ace boomed.

As Benny dropped to his knees, he began to whimper and weep like a baby. A wet spot soaked through the front of his pleated Dockers.

"Please!" Benny begged, blubbering sloppily. "Please don't kill me."

"Why did you kill her?" Ace hissed, beside himself with grief and anger. "Why her? Why didn't you come after me? Why not fight me like a man?"

"Please," squeaked Benny the Weasel. "I'm beggin' you!"

Ace put his hand to his head. His heart pounded in his ears.

Without warning, Ace's field of vision swirled. His universe spun like the cylinder of a handgun, and when it clicked back into place, he found himself on his knees, with the end of a cold gun barrel pressed hard against his forehead. He looked up, astonished.

"Frankie?" Except for the open wound where the bullet had exited his forehead several years before, Frankie looked great. "What are you doin' here?"

"What do you think, Ace?"

"But, Frankie, you're dead!"

"No kiddin'?" Frankie smiled as he pulled back the hammer. "I thought I just caught a bad draft... through the middle of my head."

"Frankie, please, don't do it."

"Do you think I'm sparin' you, Ace? After you had me clipped? What did I ever do to you? No way, you greasy little hippie." Frankie sneered at him. "I was Joe Boy's babysitter, and it earned me a bullet to the brain. Here's your payoff, wise guy!"

Ace felt the blast slam hard against his forehead. A warm, unseen hand seized his shoulder, and he blacked out.

"Honey, wake up!" Amy said, shaking Ace's shoulder firmly.

"What?" he gasped. Ace opened his eyes and moaned. His house lay still and quiet, dark and cozy. In the next room, a clock slowly chimed the hour.

"You had a nightmare."

"Oh, baby, what a dream I just had."

"You screamed like you were being killed."

"Yeah?"

"Mm, hmm."

"Hey, Amy?"

"What, honey?"

"Do you mind if I retire early?"

"Retire?" She sat up, turning on a lamp. "Early? Like, at age 62?"

"No. I mean, like, this week."

"This week?"

"What do you think about that idea?"

"But James, can we afford it?"

"Sure. We own our house, and we've got more than ten million in treasury bonds. We're set for life."

"Of course I don't mind, James," she whispered, leaning over and kissing him. "But won't you miss your work?"

"Sure I will. Like a hole in the head."

"Oh, my," Amy replied, officiously tucking a stray hair into place. "We don't want that, now, do we?"

SOMEWHERE IN THE MIDDLE OF MONTANA, Streetcar rocked on

Wally's porch and stroked the hair of his ancient Maine Coon. Deep in thought, he watched as the sun approached the craggy rim of the western Rockies and slipped behind an elongated cirrus cloud. After several minutes of silence, he spoke.

"Sorry about all the fuss, Wally," he offered. "Did it get pretty bad?" His friend pushed back his moustache and took a deep sip of coffee before replying.

"I reckon."

"You never told me the details."

"It was a mess. A couple of days after you left, I got up earlier than usual. For some reason – I don't know why – I got dressed in the dark without turnin' on the lights. It just felt spooky that mornin'. I looked out the window, just as the moon came out, and I saw a bunch of men slippin' up the draw down there in the canyon." He pointed. "They were wearin' FBI jackets, like on TV."

"Sorry about that."

"No sweat. Anyway, I figured that this must be the big trouble you were jabberin' about before you left in such a hurry."

"So, what'd you do?"

"I went into the kitchen, turned on my iMac, and opened up a video chat with a huntin' buddy back east. I asked him to keep quiet and record a movie of whatever happened. I left the chat open, turned on the lights, and made myself a cup of coffee. I sat right at the table while it was brewin'."

"You wanted to film the whole thing?"

"Sure enough."

"How'd it go?"

"It wasn't like in the movies. It was way nastier. I left my back door open, but they busted it down anyway. They found me at the kitchen table, all peaceable. That must have ticked 'em off pretty bad, because they knocked me down and stuck their guns against my head, cussin' up a storm, as mad as hornets."

"No kiddin'?"

"No kiddin'. They had potty mouths, too. Nice rifles, though."

"M16s?"

"Nope. The new XM8s."

"Nice!"

"Yep."

"What'd they do after that?"

"They hauled me off to Butte all trussed up like a wild hog. Do you remember Sheriff Ito?"

"Sure. He drives that old Willy's, right?"

"Yep. Well, right after you left the ranch, back before the FBI showed up, I had given him a call and told him that I thought you might be in trouble with the law. He said he'd check it out."

"What happened?"

"Ito got distracted, and didn't get around to it. In the meantime, the FBI traced your cell phone to this area and identified my ranch because we were army buddies. That's how I wound up hogtied with a bunch of potty-mouthed city boys dragging me off to Butte."

"How'd Sheriff Ito figure into this?"

"He showed up in Butte and told them that I'd asked him to run your ID. That proved I was a law-abiding citizen. Turns out that Sheriff Ito records every call that comes into his office, and he brought a copy to that FBI office, so they had to turn me loose."

"I'm sorry I got you into so much trouble."

"No problem, Sally. I never get to visit the city, and I was due. Butte's like a different world now. You should see how it's grown." Streetcar leaned forward, hanging his head.

"How long were you in custody?"

"A couple'a days. My only regret is that I never got to use that iMovie. I was anglin' to get myself on 60 Minutes."

Abruptly, the sun dropped down below the western mountains. A hush fell on the land, as if the universe had closed a door. "What are you going to do now, Sal?"

"I don't know, Wally. Maybe I'll move to town. Who knows?"

"I know a widow woman in town you might want to meet. Her name is Nettie Royster."

"Is she an in-law, or an outlaw?"

"Not an in-law. But she's a pretty good woman, and she's

independent as all get-out. Who knows, maybe even an old cuss like you might have a chance with a free thinker like her. That is, if you're ready to get serious."

"Been there, done that. It didn't work."

"I never knew you for a quitter."

"Okay, then. What about you?"

"I was married to my high-school sweetheart for 24 years, Sal. When she died, that was it. I've had my share of happiness. You deserve it, too."

"I've done some real bad things," Streetcar replied softly. "The law may be comin' after me again."

"We've all done bad things."

"I guess."

"The point is, where do you go from here? Are you gonna keep on doin' bad things, or are you gonna mend your low-down ways?"

"I don't know."

"Well, that's honest."

"I want to change, but I don't know how. I keep failin', whenever I try." The distant howl of a wolf accentuated Streetcar's point. "I've got too many counts against me, I guess. I think I'm too mean to change. Like that old wolf." He scratched his chin slowly. "When I first started workin' here, I meant to live a better life. I promised God a lot of things, but I didn't follow through."

"Have you prayed for help since then, Sal?"

"Plenty."

"Then don't short-sheet your own bed. Have a little faith. Do you know what I mean?"

"No."

"Then I'll put it this way. God made the universe, right?"

"You think?"

"Then what makes you think He can't forgive? And what makes you think that He can't change folks, in spite of their meanness? Even battle-scarred, weather-beaten old cobs like us?"

"You have a nice way of puttin' it."

"Thanks."

"I don't deserve it."

"Nobody does." Wally looked away. "We've both done some nasty things in our lives. Especially back in 'Nam."

"It didn't end there for me."

"I know." Wally looked at him out of the corner of his eye.

"I didn't want to leave 'Nam."

"Why not?"

"When we were there, Wally, back in country… I don't know; I just felt alive. Really alive. We were all brothers. We put our lives on the line for each other."

"We had something special."

"I think I'm finally beginning to understand it. I went crazy after that judge stole my kids in San Francisco. I was like a dog that's been kicked too many times. It wasn't pretty."

Wally looked at his friend. Streetcar's face glistened in the dim light of dusk, streaked with tears.

"I've had my fill of revenge, Wally. I don't want it any more. I'm tired. It just ain't right."

"Tell me about it."

"I want to live in peace."

"Better late than never," Wally observed sagely.

"Don't joke."

"I ain't jokin', Sal." Wally looked at him in the moonlight. "You've picked a good place to live in peace, if that's your goal."

"I wish I could see my kids. They'd probably hate me."

"That's possible, but not likely."

"They don't know what went on back then… how their mom bribed a judge to get rid of me. I wonder if they're okay?"

"Maybe you should look into that."

"You're right." The wolf howled again, and his pack mates answered in the distance. Streetcar gritted his teeth.

"I hate wolves."

"You can't kill all the wolves in the world."

"I know."

"It ain't your mission."

"I know." Streetcar shrugged and smiled, wiping his eyes with a scarred, calloused hand. "Hey, Wally."

"Hmm?"

"I think I've learned something."

"What?"

"I think I've been handling my anger inappropriately."

They chuckled quietly in the gathering darkness. "Too bad we can't just blame it on the moon," Wally replied.

"I tried that," Streetcar offered, "but the charges didn't stick." Hearing this, Wally cleared his throat, blinking at the jagged horizon.

"So tell me, Sal. How do you feel about everything that's happened?"

"I'm not so sure. I don't feel very good about it. But at least I feel something."

"Well, now," Wally suggested, rising from his chair and walking to the corner of the porch, "I reckon we've covered enough for one session." Staring up at the stars beginning to glimmer in the sky, he twisted his moustache and smiled against the darkness.

"I think we've made some real progress."